A MESSAGE FROM CHICKEN HOUSE

I'm mesmerized by Helen Maslin's frighteningly real blend of modern romance, Gothic ghost story and a beautiful charmed and doomed tale of lost love from long ago. You know the feeling, when you can't wait for daylight to dawn and it's going to be all right again, then suddenly it's so, so NOT ! I loved it. No thanks, I don't feel like going to the beach today. Or ever again!

BARRY CUNNINGHAM
Publisher
Chicken House

darkmere

helen maslin

2 Palmer Street, Frome, Somerset BA11 1DS
www.doublecluck.com

Text © Helen Maslin 2015

First published in Great Britain in 2015
Chicken House
2 Palmer Street
Frome, Somerset BA11 1DS
United Kingdom
www.doublecluck.com

Cover and interior design by Helen Crawford-White
Cover and interior illustration (heart) © firestock/Shutterstock
Cover illustration (birds) © KANCHIT/Shutterstock
Cover illustration (trees) © winui/Shutterstock
Typeset by Dorchester Typesetting Group Ltd
Printed and bound in Great Britain by CPI Group (UK) Ltd, Croydon CR0 4YY

The paper used in this Chicken House book is made from wood grown in
sustainable forests.

3 5 7 9 10 8 6 4 2

British Library Cataloguing in Publication data available.

PB ISBN 978-1-910002-34-6
eISBN 978-1-910002-75-9

For Stephen

There was a girl in the water.

The waves were many times bigger than she was and infinitely stronger, but she fought her way through each one. She kicked and clawed and lunged even though the coldness lent every wave the impact of a hammer blow. The girl gasped, her body juddering.

It hurt.

Another huge wave came crashing down over her head like a rockslide and she knew she was going under. She flailed, panicking, but the water shrugged and flipped her over.

Then it swallowed her whole.

How could she fight something that didn't know she was there?

She wasn't even a very good swimmer.

The girl surfaced in a different wave altogether. Before she could catch her breath, a new wave rose up and tried to haul her in another direction. Her mouth was rough and salty with seawater. Already she could imagine how it would feel in her chest, her lungs.

She was horribly afraid she would die. But the alternative had been to watch *him* die. And that hadn't felt like an alternative at all.

No, she was not going to let it happen.

Because just as the sea has always been the sea, girls have always been girls.

She would not give in.

Kate

When Leo asked me if I was going away for tho summer, I nodded immediately – and untruthfully.

'Where?' He lifted his eyes to mine the way motorists switch their headlights up to full beam.

I pictured myself sunbathing in the communal garden of the flats I lived in with my mum and washing up at the pub in the evenings.

'Not sure yet . . . France or Spain, probably.'

'That's a shame.' He took another sip of his coffee.

In the pause that followed, I could hear the clunk of heavy white cups, the tinkle of teaspoons and the whoosh and gurgle of the coffee machine. We were in the school canteen. But because this was Denborough Park, one of the best private schools in the country, it was a school canteen with a stuccoed ceiling, marble columns and chandeliers. *Chandeliers!* And I was probably the only one who noticed them.

All the other students were noticing me and Leo instead. This happened whenever I sat with him. He turned me into a person to be envied rather than some kind of sociological experiment.

It had been months since I'd been awarded the scholarship to come here, but there still weren't many days when I didn't miss my old state school. Denborough Park made me wear my background like a badge of shame stitched to the pocket of my blazer.

'Why?' I asked defensively. 'Where *should* I be spending the summer?'

'At my castle.'

'Your – what?' I wondered if I'd misheard. It sounded extravagant even for Leo. 'You mean you've rented an actual castle for the holidays?'

'Nope,' he grinned. 'My aunt died and left me one.'

'A real . . . *castle* castle?'

'You don't believe me, do you?'

'No, I think you're winding me up.'

'I have a solicitor's letter and an ancient set of keys. And I'm far too lazy to go to that sort of trouble for a wind-up.'

I stared at him. If anyone our age *were* to inherit a castle, it would be Leo. He probably had a great-uncle with a chateau in Paris and a granny with a floating palazzo in Venice. His father was not only the school's Chair of Trustees but also owned a string of hotels – and had fought viciously over them during his recent divorce from Leo's stepmother. Everyone knew the Erskines.

So the first time that Leo Erskine had come sauntering towards me in the school library, it had taken all my nerve not to dart behind a bookcase and hide. He was the biggest – and scruffiest – boy in the school. I was sure no other student here would get away with a uniform so thoroughly dishevelled. Up close, the state of his tie surprised me so much I asked him – out loud – if it had been caught in a shredder. Leo had laughed and told me he liked my hair.

I hadn't really believed him, because all the other Denborough Park girls had hair that was long, gold and glossy. *Expensive* hair.

Mine was purple – I'd dyed it to match my new Doc Martens.

But Leo had found me almost every day after that to tell me he liked my hair or my boots or my black cherry-coloured lipstick. And now we were . . . friends. Or something.

'But that's just it,' I murmured. 'You *are* lazy. And scruffy – you just don't seem posh enough to own a castle.'

'Oh, it isn't a posh castle. It'll be in a shit state because no one's lived there for years. But it's still a castle. And best of all it's supposed to be haunted.'

'By one of your ancestors, you mean?'

'Hope so – that'll be hilarious. Poor thing's bound to want some company after all this time. I'll see if it wants to join the gang.'

5

'You're all going there then?'

'Yep – for the whole summer. I'm going to take Beano in the campervan, and Hat-man Dan and Jackson are going to drive down.'

I made an effort to look unconcerned, while mentally calculating the number of days I'd have to get through before I saw him again. Fifty-five? Fifty-six, maybe?

Before I'd arrived at an exact number, one of Leo's friends entered the canteen and yelled an unselfconscious '*Hey!*' at us from the other side of the room.

Hat-man Dan. He was wearing headphones and he came bouncing towards our table with a listening-to-music strut. I noticed several female heads swinging round to follow his progress.

Unlike Leo, Hat-man Dan's uniform was immaculately pressed and tailored. He was a modern-day dandy in an over-sized beanie. He wore strips of leather around his wrists, the newest trainers and a watch that all the other boys coveted. He also had one of those finely sculpted jaws and dark, shining hair. Good-looking – but too clean-cut for me.

'What happened to your tie today?' he asked Leo far too loudly. 'Tiger attack?'

'You know, there might be people out on the rugby fields who can't hear you,' said Leo, pulling one of Dan's head-phones away from his ear and letting it ping back into the side of his head. 'But I doubt it.'

Hat-man Dan laughed and tugged his headphones down around his neck. Then he swung one of the chairs around and straddled it, resting his arms along the back. 'So . . . have you persuaded the new girl to come with us yet?'

The new girl. That's what they called me at Denborough – still.

'Persuade me to come where?' I said to Hat-man Dan.

'Leo's castle, of course. Go on! My girlfriend's mum will only let her come away with us if there are other girls coming too.'

Excitement rose inside me like a whole bunch of shiny helium balloons, but I didn't want to give in too easily. 'I might consider it if you stop calling me "the new girl".'

'Brilliant! Thanks – um . . . ?'

'*Kate,*' put in Leo, and a catlike grin stretched across his face as he looked at me. 'Are you saying you'd rather spend the summer in a crumbly old castle than in France or Spain?'

I held his eye for a moment. He was really asking me whether I'd rather spend the summer with *him* and we both knew it. So much for not giving in too easily! When I finally answered him with a nod, he laughed in triumph. Leo was always laughing. He made me feel as if life wasn't such a difficult business after all.

'Right, that's two girls coming,' said Hat-man Dan, jabbing a message into his phone as he spoke. 'I'll let Lucie know . . . it'll be her and you then, Kate – and there's definitely a girl Jackson's interested in. He wouldn't tell me who, though. Do you know, Leo?'

'Some slapper as usual.' Leo was still holding my eye and grinning. 'Jackson's taste in girls is inexcusable.'

Beano joined us then, carrying a couple of espressos for himself and Hat-man Dan. He drew a chair up to the table and began to stir so much sugar into his coffee it made my teeth itch. Beano was as thin and gangly as Leo was burly. I'd heard him talk a lot about lifting weights and downing protein shakes, but it never seemed to make him any bigger.

'Your housemaster's looking for you, Leo,' he said. 'I told him you were usually in the chapel around this time, but I don't think he believed me.'

'He wants me to sign up for his Leadership course,' Leo said with a weary look. 'I've already told him it clashes with Beauty Therapy.'

Everyone laughed.

To the exasperation of his parents and teachers, Leo had signed up for the unlikeliest courses the sixth form had to offer. He did whatever he wanted and refused to take anything seriously. When he'd invited me to a party a couple of weeks ago, I had been so afraid it was a joke, I almost hadn't turned up. Would it turn out to be Transvestite Night at the club when I tried to get in?

But it was just a hot, sweaty nightclub, crammed with bodies. And music so loud the floor jumped in time with the bass. In spite of all this, my eyes still found Leo before anyone else. I sent smiles and meaningful glances across the dance floor, but his friends surrounded him as always and he didn't notice me.

I wasn't worth noticing.

After a while, I gave up and went outside to look for a taxi.

I was still there, standing under the dirty amber light of the streetlamp, when Leo came out.

A wave of relief – and longing – swept over me.

And I hated myself for feeling both those things.

He came up close and lowered his face to mine. 'Leaving without saying goodbye?'

I breathed in a mixture of cigarette smoke, cannabis and alcohol – all the things that bad boys are supposed to taste of. His closeness melted all my anger and resistance away and I let him kiss me. As he pushed me back against the wall, I heard a crowd of smokers outside the nightclub cheering him on and the muffled sound of dubstep from inside the building.

Of course I thought it meant something. But when I saw him at school the next day, he smiled at me and kept on walking. Instinct warned me not to show I cared.

I guessed even then that Leo enjoyed winding people up like clockwork toys. He'd probably kissed me like that just to see what I'd make of it. So I was careful to make nothing of it at all.

'I still can't believe you're taking Beauty Therapy,' muttered Beano now, licking sugar off his spoon. 'I'd be too embarrassed. It's not exactly manly, is it?'

'He's the only boy in a class full of girls, you nimrod,' said Hat-man Dan. 'I wish I'd thought of it.'

Leo smirked. 'We're learning about massage this afternoon.'

I caught myself looking down at his huge, powerful hands and blushing.

'What have you got this afternoon?' I asked Beano.

'Um . . . I don't know . . . Psychology or Photography, I think.'

'He gets them mixed up,' murmured Leo. 'You can imagine what the Psychology students make of his long-lens camera.'

Beano spluttered and I giggled, even though I felt sorry for him. Leo's teasing could be merciless.

He met my eye over the top of Beano's head and smiled. And I could see my own excitement mirrored in that smile. A question too – maybe even a challenge.

'You mean it then – you'll come?'

The most popular boy in school – *the boy with his own castle!* – was asking me to spend the summer with him.

'Yes,' I said. 'I'll come.'

2

One week later, on the first day of the holidays, I woke early – absurd, childlike anticipation making me too restless to stay in bed. I unpacked and repacked all my bags several times. I couldn't find my dressing-gown and it was one of my favourite things. I'd bought it from a charity shop and the silk was worn through here and there, but it was still beautiful. It was a man's dressing-gown – paisley-patterned in deepest claret silk. I thought it made me look alluring and sophisticated in a way that cheap underwear or baby-doll nighties from Topshop simply didn't. I wanted Leo to see it and think so too.

But I couldn't find it and after a while I gave up. Instead, I sat down to write a goodbye note for Mum, reminding her where I'd gone. Then I startled myself by crumpling up the note and knocking on her bedroom door to say goodbye in person.

Mum was never at her best in the mornings. She was always bad-tempered and blotchy and her breath smelt sour. This early, her room was still dark and it took my eyes a second or two to adjust. Then I saw there was a big fat man in the bed next to her. What light there was came from behind me, in a doorway-sized shaft that showed his face was highly coloured and he had the swollen nose of a dedicated drinker. There was a sheen of sweat on his skin. And he was wearing my dressing-gown – like a cape – around his shoulders.

He blinked at me a couple of times, puffy, sleep-encrusted eyelids semaphoring his indignation at me. Mum didn't wake up at all.

So I closed the door on them both and took all my belongings outside, across the communal garden and right out on to the pavement to wait for Leo. There was no way I would ever let him see that flat.

Jackson arrived to pick me up.

Not Leo. Jackson.

I looked at his battered little car and the last of my holiday excitement evaporated. I wanted to go with Leo. I wanted to ride up front in his flashy orange campervan.

'They've crammed stuff into the camper up to the ceiling,' said Jackson, pushing his tousled hair out of his eyes to look at me. 'There's no room for anyone else inside it, so I volunteered to come and get you.'

'Thanks,' I said.

His Volkswagen Polo seemed to sag with dismay at the sight of all my belongings and I eyed it doubtfully. 'It's a four-hour drive, isn't it? How far do you think we'll get before your car overheats?'

'It's never done that before,' he said, climbing out to help me stow my bags in the boot. 'Although hills might be a problem. I have to close my eyes and kind of *will* it to keep going up. It gets overtaken by lorries and tractors.'

'I can't drive at all yet, so I can hardly complain. Is it OK if I put all my bedding on the back seat?'

He nodded, and I spent a minute or two bending into the back of the car and patting down my duvet so he would be able to see through the rear-view mirror, before turning to catch him staring at my bottom. My hands curled themselves into fists.

I was wearing denim hot pants with a ribbed vest. I'd also dyed my hair platinum blonde and fluffed it out like I'd seen on an old poster of Debbie Harry. Jackson probably saw the way I looked as some sort of an invitation.

It wasn't.

This was exactly what I'd been afraid of from the minute he'd shown up. I'd never had a conversation with Jackson during which his eyes had stayed on my face. He was obviously one of those boys who couldn't see the point of a girl unless she was wearing a short skirt and high heels. And making him a sandwich. What the hell were we supposed to talk about for the next four hours?

'Have you ever tried talking to a girl, Jackson?' I asked, through my teeth.

His gaze dropped to my bare legs again and he looked

distracted. 'Huh – what?'

I climbed into the car and slammed the door behind me.

'Sure you've got everything?' he asked, oblivious, as he slid into the driver's seat and surveyed the loaded back seat over his shoulder.

'I'm sure.'

Although I hadn't been camping before, I was pretty well prepared. I'd borrowed an airbed from the man who lived upstairs. I didn't have a sleeping bag, but I'd rolled up my duvet and squashed it into a bin-liner along with my pillow. I'd brought a torch, and a wind-up charger for my iPhone, several bottles of water, vitamin pills and a huge bag of apples – since I guessed the food supplies chosen by the boys would consist mainly of beer and kettle chips. I'd remembered towels, wet wipes and skimpy underwear. Hats, make-up, swimwear, as many items of clothing as I could stuff into my holdall and a selection of different sunglasses – Wayfarers, aviators, Jackie O's and so on.

'I haven't brought much more than my toothbrush,' he said, restarting the engine.

'Shit – wait there!' I exclaimed, flinging the door open and running back inside for my toothbrush.

We met up with the rest of the gang in the car park of the local pub, then headed for the motorway in a convoy. Leo was at the wheel of his pimped-out Volkswagen campervan and right at the back was Beano – at least I had to assume it was Beano since I was only able to see his buttocks as he mooned at us through the glass of the rear window.

'Aw, gross,' muttered Jackson, slowing down so we weren't presented with such a close view.

Behind us, Hat-man Dan accelerated and gave a thumbs-up as he and his girlfriend overtook us in their Volkswagen Beetle. I wondered whether everyone in the gang had bought the same make of car as Leo on purpose.

Dan's girlfriend was a tall, thin black girl called Lucie something or other. She was one of the Denborough glossies, who spent most of her time in the cookery department learning how to make six-course meals and taste wine. I didn't know her very well, but she smiled and waved at me as they sped past. Jackson chuckled as he saw Hat-man Dan realizing exactly why we'd slowed down.

When we reached the motorway we were forced to close the windows against the rush of wind and the quietness made me hyper-aware that I was alone with someone I didn't like all that much. I wondered what had happened to the girl he'd wanted to go on holiday with. I supposed she must've let him down at the last minute. Although that didn't explain why he'd given her seat to *me*. Maybe his ego wouldn't allow him to go anywhere without a girl by his side, no matter who she was.

I wasn't in a position to laugh at him, though. It was what I wanted too – someone beside me. I'd never had a proper boyfriend. All I'd ever done was work and study. But Denborough Park, where everyone had known each other *for ever*, made me feel more alone than I could stand. I wanted to belong – not just to Leo's gang, but with another person. With Leo.

Ahead of me, the motorway stretched on for ever and still Jackson and I found nothing to say. When he finally switched on some music, I slumped back into my seat with relief.

At lunchtime, we stopped at the services for coffee and sandwiches. The rest of the gang were all there, lounging on a grass verge beside the car park, listening to the music that was pouring out of the campervan. I remember thinking how cool they all looked – as if they were in an advert or a music video. Then my eye fell upon Beano, who had hair like matted straw and was eating some sort of burger with a fried egg on top, and the illusion was gone.

I bought myself a coffee and a cinnamon bagel and headed towards Leo, only to find he was already sitting between Beano and Hat-man Dan and deep in conversation. So I turned away, pretending to be stretching my legs after the long car journey. Eventually, I sat down by Lucie who was leafing through a dog-eared sheaf of papers and photographs.

'Hi,' I said. 'I'm Kate.'

'Yeah, the new girl – I know. I'm Lucie.'

'What have you got there?'

'All sorts,' she said. 'Everything that Leo's solicitor sent him about the castle – deeds, letters, photos, other bits and pieces. There's even a postcard, look.' She handed me a small, faded postcard with a picture of a castle on a muddy hillside, surrounded by dark, dun-coloured woods. There were a couple of bored-looking brown cows hanging about in

16

the foreground. Turning it over, I read: *Darkmere Castle – from a painting by A. R. Quinton.*

'Wow!' I said. 'I'm still having trouble believing it's an actual castle.'

'It isn't,' she said. 'One of Leo's uncles offered it to the National Trust in the nineteen fifties, but they didn't want it. There's a copy of the report here. Listen, it says: *Darkmere Castle is of no architectural value or historical interest. Neither is it in fact a castle. It was built in 1825 and named Darkmere House, but became known as Darkmere Castle by local people because of its castellated architecture.*'

'Oi! Lay off my fucking castle!' called Leo.

'*Darkmere Castle,*' she went on, ignoring him, '*is no more than a Victorian folly.*'

'Ha!' said Hat-man Dan. 'Folly was probably typical of your ancestors, Leo. Bad blood going back right through the ages.'

Leo shook his hair back out of his eyes and lit a roll-up. At least, I hoped it was only a roll-up – with Leo, you could never quite be sure, and we were in a very public place. With the shaggy brown hair of a beach bum, well-worn combat shorts and a shrunken T-shirt, he was looking every bit as scruffy as he always did at school.

'Well, the rest of my family can fuck off,' he said, breathing out smoke and lowering his jet-black eyebrows. 'Because *I* am the master of Darkmere now.'

All the boys laughed. The way he'd said it was intensely theatrical and I felt certain he was misquoting from a book or a film, only I couldn't remember which one, and there was something in his tone – along with those implacable eyebrows – that made me shiver.

'Hey, Lucie?' called out Beano. 'Does it say anything in there about the Darkmere ghost?'

'No . . . I don't think so. It does mention a curse, though.'

'*Whoooo-ooo!*' said all the boys at the same time.

I hung over her shoulder as she began to read aloud from an old newspaper article that someone had photocopied and added to the stack of information about the castle. The headline was: *CASTLE UNDER A CURSE.*

Underneath was a black-and-white photograph of the castle taken from a different angle to that of the postcard. It looked huge and forbidding with several broken windows. The flagpole appeared to be tilting like the mast of a ship riding a wave. At the top of one of the towers was a black-faced clock with roman numerals.

Lucie tutted as my head cast a shadow over the words of the article, and I moved back.

'*Once home to generations of the wealthy St Cloud family,*' she read, '*Darkmere Castle now stands uninhabited and unwanted – feared by local people and forsaken by its current owner. Legend tells of a curse laid upon the castle and its heirs by the first mistress of Darkmere and it has certainly been the scene of several unexplained disappearances since it was built in the nineteenth century.*'

The silence that followed was broken by a chuckle from Jackson. 'So what does the new master of Darkmere reckon to all that?' he asked. 'You're next in line for the curse, mate.'

Leo shrugged and squinted into the sun. 'Bring it.'

Lucie caught my eye and pulled a face at his bravado. I smiled back. She had to be sixteen or seventeen like the rest of us, but she had a knack of appearing to be about twenty-one, because she was so poised and polished. I wasn't quite sure whether we would be friends yet.

'I don't like places where there's been lots of unhappiness,' she said. 'You can always feel it in the atmosphere. I wonder why the mistress of Darkmere cursed the castle.'

Hat-man Dan leant over to slide his hand under her hair. 'Luce, anyone trying to find romance with a member of Leo's family is bound to be in for more than their share of unhappiness.'

'Hmm . . . I guess it's lucky I'm going to the castle with you then and Kate's going with Jackson.'

No, I was not *at all* sure she and I would be friends.

I waited for Leo to correct her, but he only smirked as if she'd said something amusing. And then I caught Jackson grimacing . . . he was *embarrassed*. The unfairness of it sent pounding hotness up the back of my neck and into my face, and I wanted to hit him.

'Actually it was Leo who invited me,' I said, hating how defensive my voice sounded. 'But there wasn't enough room in the camper.'

Everyone looked surprised – apart from Leo, who roared with laughter.

'We can always make room,' he said, nudging Beano with his foot. 'I've had enough of you making bare naked arse prints on my windows. You can do the rest of the journey with Jackson, and Kate can come with me in the camper.'

Not long after, he crumpled up his sandwich wrapping and announced he was ready to get back on the road. Beano scowled, but followed Jackson to his car.

As he lowered himself into the passenger seat, I heard him mutter to Jackson, 'Your famous charm isn't working with this one, is it?'

Jackson must have stamped on the accelerator then, because the Polo roared away with Beano's left leg sticking out of the open passenger door.

I didn't care. I'd won Leo's approval and that was what mattered. I threw the last of my coffee into the grass and climbed up next to him in the campervan.

'Sure you're not too scared of the curse to come with me?' he asked, with a wink.

'No,' I said, echoing his words from earlier. 'Bring it.'

Our journey continued through the afternoon. I was content to sit there on the hot leather seat next to Leo, tapping the route planner on my phone, both of us trying to work out how much further we had to go. In the rear-view mirrors, I could see Jackson and Hat-man Dan's cars trailing along in the camper's wake. Sometimes I lost sight of them as we flitted around bends in the road, dropped down over a hill or disappeared into a tunnel of overhanging trees, but they always caught up after a while. I suppose the vivid orange of the camper must've been easy for them to spot.

We were off the motorway now and into a tangle of country lanes. The campervan wasn't too happy about the way the lanes climbed almost vertically and then shot downhill again – usually with a bend or two thrown in for good measure. I hadn't been this far south before, though, so the scenery was fascinating to me and it more than made up for the bumpy ride.

'It's so wild,' I said to Leo. 'I've never seen countryside this rocky and uncultivated.'

'It feels like anything could happen out here, doesn't it?'

'You don't really think there'll be a ghost, do you?'

He chuckled. 'I'm sure Lucie'll see one if she puts her mind to it.'

'One of your cursed ancestors?'

'It doesn't have to be a St Cloud. Ghosts are usually some-one famous, aren't they? Anne Boleyn probably stayed at Darkmere for a long weekend and now she walks up and down the North Passage every time there's a quarter-moon or something. At least, that's the sort of thing I'll be putting in the guide books when I throw my castle open to the public.'

'I wouldn't,' I cautioned him. 'I'm pretty sure Anne Boleyn died before 1825.'

He shook his head and smiled at me. 'I've never met anyone as keen to have the last word as you always are.'

I opened my mouth, but caught his eye and closed it again. He wasn't used to being argued with. Even his best friends rarely stood up to him. Honestly, if ever there was a boy less in need of the Denborough Park Leadership course, it was Leo Erskine.

I was still watching him when he steered around yet another impossibly sharp bend and gestured at the right-hand windscreen with his thumb. The sea! It appeared as a pale cloudy mist on the horizon, then deepened in colour and separated itself from the sky, becoming a smooth, calm expanse of ultramarine and I wanted to point at it and shout out loud with excitement. Leo's phone rang, and as he answered it, I could hear Hat-man Dan and Lucie whooping on the other end.

Yes,' he said, grinning. 'We can too.'

We seemed to be following the coast now, so the sea flashed in and out of sight, through dips in the countryside or gaps between the trees. There were fewer villages and farm buildings to be seen, and the country grew wilder – mostly woods or hills covered with scrub. Then we passed a campsite that I'd noticed before because although it covered a vast area, it had only two caravans and a forlorn-looking shower building. The rest of the site was strewn with weed-covered stones and patches of ancient rubble – like the foundations of something that had long since collapsed.

'Déjà vu,' I murmured. 'Could we have gone round in a circle, do you think?'

'Probably – I'm totally lost.' Leo took out his phone. 'I'll see if Jackson has any ideas.' He frowned at the phone before tossing it on to the dashboard. 'No signal.'

I took out my own phone, hoping there was something wrong with Leo's. But all the signal bars at the top of my screen were gone too. I felt as if I'd lost one of my senses.

'Jesus,' I grumbled. 'What century is this?'

We continued to follow the rough, winding lane, with Hat-man Dan and Jackson still hanging on behind. Then, unexpectedly, the land fell away on our right-hand side and became the edge of a cliff with the sea just there – almost beneath us – sparkling with a million silvery diamonds in the late afternoon sun. It was magical. I could smell it through the open window – there was salt and sand and something slightly rotten, seaweed perhaps.

The road climbed and wound along the top of the cliffs. It wasn't too steep, which was a relief because the camper had started to wheeze. After another ten minutes, a peeling wooden signpost offered us a choice between *Hangman's Hill* and *Darkmere Castle*. Leo and I gave a cheer.

And then, at last, there it was, high above us on the hillside. Just like the picture on the postcard – with turrets and a shroud of ivy – but now in high definition with sound and movement. The dark trees swayed all around it, the windows flashed in the sunshine and the sea made a constant hushing on the air. I could see the clock tower right at the front – time frozen for ever at five past twelve. It was Leo's castle.

Our castle!

And it was awesome. It was just . . . awesome. I could hardly believe the – the *castleness* of it. My breath caught, and when I glanced across at Leo he seemed, for a moment, like the prince in a fairy tale – he really did have his own castle!

It seemed to dawn on him at the same moment. His face was suddenly electrified. I could see a fierce pride in his eyes. Fascination too . . . excitement . . . and a burning curiosity about this place where his ancestors had lived and died. He looked completely different to the boy I'd been talking to a moment earlier. Although I was ashamed of myself for thinking it, he *did* sort of look like the master of Darkmere.

'My castle . . .' he said, half to himself. Then he flung an arm around my shoulders and turned those blazing new eyes on me. 'You see? I *told* you I had my own castle!'

I was unnerved by the way he said it. It was as if Darkmere had somehow added to his consequence and lessened my own. That's how it felt anyway. But how could I not be dazzled? How could *anyone* not be? Even the first mistress of Darkmere must've been impressed when she'd been presented with all this.

'Fine, I believe you,' I muttered as I stared at the gigantic arched doorway and wondered what the hell I'd let myself in for. 'Just don't make me curse you, OK?'

3

Dust.

Dust as thick as an eiderdown covered *everything*. It hung in long cobwebby skeins from the vaulted ceiling, it darkened the windows and it rose up around our feet in great choking clouds as we jostled our way in through the heavy door that Leo had unlocked. We were standing in a great hall as gloomy and cavernous as the inside of a cathedral. Like the others, I gazed upwards and turned around in a slow circle. The hall was two storeys high and panelled in heavily carved wood as dark and dull as last year's conkers. A magnificent staircase with ornate banisters rose up to a small half-landing where it split into two and doubled back on itself, leading to a minstrels' gallery at the top.

'Whoa,' said Leo softly.

A frisson went through the atmosphere – as if his voice was

the first to sound here in *years*. The wondering silence that had fallen over us was broken and we laughed and exclaimed as we ran up the stairs, darted in and out of the adjoining rooms, calling out to each other and exploring. Leo swung his big, old bunch of keys like a jailer, trying them in every keyhole and opening every door he could find. The dust overwhelmed us before long though, and we retreated back outside coughing, spluttering and wiping our eyes.

The boys opened bottles of beer and raided the fridge in the camper for cold chicken, sausages and slices of pizza. Then we sat and picnicked in the ruins of the gravel driveway, taking in the spectacular view. At our backs were the ivy-covered walls of the castle and circling around on both sides, endless woods. The hillside before us sloped steeply down to the clifftop and beyond that, was the sea.

I ate one of my apples and sifted through the bundle of papers that Lucie had been looking at earlier. There was an estate agent's floor plan which marked all the different rooms of the castle with names, such as *Library*, *Principal Staircase* or *Tower Dressing Room*. The only room we'd been in so far was the *Great Hall*.

Stuck to the back of the floor plan was what looked like a ripped-out page from a local guide book, which read: '*Darkmere Castle was built in 1825 by George Francis St Cloud as a wedding present for his young bride, Elinor. Tragically, Elinor took her own life during the second year of her marriage, and local legend has it that she died cursing her husband and his male heirs. When St Cloud remarried, two of* his sons died in infancy and a third disappeared within a few months of inheriting the castle.'

'What does it say?' demanded Lucie, who was watching my face.

'It says she killed herself,' I answered. 'The first girl to live here, I mean. She killed herself right after she cursed her husband and his family.'

'Why, though?' asked Lucie. 'Why would anyone do that?'

'It doesn't say.' I shrugged and read the rest out loud: 'In 1859, Darkmere Castle passed to St Cloud's only surviving child – his daughter Mary. Since the decline in the fortunes of the St Cloud family, the villages and the farms belonging to the castle were sold or allowed to fall into ruin. Local people became reluctant to work on the Darkmere estate, claiming that tragedy and misfortune . . .'

Leo's face appeared above me then, blocking out the sun. His eyes widened and he grimaced. Then he clutched at his throat with both hands before collapsing on the driveway. There was a moment in which I humiliated myself by leaping to help him, before realizing he was shaking with laughter.

'Funny!' I said, standing up and kicking him in the ribs. 'Hilarious!'

He jumped up and gave me a bear hug. 'Stop predicting my death then,' he said, crumpling up the paper I'd been reading and tossing it over his shoulder. 'Come on, there's dust to be dealt with.'

'Too much dust really,' said Lucie in an anxious voice. 'Maybe we could camp outside. I-I mean, it's beautiful out here and it's much too dirty inside the castle.'

'Too dirty for you . . . or too cursed?' teased Hat-man Dan.

'No one's using the dust as an excuse to bottle out,' said Leo. 'We just need a plan of action, that's all. I've got a broom in the van—'

'We need ten brooms,' said Beano.

'Shame your mum's not here,' said Jackson. 'She's a right scrubber.'

'Hilarious,' said Beano. 'The old ones are the best, aren't they?'

'Yeah, they say that about your mum too.'

Beano picked up a broken tree branch from the driveway and brandished it like a multi-stranded whip. Jackson fled down the hill with Beano at his heels.

'Now, that's an idea . . .' murmured Leo.

Minutes later, he had the boys climbing and swinging on the branches of the trees that lined the drive, until they had all broken off their own makeshift brooms. They stripped off their T-shirts and tied them across their noses like bandits and stormed the castle, flicking at the floor and the walls with their branches until the dust flew in all directions. They went through every door that opened out of the Great Hall and prised open some of the windows too. Every so often they dashed, coughing and wheezing, into the driveway for some fresh air, their hands and faces streaked with grime.

Outside, Lucie and I decided to uncover as many of the tall arched windows on the ground floor as we could reach. Leo parked the campervan close to the front door and helped me climb up on to its roof so I could yank down the long sprays of ivy that curtained the windows over the door. As I tugged, bits and pieces of aged masonry came away with the creeper and clunked down on to the camper's roof.

Hidden under the ivy, I found a worn engraving of entwined initials in the crumbling stone. I stretched up and traced the letters with my fingers, feeling a prickly little thrill of recognition. They must be Elinor St Cloud's initials. This had been *her* castle, of course. The engraving was jagged and sticky from the torn ivy stems – some of which were still clinging fast – and the tiny suckers had burrowed into the curves of stone, destroying the shape. My excitement gave way to disappointment, though, when I realized the first few lines didn't follow the shape of an 'E' at all.

When the dust inside had been beaten into submission, we moved our bedding and our belongings into the hall. Hat-man Dan set up speakers and put some music on, Jackson handed around beers and Leo began to skin up. After that, it was just like any other evening back home – only without the threat of irate parents bursting in and demanding we turn the music down.

I peered into a couple of the rooms which opened off the hall and consulted Leo's floor plan to find out what they were called. Through a door on the left was the dining room, which had an elaborate plasterwork ceiling and a beautifully carved mantelpiece with a marble inset of cherubs, grapes and flowers. It was probably worth a fortune.

From the dining room, a couple of steps led into the clock

tower which had obviously been used as a library. It was strangely yet beautifully proportioned. Two storeys high – like the hall – and hexagonal in shape, its walls were lined with empty shelves, right up to the ceiling.

A pale green flash caught my eye as someone flitted past the window, and prompted me to return to the hall to see what the others were up to. They were all still sitting around and chatting, so I went and sat next to Leo on his airbed and he offered me the joint he was smoking.

I took it gingerly and smiled at him. 'What do you think?' I asked.

'Hmm . . .' He gazed around at the towering walls, the beams that criss-crossed the ceiling, and the evening sunlight slanting through the high arched windows. 'I think it's like being in the school chapel.'

'*That's* what it is,' said Jackson, overhearing. 'I knew it reminded me of something.'

Leo grinned at him. 'But it's been a while, right?'

'I don't believe you've ever set foot in the chapel,' I said, unable to imagine it.

'We were choirboys,' said Leo. 'Weren't we, Jack?'

'Yep, we joined up after we heard a rumour that they were giving out free wine.'

The two of them exchanged the kind of conspiratorial grins that made me suspect they probably *had* drunk a bottle of wine meant for Holy Communion at some time in the past. Leo and Jackson had a shared history of misbehaviour that I knew nothing about, and I often saw them exchange winks and smiles – triggered by a chance remark or a song heard on the radio or a line from a film, anything, really. As always, I felt instantly excluded and I wished Jackson hadn't come here with us.

'So what *are* you going to do with all this?' he asked Leo. 'You're not really thinking of opening it to the public, are you?'

'Nope . . .'

'Because there aren't any public around here. Not for miles.'

'But that could be a good thing in terms of noise regulations' – Leo swept the room with a meditative eye – 'and gate-crashers . . .'

'You're going to have parties!' Jackson was right there with him instantly.

'Sweet!' said Beano, coming to join us.

'There's plenty of room,' said Leo. 'And this floor was built for dancing on.'

I glanced at the long dark, narrow floorboards and pictured the ghosts of Leo's ancestors stomping and spinning, waltzing and whirling all around the Great Hall. He was right, of course. A flurry of enthusiastic suggestions came from the others.

'You could have a DJ up in the gallery.'

'What about a bar over there?'

'You'd have to bus people in on coaches.'

'Maybe you could open up some of the rooms and people could stay over – it'd be a party hotel!'

Leo sat back with a lordly little smile, enjoying the excitement he'd created. I really believed he might accomplish it all. He was the perfect mix of party host and entrepreneur.

'I'd like to see the Darkmere ghost trying any funny business with that sort of crowd,' said Hat-man Dan. 'It wouldn't stand a chance.'

'It'll have to learn to get with the times,' Leo said sternly. '*I am—*'

'*—the master of Darkmere now!*' chorused Jackson and Beano along with him.

As the sky outside darkened and all the shadows lurking in the far corners of the room began to steal closer, Lucie went outside to call her mum and Leo decided he wanted a fire. It wasn't a cold night, but he said the firelight would save the batteries in our torches. It took him a while to clear away the great pile of leaves and twigs and assorted crap that had fallen down the chimney over the last half-century, but he persevered. Then he leant into the fireplace, trying to see if the flue was clear.

'You always have to make a fire,' said Jackson. 'You made a fire that time we went to the seaside, and you made a fire when we had that party in the graveyard—'

'I remember that!' said Beano. 'It turned into a massive bonfire and the police came and chased us.'

'Oh, God,' I muttered. 'I'm going to be sleeping in a wood-panelled room with a pyromaniac.'

'Doesn't sound like the worst thing a girl's ever called me,' said Leo, poking around in the chimney with one of the tree branches they'd used for sweeping. 'This looks clear enough – it'll be fine.'

'It's bound to be blocked,' said Beano. 'And we'll all get smoked out.'

'It's not the smoke I'm worried about. If I set fire to the chimney, I'll probably burn the whole castle down.'

'The fire brigade'll never find us here,' said Hat-man Dan. 'I don't think you should risk it.'

Words of caution seemed to act upon Leo as a spur – I was beginning to notice that now. The lower part of his face took on an intractable cast and he started to break up all the discarded tree branches and assemble them into a fire.

'Maybe we should send Beano up first,' said Jackson. 'He's the same size and shape as a sweep's brush.'

'Only compared to the rest of you fat bastards,' Beano muttered, giving Jackson the finger. 'You lot are the reason I work out.'

Leo's luck held and the smoke drew upwards. After a while the fire was blazing and everyone had stopped worrying about it. The dark wooden panelling turned red-gold and the shadows began to flicker and dance. Deep in the fire's heart, I could see flames that were green or blue or purple – and it gave out wonderful crackling, snapping sounds.

Music continued to blare in the background. The boys played a game of poker with their own – insanely complicated – system of rules and scoring. I lay on my airbed, eating an apple and listening to them squabble.

Somehow, their noise didn't seem intrusive or disrespectful in this place that had known only silence for so long. In spite of the soaring ceiling and the imposing doorways and a religious-looking carved oak screen, the Great Hall didn't *feel* remotely churchlike. I sensed that card-playing, swearing and bad behaviour might well have carried on at Darkmere down through the decades and that Leo's ancestors had probably never been noted for virtuous behaviour. One of them – Elinor St Cloud – had killed herself before she'd been married much more than a year! Was it was her husband she'd wanted to escape from? Or this castle?

I seemed to be the only one here who'd given it a second thought.

But then Lucie came stomping through the big door, gripping her mobile phone as if she wanted to throw it against the wall.

'Nothing!' Her voice wavered between anger and tears. 'Nowhere! No signal – no matter where I go! I've walked over this entire fucking hillside and there's no coverage – not anywhere!'

'You're right,' said Leo thoughtfully. 'I suppose I'll have to sort out some kind of signal before I can organize parties here.'

'That is *not* what I fucking meant!'

Tears, I decided. She still sounded angry, but she was definitely leaning towards tears.

'I promised my mum I'd call her every night. It's the only reason she agreed to let me come here.'

'Don't worry, we'll find somewhere you can call her from in the morning,' said Hat-man Dan, not lifting his eyes from his playing cards. 'She's bound to understand when you tell her that the mobile coverage is patchy here.'

'Yeah, chill out, Luce,' advised Beano. 'Come and have a beer and a smoke – and we'll deal you in on the next hand.'

Lucie scooped up an empty beer can and threw it at Beano's head. It struck him neatly above the left temple and bounced off with a metallic *doink*. I heard Jackson chuckle and knew he was probably exchanging another of his amused glances with Leo.

Lucie turned back to Hat-man Dan, tossing her hair and sending dozens of shiny black spirals quivering furiously about her head. 'It is *not* fucking patchy! It's non-existent! And my mum will not be in an understanding mood tomorrow morning because she won't go to bed until she's heard from me. In fact, she'll probably be on the phone to the police before midnight!'

'Well, they won't take any notice of her. Because you're virtually a grown-up.'

That did it. Lucie burst into a flood of ungrown-up tears and stamped her sparkly little Keds on the floor. '*But I promised her!*'

Hat-man Dan went and wrapped his arms around her. 'Shh . . . shh,' he whispered, to the undisguised glee of his watching mates. 'Come on – shh – you know there's nothing we can do now.'

'Dan, you have to drive me somewhere I can call her. There

was a weak signal when we passed that run-down campsite, I remember it.'

'That was a twenty-minute drive away!' Hat-man Dan sounded aghast. 'And my car's almost out of petrol.'

'You can take mine,' murmured Jackson, blowing out smoke through his nose. He was now so stoned his eyes appeared to be crossing.

'Thanks,' said Hat-man Dan, clearly not meaning it at all.

Jackson grinned and joined Leo and Beano in sniggering behind their hands – although not so far behind their hands that Hat-man Dan couldn't see them doing it.

'The answer's no,' said Dan. 'I'm too drunk and stoned to drive you anywhere.'

'I don't care,' sobbed Lucie. 'There's nothing out here you could hit. There's only hedges.'

'Only hedges?' said Leo. 'Don't you remember, Lucie? The road runs along the top of a *cliff*.'

'Now you mention that,' said Jackson, 'I think I'll retract the offer of my car.'

To my dismay, Lucie appealed to me – loudly enough for Leo to hear. 'What about *your* mum, Kate? Surely she'll worry if you don't ring her? Leo could drive us both back to the campsite and you could let her know you've arrived safely. I'm sure we'll be OK if he drives slowly – and it wouldn't take all that long. Please? I know you could persuade him if you wanted to.'

Could I? I wasn't so sure. Any influence I might have over Leo was so new and hard-won that I wasn't ready to test it yet.

I shrugged. 'My mum lets me do whatever I want.'

I knew it was the wrong answer the moment I said it. Oh, it was true – my mum really didn't mind where I was or what I was doing – but it was wrong nonetheless. I saw Leo smirk as Lucie turned away.

Guiltily, I dropped back on to the airbed and gazed straight up into the deep black shadows of the ceiling. Leo leant over and offered me the end of the joint he was smoking. I let him place it between my lips and breathed in slowly, wondering whether I would ever come to enjoy it. The unfiltered tobacco scorched my throat, but the cannabis somehow travelled further and lapped at the backs of my knees.

My mum lets me do whatever I want. I said it so often. Airily. Boastfully even. As if I was too grown-up for petty restrictions. Too cool to phone home. I'd used the words to make myself seem superior to Lucie. It was easily done and I'd had a lot of practice. *I can stay out till any time* . . . *Of course I'm allowed to smoke at home* . . . *My mum doesn't mind what I do* . . .

The words themselves were all perfectly true. It was just the way I said them that was a lie.

The joint burnt my fingers and I sat up, casting around for an empty can to drop the end into. The room rocked slightly as I moved and I could taste tiny, bitter shreds of tobacco on my tongue. I drank some of my bottled water and felt slightly better, but I wanted to clean my teeth. As I peered around the dim, smoky room at the slumped bodies, I guessed there wasn't going to be any sort of bedtime routine unless I made my own. So I picked up my sponge bag and went outside to the campervan.

The darkness hit me with the suddenness of someone pulling a sack down over my head. Where the fuck *was* everything? No stars, streetlamps or lighted windows – it was bewildering to a townie like me – and I couldn't help remembering how short a walk it was to the edge of the cliffs.

The castle looked pretty spooky too. A flickering orange glow illuminated the windows above the doorway and outlined the gigantic door which I'd left ajar. The rest had vanished. I cast continual glances back at that arch-shaped glimmer as I scurried to the camper. There, I cleaned my teeth, washed my face and used the tiny chemical toilet, before stepping back out into the blackness. The fresh air and cold water had cleared my head and made me less jittery. I was able to stand quite still, leaning against the side of the van and listening to the sounds of Darkmere.

The trees were whispering and rustling, the sea was sighing like a weak and weary soul, and a sea breeze wailed eerily. An owl screamed, making me jump, and I could hear the tinny music and murmured conversation of the gang inside the hall, one of whom was coughing horribly – Beano, I guessed, since he'd appeared to be burning a lump of cannabis on a knife he'd heated in the fire. I could even hear the crumbling old bones of the castle settling themselves for the night; the cooling timbers and stones giving out mysterious creaks and moans which should've terrified me.

But that wasn't how I felt right now. My stubborn streak

rose up to meet the darkness and the ghostly noises head on. It was this same streak that had driven me to study my way to a scholarship at the most exclusive school in town, and then dye my hair purple on the first day so that no one would treat me like a brainiac.

No, I would not be spooked by the noises.

Nor would I feel guilty about Lucie or ashamed of my background whenever Jackson looked down his nose at me. I was staying put. Thanks to Leo, I had a new mantra and I said it again – out loud – before I went back into the castle: 'Bring it.'

4

Elinor

By the time my sister was eighteen, she was the most beautiful girl in Devonshire. Everyone said so. All the gentlemen living roundabouts were in love with her. And the village boys; they were in love with her too. Had they seen her, the boys from the neighbouring villages would probably have felt much the same way.

That's the type my sister was.

She had the kind of beauty so lustrous it cast a glow over anyone standing close to her. That was the reason we were brought out at the same time. Alone, I tended to pass unnoticed, but together, we were the magistrate's lovely daughters. Together, we were flaxen hair and fluttering ribbons, petal-pink cheeks and white muslin flounces.

Anna couldn't wait to go to London and hunt down a husband. She wanted diamond necklaces, court feathers and a satin gown. Perhaps even a title. But I was only seventeen and cared little for the idea of a husband. So I suggested we put it off for another year.

'Oh well . . . if you won't come with me, then I shan't go at all,' she threatened. 'I shall stay here and marry the curate.'

The curate was three and sixty, and had a face like a plate of pickled tripe.

Our parents were not about to see Anna's beauty wasted on any of the local gentry, tripe-faced or otherwise. So Anna got her way, and on a rainy spring day in 1825, we were both taken to London for the Season.

The noise and smells and bustle were dizzying. I'd never seen so many people jammed together in one place; and they all seemed to be shouting unintelligibly or ringing bells – post-bells, street vendor's bells and bells with no obvious purpose. I couldn't imagine how people ever *slept* here! Our coachman had to find his way through a mob of horses, carts, stray dogs and street urchins to get to Upper Wimpole Street where we'd taken a house.

'*Not* Mayfair, of course,' sniffed Mama, 'but as near as we can afford, until one of you forms an advantageous alliance!'

She was looking at Anna, not me.

Then came the parties. Balls, theatres, assemblies and concerts – and Anna was happier than I'd ever seen her. My role was mostly to be by her side as a foil – the way a paste stone enhances a diamond – but within a few short weeks, half the gentlemen in

London were at her feet and she no longer needed me there. I could retire early and curl up with a novel and whatever I'd pocketed from the supper table. The mantelpiece in Upper Wimpole Street disappeared beneath a snowdrift of invitations and visiting cards – and in the middle of May, one note even came for me!

I hurried to show it to Anna right away. She was upstairs, sitting by the window of our mother's dressing room, which afforded the best view of the street below. She was stitching dutifully, but I knew better, and fishing under the cushions of her chair I pulled out a ladies' periodical filled with pictures of all the latest modes.

Anna giggled. 'Well, you might've been Mama!'

'Mama doesn't mind the fashion plates nearly as much as my novels, you know.'

'Oh I know, but they do put her out of temper, because the gowns are so expensive. What do you think of the one on the next page – in green silk?'

'Hmm . . . it's lovely in the picture, but I wouldn't be brave enough to wear it. That bodice might as well not be there at all.'

Anna laughed. 'It's almost the same as my new gown.'

'But it's cut so low! You'll catch pneumonia.'

'Or a husband.'

I made a sound between a gasp and a giggle. Anna had already developed an extremely practical turn of mind about what was expected of her.

'Oh, Ellie, don't be so prudish. Take that old shawl you're wearing – it's warm and cosy, but quite hideous to look at. If you thought a little less about your own comfort and more about what might be pleasing to gentlemen, I daresay you'd have secured at least one respectable offer by now.'

I doubted it. Besides, I'd had this shawl for ever   it was practically a *friend*. I drew it more tightly around me and walked over to the window. 'Well, it doesn't matter what I'm wearing if I'm standing next to you,' I said.

Anna accepted this with a slight nod of her golden head. 'Although I think you must have more than fashionable clothes if you're hoping for a really eligible marriage,' she said. 'You need elegance and countenance – and the sort of gaiety that suggests you actually *like* dancing and pleasant conversation. I have to say, Ellie, whenever I see you talking to a gentleman, you seldom look as if you're enjoying yourself.'

'Well, that depends upon the gentleman, but I seldom am.'

'Last night,' Anna continued dreamily, 'I was introduced to a man who told me that my *joie de vivre* was as lovely as my face.'

I rolled my eyes. Dazzling as she was, Anna did not have the sort of beauty that romped or capered. *I* was the one who always came clattering down the stairs or hitched up my skirts and ran downhill, chasing wind-blown leaves or butterflies. Only then it was never described as *joie de vive*. No, when *I* did it – it was hoydenish and unladylike.

But Anna was smiling complacently, as if replaying the compliment in her head. And that was the point, I suppose – it was a pretty line and it had pleased her. The gentleman had said it merely to see her smile.

'He asked me to drive out with him in the park,' she added. 'But I refused, of course, because I scarcely know him. Besides,

Charles Milburn had already asked me to go with him. And Captain Hartley, who has that brand-new curricle and such pretty match greys. Has anyone asked you to drive out yet, Ellie?'

'No.' I shook my head. No one had.

'That's a shame! The spring flowers at the Botanical Gardens are quite lovely. Surely someone must've invited you to go and see them. Everyone's been there.'

Everyone apart from me, as it happened.

'Then what about the play on Saturday? You haven't been to the theatre yet, have you? Charles Milburn has taken a box for himself and his sisters; and he's particularly asked me to join them. I'm sure I could persuade him to find you a place in our party.'

'I expect I'll go there with Nick.'

'Nick? Do you mean Nicholas Calvert?''

'Yes, that's what I wanted to tell you!' I waved the unfolded note at her. 'Nick's come to town. He means to call on me this afternoon – and he's sure to want a card for our evening party next week.'

'Mama will write one for him, you know she will. You can have my best sprigged muslin to wear too, if you like. You ought to make more of an effort to coax a proposal out of him.'

'From – *Nick*?' My mouth popped open in surprise. 'Oh, Anna – your obsession with proposals is getting out of hand! Why would I want a proposal from *Nick*?'

'I thought you liked him.'

'Of course I do – everyone likes Nick. But that doesn't mean I want to marry him.'

'Well . . . why not?' Anna frowned and shook her head. 'You've never shown any interest in anyone else and neither has he. I'm sure everyone expects you to marry him one day.'

Did they? My stomach contracted uneasily at the thought. 'But he's my *friend* – that's how I see him.' My voice dropped to a whisper. 'I can't imagine kissing him or undressing before him – or – or doing anything . . . *marital*.'

'Don't think about *that* or you'll never go through with it.' Anna grinned and fanned her cheeks with her book of fashion plates. 'Just think of all the advantages you'll have instead. Mama won't be able to tell you what to do any more. You can wear satin and lace – and all the latest fashions. You can have a house in town and your own carriage if Nicholas Calvert can afford it. Personally, I'm curious to discover what wine tastes like. Married ladies can drink it with every meal, if they want to!'

'Hmm . . .' I said thoughtfully. 'I'd choose to have chocolate for breakfast, instead of bread and milk.' Bread and milk was disgusting – I hated it with a passion.

'Then all you need to say is, "Yes, thank you, Nicholas," and think of nothing but dishes and dishes of chocolate.'

I laughed along with her, but I still didn't think I could marry Nicholas Calvert. 'Perhaps I won't wear your best gown after all,' I murmured. 'If I appear too modish, Nick might think it's for his benefit.'

'Trust me, Ellie, whatever you wear you'll always look modish next to poor Nicholas. Every time I see him, I'm always relieved he isn't wearing a coachman's coat or a tricorne hat.'

I laughed. It was true, Nick *was* old-fashioned and countrified.

But that wasn't really what bothered Anna about him. No, what set him apart from all the other gentlemen of her acquaintance was that he called to see *me* rather than her. Nick had always lacked the proper discernment.

'And that old sprigged muslin is no longer my best gown,' she added loftily.

'So that's why you're at the window pretending to sew – you're on the watch for your new gown!'

'Oh, don't laugh at me, Ellie – you don't know how badly I need one. Every night I have to watch Charles Milburn's sisters parading around in all the latest modes, while I'm wearing the same old muslin – it's unbearable. Even the men are a great deal more richly dressed than I am. Last night, Charles was wearing a new silk-lined cloak and a beautiful necktie with the most enormous jewelled pin in it.'

I frowned, feeling unsettled by my sister's absolute *yearning* for nice things. 'But . . . it sounds as if you're trying to make a choice between Mr Milburn's jewellery and Captain Hartley's new curricle without a thought for the men themselves . . .'

Before I'd finished speaking, a noise from the street drew us both close to the window in time to witness the delivery of a large bandbox from a fashionable Bruton Street modiste. 'It's here,' Anna breathed. 'My first silk dress . . .'

'It must've been very expensive,' I said thoughtfully. 'I wonder why Mama agreed to order you a new gown when she was complaining only yesterday about the cost of living in London.'

'It's for our evening party next week. There's a Mr St Cloud coming. He's the son of one of Mama's cousins, but quite a stranger to London society and he's coming on purpose to be introduced to me.' Anna hopped from one foot to the other at the prospect of yet another suitor. She collected suitors as other girls caught and pinned butterflies. Sometimes I wondered whether the butterflies had an easier time of it.

'A man of large fortune, I collect.'

'At least a quarter of a million in the funds, Mama said. Why, that must bring in seven or eight thousand pounds a year – only think!'

'Then why does he not have a house in town?'

'Mama thinks that he prefers the country to the town. He lives all the way out on the coast. What an odd sort of man he must be.' Anna laughed at such absurdity of character.

'But that means that you and Mr St Cloud would not be at all well suited.'

'Oh, I'm sure I could make him buy a house in town – and I wouldn't mind visiting his estate on the coast in the summer . . .' She closed her eyes blissfully. 'They say he's building a castle there. Imagine that! A castle with towers and turrets . . . and the sea all around it.'

Only a moment ago, I'd tried to caution my sister against a mercenary marriage, but I couldn't suppress a sigh at the image of that castle. How I wished *I* was the kind of girl men built castles for.

There was the sound of footsteps on the stairs, a tap at the door and an abigail brought in the longed-for bandbox and then – oh – the excitement of a new dress!

First the rustle of layer upon layer of tissue paper, then the slither and shine of flawless silk. Even the smell of the brand-new box was intoxicating. The skirt was a gloriously swirling pouffe of peppermint green. The bodice was pleated and folded like an intricate fan – with a neckline that would make Anna's white shoulders go on for ever. The sleeves were works of art in themselves. '*Gigot*,' explained Anna, and although I knew that this meant 'leg of mutton', I thought it sounded wonderfully Parisian.

The abigail and I helped Anna to dress. We twisted her and turned her; laced and re-laced her; tied up tapes and straightened heavy silk flounces until she was as perfect as one of her beloved fashion plates. Then we stood back, clapping and cheering as she danced up and down the length of the room, twirling before the looking glass so many times she almost fell into the fire.

'Well?' she asked, sweeping us both a wide curtsy. 'Shall I captivate the rich Mr St Cloud, do you think?'

'Yes,' I said truthfully. 'Yes, I think you will.'

Anna was still admiring herself in her new silk dress when Mr Calvert and Mr Milburn were announced. I ran downstairs to find them shaking hands and exchanging rather red-faced civilities.

'*Nick!*'

It was *so* good to see him! I could feel it shining out of me – a warm blaze of affection for the boy I'd known from childhood and the grown man he'd become. Straight-backed, broadshouldered and dependable, with a sense of humour that still owed much to the schoolboy's delight in the ridiculous, Nicholas Calvert was my best friend.

He looked the same as always, and his sleepy eyes crinkled back at me with the same pleasure that I knew shone in my own. I honestly couldn't have said whether he was handsome or not – his face was just too dear to me. Anna's alarming remark about everyone expecting the two of us to get married one day went right out of my head and I threw my arms around him. He felt more familiar to me than anything else in the world.

'How are you, Ellie? How are you liking London?'

'I'm sure I'll like it much better now you're here!' I turned to Charles Milburn and gave him my hand. 'You must let me make you known to Mr Calvert. He's a neighbour of ours and a very old friend of the family.'

'How do you do, Miss Elinor?' said Mr Milburn, who had been taking stock of Nicholas with a rather hostile expression. 'Mr Calvert. You're from Devonshire then?'

'That's right. My father's rector of the parish and we're the Marchants' closest neighbours. I was an only child, so Ellie took pity on me and saved me from a great deal of boredom and loneliness when we were growing up.'

'Ah, then you're not a particular friend of *Miss* Marchant?' Charles Milburn's glower was already giving way to relief that Nick had come to visit me rather than Anna.

'Lord, no! I'm not that ambitious.'

I laughed and said, 'Charming!' before inviting them both to have some tea.

'Actually,' said Mr Milburn, 'I called in the hope of persuading your sister to a turn or two round the park in my new phaeton. Do you think she might be agreeable?'

'Oh, have you bought a new carriage? Captain Hartley's curricle will be cast quite into the shade.' I smiled innocently and Nick's lips gave a little twist of amusement. 'I'm sure Anna will be down directly.'

'How about you, Ellie?' said Nick. 'Would you care for a turn in a poorly sprung hack chaise?'

I grinned at him. 'I'll go and fetch my bonnet!'

Mr Milburn promptly invited Mr Calvert to step outside and admire the new phaeton which was being led up and down the street by a nervous groom. The horses, two obviously high-bred and spirited chestnuts, were plunging, trembling and rolling their eyes. It was a windy day and the horses started at almost every leaf or piece of litter that skittered by. When I came out of the house and saw them, I couldn't help wondering how much more restless those horses would be by the time Anna came down suitably attired for an afternoon drive.

'Wish I could take you out in a set-up like that,' said Nick, helping me into the hack.

'Oh, you know I don't care about that kind of thing.'

'Your sister does. Sounds to me as if this chap Milburn only bought the phaeton and pair to compete with some other poor devil who's chasing after her. Which of them does she mean to have?'

'Neither,' I told him. 'They've both offered, but you know Anna – there's always a greater prize somewhere on the horizon.'

'Someone with a greater fortune, you mean?'

'Anna means to marry well, Nick. You can't blame her for that. One of us must. Anna's the eldest and the prettiest, and – well, she gets all the offers.'

'I see,' he said shortly.

'I didn't mean that a man *without* a great fortune wouldn't be a good match.'

'That's a relief to men such as myself then.'

'Oh, Nick, don't be silly!'

'You think it silly that I might wish to marry someone too?'

'No – no – I only meant that *Anna* must marry for duty rather than—'

'Rather than . . . what?'

I blushed and stammered and looked away. He wanted me to say '*love*'. He knew that I dreamt – not of titles or fortunes, but of some great romance. Only he'd never caused me to blush over it this way before.

'Rather than anything else,' I said huskily.

'So . . . you *do* think I'd be a good match, Ellie?'

I nodded – because it was true. Nick was the best match in the world. But he wasn't the man I dreamt of marrying. I'd read too many novels, I suppose. I'd read of men who fought in duels or gambled their fortunes on the turn of a card or disguised themselves as highwaymen in order to win the women they wanted. And Nicholas Calvert was not one of these men. He was too practical. Too conventional. Perhaps, if I was honest, too *real*.

'You can see Anna's great catch for yourself, next week,' I said, turning the subject and pretending not to notice his chagrin. 'I'll ask Mama to send you a card to our evening party. Will you come?'

'I will if you promise to dance with me.'

'I can't. There isn't to be any dancing – only music and cards. Mama is persuaded that Mr St Cloud doesn't care for dancing or large assemblies.'

'Then I believe Mr St Cloud and your sister are far from suited.'

'That's exactly what I said to Anna!' I chuckled and then gave him a mock frown. 'But such a thing cannot signify, when Mr St Cloud has a quarter of a million pounds.'

We left the hack at St James's Park and walked over grass all speckled with tiny coloured petals. The strong winds had stripped much of the early spring blossom from the trees and bushes and whirled them all together. There were lots of sugary pink petals from peach or cherry trees, and the bright coral-coloured spangles of a flowering quince. 'Oh, it looks like a wedding!' I said, and immediately started blushing again. 'I mean – I – I do like the windy weather. Don't you?'

He smiled and said, 'I like it more than your sister's friend Mr Milburn does.'

'What do you mean?'

'I caught his hat. Did you see it? A glossy black beaver, tall as a chimney pot?'

I shook my head, glancing approvingly at Nick's countrified shallow crown.

'The wind caught it as he was climbing down from his new phaeton. I stepped out of my hack at the same moment and his shiny, new hat came bowling right at me. I didn't have time to think about it – I just caught it instinctively.'

'Sounds as if you were defending yourself against the hat

52

rather than catching it.'

'Upon my word,' he exclaimed, 'it amounts to the same thing with lightning reflexes like mine!'

'I remember thinking that you and Mr Milburn seemed a little awkward when I first came downstairs.'

'So I should suppose. It's not often one has to thank a perfect stranger for catching one's hat.' He stopped and gestured along a tree-lined walk. 'Shall we take this path and see if it comes out by the lake?'

I followed him as if we were children again – even forgetting to hold my skirts off the grass as we wandered about. 'You know,' I said mischievously, 'Anna told me she always half expects to see you wearing a tricorne hat like the one your grandfather used to wear.'

'Sensible fellow, my grandfather.' Nick's opinion of men in overly fashionable hats was less than high. 'And I'll wager those tricornes didn't fly off in a puff of wind.'

'No? Do you think they simply spun round with a different point at the front?'

He looked at me in astonishment before bursting into laughter again. 'I've missed you, Ellie – oh, how I've missed you!'

My heart sank.

If I'd *wanted* my best friend to propose to me, that afternoon in the park would've been perfect. The weather was fine, the grassy walks sheltered and the spring flowers glorious. It was a wonderfully romantic setting for a proposal.

Nick didn't let go of my arm for a moment, and whenever he looked at me – which was often – there was warmth and affection in his face. He really made me believe I was worth looking at. *This must be how Anna feels all the time*, I thought, marvelling at the sensation.

And it wasn't only me he convinced. I attracted several admiring glances from passers-by and I peered over my shoulder to see who they were *really* meant for every time. But, no – the young man on my arm who was regarding me with such frank approval was persuading strangers that I was beautiful.

For the first time, it occurred to me that he really might . . . *love* me. Not just as a friend. And not just as the girl everyone expected him to marry. But *truly*. I felt quite stricken. Until then I'd only imagined the awkwardness that we'd both feel if I rejected him. I'd never considered the awful possibility of breaking his heart.

Beside the lake, he asked me. His face was so earnest – and somehow vulnerable – that I would have reached out to him, had he not already taken hold of both my hands. 'I've always loved you, Ellie. Will you do me the honour of becoming my wife?'

There. It was out. One of his eyebrows quivered slightly with the effort of keeping his forehead smooth and unconcerned. It made me long to hug him as if we were both eight years old again.

But I didn't, of course.

I didn't say anything for a moment, then I whispered, 'I can't, Nick.'

By the time I was able to look up at his face, he was already attempting to hide how much I'd hurt him. That made me feel worse than if he'd shouted or sulked or stormed away. Nick wouldn't have done any of those things, though. He was the best person I'd ever known. I didn't deserve him.

'I'm sorry,' I said. 'I'm so, so sorry.'

He took me home in the hack and didn't say much. I sniffed and swallowed in a determined effort not to cry. I had no right to feel sorry for myself and I knew it. I dreaded having to say good-bye to him at the door. I had no wish to be needlessly unkind but neither could I give him any false hope. In the event, it didn't matter because the servant who opened the door was so white-faced and shaking that I exclaimed, 'Whatever is the matter?'

'It's Miss Marchant!' he said, wringing his hands. 'Poor Miss Marchant! She's been in an accident, Miss Elinor. The new phaeton was upset and she was thrown right out. The surgeon is with her now.'

Nick took his leave immediately and I raced upstairs to see Anna. Her bedchamber had already been transformed into a sickroom. The curtains were drawn and the lamp shaded. There were hot bricks, bowls of clean water, bloodied towels and rolls of flannel at the bedside. The dressing chest was crowded with lavender water, saline draughts, laudanum and hartshorn. Then my gaze found Anna and my hand flew to my mouth.

Could that really be Anna?

Uncertainly, I moved nearer to the bed and listened to what the surgeon was saying to Mama. None of her injuries were life-threatening, it seemed. She had a broken leg and cuts from the horses' hooves – one laceration deep enough to cause some nerve damage. He had stitched the worst of the cuts, bled her and band-aged her broken leg to a splint. He prophesied a full return to health within the next couple of months.

But her beautiful face had been totally destroyed.

None of the nerves on the left side of her face appeared to be working, so all her features were being twisted and pulled to the right. And every kind of cut – from deep slashes to delicate grazes – disfigured *both* sides.

She no longer looked like my sister.

I glanced at Mama as she thanked the surgeon and saw that her eyes were very bright and her lips tightly compressed. Although she seldom gave way to the weakness of tears, she gave way to bursts of ill-temper with alarming frequency, so I was glad when she accompanied him out of the room.

'Ellie?' It was dull and oddly muffled, but it was my sister's voice. 'Ellie, is that you?'

'It's me.' I went and sat upon the edge of Anna's bed. But Anna did not look at me.

'What's happened to my face?' she asked, addressing the ceiling. 'How bad is it?'

I could barely understand, for her lips were so damaged that everything she said came out sounding muffled. It took me a long moment to decipher Anna's request.

'You have some – cuts.'

'I have to know, Elinor. Mama wouldn't hand me a looking-glass and I can't get up because of my leg. The surgeon wouldn't listen either. He kept on hushing me like a child.'

I licked my lips – perhaps to help the lies flow more smoothly. 'You'll look much better when your face has had time to heal.'

'But I can't wait! I need to be well in time for Mr St Cloud's visit.'

'There'll be other parties, Anna.'

A silence fell and it sounded loud and accusatory. Perhaps I *should* tell Anna the truth.

'My face feels so . . . strange.' Anna withdrew a hand from beneath the covers and laid it against her mangled cheek. 'I don't mean where I can I touch it . . . but *underneath* the cuts and the stitches. It's sort of numb, not a bit how it ought to feel. Oh, Ellie – I'm so frightened!'

This was unbearable.

I blinked and looked away from her. Slung over a chair in the corner were Anna's best velvet pelisse and tippet. Both of them were torn and marked with ugly brown bloodstains.

'What happened?' I asked.

'I don't remember all of it . . .' Anna turned her head on the pillow very slowly, looking at me for the first time. 'Something startled one of the horses . . . a newspaper that had been caught by the wind, I think . . . and they both ran away with us. Mr Milburn was taken by surprise and dropped the reins . . . but the horses were heading out of the park and towards the main road' – Anna gave a sound somewhere between a gasp and a sob – 'and he jumped out.'

I picked up my sister's hand and stroked it.

'There was nothing for me to do but cling on – and I clung as hard as I could – but when one of the horses fell, I was thrown over the front of the phaeton and landed under the legs of the other horse. I truly thought I must be kicked to pieces.'

'Oh, Anna – don't!'

'Charles Milburn jumped out and left me! He said he loved me but he *left* me!'

'But you didn't love him either, Anna.'

'I don't care – he shouldn't have *left* me!' She gave another sobbing gasp and I fetched a glass of water and hartshorn. I held it to Anna's mouth, but her lips refused to move and the water trickled over her chin, forming a tiny rivulet down her neck and on to the coverlet. 'I can't!' she sobbed, and a tear slid out of her right eye and zigzagged its way down the red gash of stitches leading from her eyelid to her jawbone.

Her left eye neither cried nor closed. It simply *stared*. Every so often its iris disappeared up under her eyelid, leaving an eyeball as empty and white as a hard-boiled egg.

Much later on, when Anna had fallen into a laudanum-induced sleep, Mama summoned me to her dressing room and handed me the green silk gown which Anna had re-wrapped carefully in its layers of tissue paper.

'This is yours now, Elinor,' she said firmly. 'You'll wear it to the party next week.'

And when I opened my mouth to protest, my mother shook her head. 'No,' she said. 'It's no use to your sister any more. You'll be introduced to Mr St Cloud in her place.'

5

Kate

'Leo – no!'

It was my first morning at Darkmere and already my anxiety level had shot right up to terror. I felt sick and dizzy with it. I'd read all those stories about teenagers messing about on clifftops – tombstoning, abbing, planking or whatever – and now I was *in* the story and someone I knew was dangling fifty metres above sharp, pointy rocks.

Way – *way* – below Leo was a tiny, unkempt beach. A crescent of glittering grey sand surrounded by cliffs. It was littered with debris from the sea – tangles of dried seaweed, heaps of driftwood, mangled beer cans and unidentifiable bits of plastic. Clearly no one had set foot upon it for years. It was wild and beautiful, but my stomach swooped with vertigo as I looked down at it.

'Leo, mate – don't do it!'

'Leo, come back up! Don't be stupid!'

'Leo! Seriously, you're going to die!'

Only Jackson knew better than to dissuade him from whatever course of lunacy he was set on. 'Maybe this is how the curse works,' he said, his head tilted to one side as he watched Leo struggle to find a foothold on the sheer cliff face.

'I can't watch,' I said, without looking away.

Leo's scuffed Lo Top flailed and sent a shower of loose chippings hurtling down to the rocks below him. Lucie gave a little scream and hid her face against Hat-man Dan.

'It's – my – beach!' The words came hissing through Leo's teeth as his face contorted with the effort of clinging to the crumbling rock face. 'I'm – going—!'

'Yeah well, the rest of us are going to the nearest town for supplies,' said Jackson in a bored tone. 'Is it OK if we take the camper?'

I saw the black flicker of Leo's eyebrows as he considered the prospect of cliffhanging without his gasping, terrified audience. 'No – wait – for – me!' His face was sweating now. 'I – just – want – to – get – down – there!'

'We all do, you jackass,' said Hat-man Dan. 'But we're going to buy a rope or – hopefully – some kind of rope ladder before we try it.'

'Yeah, it's not that we're scared,' said Beano, nodding his head towards me and Lucie. 'We're just thinking it'll be easier that way for the girls.'

'You're so thin,' Hat-man Dan muttered, 'you could probably jump over the edge and float down like a feather. We'll buy you an umbrella and you can open it on your way down.'

Beano punched him and Jackson grinned, although no one could bring themselves to laugh out loud while Leo was still hanging over the edge of the cliff.

The rock itself looked unstable and crumbly. Tufts of grass, moss and tiny wild flowers grew around the upper reaches where Leo was clinging, but further down the cliff face darkened, became more slippery and jagged. I could see that Leo would never make it.

Maybe he was thinking the same thing. He glanced down – under his own straining arm – to the little beach so far beneath him, and his forehead furrowed. 'Oh, fuck it!' he panted. 'Give me a hand up, you lot.'

All the boys lay full-length on the patchy, close-cropped grass, their hands stretched out to grab Leo's arms or the back of his T-shirt. And slowly, hand over sweating hand, he began to inch upwards towards them.

'Bunch of wusses,' he said, as his head drew level with theirs and they caught hold of him. 'You were all too frightened to have a go.'

'Not arguing with you, mate,' agreed Jackson.

'No, you wouldn't want to risk your good looks, would you, Jacko?' said Beano.

'No, and you wouldn't want to risk your . . . um . . .' Jackson looked him up and down, then shrugged. 'I'm going to have to get back to you on that one.'

They were all laughing and joking now. As if Leo had entertained rather than terrified them. He was more firmly their heroic leader than ever.

'Now can we go and phone my mum?' huffed Lucie, striding back up the hillside.

Everyone piled into the camper and we set off along the cliff road to find the nearest town. Jackson drove and Leo sat beside him, scowling darkly and brooding over the view from the passenger-side window.

The new master of Darkmere had woken up with a filthy hangover, ashtray hair and yesterday's clothes glued to his massive frame. He'd wanted a shower, but had decided to settle for an early-morning swim instead. So he'd walked down the hillside, peered over the cliffs and immediately spotted his own private beach.

Leo had summoned the rest of us to help him discover the way down. Still half asleep, we'd wandered along the cliff's edge. We'd followed rabbit paths that led nowhere, found a host of wild flowers and a broken sign that said 'ANGER – NO SWIMMIN'; we'd scrambled in between the trees and undergrowth. But none of us had found a way down to the beach.

The view was exhilaratingly beautiful. I'd kept forgetting what I was searching for and simply gazed out to sea, where seabirds were wheeling and soaring and occasionally diving into the water for fish. At the furthest jutting point of the cliff-top – where the sea seemed all around us and we were completely invisible from the castle or the road – was one of the strangest buildings I had ever seen. It was small and cylindrical like a pepper-pot, with a narrow arched doorway and a huge square window looking out to sea. It was built from the same stone as the castle, although tufts of grass grew from its roof and the walls were lichened and half hidden by a mass of brambles, ferns and nettles. The tiny building must have been used as some sort of observation post or signalling spot, and yet it had given me the uncomfortable sensation that *I* was the one who was being watched.

Leo had shinned up on to the roof and gazed down at the swirling sea below. 'I reckon I could jump from here,' he'd said.

We'd all seen what he meant. The lookout building almost *overhung* the sea. It was a perfectly straight drop from the roof down into the water without any sign of rocks underneath. It looked easy – just a step – although it must've been more than fifty metres in reality, and I felt that horrible vertiginous plunge inside me as I gazed down. The sea danced and teased, frolicked and foamed, and sang its whispery siren song to us.

Leo looked agonized. He *hated* to refuse a dare – even one from the sea.

After an hour, the sun was high, we were tired and hungry – and back where we'd started, above the beach. Lucie was making increasingly furious noises about phoning her mum, when Leo had noticed a couple of rusty iron rungs that had been hammered deep into the cliff – the remains of a ladder.

But the cliff had defeated him. As I sat behind him in the

campervan, I could see by the set of his shoulders and the rigidity along his jawline that he was sulking because he had not achieved the impossible – and I had a horrible suspicion that Leo wouldn't be content until we were all lying on his beach in the sunshine – with or without broken limbs.

In spite of Leo's bad mood, it turned out to be a good first day. We bought fish and chips for lunch and ate them out of their paper while sitting on the harbour wall, watching the boats. Lucie finally got a phone signal. Hat-man Dan and Beano bought crab lines and weighted their hooks with bits of leftover chicken or fish, then competed to see who could haul up the biggest crabs.

'You should try dangling those long thin legs of yours into the water,' Hat-man Dan advised Beano. 'I bet there'd be a crab on each of your feet when you pulled them up.'

'The old granny in the shop said to use very small pieces of bait,' answered Beano. 'So maybe you could try dipping your cock in.'

Lucie eventually finished talking to her mum and slipped her phone back into her pocket.

'Is everything OK?' I asked, moving to sit next to her.

'Well, she's not too happy, but I'm allowed to stay. And I have to phone or text her as often as I can.'

'Cool,' I said, admiring her honesty. 'Listen, Lucie, I should've made Leo drive us here last night. I'm sorry.' I meant it. I was ashamed of myself, in spite of last night's reso- lution not to feel guilty.

'That's OK. I overreacted because I wasn't happy about

being so cut off from everything and everyone. It freaked me out a bit, you know?'

I nodded fervently. I'd felt that way too.

'I shouldn't have asked you to choose me over your boyfriend, though,' she said with a chuckle. 'That was never going to happen.'

'Hey, if I was more confident that Leo actually *was* my boyfriend, I might've made the right decision.'

'Ah . . .' Her dark eyes slanted at me as if I was more interesting than she'd first thought. 'I guess he's not the commitment type, is he? But he wanted you to spend the summer here, so that must count for something.'

'Maybe,' I said, trying not to look as if I'd considered the matter.

After lunch, the boys disappeared into a dark and dingy pub, so Lucie and I wandered around the shops, looking at postcards, buckets and spades, and necklaces made of shells. Lucie bought a box of fudge for her mum and matching friendship bracelets for herself and Hat-man Dan, which I suspected the other boys would tease him about.

On one building was a sign that read 'Museum of Smuggling', and I headed towards it with poorly disguised interest. However, a much smaller sign informed us that the admittance fee was four pounds and – from peering through the dark and dusty windows – we saw that the exhibits were mainly barnacled old barrels and rusty anchors. Lucie's purse was stuffed with folded notes and credit cards, but she said she'd rather have her fingernails pulled out than pay four pounds to see a lot of old junk someone had fished out of the sea.

We caught up with the boys in a hardware shop where they were buying proper brooms and cleaning products. Leo also bought some tools, a hacksaw, and a couple of strong ropes, at which even Jackson rolled his eyes. Then it was Hat-man Dan's turn to drive us back to Darkmere, and when he switched some music on I found myself humming along.

The sky was bluer than blue, sunlight was bouncing off the bonnet and Bob Marley was singing about the joys of jamming. I muttered the lyrics under my breath and Beano overheard. For a second I thought he was going to make fun of me, then he nodded his head in time and sang along too. Moments later, we were all singing at the tops of our voices and I couldn't remember ever feeling happier in my life.

The tune stayed in my head even when we were back at the castle. Lucie had forgiven me and the boys seemed to have accepted me as one of the gang. We'd spent an entire night at Darkmere without being troubled by ghosts or curses and I was looking forward to the summer here.

Until now, we'd scarcely begun to explore the inside of the castle. Of course we'd opened a few doors and glanced in, but this afternoon – armed with brushes and brooms – we were determined to make a thorough inspection.

The grandest rooms were those closest to the Great Hall. Through a door on the right was the drawing room. This wasn't as impressive as the dining room, but it had larger windows with better views of the sea. The ceiling was decorated with garlands of oak leaves and carvings of animals with oak leaves in their mouths. I thought that perhaps they meant something, but when I suggested it to Leo he shrugged and said the oak leaves probably meant that it was all carved out of oak.

Next to the drawing room was a little tower room, magnificently panelled but no bigger than a cupboard. Sunlight poured in through the three arched windows, but they were too high up for any of us to see out of – surely an absurd design fault. On the floor plan was the single word 'mirador', which none of us understood, although Hat-man Dan said he thought perhaps the room had once been used to store cigars or tobacco.

All these rooms opened directly into one another through enormous doorways with carved wooden surrounds. But they were linked by other doors too, smaller doors that were cleverly concealed by the panelling, and which opened into dark, narrow passages marked as 'service corridors' on Leo's floor plan. It was easy to imagine housemaids, footmen and butlers sneaking in and out of the rooms, straightening cushions, dusting ornaments or clearing away meals, while the lordly St Cloud family pretended not to notice them.

Leo made *me* feel a bit that way too.

After the drawing room was a music room, then a room marked simply 'plate' on the plan. None of us could guess what that meant. It had bars at the windows and extremely sturdy doors. Perhaps to stop all the plates escaping? suggested Beano.

Although we remained on the ground floor, the rooms grew smaller and darker as we neared the domestic quarters. Ceilings were lower, the panelling and the floorboards were made of paler, cheaper-looking wood and the fireplaces dwindled in size. I pictured these rooms furnished with chairs and tables that were no longer wanted in the family rooms. Prints instead of paintings . . . threadbare rugs . . . perhaps a kettle boiling on the fire . . . Right at the back of the castle, we passed through the estate manager's office and the house-keeper's room and then, where the floors became flagstones, I knew we'd reached the kitchens. There were hooks in the ceilings, which I guessed had once been hung with pots and pans or joints of meat; drying racks high up near the ceiling in the room that the floor plan showed to have been the laundry; and shelves of cool slate in rooms that had served as pantry, dairy and scullery.

Lucie kept up a succession of squeals as cobwebs touched her hair or another cloud of dust made her choke. 'It's so *filthy*!' she exclaimed. 'My mum would totally *freak* if she saw this place. Wouldn't yours?'

'Yes,' I said. 'Totally.'

Jackson caught my eye and one of his brows twitched. He'd guessed I was lying. I waited for him to say so, but he just let me stand there, biting my lips and wishing, for the hundredth time, that he hadn't come with us.

Then I jumped as Leo let out a howl of frustration and karate-kicked a sturdy-looking door in the corner of the kitchen. When we all looked at him, he said, 'None of my keys will fit it.'

'It's probably a cupboard,' said Jackson.

'No, it isn't.' Leo shook his head stubbornly. 'There's no reason for a door this solid to be on a cupboard.'

And he kicked it again.

It became a sort of game – all the boys taking turns in launching themselves against it, kicking it, ramming it with their shoulders or battering it around the lock with their broom handles. But the door wouldn't budge.

I was oddly relieved. I didn't think a door so strongly made and securely fastened could be hiding anything good.

Then Beano emerged from the scullery, carrying a bent iron bar he'd found somewhere. Leo snatched it and renewed his assault upon the locked door. He gouged great splintery wounds in the wood, smashed one of the hinges and made enough noise to frighten every undead spirit right out of the castle.

'Don't!' I shouted, unnerved by his single-minded fury. 'Just leave it!'

Of course that made him attack the door even more ferociously, but still it wouldn't open.

He paused for a single beat of silence, before hurling the bar across the room.

'THIS FUCKING DOOR IS *NEVER* GOING TO MOVE!' he shouted, giving it one more karate-kick.

At which the lock broke, the door gave way and Leo plunged head over heels down a fight of stone steps into the darkness beyond.

6

'Leo!' we shouted, jostling each other in our efforts to charge down the steps after him. 'Leo? Are you OK?'

But Leo didn't answer, and when I took a breath it felt as if something was tearing inside my chest. Why had I shouted at him to stop? I might've *known* it would have the opposite effect.

The boys had to feel their way downward in the pitch dark-ness and Beano only managed to find Leo by stepping on him. Then Hat-man Dan toppled down the last few steps and got tangled up with both of them. With a lot of pushing, shoving and swearing, they carried Leo's apparently lifeless body back up the steps.

'Oh my God,' I said shakily.

'Is he dead?' Beano's voice was terrified.

'What are we supposed to *do*?' whispered Lucie.

'We need an ambulance,' said Hat-man Dan, reaching instinctively for his phone. His was not the only hand that did so – and then we all stopped as we remembered, once again, how helpless we were without a signal.

'Put him down here,' said Jackson. 'Somebody help me find a pulse.' He laid his fingers under the side of Leo's chin, his eyes screwed up in concentration.

Hat-man Dan pressed his ear to Leo's lips and I reached for Leo's wrist. I couldn't feel the slightest movement. Maybe my own hands were shaking too much.

'Fuck,' said Jackson. 'Do you think *this* is how the curse works?'

'Stop saying that!' snapped Hat-man Dan. 'I think he's still breathing.'

Jackson turned to me. 'Kate, go and get some water, will you?'

In spite of his great size, Leo looked oddly fragile. His hairline was dark and damp with sweat, his closed eyelids were blue-mauve and his face was pale.

As I ran for the door, I heard Jackson saying, 'We'll have to put him in the camper and take him to the nearest A & E. He could be concussed or have broken bones or something.'

I didn't hear any more until I was on my way back from the hall carrying a bottle of mineral water.

'He could be in a coma,' Beano was whimpering. 'And it's my fault. I was the one who gave him that iron bar.'

'How are you going to get him to drink it?' asked Lucie, as I

71

handed Jackson the water bottle. 'He's unconscious.'

'Yeah, I'd noticed that,' muttered Jackson, unscrewing the lid and pouring the water all over Leo's face.

The rest of us winced – it looked so callous. But Leo gave a deep, broken groan and opened his eyes.

'*Ow!*' he said feelingly.

'Yesss!' shouted Beano. 'The new master of Darkmere beats the curse once again!

'Thank fuck for that,' said Jackson, sitting back and running his hands through his hair.

Leo had a lump on the back of his head and a badly bruised coccyx, but he refused a trip to the nearest hospital, opting to self-medicate by holding an ice-cold can of beer against the back of his head.

'Ahh . . . that's better.' He opened a second can and drank deeply. 'Right! Let's go and see what's down there.'

'You're not serious?' I squeaked. 'You were just knocked out.'

'Yeah, so you probably shouldn't let me go alone.'

'But none of us needs to know what's down there.'

'We're going.' Leo stood up and swayed, clutching the door frame for support. 'Because whatever's down there is mine now.'

Each of us held a torch or a camping lantern and we all stuck close together, but still the journey through the cellars was scary. They were dark – and I mean *absolutely* dark – and cold, even though one of the hottest summers in years was beating down somewhere above us. And they were intensely claustrophobic. The walls and ceiling were close enough for us to touch and made me feel buried alive. It was a horrible feeling.

'Do you think the air's OK to breathe down here?' I asked nervously.

The boys all made choking, gagging noises, but instead of lessening the tension, the sounds echoed weirdly up and down the tunnel as if unseen people were mocking us. I inhaled slowly, ignoring the way my heartbeat had begun to batter the inside of my chest.

The tunnel sloped gently downwards, and various cellar rooms led out of it. Most of them were small and cave-like, strewn with traces of coal, firewood or what looked like mouldy old fishing nets. None of the castle's grandeur was in evidence down here; the walls, floor and ceiling were all rough grey stone with occasional green patches of some sort of mould or lichen.

The gang began to drift apart as we went deeper underground and our torches were waved around in different directions, casting each other's shadows upon the walls in horribly magnified and distorted ways. There was a distinct scurrying of rats or mice beneath the echoes of our footsteps, and one of the boys was still making an intermittent coughing, choking sound that made it impossible for me to forget my fear that the air might not be safe to breathe.

Then Beano hid in an alcove and jumped out on Hat-man Dan with a blood-curdling yell, frightening him almost to death.

'Oh God!' I clutched at the person nearest to me, not caring who he was – or that he flinched away from my touch.

Then I found I did care when it turned out to be Jackson.

'Are you all right?' he asked politely, after a second or two.

'Fine,' I muttered, cringing with shame in the darkness. 'I'm – I'm just not sure I can remember the way out.'

'I remember it,' he said quietly.

At last we reached a fork in the tunnel. The right-hand passage was widest, so we went that way, only to be stopped by a rusted iron gate like a portcullis. The bars were thick and immovable, the hinges had been sunk deep into the walls of the tunnel and the gate was locked. I think we all knew that none of Leo's keys would fit the lock even before he tried them. And when he kicked at this gate in frustration, we all moved back fearfully.

'I reckon the ceiling'll cave in and bury us before that gate budges,' said Jackson.

'I don't want to go this way,' Lucie said firmly. 'It looks like a dungeon.'

'She's right,' said Hat-man Dan, drawing back with her. 'We'll probably find smugglers' skeletons still shackled to the walls and God knows what else. I can't face it.'

Lucie shone her torch directly into his face. 'I can't tell whether you're taking the piss out of me or not.'

'A bit,' he admitted fondly. 'But not entirely.'

So we all followed them back to the left-hand passage which was narrower, danker and seemed to slope downhill more.

'It's like walking into a grave,' I murmured, making Lucie whimper.

There was a slight bend in the tunnel then, and as we all rounded it a distinct breath of cold air blew over us, lifting every hair on my body – even the invisible ones on my arms and the back of my neck. I felt Jackson shiver beside me and Lucie screamed.

'I *knew* it!' Still clutching the base of his bruised spine, Leo began to jog down the sloping floor of the passage into the draught.

Soon there was a glimmer of light. After the darkness it was wonderful. And suddenly we were all running. The daylight turned into sunshine streaming in golden rays through a mountainous heap of driftwood, seaweed and rubbish blocking the mouth of a cave.

Leo dived forward, kicking, pushing and tossing bits of driftwood behind him. He'd reached his beach at last.

Stepping out of the darkness on to that beach was one of those weird moments when I seemed to feel the beauty of it inside me as much as I saw it with my eyes. The sea was right there – endlessly rolling and crashing – flashing silver and gold in the sunshine, and drawing me towards it. The warm sand shaped itself around my every footstep. There were rocks with tiny flowers growing on them. There were coloured pebbles and pretty shells. There were seabirds bobbing on the water. Oh, it was the loveliest place I'd ever seen, and I thought, *This* – this – *is the reason the first St Cloud built a castle here.*

It was wild and secret. The evening sun was slowly sinking into the sea and setting fire to every wave as it went. The sand and the water retained the heat of the day – as if they'd soaked up every last drop of sunshine, but the air cooled around me, making me conscious of being alive and young and happy.

The others must have felt it too. We chased each other in and out of the waves, kicking up great sprays of rainbow droplets and shrieking as they soaked us. Leo and Beano dared each other to wade out further and further until they were all but swimming fully dressed. The rest of us climbed on the rocks and paddled through warm, soupy rock pools, collecting smooth, flat stones to skim across the water.

Eventually the sun seemed to explode on impact with the horizon, illuminating both sky and sea with a fiery orange blaze, shot through with steaks of purple and gold. It was breathtaking. I flopped down on to the sand next to Leo and sifted handfuls of the coarse grains through my fingers, digging my toes into it at the same time.

'You like it?' he asked, smiling.

'I love it,' I said, that mood of perfect happiness sweeping over me again. 'It's my best holiday ever.'

'Already?' He moved closer, his smile hovering over my lips. 'This is only the first day.'

'I can't imagine anything better than this.'

Then he kissed me very firmly and said, 'How about now?'

When I opened my eyes, he was already sauntering back

towards the water, where Beano had found a piece of rusted metal that looked as if it had once been part of a boat. Leo helped him drag it out of the water and I leant up on my elbow, liking the thought that it had been one of his own ancestors who had kept a boat here long ago.

Then I noticed Jackson's face in the background, and everything was spoilt. His lip was curling with contempt and his light brown eyes were like a thunderstorm. Slowly, he turned his gaze out to sea. But he'd obviously been watching me with Leo, and his disapproval had intensified into something more.

Why didn't he like me? The unfairness of it brought me to my feet and I marched over to him without even thinking about what I might say when I got there. Of course nothing came to me, so I dug my foot deep into the shingle and kicked a gritty shower of it all over him. He jumped to his feet, his fists clenched.

'What is your problem?' I demanded, squaring right up to him. 'What is it?'

'Right now?' He blinked, wiping his eyes and shaking the grit out of his hair. 'All this shit you just kicked over me, I suppose.'

'No, I meant what's your problem with me and Leo? Is it because I'm not one of those shiny-haired, rich girls with all the right vowel sounds? Is that what this is about? Me not having money like the rest of you?'

'What?' He sounded genuinely shocked. 'No! I don't have any money either.'

'Yeah, right! How did you get into Denborough Park then?'

'I got a . . . a bursary,' he said. 'It means . . . well, it means Leo's dad pulled strings.'

I felt a jolt of surprise, but I'd built up too much momentum to stop sniping. 'That must be nice for you.'

'Must it?'

No, I thought, remembering my own dread of becoming some rich kid's charity project. *It probably sucked to owe so much to a classmate – even a friend.* I could feel my anger ebbing away.

'Why then?' I repeated. 'What's wrong with me?'

'There's nothing wrong with you, Kate.'

He had turned away from me to look at the sea again, so I could hardly hear him, but I knew it was the first time he'd used my name.

'For some reason . . .' I said, pausing to listen to the slow crash of the waves mingled with the shouts from the rest of the gang. 'For some reason, you don't think I should get involved with Leo, do you?'

'I think . . . when it comes to girls . . . Leo has a very competitive streak.'

I had no idea what he meant. 'Leo's your friend, though,' I said at last.

'Exactly. You don't know him like I do.'

My mouth opened, but he shrugged and walked down to the sea.

I sat down where I was, my chin resting on my knees as I watched the sky darken and the sea turn the colour of gunmetal.

Of course Leo insisted upon lighting a fire. Although the tide had come in fast and there wasn't much beach left, there was still a bonfire-sized heap of driftwood and seaweed close by the mouth of the cave and he couldn't resist it. Once he'd got it ablaze, it crackled and roared, and the bladderwrack made sounds like popcorn. Showers of golden sparks shot up into the air and floated down again as tiny feathers of ash. The firelight gilded everyone's faces with mysterious shadows as if we all knew terrible secrets. I wished I could look like that always. Especially first thing in the morning.

You don't know him like I do . . . What was it that Jackson knew?

Hat-man Dan laughed then and caught my attention. He was leaning back on his elbows and shaking his head at whatever Lucie was saying. It must've been something about the castle, because I heard him laugh again and say, 'How can this place be cursed? I don't believe it. It's like paradise here.'

'It was easier to believe in the tunnel,' she conceded. Then, raising her voice, 'So who left the castle to you, Leo? And why didn't the curse affect them?'

'Don't you remember what it said?' Leo paused in the act of skinning up one of his huge spliffs and shook his head. 'The death curse is only supposed to work on us *male* heirs to Darkmere.'

I remembered. But I also remembered the way Leo had laughed at that article and chucked it over his shoulder. Now it seemed as if he'd been paying more attention than he cared to show.

'The women in my family were obviously a bunch of tough old birds,' he added. 'Apart from my mum, of course – she didn't even stick around long enough to inherit the castle. It came to me from her sister, my Auntie Hester. She died in May – breast cancer like my mum.'

'I'm sorry, Leo, I didn't know your mum had died.' Lucie's voice softened. 'How old were you?'

'I was seven. I moved in with my dad and my stepmum. They bought me a PlayStation, a flat-screen TV and a digital camera to make up for it.'

I watched the derisive curl of Leo's lip as he returned his attention to his half-finished joint, running the cigarette paper along the edge of his tongue and sticking it down in one swift motion.

I thought about my own mum. She wasn't a whole lot of use to me. *Would I swap her for a TV, camera and games console?*

Leo suddenly put back his head and laughed. 'Stop looking at me like that, Lucie. I'm not going to cry. It was ten years ago. I'm over it, all right?'

She shrugged and looked away, but I don't think any of us believed him.

'So, who was the last male heir?' asked Jackson.

'Ah, my long-lost Uncle Peter . . .' Leo paused and attempted to light the joint from the bonfire, almost losing a forelock of hair before Hat-man Dan tossed him a lighter. 'He inherited Darkmere right out of the blue when he was sixteen years old. My Grandma Edie told me that a solicitor's letter containing the deeds to the castle arrived with all his birthday cards.'

There was another crackling silence while we all waited for someone to ask what had happened to Leo's uncle. I thought it would be Lucie, but she stayed quiet. So I cleared my own throat and without making it sound like a question, I said the words I knew we were all thinking. 'So . . . he just went missing.'

Leo nodded. 'Yep. Right after he got the castle.'

I stared at him, feeling my mouth open of its own accord. 'But – but – how can you say you don't believe in the curse after that?'

'Because shit happens. It just does, Kate. Not because of stupid supernatural curses, but because that's how life is. Sometimes it just fucking sucks. My mum and her sister died of cancer and they both left kids behind. So why' – here he paused quite deliberately, drawing smoke deep into his lungs and closing his eyes then opening them slowly, like a cat – 'would I think that my *uncle* was cursed?'

I couldn't answer that. All I could do was sit there feeling small and stupid. I stared into the fire without seeing it, hoping the orange glow would hide my burning cheeks. Since when had I ever believed in curses or anything supernatural anyway?

'What do you think happened to him?' asked Jackson.

'I think he wandered off,' said Leo. 'My mum told me he'd fallen in with a gang of travellers. Real crusties with an old black ambulance, you know? They were supposed to have camped here for a while, and were long gone by the time my gran contacted the police. But who knows?'

I think we all knew. He'd been at Darkmere with a gang of mates – just like us. And that was the last anyone had seen of him . . .

Fear squeezed the inside of my chest and made it hard for me to take a full breath. I'd always thought superstition was for flakes and hippies, but there was something dangerous at Darkmere – whether any of us believed in the curse or not.

'Oooh, it's spooky,' said Lucie with a stoned little shiver. 'Didn't your gran look for him, Leo?'

'She never stopped,' he said, flicking the end of the spliff into the fire. 'She's still searching and hoping and waiting. My Grandma Edie leads the most depressing fucking life ever. My mum and my aunt were the same. My mum died hating her brother for ruining everyone else's lives.'

There was a long silence. The fire was too bright now and I looked away from it towards the blackness of the sea. At least . . . I *knew* the sea was there, but however hard I stared, nothing visible took shape. The smoke was bothering me too. I could taste it at the back of my throat and it was making my eyes itch. Then I realized I was tired. It was long after midnight and we were all worn out, twitchy and stoned. The mood had become dangerously confessional.

'But she didn't really mean it,' Lucie said quietly. 'He was her brother. She would've been pleased to have him back *really*.'

'I don't think so,' said Leo.

Lucie stared at him. 'But we all say things when we're angry that—'

'I bet she meant every word!' huffed Beano, his thin face stretched tighter than ever over his cheekbones. 'That's how I felt about my sister when I was growing up. She was the one our parents worried about and fussed over. Total fucking drama queen. If I ever had a problem, they didn't even notice!'

'Hey, you'd be more noticeable if you ate something, Slender Man,' said Hat-man Dan.

'I'm tired,' said Beano. 'Mostly of you, Dan, but I'm going to bed anyway.'

His footsteps went crunching away in the direction of the tunnel and the rest of us looked at each other across the fire, exclamation marks in our eyes.

'Did he say he had a problem?' said Lucie. 'What problem?'

'It can't be my jokes about how skinny he is,' said Hat-man Dan. 'Because they're hilarious.'

Leo put his head on one side. 'Maybe they're wearing a bit thin.'

'*I'm still in fucking earshot!*' said Beano, his voice echoing eerily from the cave mouth.

Silently, his huge shoulders shaking, Leo began to laugh . . .

Before long the rest of us followed Beano inside, yawning and rubbing our eyes with tiredness.

I was one of the last into the underground passage and I tried to tell myself quite firmly that it was no scarier at night than it had been in the day. Why would it be? It was dark either way. So there was no reason for the tightness in my chest . . . or the panic that had started to crawl all over my skin.

I'd forgotten how musty and dank it was in here, though. The air held a smell of decay that made the contents of my stomach rise up in revulsion. The noises were even worse – a hundred echoes took the boys' voices and footsteps and turned them into live things that crept backwards and spiralled around me or multiplied into a Greek chorus. My legs began to shake and I slowed right down.

There were other sounds now too. Dripping water . . . scuttling things . . . rustly little draughts . . . It was like a rising, quickening susurration that would, if I remained underground long enough, grow louder and faster until I was caught in the middle of a deafening storm.

'Probably rats,' said Leo, who cannoned into me when I finally stopped altogether.

'As if that makes it any better!' I said, my pulse racing to keep time with the noises. 'It's horrible – like – like dead people's heartbeats.'

He laughed. 'Dead people don't have heartbeats.'

'Huh, the ones at Darkmere probably do.' I moved to catch up with the others, but Leo's arm had gone around my waist.

'I like it down here. Stay for a bit.' His voice was thick with suggestion and I realized he was genuinely unaware just how horrible the atmosphere was down here. Perhaps he even thought I'd lagged behind on purpose; that I was waiting for him in the hope of being kissed again. I closed my eyes, hoping to feel that feathery spiral of excitement uncurling in my stomach – but my stomach was already too full of fear.

Please don't ask me to do this now. Not down here, in the whispering, watching darkness . . .

But I felt his face nudging my hair aside and he began to kiss my neck. Both his arms slid around my waist and locked there. I put my hands on his forearms, feeling the massive hardness of his muscles under my palms. They were like iron bands. I suddenly wished he wasn't so strong and so big. I wished I knew him better too – trusted him. The bad boy wickedness that had attracted me to him felt dangerous now.

Leo squeezed me even tighter, sucking my entire earlobe into his mouth. Oh God! My ear was so *wet* now. My shoulder jerked upwards reflexively, but Leo's mouth fastened on that too as he yanked down my vest-strap with his teeth.

This wasn't how I'd felt when he'd kissed me outside that nightclub – or when we were on the beach. I didn't want this. But Leo still hadn't noticed. It felt like I was hardly there at all. He could have been kissing *anyone* in this suffocating darkness. I began to feel the kind of panic that made me want to kick and scratch and run away.

What was wrong with me? This was Leo. Leader-of-the-gang Leo.

I turned my face into the solidness of his chest, my eyes shut tighter than ever as I tried to pretend we were somewhere else. *Anywhere else . . .*

That was when I choked. Leo seemed to be wearing some

sort of . . . aftershave? Acid-sharp and lemony. Caustic even. Surely I would've noticed if he'd worn it before now – I could've sworn he *never* had. It was mingling with the already poisonous air of the tunnel and stinging my nose and throat. Jesus, why had he suddenly drenched himself in such awful stuff?

I couldn't do this – I *couldn't*.

But before I could say anything, I heard the sound of footsteps and realized one of the others was coming back. Relief overwhelmed me. He'd have to stop now – he'd have to let me go. The footsteps grew louder and faster – someone was almost running towards us, but Leo didn't stop and no one appeared.

There was no light either. Why would anyone be running around down here without a torch?

'Leo . . .' I said, and there was a whimper in my voice. 'Leo – stop!'

The footsteps were upon us now, but still no one appeared and the air around me felt as cold as ice.

'Leo – please!'

I don't think he even heard me. When I turned my head to speak louder, his breath hit me in the face, hot and sharp with alcohol. Then I felt his teeth and tongue against my open mouth and he pulled my vest-top down further. I tugged at his arms, twisting and squirming against him – even this he seemed to take for encouragement.

'Leo, don't!' I shouted. 'I don't want to!'

He let me go.

I felt nothing but freezing air all around me and I drew in great shuddery breaths of fetid blackness.

'What's the matter?'

'I . . . I just don't want to.'

'What? Why not?'

'Because it's so horrible down here! Didn't you . . . didn't you hear those footsteps?'

'Footsteps?' His voice couldn't have been less amused. 'What are you talking about? Did someone put you up to this? Beano? No – Jackson, I bet it was Jackson?'

I couldn't think how to answer him. My thoughts were still flittery with fear, but as I paused an image of Jackson came into my head, saying, '*Leo has a very competitive streak . . .*'

'Why did you invite me here?' I asked him.

'I don't know – probably because I thought you'd be more fun than this.'

'Was it something to do with Jackson?'

'Fuck Jackson!' He gave a snort of exasperation and tried to grab me again, but I slapped his hands away and dived out of reach. With my arms outstretched and my head ducked low, I sprinted all the way through the tunnel and back up to the castle, leaving the master of Darkmere alone with his ghosts.

7

Elinor

I was perched so high above him that the first thing I noticed about St Cloud was his hair.

It was thick and wavy – and not nearly as neat as it ought to have been. I liked its not-neatness right away but I knew Mama would give him one of her lizard-eyed glances, and I hoped he wasn't the kind of man too easily discomfited.

He looked up then and saw me watching him through the banisters – and I accidentally let my mouth fall open in dismay. We'd been in London for almost a month and I'd crouched here on many nights, spying on the ladies in evening gowns and the gentlemen in their long-tailed coats. Although Anna could swish downstairs into the throng without hesitation, I always needed a little extra time to work up the nerve to go down. No one had ever noticed me before. But St Cloud did.

Perhaps it was because he was taller than most men. Broad too, with powerful shoulders and enormous hands and feet. He looked old enough to be a friend of my father's and I felt my lack of years at once. My lack of beauty and polish too. My dress didn't even fit properly! I couldn't help it – I sprang up and turned to run away.

He laughed at me.

I heard him. And I caught the gleam of his teeth in the brightness of the hall. Extra candelabra had been put there and the chandelier was dripping with candles on account of the party. Half-risen from my childish hiding place, I sent a glare right back at him.

I didn't mean to do it. Lord knows, I'd watched my sister and practised all her seductive smiles, coquettish little tosses of the head and an especially flirtatious sort of . . . *simper* that she used for this kind of occasion. He didn't get to see any of them, though. I stomped downstairs, ungracious as could be.

Later on, I learnt that sophistication bored him, so I suppose it was for the best. Besides which, Mama had asked me if I had the toothache when she caught me practising that simper in the looking glass.

I wasn't in the mood for a party – it was barely a week since my sister's accident – and I didn't want to simper at men who laughed at me. How could I chatter and flirt and play card games when I was so worried about Anna? I still felt guilty about Nick too. I wanted to go back home to the country where we could all be comfortable again. I intended to cross the hall with no more

89

than a nod in Mr St Cloud's direction, but my father came out of the drawing room to receive him, with my mother not far behind.

'Ah, St Cloud,' said my father. 'You're here in good time, I see.'

At the same moment, my mother caught sight of me and said, 'There you are at last, Elinor. I was beginning to wonder whatever could have become of you.'

I thought St Cloud's eyes twinkled at the way we'd managed to be both late and early, but he maintained a politely bland expression as formal introductions were carried out and rubbers of whist were proposed for later in the evening. He offered me his arm and we passed together into the drawing room.

It was disconcerting to see how much attention we attracted together.

So many eyes! I was suddenly unsure about the way I was holding my head. *What on earth did I usually do with my chin?* And I couldn't remember how I usually managed my skirts in order to walk naturally. *How did I avoid leaving nervous handprints on the silk?* Anna's new green gown swirled and shone like Christmas, but I would've been happier in muslin. Silk was so cold. It made me shivery with goosebumps and I longed for my thick woollen shawl. There was so much bare skin at my throat and shoulders and I felt certain I must be blushing it all into blotchiness.

When St Cloud's voice broke into my awareness – asking me how I liked the harpist – I stared at him in surprise and blurted out that I hadn't heard a note.

'Good God,' he said with a quiet snort. 'How are you managing to block it? That's a trick you must teach me.'

'You're not fond of the harp? What instrument do you prefer?'

'I don't know . . . military airs? Trumpets and drums?'

'I don't believe Mama considered trumpets,' I said gravely as I took a seat on a spindle-legged sofa against the wall. St Cloud lowered himself down beside me and the sofa creaked a complaint – which made a nearby dowager frown at him. The sofa shook and creaked again as he laughed unrepentantly.

The young harpist played quite prettily and made up for any lack of technical skill with soulfulness. As she plucked at the strings, she closed her eyes in a sort of solemn ecstasy and I felt a burst of hysterical laughter rise inside my chest. I gazed into the middle distance and tried to think about something else.

'You seem quite transported,' whispered St Cloud. 'I envy you that.'

'Hush,' I said. 'It makes me think of angels.'

'Really? Are they drowning?'

'I beg your— What?'

'No, I mean it,' he said earnestly. 'Can't you hear all their little voices crying out for help as their mouths fill up with water? The music has that plaintive, bubbling quality.'

I gulped and coughed, aware of my mother's presence across the room and, closer at hand, the dowager's scowling disapproval. 'I suspect the harpist is that lady's granddaughter, sir.'

'Ah . . .' He met the older lady's frown with perfect unconcern. 'I'm surprised she can have any wish to think of angels at her age.'

The harpist played on, her expression becoming almost pained at the aural beauty she was creating – and I had to try so hard not to giggle that my eyes watered.

'You really are moved, aren't you?' said St Cloud.

I bit the insides of my cheeks. 'I've never heard such – such richness of tone and feeling.'

He held his chin between a considering finger and thumb. 'It puts me in mind of the time one of the maids dropped a tray of pastry forks down the stairs. Although that *was* more tuneful, of course.'

I laughed out loud at that and the music-lovers who surrounded us made so many noises of annoyance that I nudged St Cloud to lead me away into the adjoining room. I was as shocked at myself as I was at him. And Mama was probably devising all manner of dreadful punishments for me.

The card tables in the other room were already made up, but there was a pedestal table tucked away in a corner with a chess-board laid out and two empty chairs. St Cloud drew me over to it.

'I'm not very good,' I said.

'That's probably just as well. I can't even remember the rules. Let me fetch you a drink before we begin.'

As soon as he was gone, Captain Hartley came up and asked after Anna. I explained that she had broken her leg and was indisposed, but we hoped she'd be better soon. When St Cloud returned with a glass of wine for himself and some lemonade for me, I introduced him to Captain Hartley. Until that moment I hadn't known it was possible for one man to smile amiably at another, yet give the impression that he was about to throw him through a window.

I suppose it was all to do with St Cloud's size. The captain's eyes had to travel up over his broad chin and prominent nose before they reached his eyes. It was an odd, fraught moment. Then St Cloud clapped him on the back and laughed before taking the seat opposite me. I think Captain Hartley sort of evaporated.

Far fewer men than I was expecting approached me to ask about Anna.

'How long are you planning to remain in town?' I asked St Cloud. 'I know my sister most particularly wishes to be introduced to you, but not until she's recovered from a carriage accident she was involved in.'

'I'll stay until my business here is resolved . . . one way or another.' He looked at me over the rim of his wine glass and his eyes twinkled again. 'I'd be glad to know your sister, of course.'

'Good . . . I'll tell her.' There wasn't anything more to say. I could hardly make him promise not to offer for anyone else until Anna's looks were restored to her. But neither could I pretend my beautiful, broken sister did not exist.

'I'd like to see something of you while I'm in town, if you've no objection.'

I shifted one of my chess pieces – I had no idea which one – and mumbled something incoherent.

'As it happens, I have business with your father tomorrow morning. Will you drive out with me afterwards?'

'You're coming to speak to my father?'

'Don't look so alarmed. It's estate business.' He drained half his glass, and without any noticeable thought picked up a black knight and dropped it amongst my startled pawns. 'Well . . . not exactly that, but it isn't a subject fit for your mother's drawing room.'

'Won't you tell me anyway?'

He hesitated and I looked away, biting my underlip and wishing I could learn to think before I spoke. Then he said, 'I've had word that a couple of men who used to work on my estate will be coming up before your father at the Easter Sessions and I'm going to urge him to be lenient in his sentencing.'

I smiled at him in surprise. I'd been so certain he would brush my question off with some kind of joke about my delicate young-lady ears. But instead he had explained the matter to me quite seriously – as if I were a grown-up. Nothing could have won me over more completely.

'Oh, if they're innocent, he'll find them so. Papa's always fair.'

'And if they're not?' Eyes gleaming again, he picked up his queen – tiny in his large hand – and rolled it between his fingers. It mesmerized me somehow and I couldn't look away. 'I have a sneaking suspicion that they may've fallen among thieves. But they both have wives and children who've done no wrong at all. So I thought to vouch for the men and pledge my word that they'll return to their families in the village and go back to working in my quarries.'

I wasn't avoiding his gaze now. I was looking right back into the warmth of his eyes and letting it melt me slightly. 'Most men would send an agent with a letter, I think.'

'I intended to, but one of the men's wives pleaded with me. The poor woman had heard that your father had a reputation for severity. Forgive me, Miss Marchant.'

'He *is* too severe – I know it!' I coloured and clapped my hand to my mouth. 'I oughtn't to have said such a thing about Papa. You must be shocked at me.'

Later, of course, I understood that St Cloud was utterly unshockable. But then he only laughed and sought to distract me by capturing my queen with a bishop that hadn't been anywhere near it.

'Put that back!' I exclaimed. 'That's not allowed! You can't make up your own rules like that.'

'How do you mean to stop me?'

'Why, I shall . . . I shall—'

'Just as I thought.' He grinned, showing all his teeth. 'I can't see the point in playing by anyone else's rules.'

I'd never met anyone like him. He was irreverent, arrogant and strong-willed. But he had the kind of charm that made my mother overlook his untidy hair and badly tied cravat, and which would – later – persuade my father to give him back his quarry workers. He made people do whatever he wanted, and his arrival lit up my London season like a lightning storm. I was dazzled by him.

That night, I was still laughing and attempting to make him give up my queen when Nick came in.

I didn't notice him until he was halfway across the room. Then my chest contracted in shock and I started up from my chair with the intention of running away. There was nowhere to go, of course. Everything inside me cringed at the thought of an impending scene. I knew Nick must be feeling the same way – it would've been torture for him to behave in a way that would draw the censure of a roomful of people, but he was forcing himself onwards. Towards me. He was trying to look dignified and purposeful, but his face was too set, his shoulders too high and his fists too clenched. He looked like an angry boy.

'I came to enquire after your sister,' he said, his voice as tightly reined as his face. 'I'd assumed your party must have been given up when I received no card. Does all this revelry mean that Miss Marchant is recovered now?'

'No . . . Anna's upstairs . . . she's not quite well yet . . .'

My words ran out and I fixed him with my eyes, entreating him to understand. I hadn't wanted to come down at all – of course I hadn't. I was only here in obedience to my mother. But it didn't work. He'd already seen me laughing with this tall stranger while my sister lay up in her room, wretched with misery and pain. I felt like a monster.

'She must be very unwell indeed to miss a party.'

'But . . . but this isn't really a party . . .' My mother's arguments were weak and halting on my lips. 'It's merely cards and Miss Flinton-Foster with her harp. Because, you see . . . some of our friends had travelled so far to be here. Such as Mr St Cloud . . . May I introduce Nicholas Calvert, my – uh – a neighbour of ours?'

Nick's fingers fastened on the edge of the table and he nodded in St Cloud's direction without a glance. 'Ellie, this doesn't sound like you. Can't we at least be friends? I spoke too soon, I know it. Don't do this to me, I beg.'

'I'm sorry, Nick. I asked my mother to send you a card, I really did.'

'Listen, I took too much for granted – I took *you* for granted. It was unforgivable of me, I see that now. We always suited each other so well that everyone assumed we would be married – my father and your father – oh, everyone. I assumed it too. You must've felt *conscripted* into marriage with me. Thing is, Ellie, I never imagined any future for myself without you in it. You're the only girl I ever loved and I can't be happy without you.'

'Oh Nick – don't! I can't bear it!'

'Ellie, you *do* love me, I know you do. Just promise me you won't—'

There was a footman at his shoulder now and Nick jerked round angrily, wrenching his sleeve out of the man's fingers. 'Take your hands off me – I *will* speak!'

My father appeared at Nick's other side. 'Come now, Nicholas, I can't have you upsetting my daughter like this. I'm sure we're all very much obliged to you for your attentions but this is a small family party, you know. It's time for you to leave.'

'*He's* not family!' Nick pointed at St Cloud, apparently noticing him for the first time.

No one ever argued with my father. Not unless he'd just sentenced them to transportation or hard labour – and even then it irked him.

'Young man, you are not suitably dressed and you were not invited. I repeat that it is time for you to leave.'

'But you *can't* object to my friendship with your daughter! You never have before!'

My father gave himself away then. His furious gaze swung from Nick to St Cloud, sitting so much at ease beside me, then

97

back again. It only took that moment for Nick to understand that the other man was worth more to my father financially.

'That's how it is, is it? So much for the Honourable Jonathan Marchant JP and all his integrity!'

'How dare you!' My father gave up his struggle to find words of weight and reason. He narrowed it down to just one more. '*Medcroft!*'

Medcroft was the butler. He took hold of Nick's right arm and signalled the footman to seize his left. Nick shook them both off.

'Ellie, I can't lose you – *I can't!*' He moved to take hold of my hands – as if words were no longer enough and he needed to hold on to me physically to convince me of the strength of his feeling. He really *couldn't* let me go.

And that was when St Cloud stood up.

The table and all its chessmen went crashing to the floor as he stepped toe-to-toe with Nick, towering over him as he had with Captain Hartley.

'You can,' he said, 'and you will.'

Only Nick did not evaporate as the captain had. He tried to look down his nose at St Cloud – although it meant looking upwards. 'Your kind doesn't intimidate me.'

'No? Perhaps I'll stop trying and break your spine instead.'

The threat of such violence was made so lightly – so *casually* – it took my breath away. Surely he couldn't mean it.

Nick put up his fists and St Cloud smiled very slightly.

'Oh, pray – don't hurt him!' I cried, and poor Nick reeled, my words hurting him worse than any blow. St Cloud, however, bowed in my direction and – very gently – assisted the two footmen and a groom who'd been summoned from outside, to bundle Nick out of the room.

Later, I cried for a long time.

I'd imagined men fighting over me *dozens* of times – mostly when I'd read similar scenes in one of my romantic novels or listened to Anna and her friend, Miss Milburn, describing their suitors' squabbles – but it was horribly different when real people were involved. How on earth had Anna been able to bear it? How could I? Nick's face had been so red and shiny – and not at all heroic. I kept remembering it:

I never imagined any future for myself without you in it . . .

Well, he'd lost me for ever now. And I him. With this realization, my own view of the future tilted sharply like the deck of a ship – sliding Nick out of sight along with everything that connected us – until there was nothing familiar left.

As the season drew to a close, St Cloud became a frequent visitor to Upper Wimpole Street. He took me out driving. He escorted me to the shops and Hookham's library for the latest novels. He bought me things: little volumes of poetry, bunches of flowers, rose-scented gloves, ribbons and lace – anything I exclaimed over or let my eye linger on for too long. Somehow he made me feel ungracious if ever I tried to protest. I had no experience or guile – no defences at all against a man like St Cloud.

One day, in Grosvenor Street, he bought me a diamond butterfly clip. It was the most beautiful and delicately wrought thing I had ever seen. I wanted it so much it gave me an inkling of just how deeply in his debt I was placing myself.

'No,' I told him. 'This time I mean it. It's too costly and I won't accept it.'

'Very well,' he said, stretching out his large hand with my delicate butterfly on its palm. 'Then I shall release it back into the wild.'

He made as if to toss it under the wheels of a heavy cart passing along the busy thoroughfare, and I leapt to catch his hand with a shriek.

'*No!*'

'What then? Do you mean for me to give it to some other lady?'

My hands and his own were now holding the little clip. My eyes went to his and I shook my head.

'I could give you far more than this, Elinor.'

He told me about the castle then. He told me that it stood on a steep green hillside with the sea all around, and that when the sun sank into the water, the windows would flame as if the castle were on fire. There were cannon high upon the battlements, he said, and a plate room filled with gold and silver. There were dark woods where owls screamed at night and a sheltered cove full of oyster beds. He told me I could rule over that castle like a queen from a fairy tale and he would have my name inscribed upon its tallest tower.

There was a fierce ache somewhere behind my ribs, but I kept my eyes on the tiny butterfly and said, 'I should not accept it, sir.'

'No, likely you shouldn't.' He pulled the ribbons of my bonnet undone. 'But that doesn't mean you *can't* – it only means you mustn't let your mama discover that you have. Now, are you going to let me take this bonnet off so I can fasten it into your hair?'

I let him and he spun me around so I could see my reflection in the jeweller's shop window. The butterfly sparkled in my hair and my eyes were huge. St Cloud was standing close behind me, so tall that my face was level with the buttons on his coat. 'Thank you,' I mouthed, and his reflection smiled back as slowly and surely as if I'd given *him* something.

I hadn't, though . . . had I?

There was no one I could ask. I knew Mama expected me to make myself as agreeable to St Cloud as possible – she had even given me all my sister's prettiest gowns to wear whenever he took me out. As a result, Anna was now too distraught to see me or speak to me.

My best friend was gone too, of course. After his shameful behaviour at the party, Nick had been sent abroad by his father to 'continue his studies'. That was all Mama would tell me and I had no means of finding out anything more, since she had gone on to destroy all the letters Nick sent to me – even the one he'd wrapped around a gold coin and addressed to one of the servants. Mama had allowed the dutiful footman to keep his guinea and thrown the accompanying message on to the fire before my eyes.

Everything conspired to drive me closer to St Cloud. Whenever I wasn't with him, I was terribly lonely.

And when he proposed, I was more than ready to go away with him.

After that, it all happened so fast! Within a week, he and my father had arranged the wedding between them. The lawyers began their legal wrangling and the dressmakers set to work on my wedding dress and all the additional gowns and petticoats that would make up my trousseau. Two weeks later, St Cloud left London again, in order to make his home ready to receive its new mistress.

At the first fitting, I discovered my wedding dress was to be cut quite as low as the green silk gown and left me feeling horribly exposed. I stretched my hands across the bare skin below my collarbones and caught my mother's eye pleadingly.

'I can't,' I whispered. 'Oh, I can't!'

She started to frown, and then changed her mind. 'Perhaps you're right – Mr St Cloud may well prefer virtue to vivacity in a young bride.' She indicated to the dressmaker that the neckline must be made higher. 'And Lord knows you don't have your sister's figure for it.'

'I don't think her figure is much of a consolation to her at the moment, Mama.'

'She must be made to see reason. I shall have her fitted for a bridesmaid's dress of pale pink gauze over rose satin. That ought to draw her out of her bedchamber.'

'She won't do it,' I said, remembering how the maid who emptied the ashes from Anna's fire had told me the grate was choked with the charred scraps of Anna's beloved fashion plates.

'Then we'll ask a couple of the other girls who are out this year. Perhaps Miss Flinton-Foster and—'

'If I can't have Anna, I won't have anyone.'

'It'll create a very odd appearance, Elinor.' Mama looked me over as I stood in the centre of the room in my long gold dress, my head high and my eyes full of sadness for my sister, and once again she changed her mind. 'But you must decide, of course.'

This, more than anything, made me feel as if I had changed – as if I had become someone else since my engagement. Mama still disagreed with my every word, but she let me have my way. I was the bride elect now. It made me feel panicky and breathless – and less grown up than ever.

When it was finished, my wedding dress was as smooth and shining as rich cream poured over an upturned basin. The sleeves were diaphanous clouds of blond lace and the bodice was embroidered with gold thread and tiny seed pearls. Mama took it away and hung it in her own dressing room. 'Otherwise you'll be tempted to keep trying it on and parading around in it,' she said with an accusing sniff.

But she was wrong. Although I crept into her room to look at it a great many times, I never felt any inclination to wear it. I regarded it in much the same way that Sleeping Beauty must have looked at the enchanted spinning wheel – it *drew* me, but I couldn't bring myself to touch it. In the light of my single candle, the wedding dress glowed, shining and golden. I felt a great deal of reverence as I sat before it in my old shawl and nightgown. Excitement too, for the strange new life it represented. But I never once convinced myself that the dress I was staring at was mine – no matter how many times I sat there.

The detached feeling persisted even as I dressed for my wedding day, my fingers cold and trembling as they smoothed the heavy silk. I knew I would remember the texture of it always. I shredded sprays of orange blossom and tore creamy rose petals as

I tried to help with my hair, until Mama and her dresser begged me to be still. With nothing else to distract me, I stared at myself in the glass and counted the days since I'd first met St Cloud. Fifty-five? Fifty-six, perhaps? Two short months and here I was, dressed as his bride.

Too soon, I heard the carriage arriving at the door and the sound made me feel so faint I was sure I must be ill. But no one would believe me, and I was driven to the church of St Clement Danes where a host of my parents' new London friends were waiting for us.

I'd always imagined I'd be married at home, of course, but being married by Nicholas Calvert's father was now out of the question. So I was to be married here – in an unfamiliar church, before an unknown congregation. And St Cloud – who waited for me, dressed more smartly than I had ever seen him – he was a stranger too.

My father bore me down the aisle and I knelt before the altar, but none of it was mine. Not the dress, the wedding or the husband. It wasn't happening to me. Not really. This was the wedding of someone else – someone more beautiful and golden.

Someone like my sister.

8

Kate

The Great Hall was lit only by moonlight and a small candle that no one had bothered to extinguish, but I was relieved to see anything other than blackness after the dark of the tunnel. The others were bundled up in their sleeping bags and I stumbled past them before collapsing on to my airbed. I must have been down in the tunnel longer than I thought. After a few minutes, I realized my bed was right next to Leo's, so I got up and slid it and all my belongings into the furthest corner of the room.

I lay awake for a long time, but I never heard him come into the hall. For a while, I dreaded the sound of his footsteps, then – after an hour or so – I started to worry. What if something had happened to him? It was so dark down there – and it felt so unsafe. Would it be my fault if something happened to him?

I gazed up at the dark shapes on the ceiling and saw that the straight, symmetrical banisters around the minstrels' gallery cast uneven shadows. Sharp and spiky, like tree branches or the misshapen fangs of monsters. I shivered and remembered how much fun this holiday had sounded when we'd talked about it in the safety of the school canteen. It felt so different now. An owl shrieked out in the woods and I shivered again. I was still twitching with unease as I fell asleep.

When I woke the next morning, Leo was sprawled across his airbed, snoring like a drunken wolfhound, and I let out a sigh. He was indestructible.

Later I watched him prowling around his domain, sticking candles into empty bottles and jamming them into holes in the carved wooden screen until the whole thing took on the appearance of a shrine in a church. This was *his* castle and I was no longer welcome here – the hardness in his eyes whenever he glanced at me told me as much.

I didn't know what to do. I wished there was someone I could talk to and ask for advice. But I wasn't close enough to the rest of the gang. What had happened last night had made me feel like an outsider again. The new girl.

I didn't go near Leo for the rest of the morning, but he seemed to be the same as always. He laughed and joked with the others and I realized he wasn't about to tell anyone I'd run away from him. He certainly wasn't going to let any signs of anger escape him – nothing would ever show he minded.

Apart from the way he looked at me. *That* was excruciating.

By lunchtime, I'd had enough, and when he finally wandered away on his own, a mug of tea in his hand, I followed and found him in the tower room with its too-high windows and heavy panelling. The room was so small it was like being stuck in a lift with him. His resentment surged around us, filling what little space was left.

'What are you doing in here?' I asked.

He stared at me for so long I didn't think he was going to answer. 'Nothing,' he said eventually. 'I just like this room.'

'Leo, I'm sorry,' I said in a rush. 'About last night, I mean . . . I panicked – I don't know why . . . but I'm sorry, OK?'

'OK,' he said slowly. 'Fine.'

It didn't feel fine.

'So . . . can we take things a bit slower now?'

'There's nothing to take slower. I was drunk and you were there.'

He didn't take his eyes away from mine the whole time. Even when he'd finished speaking and took a sip from the mug he held, he continued to watch me over the rim.

'I can't stay,' I said, shaking my head. 'Not now it's like this – it's too awkward. I'll ask Jackson or Dan to give me a lift to the nearest station.' I wondered if either of them would.

I turned to go, but Leo said, 'Well, we'll all go and get packed then.'

'What do you mean?'

He'd brought biscuits to have with his tea. I watched him tear open the packet with his teeth. He didn't offer me one.

107

'If you leave, Lucie'll have to go too – you know that.' He slid an entire biscuit into his mouth and crunched it, taking his time. When he continued, his words were thick and crumb-covered. 'She'll make Hat-man Dan take her home and she won't want to spend the whole summer without him. So he'll end up going with her. Jackson will probably go back too. Like I said, you might as well wait for us all to get packed.'

My eyes widened in dismay as I tried to imagine what the autumn term at Denborough Park would be like if I was not only excluded from the gang, but responsible for ruining their summer. Bloody hell . . . like it wasn't hard enough anyway.

'So . . . it won't bother you if I stay?'

He snorted. 'Seriously, why would I care?'

'I-I suppose I could stay for the week . . . and see how it goes.'

Leo only shrugged and I returned to the hall, feeling very uncertain about my decision. Had it even been *my* decision? The others were getting changed to go down to the beach, so I stopped thinking about it and scrambled into my bikini. Although I wasn't sure how long I'd be staying at Darkmere, my stomach lurched at the thought of being left behind to face the tunnel on my own.

Leo joined us on the beach and organized a game of cricket with beer cans and empty bottles. The boys had a dinghy and a couple of surfboards – although the waves weren't the right kind for surfing on, so they took turns at lying on the boards and bobbing about like human driftwood.

Lucie stretched out on a towel, wearing a sunhat as big as a satellite dish and leafing through a magazine. She looked very pretty and slightly bored. I drew patterns in the sand and hunted around for interesting shells or pieces of sea glass. Eventually I wandered all the way to the water's edge and stared down into the shallow waves until it seemed that the sand was moving and the sea was still.

Before I looked up, something startling happened. There was a slap of running feet and Hat-man Dan was beside me.

'Oh, shit!' he said, his eyes starting from his head. 'Oh, *shit* – look! We have to help her!'

I gazed out to sea and saw nothing there.

'What?' I said, puzzled. 'Help who?'

'That girl – look! Oh, shit – she's not swimming – she's – she's just *floating!*'

'I don't think so, Dan,' I said uncertainly.

Only he didn't seem to hear me. He charged into the water and began swimming full tilt at the horizon. After a minute or two, I saw him pause, his head snapping from side to side as he cast about for whatever – or whoever – had caught his eye.

But there was no one else in sight.

He swam out further than any of us had dared go. I yelled at him to come back and I heard the other boys shouting too.

'Whoa! You being chased by a shark, Dan?'

'Dude, you're going to end up in Iceland or somewhere!'

'Seriously, come back!'

But Hat-man Dan was soon so far into the sea that his head was no more than a distant speck. Then a wave rolled right over him and I couldn't see him any more.

That was when Jackson plunged into the water and powered after him. Leo too. Lucie, Beano and I stood knee-deep in the waves – startled into silence and immobility. Dan didn't surface. I guessed some kind of undertow had dragged him right under.

Leo was the strongest swimmer and he was the one who reached Dan first. He dived under and came up with him in his arms. Together, Leo and Jackson helped Dan back to the shore and dragged him up the sand.

He coughed and gagged and spluttered. 'I couldn't—' he kept saying, in between gasps. 'I couldn't get there . . . I couldn't reach her . . .'

'There wasn't anyone there,' Lucie shouted, trying to drape a towel around Hat-man Dan's shoulders. 'Calm down!'

Jackson held on to him too. 'Honestly, Hat-man! One of us would've seen her too. It must have been a trick of the light or something.'

But Hat-man Dan curled up on the sand, unable to stop shaking. 'She was there,' he sobbed. 'She was there.' He was unrecognizable as the unruffled dandy I'd come to know. His hair straggled over his face and his body was caked in sand as he lay there choking and sobbing. He looked like a piece of jetsam, spat out by the sea.

His misery affected us all. We were quieter then, more subdued. We put our earbuds in and sunbathed, or sat gazing at the horizon. When I walked through the shallow waves again, a tangled clump of fine yellow seaweed washed up against my ankle, before floating away like fair hair. I mentioned it to Hat-man Dan, but he shook his head stubbornly and wouldn't meet my eye.

Later that day, Leo surprised us by appearing on the roof of the pepperpot building on the clifftop, his semi-naked form outlined sharply against the brilliant blue sky. He bounced up and down on the balls of his feet, flexing his arms into a diving position.

'Go on!' the boys shouted. 'Go on, Leo – do it!'

But he didn't jump. It really *was* too high.

'I'll do it before we leave,' he said, strolling out of the tunnel ten minutes later. 'I'll get totally wasted and do it on the last day.'

'Ah, that'll be a lovely end to the holiday,' said Lucie. 'Taking you home in traction.'

Leo only laughed. He wasn't afraid of anything here.

After that day, the weather continued hot. The sun came into the castle through the small window panes and landed upon the floor in bright golden ingots. It was impossible to resist it and stay inside. Our days fell into a casual sort of routine. We'd wake up in the vast, panelled hall and lounge around in our shorts or bathrobes, chatting, drinking tea or eating bits of toast. Then, when the sun was high enough to have warmed the sea for us, we'd make our way down to the beach for a swim.

During that first week, Leo examined the walls of the tunnel and discovered hollowed-out niches set at regular intervals, each one spattered with drips of ancient candle grease. He stood new candles inside and left them to burn. Visibility improved, but the candles he'd filched from his stepmother were heavily scented and the noxious air of the tunnel became overly sweetened by cloying wafts of smoke. Gardenia, lavender and lily-of-the-valley mixed with mouldy must. Worst of all were the times the cellars filled up with that sharp lemony scent that made my throat close up.

I never stopped hating that underground passage between the castle and the beach. After a day or two, it began to seem much shorter and less winding, and I no longer had to think about which direction to take or remind myself to duck my head at the low bits. But I couldn't stop casting those quick, nervous glances around each bend in case something lurked there.

I never stopped listening for footsteps either.

Leo set to work with his new hacksaw – trying to saw through the hinges of the portcullis-like gate that blocked off the wider, right-hand passage. He was hopelessly lazy so progress was slow, but whenever he had nothing else to do, he settled himself down in the semi-darkness and sawed away at the bars, sending a hideous, rasping, scraping noise echoing around the cellars.

And after a while, I would brave the cellar and the noises. I would take him a cold beer or a snack. I would smile my best smile and say something friendly as if I hadn't noticed the hardness of his eyes. It gratified him, I think – made him feel as if he was the lord of the manor and I was some lowly serving wench. To be honest, I wasn't sure I even *liked* him any more.

But I remained a member of the gang, and gradually I relaxed around him again. It was impossible not to, as we all began to unwind. Our phones went uncharged and we lost track of the time and which day of the week it was. It stopped mattering. Sometimes Dan drove Lucie to the dilapidated campsite so she could phone home. He even persuaded the local farmer to let us use the shower building there, but whenever Leo and Jackson suggested we drive into town for proper coffee or pints of beer at the pub, they were outvoted by the rest of us. We found ourselves increasingly reluctant to leave the splendid isolation that we'd found at Darkmere and go back to the real world.

'Tomorrow,' one of us would say with a yawn and a stretch. 'We'll drive into town tomorrow . . .'

Evenings, of course, were for beach parties, bonfires and barbecues. If the tide was in, Leo had to build his fire right at the mouth of the tunnel, and the sea, black and gleaming in the dark, came up close enough to reflect the golden light of the flames. We'd sit around the fire, talking and laughing and holding long, rambling, drunken conversations about what we wanted and where we were going in life.

Leo told us his endless schemes for turning the castle into some sort of mad party hotel and how he would make Jackson the bar manager. Hat-man Dan was planning to start his own graphic design company and Lucie was going to work for her parents' organic food business. I listened in silence. *This* was the difference that Denborough Park had really made: it had taught them that they could achieve whatever

113

they wanted. Even Beano believed it – and his ambition was to be a high-class gigolo.

On one of these nights, towards the end of the first week, Hat-man Dan told us he'd heard footsteps behind him and, turning, had found nobody there.

'It's happened in the tunnel a couple of times,' he said. 'I suppose one of you funny bastards is doing it.'

'It's me.' Beano raised his beer can. 'I use my cloak of invisibility and my robo-boots.'

'Shut up, Beano,' said Jackson. 'It must be the weird echoey acoustics in the tunnel. I've heard some odd noises in there. Footsteps, rustling, coughing . . .'

'I've heard that,' I said.

Leo's gaze flashed in my direction for just a second as he remembered when I'd heard it, but his face didn't change.

'Don't be a sap, Kate.' Beano gave me a prod with his beer can. 'They've planned this conversation to try and freak us all out. They want one of us to have screaming nightmares about the ghost of Darkmere. They'll find that hilarious.'

'There's something else,' said Hat-man Dan, after a pause. 'You know I trekked up to the farm on Hangman's Hill the other day?'

'Yeah – you brought back eggs and milk and bacon,' said Beano approvingly. 'You should go up there again. I love fry-ups!'

'I didn't go up there for food. I went there to ask about that girl I saw in the water. I thought maybe she'd been camping around here somewhere . . . and I wondered if anyone had reported her missing.'

'Oh God, not this again,' said Lucie.

'The farmer knew who she was,' said Dan. 'He told me that people have seen her wandering through the woods or walking along the clifftop *for the last two centuries*.'

'Of course he did,' said Leo. 'He was trying to work out how gullible you were before selling you that overpriced bacon.'

'Shh, I want to hear this,' said Jackson. 'We've got the campfire, the dark cliffs, a secret tunnel and a haunted castle. This is the perfect time for a ghost story. Who is she, Hat-man?'

'Local people call her the Lady of the Lake. She's the reason no one goes near Darkmere any more.'

'Bollocks,' said Leo, finishing his can of beer and belching extravagantly.

'There have been accidents up on the cliff road.' Hat-man Dan pointed up above us. 'Cars have swerved to avoid a young girl who appeared in the road right in front of them. She's mentioned in all the police reports, but after a while the local police stopped trying to find her – they knew who she was all right.'

'Double bollocks,' said Leo.

'What did she look like?' I asked. 'Does she wear old-fashioned clothes? Or a shroud or what?'

'It's usually something long and floaty,' said Hat-man Dan. 'Although when the farmer saw her last, he said she was wet through. She had long, streaming-wet hair and a dress that was trailing water. He told me that people have stopped their cars to help her, thinking she'd fallen into the sea – or even tried to commit suicide – but she never seems to hear them. She always carries on her way as if she's dreaming. Or in some sort of trance.'

'People say that about me.' Leo inhaled smoke from his habitual spliff and allowed his head to roll back on his shoulders. His eyes were reduced to narrow, glittering slits.

Jackson chuckled. 'Are you saying the Lady of the Lake was the local stoner?'

'No, it's more than a trance,' said Hat-man Dan in a whisper. 'The farmer said she had white eyes – not only the parts that are supposed to be white, but the irises too. He said they were misty and white like milk.'

'Like the eyes of a drowned person,' said Beano.

'Maybe it's because I'm stoned,' said Lucie, 'but I'm start-ing to feel a bit spooked.'

'Me too,' I murmured. 'Can we not talk about the Lady of the Lake any more?'

'You know,' Leo said thoughtfully, 'there ought to be a lake here too.'

'You've already got a castle and a beach. Isn't that enough?' asked Jackson.

'No, I mean there *should* be a lake here somewhere,' said Leo. 'The castle's called *Darkmere*, isn't it? That means a dark lake. So there must be a lake in the grounds somewhere. I'm going to have a look around tomorrow.'

Although he'd changed the subject, our heads remained full of ghosts. We stuck close together in the tunnel on our way back into the castle and talked in whispers. Our collective mood was jittery and tense. Even Leo and Beano found very little to say.

Back in the Great Hall there were a couple of guttering candles on the mantelpiece which left most of the room in shadow. We all climbed into our sleeping bags or wrapped ourselves in our duvets, but it was a long time before any of us fell asleep.

I found myself straining my ears to catch the least sound. After a while, one of the candles went out with a hiss as the wick fell into the pool of hot wax and my heart bumped into my ribcage with fright. It was ridiculous!

I could hear everyone's breathing, their legs shifting position under the covers. Nearby, Jackson turned over restlessly and yawned. Hat-man Dan was listening to music and his headphones made a continuous *chach-chach-chach* sound.

I guessed it was somewhere in the early hours, which didn't leave more than, say, four hours of this eerie flickering darkness until the sky began to lighten. But with all my nerves prickling and jumping, four hours felt like a long time.

As the remaining candle faltered . . . flared . . . and finally went out, the room grew darker still. My ears seemed to grow keener in response. I could hear the sea and the wind outside in the trees. When an owl screamed, Lucie and I gasped simultaneously – then giggled at our own stretched nerves.

I hadn't realized she was still awake.

'Oh, for God's sake,' huffed Beano. 'Go to sleep, women!'

'Tell me, Beano . . .' Lucie's voice came sweet as sugar

through the darkness. 'Why is it that you don't have a girlfriend?'

There were a few chuckles at that, but gradually everyone else's breathing relaxed as they each fell asleep in turn. *Why couldn't I sleep too?* I wondered despairingly. *Why?*

If some horrible apparition were to show up and float among us, I wanted to be as blissfully unconscious of its presence as everyone else. Wakefulness wouldn't save me – I couldn't run or hide. We were miles from civilization. I didn't feel bold or adventurous any more – that hadn't lasted long after my first night here. Instead, I felt very far from home.

It seemed to me that one of the shadows by the door to the dining room was moving. After I'd noticed it, I couldn't tear my eyes away from it. I even began to wish it would move *more* – so I'd know for certain. My eyes started to water. I knew that if I looked away from the shadow, whatever was hiding there and watching me would seize the opportunity to creep up on me. Slowly . . . silently . . . and with infinite caution, I reached out my hand for my torch and switched it on, flashing a thin white beam into the corner by the door.

There it was – a black cowled monk hovering above the ground!

Then the monk resolved itself into Leo's black hoody hanging from the corner of the door by its hood. I sighed and massaged my aching chest. This was pitiful. I was going to go to sleep now.

Just as soon as I'd checked the shadows by all the other doors.

And this time I caught a dark moving shape in my tremulous beam of torchlight and instantly dropped the torch in horror. '*Jesus-Jesus-Jesus!*' I said, breathing so fast my own airways threatened to choke me.

'What are you doing?' someone hissed. It was Beano . . . I think.

'Jesus!' I said again – more in relief than panic now – and scrabbled for the torch. When I'd found it, I retrained its beam upon him and saw he was half crouching in the darkness, one leg still inside his sleeping bag and the other on the dirty wooden floorboards. It was no wonder I'd been sensing stealthy movements in the room.

'I was just going out for a piss,' he said. 'If that's OK with you.'

Then he sped across the hall, past the slumbering shapes on the floor, and disappeared out of the door, making no more noise than a ghost. I lay back down, but stared after him for a while. Although Beano acted like each day was one long comedy routine, for some reason, he was having as much trouble getting to sleep as I was.

In the morning, I woke with a start. I sat up, tousle-headed, and squinted around the room. Everyone else still seemed to be asleep and there was a blueish morning light at the windows. There was no movement or sign of activity anywhere in the hall. But I'd heard another noise, I was sure of it.

I slid out from under my duvet and padded over to the

dining-room door. I reached up and unhooked Leo's hoody, wrapping it around myself like a dressing-gown. Its sleeves shot down over my fingertips and the hem fell to mid-thigh. It smelt of sweat and smoke and something I couldn't place immediately. Then I remembered it was Leo.

Weirdly, there was no hint of that acid lemon cologne I'd smelt on him when we were down in the tunnel.

I went to the front door and opened it to look outside. I couldn't see much. The hillside was still cloaked in a thick blue veil and the campervan was indistinct. I stepped gingerly over the gravel and climbed into the camper. I had a wash and switched the kettle on for a celebratory mug of tea. It was always a small victory to be the first into the campervan in the morning.

After that, I returned to the hall and wandered through to the drawing room, sipping my tea and exploring idly. I continued into the tiny tower room, where I'd found Leo on that day I'd told him I was going to leave. He seemed to be drawn here quite often, which puzzled me. I stood in the centre with my arms outstretched and I could almost touch two of the opposite walls – that's how small it was. Though it was built on the corner of the castle nearest to the sea, its windows were too high to afford any view at all. I looked up at them, admiring their ornate wood-panelled surrounds and wishing I could see out.

There were some scratches on the underside of one of the windowsills. Initials. They wouldn't have been very noticeable to anyone taller than me, but I could see them distinctly.

There was an 'E' and a 'C' – and another letter in between which had been scratched over until it was obliterated. I guessed it had once been the 'S' that would've completed Elinor St Cloud's initials. I felt the same prickle of recognition as when I'd uncovered the inscription upon the outside wall, but this time I could see Elinor more clearly. She'd scarred the beautiful panelling like a rebellious teenager.

Like one of us, in fact.

I put down my mug of tea and tried to shin up the carved wood panels of the wall to reach one of the windows, grabbing at the many projecting bits of carving to pull myself upwards. To my alarm, a pretty wooden rosette that my fingers had lighted upon came away from the wall and, for a moment I thought I'd broken a piece off Leo's castle.

Instead a set of four polished wooden steps unfolded themselves from inside the wall. I leapt backwards with a gasp. The rosette was a lever! *This was how the people who had lived here before had reached the window!*

'Jackson!' I shouted. 'Leo! Come and see what I've found!'

Without waiting for them to join me, I bounded up the steps to look out of the window. There! It *was* a beautiful view. As dawn began to lighten the sky, I could see the green hillside leading away to the edge of the cliffs and the misty sea beyond. I could see the beach . . . somehow. *How could that be?*

I looked more closely at the window, certain there was some sort of optical illusion at play. The window was made up of three long, thin arched panes – a triptych. The outer panes were positioned at forty-five degree angles to the central pane, with heavy wooden panelling all around. But while the middle pane showed the view of the hillside that I'd been expecting to see, the other two . . . did not.

I put my face up close to the left-hand pane. It was heavy-looking, silvery and spotted with age; but it wasn't a window pane at all. It was a mirror.

I understood then. There was another mirror somewhere outside – on the cliffs perhaps, or that little hidden lookout building we'd found – and it was fixed at the precise angle that reflected a view of the beach. It was clever and mysterious. Why had the St Clouds needed to keep such a close watch upon the shore?

As I transferred my attention to the right-hand mirror, I was aware of the thud of bare feet in the drawing room behind me – someone was coming to see why I'd called out.

The right-hand mirror somehow magnified the view shown in the left. It was definitely Leo's beach. I could see the foot of the cliffs and the mouth of the cave. A shimmer of pale green flashed across the darkness as if a figure had whisked out of sight. I blinked and stared harder. The view was distant and blurry, but I could make out heaps of driftwood and debris . . . and a stretch of clean, freshly laundered shingle . . . and there, by the black rocks I could see . . .

I backed away reflexively and almost fell down the steps on to Beano who'd just arrived.

'Hey, cool find,' he said, starting to come up.

'No, don't,' I argued, pushing at him with my hands. 'Don't!

It's . . . it's nothing . . .'

Beano, however, had a radar that was horribly acute for anything sensational. Even before he saw, he *knew*. His eyes glowed with anticipation as he bustled me aside and leapt right to the top step. Leo followed close behind him. Jackson too. Within seconds they were all at the window whooping, cheering and hooting with laughter.

Hat-man Dan and Lucie were down on the beach.

Naked, thin as wishbones.

It must've been the sounds made by the two of them sneaking out that had woken me.

Jackson jumped back down and landed on the floorboards beside me with a bang. 'Don't stay up there perving on them,' he said, giving the ladder a kick. But Leo and Beano continued to watch and giggle. As Jackson passed me on his way out of the room, his scowl swept across my arms and shoulders, making me aware that I was still wearing Leo's hoody.

'Ooh, look!' I said, pointing at the road ahead. 'A badger!'

'Doesn't look much like a badger,' said Jackson, who was driving. 'Looks like an old dead bathmat.'

'The countryside's pretty, though,' I said. 'Hills . . . trees . . . hedgerows—'

'Roadkills,' muttered Jackson.

'Are you in a bad mood?'

'No.'

'Are you sure?'

'I had too much to drink last night, so I don't want to look at the trees and the hills. I just want to get into town and buy some food and a cup of coffee that doesn't taste like hot water with dust in it, OK?'

I started to argue but was distracted by a bunch of feathers protruding from a pink pulpy mound at the roadside. 'Is that a pheasant?'

'Not any more,' said Jackson, scowling. 'I hate the country. It's full of death and it stinks of shit.'

So I gave up trying to talk to him and gazed out of the window. We were driving into town behind the campervan. I'd asked Jackson if I could go with him this time – in a deliberate reversal of our journey down to Darkmere – and I was attempting to win him over with my observations of nature.

It wasn't working.

But I hadn't been able to face a ride in the camper. Leo barely spoke to me any more, although he sometimes threw me a questioning glance as if he was trying to work out the point of my existence. Beano was his usual boisterous self, but there had been a wary, resentful look in his eyes since last night, and I wondered if he was afraid I'd tell the others he was having trouble sleeping. Hat-man Dan was in a temper – and that was my fault too. Lucie had been so mortified by the round of applause she'd received upon her return from the beach that she'd burst into tears and refused to come to town with us. I would've given anything *not* to have called out when I'd found those steps and the mirrors that spied on the beach. But it was too late now, of course. I was doomed to do the wrong thing at every turn.

I was beginning to seriously consider going home.

Jackson parked behind the camper, in a road close to the harbour, and we all headed for the high street in a gang. As we walked, we bumped into each other or trod on each other's heels because we were reading the rush of emails and texts which had reached us after we'd passed the run-down campsite and came within range of a signal.

We went to a pizza place for lunch and then Leo announced his intention of spending the afternoon in the pub.

'We should probably get back soon,' said Dan. 'I don't think Lucie'll want to be left on her own too long and I'm in enough trouble as it is.'

'Give her time to get over it,' said Leo. 'Come and have a pint.'

'We have to do some shopping first,' Jackson reminded him. 'We need more supplies.'

'Oh God, you're such a bunch of old women,' said Leo. 'I need a drink and I'm going to the pub.'

But I couldn't face it and I began to look up train timetables on my phone. To my dismay, I discovered there was no station here and I was going to have to take a bus to the next town – twenty-five miles away – before I could catch a train home. I took out my purse and inspected its contents gloomily. I had just over fifty pounds left – and I wasn't sure it would be enough.

'You going to treat us to lunch, Kate?' Leo asked.

'I can't afford to,' I said, reddening.

Leo laughed in my face.

'Some of us have to earn it,' said Jackson in his most bored voice.

'Aw, you're such a hero, Jackson,' said Leo.

'Where do you work?' I asked.

'In the pub opposite the theatre,' said Jackson.

'It's a pretty cool job,' said Hat-man Dan. 'He knows all the night people – the bouncers and doormen, the dealers and the barmen. He always knows which bar is having an after-hours lock-in or which club is about to get raided.'

'That's not true,' said Jackson signalling for the bill. 'It's not remotely cool. It's endless washing-up and wiping down tables, and it means I'm useless at getting to school on time in the mornings.

'You won't have to put up with hours like that when I get Darkmere up and running,' said Leo, clapping Jackson on the back. 'We can sleep all day and party all night.'

He led the boys out of the pizza place and straight back to the pub they'd been to last time. No one asked me to come in. So after a moment's pause, I carried on walking along the high street on my own. I passed the supermarket, the cafes and the little souvenir shops. The town hall was covered with scaffolding because its roof was being repaired – and every inch of it was covered with seagulls. They watched me beadily, heads twitching like security cameras as I wandered past.

At the end of the street, I sat on the stone window ledge outside the Museum of Smuggling and studied the local bus routes on my phone. Bus timetables were *complicated*. Ten minutes passed and I still hadn't worked out where to find the right stop. I peered in through the window of the museum; the woman behind the counter looked exactly the type to know the way of the buses. Old. With gold spectacles on a chain and completely rigid hair like a sort of bouffant crash-helmet.

So I went in and asked her where I should catch the bus. The museum was cold and musty like the rooms at Darkmere, making me think of ghostly footsteps, strange noises and unsolved mysteries . . . and somehow I ended up handing over four pounds to look around. There were model ships, mouldy old barrels with secret compartments for contraband and, of course, the barnacled anchors – along with other unrecognizable salt-encrusted objects which really ought to have been thrown straight back into the sea.

In one corner of the room, I came upon a life-size mannequin with a crazily blackened face. He was wearing an old-fashioned farmer's smock and a wig made from a piece of doormat. In his hands, he held an enormous wooden stave. I snorted out loud and immediately glanced at the woman behind the desk to see if she disapproved of such levity in the museum. She didn't look up. Quite rightly, she'd been avoiding my eye ever since she'd taken my four pounds.

So who or what was this mannequin supposed to be? The card on the wall informed me that he was Ned Scathlock, a notorious local smuggler who'd been hanged for murder in 1827. I wondered if he'd been hanged on Hangman's Hill, but the card didn't say.

I wound my arm around the smuggler's neck, held my cheek against his black one, and took a selfie with my phone.

That cheered me up and I began to look around with more enthusiasm. There were drawers full of delicately pinned moths and butterflies with iridescent wings. There were shelves of stuffed animals with beady glass eyes, including a couple of mangy foxes, a badger much like the one we'd driven past on the way here and a horrible old pike with scale-rot. The name on the accompanying card caught my eye and I read that the stuffed animal corpses had been donated by someone named Mary St Cloud in 1915. I was careful to scan each of the little cards by the exhibits after that.

The name appeared again on a card beside a group of mannequins, dressed as if attending an especially dowdy fancy-dress party. There was a soldier on leave from the Peninsula War in his dirty red jacket with moth-eaten epaulettes; a shapeless bride in an awful net curtain of a wedding dress, and next to her a debutante in a sagging old ball gown that had once been green. It was the exact colour of seasickness, and not in the least like anything I'd ever wear myself. Yet I had the strangest feeling I'd seen it somewhere before.

As a kind of parting shot, I snapped a photo of the dummies and forwarded it to Leo with the message: *Your family looked like this!*

I'd seen all there was to see here, but I felt a nagging dissatisfaction. I hadn't found answers to any of my questions about the St Clouds – apart from the fact that they had liked shabby dresses and dead animals. So I returned to the desk and asked the woman if she had any information about Darkmere Castle.

Her expression said she doubted it, but she offered to go

and hunt around in the archive all the same. Before she left, she cast a suspicious glance at me over her shoulder – as if my question was a ruse to get her out of the room so I could steal all the barnacled anchors. I couldn't really blame her – I didn't look like anyone's idea of an historian with my peroxided hair, denim hotpants and Hello Kitty sunglasses perched on my head.

But when she reappeared, she was holding a dusty folder. She even found me a chair to sit on while I looked through it. I found myself grudging her the four pounds entry fee less. Not entirely, but less.

The folder contained a handful of newspaper clippings and some black-and-white photographs. One of them was an interior shot of the Great Hall fully furnished, and I studied it in fascination. I was so used to the hall as I knew it now – the bare floorboards covered with our dusty, sandy footmarks; the walls above the panelling empty of anything but grime; the high vaulted ceiling festooned with long cobwebs that none of us could reach; and our bedding, clothes and belongings strewn about all over the place. And now here was a sepia photograph of the same room crammed with the St Cloud family's possessions.

At first glance, there were an awful lot of antlers: rows and rows of them jutting spikily above the familiar doorways and all along the banisters of the minstrels' gallery. Leaning in even closer, I could see that – ugh! – the skulls of the stags still seemed to be attached. They were pathetically small, their bone-whiteness bleached to a blur by the flash.

There were pictures on the walls, long, low sofas, high-backed armchairs and knobbly carved wooden chairs which looked extremely uncomfortable. Over the fireplace, I could see a large mantel clock, a row of plates and two small busts – no, wait – it was a pair of those Chinese-style vases. A hundred other tiny details were too small or too blurred for me to make them out – and while there was still a chance I might recognize something else, I couldn't bear to replace the photograph in the folder. Instead, I slipped it under my T-shirt and tucked it into the waistband of my shorts, where it crackled faintly whenever I moved.

Beneath the photographs, I found a small faded booklet listing the entire contents of the castle. It was an auction catalogue dated September 1943. So that was the last time that the castle had been furnished as a home – during the Second World War. I thumbed through the catalogue and saw that among all the Dresden and the Sheraton there were hundreds of mundane little items such as 'copper coal helmet', 'plated butter dish and toast rack' and 'three feather pillows'. They made me feel sad, although I couldn't have explained why.

At the back of the catalogue there was an old map showing various farms, buildings, and hundreds of acres of land which had been divided up into lots and sold at the auction too. I ran my finger around the outline of the castle and what had once been the gardens – now swallowed up by trees. Then I turned the map around and frowned. It took me a while to realize that the coast road I knew so well simply hadn't existed in 1943. In those days the castle had been reached by a twisting driveway that ran through the woods and along the top of the hillside.

I followed this old road with my fingertip and came to the run-down campsite. It hadn't been a campsite back then, of course; it had been a small village called Merestone. And it was much closer to the castle than I'd realized – there was a shortcut right through the woods.

No, it was no good – I couldn't leave this behind either. I stuffed the auction catalogue inside my hotpants with the sepia photograph, and for perhaps the first time ever, I found myself wishing that my clothing was a little more capacious.

After that, I drew my knees up under my chin and began to read a story from a 1942 edition of the local paper. It was headed: *RESPECTS PAID TO CLIFF TRAGEDY BOYS* and accompanied by a tiny photograph of the cliffs at Darkmere:

Tributes have been pouring in after the deaths of two fourteen-year-old members of one of our most prominent local families. Mstr Philip St Cloud Curzon and his cousin, Mstr Roger Claydon were reported to have slipped from a rock face and plummeted over 150ft on Wednesday afternoon. Police and the Coastguard rescue team attended the incident which occurred close to Darkmere Castle, home of the boys' grandmother, Mrs Harriet St Cloud. A police spokesman described the deaths as 'a desperately tragic accident'. He said that the children had recently arrived at Darkmere and were engaged in a search for gulls' eggs when the fatal accident occurred. The two young sisters of Mstr Philip St Cloud Curzon told how they were playing around the castle and clifftop before boys had both taken the fateful decision to climb down to the beach via the remains of an ancient cliff ladder. Ten-year-old Celia St Cloud Curzon, and her seven-year-old sister Edith, saw Mstr Roger Claydon lose his footing and clutch at Mstr Philip St Cloud Curzon as he fell. Owing to the remote location, it was almost an hour before the Coastguard could be alerted to the plight of the two boys. Mstr Roger Claydon was found to have landed on the rocks and, despite being taken to hospital in a critical condition, he died late on Wednesday evening. A full-scale search for Mstr Philip St Cloud Curzon, whom his sisters had seen unconscious in the water, continued throughout Wednesday night and Thursday morning. However, the boy's body was not found and the search was eventually called off.

I sat for a while, holding on to the newspaper clipping and remembering Leo's attempt to climb down those rusty old rungs in the cliff face. Horrible! The exact same tragedy had so nearly happened again – right before my eyes.

Of course, it couldn't be a coincidence that the contents of the castle had been sold so soon after the deaths of these two boys. The St Cloud family must've been unable to live there any longer and had abandoned the castle altogether. I thought about Leo's 'Grandma Edie' who had watched her brother fall when she was only seven years old. No wonder she had never returned to Darkmere. When the deeds had arrived for her own son, she must've been scared to death.

I shuddered and put down the clipping, coming back to the present. After a moment, I stood up to stretch the muscles in my legs and realized I was feeling quite sick. Before I could reach for another of the newspaper articles, the sound of the museum's main door opening and the voice of the woman on the desk made me look up in surprise. To be honest, I hadn't anticipated any visitors to the Museum of Smuggling other than myself.

I couldn't see who it was, but a smoky murmur made me slide my chair backwards until I had a view of the front desk.

Jackson looked as out of place in the museum as I did. His hair was tousled, his jeans were torn and his T-shirt didn't go low enough to be tucked into them. He had that just-crawled-out-of-bed look that comes from camping in a derelict castle for weeks on end.

'What are you doing here?' I called out to him.

He grinned and came over. 'Looking for you, of course.'

'But why? What's wrong?'

'I don't know . . . I was getting a bit . . . not exactly worried.' He shrugged with one shoulder and moved to examine the stuffed animals. 'I thought maybe you'd given up on us all and gone back home.'

'But why would—' I looked at my watch as I spoke and let out a yelp. 'Holy shit, I've been here for *hours*!'

'Ha! You're such a geek.'

'Shut up, I'm not!

'You are. You're a total geek.'

I could feel myself blushing. 'How did you know where to find me?'

'Looked in all the geekiest places in town.'

'*What?*'

He nodded solemnly. 'I tried the library first, obviously.'

My face must've fallen because Jackson burst out laughing. 'That photo you sent Leo was a pretty big clue.'

I tried to laugh with him, but I was still too embarrassed that this boy – who worked nights in a neon-lit bar, who listened to reggae and drank strong black coffee – had found me here. In a museum of crazy mannequins and barnacled anchors.

'So . . . are you ready to come back to the castle?'

'Um . . .' I stalled, shuffling the papers and photos, although I wasn't really seeing them. 'I haven't finished looking at everything yet . . .'

Jackson rolled his eyes and sighed. Then he lifted up his Jimi Hendrix T-shirt and offered me his waistband in a submissive gesture that made me give a peal of laughter.

I stuffed a couple of photos and unread newspaper stories into Jackson's jeans and smoothed his T-shirt down over them. Halfway through, I had a sudden memory of the fury I'd felt when I'd caught him looking at my bottom while I was putting my stuff in his car. It flustered me and I tried to hide the remaining papers without touching him or noticing his stomach muscles.

'Ready now, geekmeister?'

I nodded and darted a quick glance at the woman behind

the counter, but she appeared to have caught sight of her own reflection in one of the glass display cases and was patting her rigid hair into shape – *tap, tap, tap*. Was this an effect Jackson had on women? I wondered why I hadn't noticed it before . . .

'Ironic really,' he murmured, as we sidled out of the museum, 'that you're making me smuggle stuff out of the Museum of Smuggling.'

10

Elinor

*D*arkmere was not just remote but *hidden*.

St Cloud and his coachman knew their way, of course, but I had small hope of visitors ever finding the driveway. There was no lodge or gatekeeper, just a low wall broken by a pair of simple stone gateposts and nothing but a farm gate leading into thick woodland.

We'd been travelling south for two days and were already far beyond the countryside around my own childhood home. It was wilder here – almost desolate. St Cloud spurred his horse into leafy darkness eagerly, but I looked through the window of the chaise and shivered with reluctance.

The tenants had come out to stare at us. I glimpsed villagers or farm workers standing at the edge of the drive as it snaked through the woods. Some of them waved or cried out good wishes. Others simply watched, half-hidden behind the trees. Eventually, the trees thinned and the chaise emerged from the woods into the glimmering dusk. The hillside that St Cloud had described was there, smooth as velvet, and beyond that I could see the shifting inky-blackness of the sea.

I found myself bouncing from window to window, unable to be still until the horses were reined to a halt and Darkmere was right before me. Then . . . I think for a moment I forgot how to blink or breathe – I could only stare.

The castle's creamy walls blazed like gold in the light of enormous flambeaux. Each corner, turret and windowsill was composed of clean straight lines. Age had not yet blurred or softened its appearance. There were no crumbling bricks, no rain-blackened stonework, not a trace of lichen or ivy. It was as perfect as a colour plate of a castle in a book.

St Cloud dismounted and came to hand me out of the chaise. 'Welcome home,' he said, helping me down on to the drive. I heard the sea then – and smelt it too – for it lay all around the hillside, like a dark mirror. It was almost too much beauty after such a long and uncomfortable journey and I felt tears prick behind my eyelids.

St Cloud moved towards the crowd of people watching us from the entrance to the castle. House servants, I supposed . . . kitchen workers . . . grooms and gardeners . . . they were all staring as one. But my gaze was pulled back up the castle walls again, and with yet another thrill I saw my own brand-new initials and the date of our wedding inscribed above the front door. This really was too much and the tears spilt down over my cheeks.

Then I blinked and my hand went to my cheek as if someone had slapped me. Because they *weren't* my initials.

ASC.

Anna St Cloud.

Oh, how my sister would've loved such a gesture! My eyes streamed harder than ever and I wiped them with the back of my hand. I felt almost as sorry for Anna as I did for myself. Of course, it was she who St Cloud had originally been invited to meet. He must've made up his mind to marry her before he'd even set eyes on her. These ornate initials were a measure of his absolute certainty that she would accept him. And he'd been quite right – she would've done.

Occasionally I'd wondered which of us St Cloud would've chosen if he'd ever seen Anna at the height of her beauty. Would he have even noticed me?

Probably not.

At least, that's what I'd told myself at the beginning. But my fascination with him had grown, and I'd stopped wondering about the answer to that particular question. Instead, I'd persuaded myself that I was the one he wanted. Not my sister or any of the season's most eligible debutantes, but me.

Only now, when I was standing before my new home and look-ing up at someone else's initials upon it, did I finally understand that he'd come to town for a bride, and either one of the Marchant sisters would've done. I think if I'd been at home, I would have fled upstairs to my bedchamber. But here, there was nowhere to run. I felt humiliated to the very core of my soul.

St Cloud didn't notice my distress. He bore me down the row of domestic staff and in through the great wooden doorway, and then almost immediately, he disappeared to talk over estate business with his steward. I was left staring about me at the vast hall with its magnificent panelling, carved screen and grand red-carpeted staircase. It was Mrs Thorne, the steward's wife and housekeeper at Darkmere, who stepped forward and took me over the principal rooms – the hall, the dining room, the library and the plate room stuffed full of treasure and antiques – before accompanying me upstairs to my bedchamber to rest before dinner.

'Summer cold,' I muttered to her, rubbing my eyes and blowing my nose. 'Such a nuisance.'

'Of course, my lady.' She pushed open one of the big arched doors. 'This is the south-west chamber, made ready for you on the master's instructions. You have only to ring if you need anything. More hot water or a fire made up, perhaps? Or a draught from the apothecary?'

The sneer was so delicate I'd almost missed it. But she didn't believe I had a cold. Perhaps she had noticed that St Cloud had forgotten to have the initials over the door altered when he'd married someone with a different name. Perhaps she – and all the other servants – had been laughing at me before I'd even arrived.

How could I face any of them after this?

I knew that St Cloud would laugh too, if I pointed out the mistake. I was familiar enough with his sense of humour for that! No . . . I wouldn't mention it. Not ever. It would be a – a *vow* never to let any of them see that I cared. My husband's blunder would remain quite beneath my notice.

The room was lovely. It had a rolling yellow and green carpet, sprigged with flowers and as vast as a meadow. Arched windows overlooked the sloping hillside and the sea, pink brocade curtains framing the view. Someone – perhaps Mrs Thorne – had arranged a jug of flowers upon the dressing chest. Mechanically, I laid out some of the toilet appointments I'd brought from home, bathed and changed out of my travelling dress, and then lay down upon the bed and sobbed into my pillow.

I hated the lovely room. And the castle. But most of all – I hated St Cloud! Wave after wave of homesickness engulfed me. I even cried for the rented house in London, and I'd never known much happiness there. Mostly I missed the draughty old house in the country where I'd grown up. I longed for the comfort of familiarity – to hear my parents sniping at each other across the dinner table while my sister ran in late because she'd been arranging a knot of new ribbons in her hair. And Nick, of course, had always been close at hand whenever I needed a friend. We had played together, shared confidences and quarrelled with each other almost daily. If home could be just one person, it had always been him.

I was red-eyed at the dinner table that night. My head ached and I had hardly any appetite. St Cloud was more at ease than I'd ever seen him, though. He lounged in his seat at the head of the table, with his long legs stretched out and his face tilted towards the open window, as if he were reacquainting himself with the sight and smell of the sea outside. I tried to smile at him across the silverware, but it was a wan and watery attempt.

This was the first time we'd dined alone together. In London, my father had always dominated the conversation. He'd talked a great deal about his duties as a Justice of the Peace, and how he had the ear of some of the country's most important lawmakers. In response, St Cloud had generally worked his way down a bottle of burgundy and eyed my father with boredom.

Tonight, I learnt a little more about my husband. He told me he was glad to be away from town and that he was looking forward to sailing and fishing and taking a gun out into the home wood. The independent and active life of a country gentleman suited his tastes. His inheritance had come to him unexpectedly, he said, and he appreciated it all the more for that.

His two brothers had been much older. The first had broken his neck going at one of the most notorious raspers in the county; and the second, who had persuaded his father to buy him a pair of colours, succumbed to a bayonet wound at Talavera before he could be summoned home to step into his brother's shoes. Although he spoke scornfully of his brothers' recklessness, I could tell St Cloud didn't lack their daring. He simply preferred to watch and wait. Already I was beginning to regard him as the most guarded man I'd ever met.

He said little about his parents and appeared to feel no affection for the family home back in Ireland, having chosen instead to set up his own establishment here at Darkmere, on this wild and secretive stretch of coastline that obsessed him.

'Well, madam wife?' he said in his lazy drawl. 'And what do you think of my castle, now that you've seen over it?'

'Beautiful,' I said quickly. My gaze swept the dining room

142

with its distinctive panelling, the fireplace with its carved marble inset and the heavily decorated ceiling. It was strange to think that I would be eating in this room for many years to come. 'It's so . . . quiet here.'

My words instantly made the room seem quieter still, and in the pause that followed I wished them unsaid. A clock ticked upon the mantelpiece. Presently a door in the panelling opened soundlessly to admit the butler with a dish of partridges.

'Surely that's an advantage,' said St Cloud. 'To have thick carpets and well-trained servants.'

What I'd really meant was that wherever I was in the castle I could hear the hush and sigh of the sea and I found it unsettling.

'Of course,' I said. 'I'll soon get used to it.'

'There's much that you'll have to get used to, Elinor.'

I stared down at my plate and the silence came again, louder this time. I couldn't be sure of his meaning, but I could feel my cheeks flame as I guessed at it.

St Cloud did not leave the dining room with me and I spent a long and lonely hour waiting for him to join me in the drawing room. When at last he came, he stayed only a moment or two, before closeting himself in the little tower room at the corner of the castle. Somehow it felt more like a reprieve than a slight, and I retired to my bedchamber to wait once more.

I read page after page without once escaping into my book. I paced around my unfamiliar room and stared out of the window at the strange blackness beyond. In a sudden fit of piety, I knelt and prayed, but it didn't seem to help. When I opened my eyes again, they itched with tiredness and my headache became a swirling, nauseous pain. I opened the window and the sea hissed at me like an angry crowd. Such a strange, restless noise! Would I ever become accustomed to it? Somewhere close by, an owl screamed with a sound that terrified me. I climbed into bed and pulled all the covers over my head.

Only in the early hours, when silence had long since fallen over the many rooms and passages of Darkmere, did St Cloud finally come. It was so quiet that I was able to hear his footsteps drawing near to my room in spite of the soft new carpet that ran all the way along the corridor outside. At home there had been worn drugget along the upstairs passages – and in some places, nothing at all to hide the bare boards. Stealth had been almost impossible.

My husband's steps halted outside the door and I stared at its huge arched shape, steadying myself for the sound of his knock. Then the handle turned and the door moved towards me. There was a brief tap accompanying the movement, but St Cloud – apparently – did not require my permission to enter.

My hair was loose and I was wearing one of the new night-dresses that had been part of my trousseau. All my night-things had been chosen by my mother and packed in the highly polished dower chest that she had brought to her own marriage. Mama had added hemstitched linen sheets, pretty bedspreads, tablecloths and runners. Anna had been given the task of trimming my new nightcaps, but tears from her undamaged eye had drenched each one and the stitches were clumsy and uneven. I had chosen to leave those in the chest.

St Cloud was holding a branch of candles and shielding the

flames with his free hand. The soft orange glow illuminated the left side of his face, while his long, aquiline nose and prominent eyebrows threw black shadows across his forehead and right cheek. His was not a handsome face, but it was compelling. The harsh features – the slants, planes and angles – all suited him somehow. And his *eyes* . . . his eyes reflected the candles' tongues of fire and made me think of demons and souls in torment.

How I wished I knew what he was thinking, now – more than ever. But he seemed to prefer secrecy to intimacy. I knew him no better than when I'd first met him, on the evening of that fateful party. And now, here we were – married and at Darkmere.

He turned and locked the door before advancing further. With his branch of candles, he lit those upon the dressing table and the mantelpiece. Then he came and sat upon the bed next to me and I quailed at the shock of his proximity and the way the mattress dipped and bounced beneath his weight. St Cloud smelt of brandy, and tobacco from the little black cigars he smoked in the evenings. I did not dislike the scent of tobacco, but it was yet another foreign quality that unnerved me.

'What . . . should I do?' I stammered.

'Whatever I ask of you,' he replied. 'Isn't that what you promised?' He had already removed his coat and his waistcoat hung unfastened. Slowly, he began to untie his neckcloth and pull it free of his collar.

Panic rose inside me and I froze – completely rigid, too numb with dismay to frame a single word of protest. St Cloud began to kiss and caress me, but my veins seemed to run with iced water and my body grew colder wherever he touched. Oh God! I watched from outside myself as he pulled my nightgown up to my neck and looked down at me. *Is that really me?* I thought wildly. *Why can't I move? Why don't I feel anything?*

My body no longer seemed to be under my own command. I could not make it relax or bend to my husband's advances. I wanted so much to win his affection and to love him in return. I wanted to talk over all our shared hopes for the future and learn to understand him better. Instead, I closed myself against him instinctively, and when he forced his way into me the pain made me cry out in horror.

St Cloud was indignant. 'You're my wife,' he hissed. 'My wife! Why in God's name do you think I married you?'

'I'm sorry,' I said, trying not to cry with shame and mortification. 'I'm sorry . . . I'm sorry . . .'

But I didn't want to be married any more.

He continued to move inside me and I fought the urge to push him off. The best I could manage was not to let him see how unbearable it was. Anna had advised me to think of something else, but nothing helped. Not all the dishes of chocolate, green silk dresses or clifftop castles in the world.

Oh God, would it always be like this? How often would I have to endure it?

More than ever, I wanted to go home. I felt like a failure as a wife – and I think St Cloud thought so too. He certainly didn't stay long afterwards.

I dreaded meeting him at breakfast the following morning. Sleep had come only fitfully, and an echo of last night's headache was still fluttering around my head like a razor-winged moth. So I took the coward's way out and decided to spend my first morning at Darkmere in bed. My maid brought me a dish of chocolate and a couple of slices of bread and butter. To my surprise, she told me that St Cloud never breakfasted before noon in any case. Everyone in the castle appeared to keep quite eccentric hours – although she couldn't tell me why, since my mother had sent her with me from London and she was as new to Darkmere as I was.

I sipped at my chocolate, but found it overly sweet and powdery. Remembering Anna's advice again, I sighed, because she had been so wrong. Too much chocolate only made you sick. Too much of *anything* could make you sick.

Before the maid left, she drew back the curtains and I went to sit at the window. The sea was somehow friendlier than it had been yesterday and it held my gaze. In fact, there was a brightness and energy to the whole prospect that invigorated me. The waves were long and white-topped, and they whipped up and down as if someone were shaking out a sheet or a tablecloth. The grass on the hillside was being flattened this way and that by the wind. The sky was moving too. Like a ribbon patterned with clouds and birds, it seemed to whisk past my window as if on a reel. Quite suddenly, I wanted to go out and look around.

I dressed in a rush and left my room. The passages were wood-panelled, dimly lit and thickly carpeted. I couldn't help it, I lifted up my skirts and stole along like a housebreaker. I missed my way several times, but eventually I found a door that opened on to the minstrels' gallery and I leant over the banister to look down at the hall.

I had a vivid memory of the first time I'd ever seen St Cloud – the way he'd laughed up at me as I spied on him through the banisters of my parents' house. If he were to come striding across the hall at this very moment, my view of him would be just the same. I stood quite still for a while, watching and listening to make sure this couldn't happen.

From the gallery it took one swift run – down the stairs and across the length of the hall – to the massive front door. I let myself out into the forecourt, crossed the gravel and scampered down the hillside with the first real feeling of freedom I'd had since my wedding day.

I wandered along the clifftop, enjoying the wind on my cheeks and a magnificent view of the sea. It was so vast and so sparkling; its endlessness hypnotized me. The waves dipped and swelled, and a small boat with a full sail seemed to almost bounce over them, leaving a glorious swirling white wash behind it. A flock of seabirds circled the boat, and I felt infused with their mad, swooping curiosity. Perhaps St Cloud had gone out sailing this morning and it was his boat that I could see. I chased it along the clifftop, pushing my way through the nettles, brambles and trees in a scrambling and unladylike manner until I was at the furthest point of the Darkmere cliffs. To my astonishment, I was confronted not by a steep drop into the sea, but a little round building like a pepperpot with an arched doorway. At the same instant, there was a noise from within it – the scrape of a boot on stone – and I found myself face to face with a gigantic rough-looking man wearing a filthy neckcloth and a scowl.

I gasped. I'd thought myself to be quite alone out here. To my horror, the man took a quick step towards me.

'No! Keep away from me!' I said breathlessly. 'You've no business to be hiding in there.'

His scowl deepened in confusion and he advanced no further. 'I weren't hiding,' he said. 'I were keepin' a watch for the master.'

'Oh! You're . . . you're one of the grooms then?' A tremor of relief passed through my knees. 'I'm afraid I don't know everyone by sight yet. Or are you one of the gardeners?'

'That's right, my lady,' he said, in a way that made me suspect it wasn't the truth. 'I work for the master o' Darkmere.'

'What did you say that you were keeping watch over? Did you mean you were watching his boat? Is that Mr St Cloud sailing down there?' I pointed and looked out to sea where the little sailing boat was flashing through the waves – then, on the horizon, I spied a second vessel; this one a big ship in full sail, looking for all the world as if it had escaped from a glass bottle.

He shook his head without turning to see where I was indicating. 'I dursay that'll be a fishing smack belonging to someone from the town, my lady.'

'And that larger one?'

'Revenue cutter.' The horrible man spat – *actually spat!* – over his shoulder, in the direction of the ship.

'What's your name?' I asked him indignantly.

He hesitated, still glaring and evidently reluctant to divulge any information, but no reason to be discourteous seemed to occur to him. 'Scathlock, my lady,' he said. 'Ned Scathlock.'

'Right . . . well, I'd like you to show me the way down to the water, if you please, Scathlock?'

'There's no way down for you, my lady.' The young giant tugged his hair obsequiously and ventured to add that the master might not be quite pleased to hear that his new wife had strayed so near to the clifftop.

I was annoyed by his impertinence, but he proved to be quite right.

That evening, as I rose to withdraw from the dining room, St Cloud detained me with a gesture and said, 'Thorne tells me you were out walking rather near to the cliff's edge today, Elinor. That path is overgrown and dangerous. I'd prefer it if you stayed a little closer to the house in future.'

'Thorne? I didn't see Thorne.'

'Naturally, the man who saw you reported his concerns to Thorne.'

'What is it that Ned Scathlock does for us here, St Cloud?'

'He's one of our keepers.' St Cloud yawned and refilled his own glass. 'Quite outside the compass of your concerns, my dear. You must content yourself with the old and the sick of the village.'

I wasn't satisfied with his explanation, but my hand was already upon the door handle and I was reluctant to prolong the awkwardness of our second evening meal with further questions. So, of course, I chose escape.

I hadn't missed his hint about the villagers, though. Their welfare was in my trust now and I was keen to make a success of at least *one* of my duties as his wife. I knew that a village as tiny as Merestone was so cut off from the rest of the country that its inhabitants were bound to be suspicious of anyone new. But I meant to be so charitable and so charming that they would come to welcome my visits as much as the food or alms I brought with me.

I rose early – thanking God that St Cloud had not come to me on my second night – and rang for my maid, but my bell was answered by a much younger girl with sly, slanting eyes and untidy hair. She dragged her feet and slopped my chocolate about in its dish.

'Who are you?' I asked in surprise. 'And where's Walker?'

'Morning, my lady.' She bobbed a curtsy and giggled. 'I'm Nell – Nell Scathlock. Mrs Thorne says I'm to wait on you now, my lady, seeing as your Miss Walker's upped and gone off back home.'

'What – why?' My stomach dropped with a little jolt of dismay. I hadn't known my new maid very well, but I felt as if my last link with the outside world had gone. 'Why would she leave me?'

'She weren't really getting along with the rest of us. Didn't like the quiet, didn't like the hours – didn't like anything much. She kept right on complaining till Mr Thorne put her in the trap an' took her away.'

'But – but he can't have driven her all the way to London!'

'Lor' no, my lady. But that weren't where she said she were going. She told us she were going back to *civilization*.' Nell gave me a mischievous smirk. 'An' Mr Thorne had some business over in the next town, so he took her with him. Told her she could take the stage back to somewhere more civil from there.'

'I see,' I said. 'You haven't been a lady's maid before, have you?'

'No, nor any kind of maid really. But Mrs Thorne told me to say I were willing to learn.'

'Oh . . . very well. You may help me dress my hair and then accompany me to the village, Nell . . . *Scathlock,* did you say? Why, I believe it must've been your brother I met out on the cliffs yesterday.'

'Ah now, you mustn't judge me by our Ned, my lady.' She picked up my hairbrush and examined it. 'None o' the screws inside his head are done up tight enough, that's what I say.'

After Nell Scathlock had wrecked my hair and I'd done my best to repair it again, we went downstairs and Nell showed me the way to the game larder, where I helped myself to a couple of wood pigeons, before fetching milk and cheese from the dairy. I had an idea that some fruit from one of the hothouses would be a nice touch, but that made Nell laugh so hard I gave up the idea. Mrs Thorne gave my basket a disapproving glance but said nothing. Since she was the one who'd inflicted Nell Scathlock upon me, I took a quantity of cold beef from the kitchen table just for the pleasure of seeing her lips go even thinner.

To my surprise, St Cloud came into the kitchen while I was there. He was dressed in an old shirt and breeches and there were a couple of dogs at his heels. As usual, he made the room shrink.

'I-I was told the servants never look for you much before noon,' I blurted.

'Really? I don't believe I have any regular habits at all.' He glanced around at the kitchen staff, who – admittedly – did not seem in the least taken aback at the way he'd strolled into their midst. 'Sounds like a very dull way of carrying on. What are *you* doing up so early?'

'Charitable works,' I said primly.

'Good God! I'm only here for a pint of ale and a sandwich.'

Mrs Thorne broke in with a sniff. 'I'm afraid, sir, that Madam has just taken the contents of your sandwich to give to someone in the village.'

St Cloud burst out laughing. 'Who the devil are you planning to give it to?'

'I don't know,' I confessed. 'Who do you suggest?'

'Oh, you'll have to apply to Thorne – he has a list of all our neediest dependants. I think he's gone off in the trap this morning, though. Can you think of anyone, Mrs Thorne?'

'Well . . . there are the Barrows, of course.' She turned to me with another frigid sniff. 'One of our quarry workers has broken his back under a rockslide on the Darkmere estate and he's been taken away to the infirmary with small prospect of recovery. His wife claims she's unable to feed her children and meet her husband's medical bills. I'm sure she'd be glad of some beef and' – she eyed the wood pigeons – 'this evening's second course.'

St Cloud laughed again. He accepted a thickly cut sandwich from one of the kitchen maids and tossed some of it to the dogs before disappearing through a stout wooden door in a corner of the room. I glimpsed part of a rough stone wall before the door banged shut behind him.

'What's through there?'

'The cellars, my lady.' Mrs Thorne turned and hurried away

153

before I could ask her anything more.

Nell pulled a face at her retreating back and I didn't bother to admonish her. Because in my head, I was doing the same thing.

We went out through the kitchen courtyard and around the outer walls of the castle until we reached the driveway at the front. A mist like a fallen cloud hung over the sea and the air tasted salty and white. I led the way past the entrance to the stable yard and along the driveway towards the woods, with Nell chattering away at my side.

Before we'd reached the shade of the trees, the distinctive and brutish form of Nell's brother loomed up from the direction of the clifftop and I quickened my pace away from him. But his appearance was followed by a high-pitched scream of terror and the sound caught at my heart. It reminded me of the noise made by the little brown hares in the fields around my childhood home, when they were caught in a snare.

Only this time it wasn't a hare.

Scathlock was dragging a boy. I couldn't say whether he had him by the hair or the ear – or perhaps a handful of both – but the boy's bare feet were scarcely touching the grass and he looked mortally afraid.

'Oh no – *no!*' I heard someone crying out in protest and a moment later, I realized the cries were my own. I was already running to stand in front of Ned Scathlock. 'Put him down! Oh, pray, stop – you're hurting him!'

But Scathlock did not stop. He showed no sign that he had seen or heard me as he strode onward, his face a dreadful mask of uncontrollable wrath. The boy gave a sob and Scathlock shook him like a rat.

I hitched up my skirts and ran faster, planting myself right in Scathlock's path.

'How dare you!' I shouted. 'Put that boy down at once! Do you hear me?'

It seemed as if he must come striding right into me or perhaps even knock me aside, but I stood my ground. To be truthful, I was too angry to back down. I was angry at his manner; I was angry that he'd frightened me yesterday and I was angry that he'd carried tales to St Cloud. At that moment, I was angry with everyone at Darkmere.

Scathlock hesitated. He met my eye and flared his nostrils, breathing in through his nose like an angry bull.

I heard a sound behind me and saw that Nell had followed me down the hillside, but she was quailing and poised to run. 'My lady . . . you must not,' she whispered. 'Oh, you must not . . .'

Further back, I saw that two of the grooms were watching the scene from the safety of the entranceway to the stableyard. I was briefly outraged that they didn't dare come to my assistance, but another look at Ned Scathlock's face prevented me from judging them too harshly.

'Very well,' I said, pretending not to notice the way his eyes were burning flaming holes through my face. 'If you will not do as I say, I'll go and fetch my husband to reason with you.'

Behind me, I heard Nell's voice quaking as she added, 'You must take care, Ned. She's mistress here. You know that, dun't you?'

Ned Scathlock's face twitched unpleasantly. His jaw worked,

his lips curled and muscles bulged in his neck. At length he said, 'I were keepin' a watch for the master and I found this 'un where he shouldn't ha' been. The master's steward'll want to see him chastigated.'

'Put him down.'

Scathlock looked at the boy and his face continued to work as if it was costing him a great effort not to snap the boy's neck. Then he dropped him. I half expected the boy to flee, but he only threw his arms over his head and cringed there on the ground.

'Who are you?' I asked him, dropping to my knees. 'What are you doing here?'

'Trespassin',' supplied Scathlock, from high above me.

'Yes – thank you,' I said, trying to sound as if I expected him to obey me. 'You may go about your duties now – whatever they may be.' I turned back to the boy. 'Are you much hurt?' I asked.

He uncovered his head, but couldn't answer. He looked from me to Ned Scathlock and his eyes popped. He reminded me of one of the little brown hares again. Instinct was urging him to keep still, but his fingers worked of their own accord, twisting and turning the hem of his ragged smock. A ribbon of blood trickled from his torn ear. At last, Ned Scathlock spat on the ground and tramped off towards the castle. The boy scuttled back from us like a crab. From the darting of his eyes, he seemed to be wondering whether to make a dash for the woods.

'We're going that way too,' I said. 'I wish you would come along with us – and perhaps tell us your name.'

'*I* know who he is,' said Nell. 'He's Jemmy Barrow, who lives down the end o' Wick Lane. It's his ma you're on your way to see, my lady. She takes in laundry and goes out scrubbing floors – and there's you wantin' to bring her peaches!'

She sniggered and I noticed Jemmy's eyes flashed at this description of his mother.

'Is that true?' I asked him. 'Was it your father who had the accident?'

He nodded, holding his sleeve to his bloody ear.

'And how does he go on? Do you know?'

Jemmy's nervous fingers moved to his lips as if to check any words that might prove to be wrong. Then he muttered, 'Ma says it dun't seem like he's comin' back.'

'Course not,' said Nell cheerfully. 'He'll not get out o' that infirm'ry bed. His back's broke, in't it?'

'I'm sure he'll be well again soon, Jemmy,' I said, making a mental note to find as many extra chores for Nell as I could. 'And my husband will take care of the infirmary bills. Do you think your mother will be pleased with a few provisions?'

He nodded his head vigorously at the basket of food and said, 'My name's jus' Jem, my lady – because I'm the man o' the house now. That's why I was tryin' to help out.'

'Help out how?' I asked.

'You can help *me* out by carryin' this,' put in Nell, handing him the rush basket.

'I were diggin' for lugworms on the beach,' he explained. 'I thought to sell them to the fishermen. Only they were too quick for me. An' then I saw . . . I saw the master—'

'Course they were too fast for you, cocklehead,' Nell said scornfully, cutting him off. 'You need a special fork – a lugfork.

157

My pa makes 'em at the forge.'

'I wish I had one,' he said, swinging the basket. 'I'd like to jam it in your brother's neck!'

'I dursay our Ned wouldn't notice.'

'Perhaps I could buy one for you,' I suggested, touched by the little boy's desire to help his mother.

'No, I'm afeared o' going down on the beach again. Ned Scathlock caught me at the top o' the ladder and said he were goin' to drown me.'

'Why then, I'll find you a job at the castle!' I said, coming to a stop under the dappled light of the trees. You can be a – a boot boy or something.' Nell gave a gurgle of laughter and I glared at her. 'Jem will make a better boot boy than you make a lady's maid, Nell Scathlock!'

'Oh, the master'll not like this one bit,' she said, wiping her eyes. 'Not one bit!'

And she was right.

This time, he didn't even wait until after dinner to let me know. He hunted me down in the library, where I was curled up at the fireside reading a book. 'Tell me, Elinor,' he said, leaning his folded arms on the back of the armchair across from my own. 'Why is my steward under the impression that you've hired some half-witted boy to ruin my boots?'

'I wanted to do something for the Barrows, St Cloud, you see—'

He held up a hand. 'Then you send them something from the kitchen garden or the larder. You don't introduce untrained village brats into the house.'

'What about Nell Scathlock? She's not—'

'The Scathlocks are different.' His tone was final. 'And I approved Mrs Thorne's decision to employ her.'

'But Jem could be trained! Only last night, you teased me to make an effort with the tenants. I was trying to please *you* as much as I was hoping to help Jem and his mother.'

'I also asked you not to interfere in that which doesn't concern you.'

'Well, it ought to concern someone other than Mr Thorne. The tenants all look to him for charity and repairs to their cottages – and I don't believe they meet with much generosity at all.'

'Do you know why I employ Mr Thorne, Elinor?'

I frowned and shook my head. Nell had told me that all too often Mr Thorne would increase the rents or think up reasons why necessary repairs should not be made. Jem had said the same. To me, the steward seemed disagreeable beyond all bearing.

'Because – unlike you, my dear – Mr Thorne does exactly what I tell him.'

'The servants ought to do what *I* tell them as well,' I said, remembering the complacent little smile Mrs Thorne had given me when I'd instructed her to see that Jem was trained as the kitchen boy: '*Certainly, my lady . . . if the master wishes it.*'

'*I* wish it!' I'd said and she'd regarded me levelly – right in the eyes – with that hateful sneer of hers, and said nothing.

Yes . . . both the housekeeper and the steward did exactly what St Cloud told them. He seemed to share a sort of unspoken cama-raderie with them – with *all* his servants, in fact – as if they were bound by a secret understanding. Oh, they obeyed him of course, but at the same time there was this sense of – of *collusion*. I couldn't describe it any better than that, but I knew most of the villagers were party to it as well. From the forbidding steward and the Scathlocks right down to the boy who swept the village street, they all conspired to make me feel my *outsideness*.

Today, I'd thought to change that. Jem and his mother had been the first to talk to me as if my words might hold sway – as if I really were the mistress of Darkmere. Only now it seemed I was not to be allowed to help them after all and I flung my book on to the floor in disappointment.

'Temper tantrums won't get you your own way.' St Cloud's face darkened as he bent to pick it up and I felt a twinge of misgiving. 'You should remember that.'

I stood up and drew my shawl higher around my arms, meaning to stalk past him with my chin held high. But he stepped in front of me and cupped my furious face in his huge hands. 'Well?' he said, an odd smile flickering over his lips. 'I'm told you confronted Ned Scathlock today. You can't imagine I'm going to let you walk away without a word about it.'

'That man's vicious! A-a bully! So I stood up to him.'

'Oh, undoubtedly he's a bully – that's not what troubles me.'

'What then?'

'No one's ever stood up to him before.' St Cloud's tone seemed almost as impressed as it was disapproving. 'No one who lived to tell about it anyway. And yet here you stand – half, no a third of the man's size – and you have no idea why that should trouble me? I'm afraid, Elinor, that if you can defy Ned Scathlock like that, then you're more than capable of defying me too.'

'I don't wish to – oh, you don't understand—' It was hard to explain how I felt while he was watching me so closely, dark eyebrows lowering above those dazzling eyes of his. 'Oh, St Cloud, you may have given me your name, but I'll never really be mistress of this house unless you let me!'

He looked at me for a lengthening moment – an adult regarding an angry child. 'Darkmere's mine,' he said softly. 'And I chose you for my wife because you seemed so . . . biddable, Elinor. You knew nothing whatever about me, yet you married me, simply because your mother and father willed it. You did what you were told. That was all I wanted.'

His words made me despise myself as much as I despised him. 'Perhaps you should have engaged another servant,' I said in a low tone.

'No, I wanted a wife and I'll treat you as a wife. But *I* am the master of Darkmere – even Scathlock understands that. Do *you* understand it, Elinor?'

I sensed that he meant to go on holding me there until I submitted to his will. So I made myself nod against the pressure of his hands. 'Ned Scathlock didn't obey me,' I muttered. 'Not really. He only let that boy go when I threatened to fetch you. It was *you* he was obeying, not me.'

That satisfied him and he smiled at last. 'Still . . . it was very brave of you to interfere with him at all. I had no idea you had it in you.' He drew me against him and kissed me, but his touch felt proprietorial rather than affectionate. 'If you promise you'll never do anything without consulting me again, I'll let you have your kitchen boy, how's that?'

I nodded even as I wanted to cry. Because no matter what he said, I could see no difference between my own role and that of a servant. Nell Scathlock might as well have been mistress of Darkmere.

11

*N*ell Scathlock.

The blacksmith's daughter. Barely sixteen years old, she gossiped, chattered and flounced in a way that rather reminded me of Anna. I suppose that's why I bore with her so patiently. Although she showed *me* scant deference, the sight of St Cloud had her in a flutter of pink-cheeked confusion, and all too often I found her – in company with one or two of the kitchen maids – hovering outside my husband's dressing room, the library or the workroom he'd set up near the stable yard.

This was a curious room, part chemist's laboratory and part inventor's workshop. St Cloud's instability of character had caused him to take up and abandon many different studies and his workroom betrayed his interests in astronomy, botany, mirrors and other optical instruments – even taxidermy. The walls were arrayed with curious tools and implements that made it look a bit like a tack room, but there were shelves holding jars of deadly-looking powders or liquids too. There was a working furnace and an anvil, a copper boiler, and a workbench that held whatever St Cloud had designed most lately . . . a new piece of fishing tackle . . . a part he'd made for his yawl or his chaise . . . a trap or a snare for use in the home wood. These last served St Cloud's enthusiasm for taxidermy and whatever creature was unfortunate enough to fall victim to one of his innovative home-made traps was then likely to end up dissected upon the workbench or filled with sawdust and displayed – grinning helplessly – upon his mantelshelf.

Sometimes, when he sat across the table from me at dinnertime, or came to my room at night, I felt his eye upon me as if I were a specimen in one of the scientific studies he was conducting. He didn't deliberately frighten me, but neither did he take any pains to set me at ease in his company. It was this air of detached indifference that fuelled my recurring nightmare that I would fall asleep beside him one night and wake to find he had dissolved my entrails in acid, filled me with sawdust and set me high up on a shelf amongst his collection of stuffed animals.

My new life was solitary and cold. Friendless. There were no parties or entertainments at Darkmere. No picnics or excursions in the chaise. There weren't even any neighbours for miles around – certainly none that St Cloud thought it worthwhile to associate with.

I wondered how my giddy, society-loving sister would have fared had *she* become Mrs St Cloud. She would surely have been tearing her long, yellow hair with boredom in less than a week.

164

Although according to the last letter I received from Mama, Anna's face had shown little improvement and she now chose to live in virtual seclusion, so I suppose Darkmere could have been the perfect home for her after all.

I spent most of my time in the library, reading or writing letters. My visits to the village hadn't been very successful. My shyness made me inarticulate where I ought to have been gracious and charming – I'm afraid many of the villagers even mistook it for disdain – and I met with a great deal of empty forelock tugging, bowing and curtsying. Again and again, I was made to feel as if *everyone* at Merestone knew something I didn't – as if they'd all read the same book, but the last page had been torn out of my copy. It made me feel small and young and alone.

As the summer gave way to autumn, I fell ill.

It felt like seasickness. I'd never been on board a ship in my life, but when I sat watching the up-and-over roll of the distant surf after breakfast one morning, my stomach mirrored the motion exactly. I suppose that's why sickness is so often described as coming in waves – because it really does.

I could taste the sea too. The tang of salt was always there on my lips and tongue – it was in the air I breathed. And that morning, I felt as sick as if I'd drunk a gallon of the warm, briny water. I turned away from the sight of the sea and gazed up at the sky instead, shifting my position on the hot leads of the castle roof. This was one of my favourite places because no one was allowed up here. Of course that meant that *I* wasn't allowed up here either, but the only thing that gave me any pleasure nowadays was to discover petty and unnoticeable ways to defy my husband. Yesterday I had spent almost an hour spoiling the panelling in the tower room, because it was *his* favourite place. I knew he used that room to spy on his own servants and workers – and when I looked at those mirrored windows, my fingers curled themselves into fists. I'd felt a rage so *furious* it had filled me right up and threatened to come bursting out of the top of my head like a volcano. I'd longed to smash every inch of that little room. Oh – the irresistible shivering-shattering sound all that heavy glass would make if I smashed it all!

I hadn't, of course. I'd carved my initials into the wall instead. Then I'd realized they were *his* initials too, so I'd scraped away the middle letter, leaving my initials as they would've been if I'd married Nicholas Calvert.

Because I missed Nick.

Sometimes when I came up here to the roof of the castle, I'd stride up and down the battlements, imagining myself as a medieval lady waiting for an armoured knight to come and storm the castle. He would bring a fleet of ships, foot soldiers and archers, and a team of horses dragging a battering-ram or a trebuchet. I'd hear the shouts, the clash of weapons and the whinnying of the horses. But the knight wasn't bold or reckless like the imaginary heroes of my childhood. He wasn't a mysterious stranger. He had a face that I loved. He was Nick.

Oh why, oh *why*, had I turned him down?

Today, though, I felt too sick for romantic daydreams. I had come up here so that no one would see me if I hunched over and retched. Or if I curled up into a ball afterwards and wept tears of self-pity all over the roof tiles. It was awful – and it was happening almost every morning. If I really *were* a medieval lady, I would employ a poison taster.

No . . . that wasn't true. I didn't really suspect anyone in the kitchens, for the sickness often came upon me before I'd touched my breakfast chocolate. But I resented my housekeeper and the maids because I was ill and afraid – and there wasn't one among them whom I could confide in. If I'd suffered this way at home, Mama would've sent for whichever of the county physicians was the most fashionable, and our housekeeper would've dug out some ancient sickness remedy containing the bitterest herbs and the skin of a live toad. Yes – that toad would've been bad, but it was worse here, where no one noticed or cared.

I leant back against one of the chimneys and gave myself over to the tragic vision of my illness worsening until I lacked the strength to go back inside. I was quite alone up here. There was nothing but a couple of old cannon, a naked flagpole and the parapet wall. Everything else was sky. I would die here against this chimney and no one would find me until the gulls had picked at my bones.

After a while, the roof became too hot for me to lie there thinking about death. My chemise was damp against my back and my stockings felt glued to my legs. I stood up and tried to loosen my bodice, but it didn't help much. Of course I knew it must be my mood that was too tight, not my dress, but the constricted feeling was making me sicker than ever.

The air up here was as warm as the heat from an oven. But when I looked out across the battlements, I could see there was a breeze over the sea. What else could be whipping up the waves and tossing them towards the land so swiftly? My sticky, over-heated skin yearned to feel it. I remembered splashing in the rectory lake with Nick when we were children. How we dared each other to duck right under, until our ears were singing with coldness. The memory alone was enough to make me feel cooler. If only I could get down to the sea somehow . . .

I closed my eyes and imagined how I'd lift my petticoats and paddle through the shallows, icy water separating each of my toes. I'd turn my face to the fine spray where the waves smashed against the rocks and I'd feel the sea breeze lifting the damp curls of hair from the back of my neck – oh, I was sure it would make me feel well again!

Half in a trance, I climbed down through the trapdoor that opened into the castle and went past the servants' bedrooms and along the upstairs corridor. Instead of the dark panelling and the arched doorways, I could see the rough grass and thorny bushes that grew along the clifftop – and I could hear Jem's voice saying, '*Ned Scathlock caught me at the top o' the ladder.*'

There was a ladder – a way down to the sea! I'd forgotten he'd mentioned it. All I'd remembered was Ned Scathlock telling me there was no way down. Which meant that St Cloud wouldn't want me to go down there either – and *that* of course, settled the matter. If he was determined to treat me like a defiant child, well – I was prepared to behave like one.

I ignored the main staircase and took a little-used flight of stairs leading to a side door. Then I skirted the kitchen courtyard and passed through the kitchen garden. I was breathless now and hotter than ever, but a hint of a breeze came up the hillside to meet me. The slope sped my steps, my little square-toed slippers chasing the promise of a cool wind and icy water. I was wary, though, glancing this way and that as I ran, expecting Ned Scathlock to loom before me at any moment. But perhaps he wasn't on lookout duty today because I met no one.

The sun still weighed on me, making my spine trickle and my stomach lurch, but the breeze was stronger along the cliff edge. It picked up my skirts and compelled them to dance. I shaded my eyes and scanned the cliff edge. Within moments, I saw a place between the rocks and brambles where the grass became sloping rock. It was obvious now I was looking for it. I crawled to the edge on my hands and knees and peered over. *Oh* – my stomach seemed to go swooping over the cliff ahead of me. I had to sit back and press my handkerchief to my lips for a while before I could contemplate the ladder a second time.

It dropped, straight as pump water, to the bottom of the cliff.

I turned and shuffled to the edge backwards – easier not to look – and pointed my toe, feeling for the first rung. Even when I had it under my foot, it took all my nerve to keep on going backwards. And then I was over the edge and there was no going back.

Blood rushed to my head and my vision went cloudy. I squeezed my eyes shut and clung to the ladder. Now that I considered the matter, it had been a while since I'd done anything quite this unladylike. Perhaps I *should* try to go back up.

But . . . when I could see again, I carried on down. The wind seized my hair, whipping it across my face and I couldn't stop it. My skirt and petticoats billowed, my hands sweated and slipped on the rungs and my heart was pounding so high in my chest it was almost up to my throat.

I was petrified. But I felt utterly alive.

I began to climb down faster as I remembered how to trust my own muscles again. I wanted to run and jump and turn cartwheels along the beach. I wasn't made for sipping tea in the drawing room or driving sedately to church in the trap when St Cloud remembered it was a Sunday! In my haste, I missed a rung and lost a shoe, but I knew better than to look down. A moment later, I lost my handkerchief too – I hadn't tucked it into my pocket properly and I saw it go fluttering away on the breeze, like a drunken seagull. I laughed out loud, the sound bouncing off the cliff face.

But as the handkerchief disappeared from view, something out on the horizon caught my eye and I twisted, staring. It was a Revenue cutter, sails whiter than the clouds, racing across the water. A smaller craft – a yawl like St Cloud's – was hastening away from the larger vessel. There was a bright flash of colour and I realized the Customs men were signalling with flags. But whatever order they gave, the men sailing the yawl paid no heed to it.

It seemed strange that the Customs men should be so active along this stretch of coast when the only landing place was . . . right below me. Darkmere's private beach.

Without meaning to, I looked down.

The blood rushed to my head again and nausea rose up with it. I squeezed my eyes shut and clung to the ladder blindly. I felt sick and faint – and I couldn't have turned a cartwheel now if my life depended upon it.

I tried not to think about the cutter – just as I was trying not to look at it – but my mind refused to stop working. I thought of Jem, who had 'seen something' on the beach . . . I thought of the villagers with all their secrecy . . . And of course, I thought of my husband who now wrote letters of complaint to his father-in-law. He'd told me that my father's friends on the Board of Customs ought to be informed of the way the Revenue cruisers interfered with the local fishing trade and laid waste to his oyster beds, and how the Customs men had been brawling with the villagers. But I hadn't listened, not really – I barely understood what any of it meant. I had no idea my father's influence extended this far south.

St Cloud had known, though – he'd known it when he met me. And he'd known it when he'd married me.

I didn't want to go down to the beach any more. God only knew what I'd find down there! I didn't want to discover anything else – I didn't even want to *think* about any of it. Instinctively, I began to climb back up the way I'd come, but my legs had started to shake. So I stopped trying to climb the ladder and let my eyes crawl up the rock face between the rungs until my head was tilted back against my shoulders. The cliff went on for ever – I could hardly believe I'd come so far! There was no way I'd have the strength to make it all the way up again.

Up above me, something moved among the rocks. Someone's head. Ned Scathlock was peering down at me.

So I hung there in space, not knowing what to do. My arms ached and my throat burnt with sickness. None of the distant shouts made sense any more and the whole world tipped sideways. When another wave of faintness swept over me, it was almost a relief – because I knew that I hated Darkmere and St Cloud – and now I didn't have to decide what to do about it or which way to go.

I simply fell.

Kate

When we got back to Jackson's car, I looked around for the camper in confusion. 'They've already gone back to the castle,' he said.

'Oh – but what about the shopping?'

'We did it without you.' He paused, one leg already in the car, hazel eyes watching me over the roof. 'Was there anything special you wanted?'

'No, not really . . . I think my apples ran out, but I'm not all that bothered.'

'I bought you some more,' he said, disappearing into the car.

I gazed into the empty space where his head had been. Then I swung myself into the car and stared at him hard.

Jackson concentrated on starting the car and avoided my eye.

'Chill out,' he muttered his eyes on the rear-view mirror. 'It's only apples.'

'OK,' I said meekly. But although I wasn't sure what those apples were yet, I knew they were definitely more than apples.

The atmosphere in the car had started to thrum with tension, as if we were driving under the kind of heavy power cables that linked electricity pylons. I shifted in my seat and darted little glances at him.

'So, you really thought I might've gone home?' I asked eventually.

'Uh . . . I noticed you looking up train times at lunchtime.' He did the one-shouldered shrug, which I was beginning to realize was characteristic. 'I'm glad you stayed, though.'

I gave him another sharp look, wondering why it would it have made any difference to him. Maybe he was being polite.

'I *was* thinking about leaving,' I admitted.

'Does that mean things aren't working out for you and Leo?'

'Uh-huh . . .' My voice came out huskier than I'd expected and I stopped to clear my throat. 'He just . . . I don't know . . . he seems different at Darkmere to how he was at Denborough.'

Jackson kept his eyes on the road, but he looked amused. 'He isn't.'

'No, I think he is . . . a bit anyway. But you were right before

– when you said I didn't really know him.'

I'd thought about it a lot over the last week or two. Had I fallen for Leo because he was so self-assured, so privileged? Everyone admired him – he never had to try. He simply did whatever he wanted. He was, I'd supposed, all the things that were missing from my own life. Maybe I'd wanted him for *what* he was, rather than *who* he was.

Not that I was planning to share any of this with Jackson.

'So what are you going to do now?' he asked, slowing for a bend in the road.

'I don't know . . . It's Leo's castle and he doesn't really want me around.' I tilted my head back against the headrest and closed my eyes with a sigh. 'To be honest, I can't understand why he invited me here in the first place.'

'Because I asked him to.'

I opened my eyes. Stared at the crooked sun visor.

Whoa . . . wait . . . what?

Jackson didn't say anything else, and this time I gave him a stealthy, sidelong glance. He carried on watching the road ahead. My stomach had dived – *was still diving* – endlessly downwards. Only this time I wasn't peering down over the edge of the pepperpot building. I was looking at Jackson. *Did he mean . . . ? What was he . . . ? Oh . . . whoa!*

Then he stopped the car. He didn't turn the engine off; just pulled over to the side of the road. I had no idea what was coming next, so I sat there, twisting my fingers together and trying to breathe normally. The car felt as hot as an oven.

'Do you want to go home?' He turned to face me at last, his

eyes searching my own. 'This is the turning for Darkmere, but I'll drive on to the next town and take you to the station if you've had enough.'

It was the perfect solution. He would take me to the station and make sure I got on the right train – I knew that instinctively. He'd probably lend me money for my ticket if I didn't have enough. I wouldn't have to worry about it any more.

And yet I hesitated. 'Um . . . I think . . .' The gruffness was back in my voice. 'I think I should check with Lucie before I go home . . . she might not want to stay on without another girl there . . .'

Wow! Jackson was *really* good-looking when he smiled. The excitement that I hadn't felt with Leo – not in the club or on the beach, not even when his great big hands were all over me – began to uncoil and writhe around in my stomach.

'Definitely best to check,' nodded Jackson. He appeared to have exhausted his ability to meet my eye and was now addressing my right kneecap. 'I promise I'll take you home next week if it doesn't work out.'

He seemed to catch himself looking at my legs then, and wrenched his gaze back to the steering wheel, in half-laughing embarrassment. Instead of the usual surge of righteous indignation, I was only aware of a little fizz of shyness. I flushed and fidgeted, somehow feeling as if I was all arms and legs and bare skin.

The drive back to Darkmere was beautiful – like a string of holiday postcards, but I don't remember seeing any of it. I was too occupied in trying to untangle my own feelings. I was aware that I didn't dislike Jackson any more. Had come to trust him even. But it was a shock to learn he was so interested in me.

He must have asked Leo to invite me on this holiday *ages ago* – while we were still at school. And Leo had. But Leo had also kissed me and flirted with me . . . whenever Jackson wasn't around to see . . . It must've appeared to Jackson as if I was pursuing Leo without any encouragement at all.

Then I'd refused to travel down here with him. I'd glared at him or ignored him. Oh, and I'd kicked sand all over him on our very first trip to the beach. But he still wanted me to stay.

Without meaning to, I grinned a great big stupid grin.

'What?' he said, glancing at me.

'I'm glad I didn't go home,' I said.

'Lucie might want to leave anyway,' he warned me. 'She was pretty upset this morning . . . you know, about everyone watching her and Dan.'

'You were a bit moody yourself earlier on,' I said, remembering

He groaned, taking his hand off the wheel and rubbing the back of his neck. 'I know.' His bicep stood out below the thin fabric of his T-shirt. 'I was jealous, I suppose.'

'Of Hat-man Dan?' I asked, thinking how pretty Lucie was.

'No . . . of both of them. Being together, I mean. I'm tired of getting wasted every night and playing poker with bloody Beano, while Leo maps out my future career. Working for *him*, of course. Jesus! That isn't what I want.'

I nodded, feeling a rush of recognition. I was tired of

working and studying and being alone too. Without thinking, I pressed the button to slide my window down, but it was already as low as it would go. The hot sun poured in and that strange electric charge continued to surge through the air around us. I don't think I'd ever been so *aware* of anyone before.

Back at the castle, Beano and Hat-man Dan had already gone down to the beach for a swim. Lucie was lying on her airbed, flipping through a magazine and arguing with Leo, who was packing some of the new groceries and bottles of beer into his coolbag to take down to the beach for the evening's barbecue.

'Why can't you give him a day off?' she demanded. 'Just one day when you don't insist on getting Dan drunk or stoned. It's making him totally paranoid.'

'I'm not his mother.' Leo rolled his eyes at Jackson and slipped a bottle opener into the back pocket of his shorts. 'And neither, for that matter, are you.'

'But he can't handle it like you can. He keeps seeing things – things I can't see at all – and it's freaking us both out.'

'Sounds like he needs more drinking practice not less. That's the way to build up his tolerance.' Leo crammed one final bottle of beer into the bag and forced the zip closed. He looked at Jackson again. 'You coming down for a beer and a swim, mate?'

'Sure.' Jackson gave him a nod.

'What about you?' I asked Lucie. 'Aren't you coming down to the beach?'

'No, it's too hot,' she said, pouting crossly. 'I've got a headache. This bloody castle seems to be surrounded by its own little micro-climate.'

'The weather's been fucking amazing!' Leo said in outrage. He rummaged around in his belongings, located a huge box of prescription-only codeine tablets and tossed them to her. 'Here! I'll leave you to enjoy your PMT in peace.'

'I have *not* got PMT!' Lucie sat up and hurled her magazine at his departing back as he hefted the coolbag on to his shoulder and left the Great Hall through the drawing-room door.

'I get headaches in the heat too,' I murmured, picking up the tablets and inspecting them. Leo had a medicine chest in his campervan and he kept it stocked with an assortment of weird and wonderful substances – many of which were illegal. 'God, I bet these are strong. Do you want me to fetch you some water so you can take them?'

'Yes, please,' she said, slumping back on to her airbed with a sheepish look. 'Actually I *do* have PMT – and I've had yet another row with Dan, so I'm going to stay up here and keep out of everyone's way.'

I handed her a bottle of water. 'It's too hot for me as well. I think I'll change into a sundress and go for a walk in the woods where it'll be a bit cooler.'

'Sounds good,' I heard Jackson say.

'No, it's not just the heat,' Lucie grumbled. 'It's everything. I don't want to have my period with only that stinky chemical toilet or the grotty shower block that's twenty minutes away. I want a proper *clean* toilet. And I want a bath. A really deep, hot bath with bubbles in it. I'm fed up with roughing it . . .'

I barely heard her. As I bent over my rucksack, rummaging for some sort of dress, the blood was rushing through my veins so fast I could hear it roaring in my ears. Was Jackson coming with me?

'. . . there's sand in my hair,' Lucie went on. 'It's in all my clothes – even my make-up. I want my bed and my TV and my mum's cooking. Don't you miss smooth, clean bed sheets?'

'Um . . . my mum's not really the homemaker type,' I muttered vaguely, cheeks flaming. 'Clean sheets do sound nice, though.'

'I'd like to have a look at the woods,' said Jackson. 'Mind if I come with you?'

'*Really?*' said Lucie, surprised out of her self-absorption for a moment. She swivelled her head, looking from one of us to the other. 'Oh, *right* – the woods. I see.'

'No – no, there's supposed to be an old driveway,' I said, hopelessly flustered. 'I read about it at the museum. And um, I want to find out where it used to be. Maybe see if the old gateposts are still there . . .'

'*Gateposts!*' muttered Lucie, retrieving her *Grazia* and burying her nose between the pages. 'Yeah, Jackson's well known for his interest in old gateposts, isn't he?'

I fled into the campervan to wash and change my outfit. My hands were shaking and my fingers were clumsy and damp. Why on earth had I mentioned gateposts? Jackson had been quite right when he'd accused me of having a nerdy streak. I hid it under skintight outfits and attitude, but he'd come dangerously close to seeing through all that.

I splashed cold water over myself and pulled on a long T-shirt dress – adding my Doc Martens in case of stinging nettles.

Jackson was waiting for me in the shade of the front door. We followed the gravel drive along the top of the hill until we reached the point at which it curved to the left and swept gracefully downhill to meet the coast road. Here, we stepped on to the rough grass and continued straight ahead into the trees. The cliffs, the sea and the castle all disappeared from view. We followed the old estate drive easily; the path was wide and there was a scattering of loose stones among the moss and earth underfoot. Then, after the first fifty metres or so, the trees began to close in on us and the ground became soft and uneven. We went on, deeper into the woods.

I was too aware of Jackson beside me to take in much of our surroundings. Every now and then he glanced at me with a look that was somehow *physical* – as if he'd actually touched me. I began to feel damp with sweat between my breasts and at the small of my back. And I stumbled over the fallen branches and brambles.

I couldn't see anything ahead except more trees. The air around us was cool and green, almost shimmery with intimations. The only rays of sunlight to reach us came filtering down through so many interwoven leaves and branches they'd lost all heat and brightness – they were hazy, almost celestial-looking shafts of light.

I wondered how long Jackson wanted to keep on walking. Maybe he was leaving it up to me to decide. We must have walked for a mile at least, and these trees could go on like this for ever. I'd have to say something, take control of the situation somehow. And then he spoke and his voice made me jump.

'Do you think we'll ever find them?'

I blinked at him. 'Find what?'

'Aren't we looking for gateposts?'

'Oh! Right – yes!' I'd totally forgotten. 'Yes, that's what I thought you meant.'

He reached across the tiny gap between us and put his hand on my back. His palm was hot and I jumped as if he'd burnt me. It was more than the heat, though. I felt his touch not just on my back, but all over my body – right down to my toes. Furious at my overreaction, I stepped quickly out of his reach.

'Listen,' I said shakily, 'whatever other ideas you might be having, I really *do* want to see the gateposts.'

'Yeah, me too.'

'I'm serious.'

'I know. I wonder how big they'll be.'

'Shut up, Jackson.'

I stomped ahead, trampling leaves and sticks. An oniony scent drifted up through the air and I noticed I was treading on the smooth, cool leaves of hundreds of wild garlic plants. The flowers were drooping and dying, their long skinny stems lying like fallen warriors. There were intricate ferns too and moss-covered logs. Behind me, I could hear the crunch and crackle of Jackson's footsteps and my stomach twisted with a churning mixture of panic and excitement.

I was brought up short by an ancient five-bar gate. In fact, I almost marched slap into it. There was dense, impassable undergrowth at each end, and the trees continued beyond it. It could be climbed over easily enough, of course, but its being there surprised me.

'Why?' I wondered aloud, 'has somebody put a gate *here* – in the middle of a wood?'

Jackson walked up to the gate and inspected it. 'I think,' he said, 'because it's attached to your gateposts.'

A rueful laugh burst out of me. I hadn't managed to keep those gateposts in my head for more than half a second. Maybe I wasn't as nerdy as I'd thought.

Jackson was right. Each end of the gate disappeared into huge clumps of ivy and bramble cables. What I'd taken for trees or overgrown shrubs were two huge columns of rough stone – the same stone that the castle was built from – absolutely hidden by creepers. They were taller than me, but much closer together than I'd expected, and I stretched my arms wide trying to reach them both at the same time. Neither Jackson nor I could touch them both, but they were only a few centimetres away from our outstretched fingertips.

'Maybe these aren't the gateposts,' I said. 'I can't believe a coach and four would've been able to drive between these too easily.'

'No, I think it would.' Jackson was pulling strands of ivy

away, and stepping towards me. 'I could get the car through here OK.'

'Still . . . I was expecting – I don't know – something grander, I suppose.'

'Like what? Marble columns topped with lions or something?'

I flushed and nodded. 'Well, Darkmere *is* a castle, after all.'

'It's a shame.' He took one last step and put his arms around me, his eyes on my lips. 'We walked all this way and you're disappointed.'

My eyes went to his lips too – I couldn't look anywhere else. My eyelids lowered until I was watching his mouth through my lashes. Hypnotized. He leant in, bowing his head until the side of his nose brushed my own. I sensed the way his lips would feel a moment before they touched me. My own lips parted in a little plea of wanting . . . *I wanted . . . I wanted . . . I wanted* . . . and when he finally kissed me, I embarrassed myself by going all rapturous and shivery.

Jackson kissed me as if he would never stop. Long, slow kissing, until I was light-headed and swoony – and not at all certain my body was going to keep on holding me up. I clung to him more tightly, clutching hard enough to leave finger-marks on his skin. It was all I could do to stop myself biting him.

I was aware that we were completely and utterly alone out here. There wasn't another living person within a mile of us and it made a difference. It made me feel wild and bold and reckless. And kind of vulnerable too.

When he drew back to look at me, his breathing was ragged and his hands were unsteady. I was astonished to see the green branches arching above us. Like someone drowning, I had lost all idea of which way was up and which was down.

'Can we come out here and look for gateposts every day?' he asked.

'OK . . .' I was instantly distracted by the way his T-shirt was all rucked up, and without another thought I slid my hands underneath it, because I'd been wondering how that might feel ever since he'd helped me hide those papers at the museum. Jackson seemed to lose control the moment I touched him and I think it was somewhere around this point that we both fell over and toppled to the ground.

It wasn't smooth or sophisticated – the way I'd dreamt it would be. But that was my fault. When he rolled on top of me, I wriggled and squirmed. When he touched my breasts, I twisted and turned from side to side. When he ran his hand along my hip bone, I gave a muffled squeal and clamped my thighs together. I was infuriated with myself but I simply couldn't help it.

Even then, I couldn't compare it to what had happened with Leo. Because I knew in my head that I *did* want to do this.

Here. Now. With Jackson.

But I'd built a lot of walls around myself – to protect me from ending up like my mother, who gave herself to men so easily – and they didn't come down without a struggle. So we rolled around together, kissing, tumbling, pulling at each other's hair and remaining clothing, until his jeans were bright with mossy stains and my hair was filled with leaves and twigs.

The ground was soft. Not earth, but a sort of feathery mulch made up of a hundred autumns' worth of fallen leaves which had lain here undisturbed until they slowly disintegrated into a soft brown dust. Over this lay the cool, crumpled sheet of wild garlic leaves that tickled us and stained our skin, and gave off that mild oniony scent that reminded me of picnics and summertime lunches.

After a while, I began to feel drugged by the cool green air, the earthy scents and the sensation of Jackson's skin against my own. Gradually – almost imperceptibly – my struggles stilled as my senses were taken over by the way his body felt and smelt and tasted. Salty and smoky and warm – and sort of *manly*. Yes, I really did want him.

I *really* did.

As he lay on top of me, his mouth trailing heat across my skin, I opened my eyes for a moment and saw the faintest patch of blue sky way up between the leaves, no bigger than my thumbnail. And every inch of me was so high with dreamy, languorous happiness I felt like I was floating up, up towards it as if I were lighter than the air itself.

Elinor

I was falling . . . too fast to catch my breath. The air around me offered no resistance – I was falling faster and faster, so fast I might have been made of stone. My body tried to curl as I braced myself for the inevitable bone-smashing collision, but my arms and legs still flailed – refusing to give up the hope of clutching at something and saving myself. The movement made me twist and fall in spirals. Somewhere inside, I was screaming in terror, but I couldn't force the sound out of my mouth any more than I could draw a breath inwards . . .

Then, as always, I hit the ground and everything went red. I woke, gasping and jerking around on my bed like a fish in a net. Every time.

'*You can breathe!*' I told myself, gulping in air. '*You're safe –
you can breathe.*'

I had that dream night after night. No matter how much time I
spent in bed, my exhaustion never really went away. Because I
kept on falling. And the room was red because I kept the window
closed and the pink brocade curtains drawn against the sunshine.
I couldn't bear it any more. The warm light, the sounds of the
waves and the gulls, the sea air – everything made me nauseous.

And yet I wasn't ill.

I'd never been ill. I'd been feeling sick and faint because I was
going to have a baby. I'd known such a thing was *possible*, of
course . . . but I hadn't believed it would actually happen. Not to
me. Why would I be having a baby when I didn't want one?

I knew nothing at all about babies. Except that they made me
feel unwell. I counted my symptoms on my fingers – the sickness, exhaustion, aches and pains, dizziness, dyspepsia. No, it
couldn't be right . . . This baby would be born with some hideous
deformity and I had no idea what to do about it.

St Cloud would blame me. He'd said as much that day I'd tried
to climb down to the beach. A doctor had been summoned from
the nearest town and had talked to St Cloud about my *condition*.
Even then, I hadn't known what was wrong with me until St
Cloud had leant over my pillow and said, 'If there's anything
amiss with the child, Elinor – if he's an idiot or worse because of
what you did today, I will not forgive you.'

After that, I'd worried about it incessantly. Every time I developed some ailment or unusual symptom, I saw it as a sign that
something was wrong and I felt like a murderess. But I couldn't

change or undo what I had done. And if I felt this awful now . . .
how much worse would it be when my time came?

I wondered – almost dispassionately – if I would die. Would it
matter so very much? After all, I ought to have died on the beach
that day – along with the unwanted baby. But we'd both survived
the fall because *someone had caught me* . . .

A man.

Worse – a stranger!

He had stepped out beneath me and I'd dropped right into his
arms like a windfall apple. I couldn't remember any impact at all.
He was so big and strong I'd thought he must be my husband. But
my eyelids had fluttered open as he lowered me to the ground and
I saw that he had blazing red hair – the colour of firelight on
polished copper, and his face was vividly freckled. With the sun
behind him, the effect was quite startling. I would've recognized
such a man if he lived in the village or worked on the estate . . .
and I'd never seen him before in my life.

'Breathe,' he said, supporting me with one arm and fanning me
with his hat. 'You're all right now. Lie still a moment and
breathe.'

I breathed. I was on the beach. My head was swimming . . . and
there was a stranger.

'I'm not sure what to do for you,' he said. 'You need water – or
a spot of brandy. Do you have no salts, ma'am?'

I tried to shake my head, but the stranger's face tipped and
tilted . . . and I had to close my eyes for another long moment.
'No . . .'

He swore then, thinking perhaps that I was too woozy to

notice. But the roughness of his language made my eyes open in alarm. My gaze fell upon the twin pistols tucked into his belt. Not just a stranger then, but a heavily armed stranger. The realization horrified me.

'Who are you?' I wondered aloud.

'Forgive me. My name is Lieutenant Higgs. I'm a Preventive Officer in the Coast Guard and I've been patrolling the cliffs around the Darkmere estate. The fact is . . . well, it seemed to me . . . this beach would be well worth setting a watch on.' His eyes flicked back to the open sea and then to the rocks behind us. 'I oughtn't leave you,' he muttered, 'but I can't afford to be found here.'

I understood. He'd been hiding among the rocks – trespassing, in the hope of obtaining evidence against my husband and the men who worked for him. And he'd given himself away in order to help me. To save my life, in fact.

I struggled to sit up, and when Lieutenant Higgs reached out to assist me, I noticed that even his hands were brightly freckled.

'Thank you,' I said. 'But pray don't – I mean, you need not concern yourself with me, sir. I'm . . . I'm perfectly well . . . Just a little off balance.'

'So I should imagine – you must've fallen more than twenty feet!' He smiled, but he didn't stop glancing over his shoulder. 'No doubt you think me quite chicken-hearted, but I truly cannot be found here. Now I really must go back up the ladder myself. I'll be sure to send word to the castle that you're—'

He broke off and looked upwards. The fear in his face was awful. I already knew who was coming down, of course – it had to be Ned Scathlock. But I followed the lieutenant's gaze anyway. Grains of shingle peppered my upturned face as Ned Scathlock's massive legs and hindquarters descended, his boots clonking on each rung.

Lieutenant Higgs backed a few steps down the beach, considering the water. I suppose he thought to take his chances with the undercurrents and try to swim around the rocky coastline rather than explain himself here. Scathlock had obeyed me before, so I raised myself slightly, preparing to try to hold him off the other man for as long as I could.

Then there was the crunch of a step from yet another direction and I looked around to see that St Cloud was on the beach. He was in his shirtsleeves, his hair lifting in the breeze. His eyebrows were drawn low over his eyes as he came near. There was anger in every line of him.

Mr Thorne emerged too, following at St Cloud's heels, and finally I realized that the crevices in the cliffs were caves and smugglers' tunnels – Lieutenant Higgs must've known that much already. When I looked at him again, he was struggling to master his fear and face the three men with his shoulders squared.

I never saw him again.

St Cloud ignored all my pleas and protests. He picked me up and carried me through a tunnel that led into the cellars of the castle and from there into the kitchens. Then he put me to bed to await the doctor from the nearest town. I suppose he returned to the beach. There was nothing for me to do then but lie there and worry about the fate of the lieutenant.

After the doctor's visit, though, I only had enough space in my head to worry about myself. Because I was going to have a baby. My entire life had fallen under St Cloud's control – and that now included my body too. It would swell and contort and eventually tear apart. Then there would be a baby. I ran my fingers over the curve of my stomach and shuddered. I was already stranded all the way out on the edge of the country in a castle that felt like a prison – and now I was trapped inside my own skin with something that was a part of St Cloud. My nightmare that he would turn me into one of his taxidermy subjects had finally come true.

I began to develop nervous habits. I jumped at the sound of a sudden footstep or a tap at the door, and I tiptoed whenever I made my way along the passages between my rooms and the library. I don't think I admitted it to myself, but I was avoiding both my husband and his steward. Servants too. I listened at the doorway of each room I entered, and I took to darting into the service corridors whenever I heard someone coming.

It was around this time that I began keeping a journal. I had nothing else to do and no one to talk to, so I poured my unhappiness into a leather-bound notebook with marbled endpapers. I slept with it under my pillow for fear of its falling into unsympathetic hands. One afternoon, upon finding the standish in my dressing room empty, I tucked my journal under my arm and crept along the landing to my husband's dressing room, where I knew I would find plenty of ink in the desk. Here, my increasing nervousness reached the point of absurdity. I heard footsteps coming along the landing and – without thinking – I opened the door of the closet and slipped inside.

It wasn't St Cloud.

Two of the maids came in and the first turned, hissing, upon the other. 'What do you mean by coming up here? These rooms are my lookout and so you know it! You'll land us both in trouble if Ma Thorne catches you up here.'

I recognized Nell's voice and my stomach turned cold at the thought of her scorn if she found me – the mistress of the house – hiding in a closet.

'Well, she won't if you hush. She thinks I'm laying out the laundry in the garden, but I wanted a bit of talk with you first.'

'And what about *Milady*?' asked Nell, with a note of unthinking contempt that stung me like a slap to the cheek. 'She might be on the wander, you know. She flits around up here like a ghost these days.'

At that, the laundry maid burst into smothered laughter. 'A ghost is right! She's as pale as a corpse and as plain as the Lord could've made her!' She slapped her hands on her apron. 'When you think how we'd heard that the master had gone up to town to offer for one of the great beauties – mercy!'

Nell giggled and I cringed inside the closet. I couldn't come out now – not even if I had to give birth in here! Why in God's name had I hidden at all? I was acting like a madwoman!

'She scarce leaves her room any more. I think she must be invalidish, don't you? It's a sign of quality. That's what they say.'

'It's a sign that Jem doesn't need your help to clean her boots – since she no longer wears them.'

'You common scrub! Go and see about your sheets before I fetch Mrs Thorne!'

'Not until you've told me what you were a-whispering about

with Jem over all them boots and shoes this morning. You'd never have helped him out like that unless he was telling you something worth the hearing.'

Nell hesitated and I guessed she was shaking her head – I knew how stubborn she could be. She was probably pretending to dust the furniture now. I'd often seen her do it whenever she was asked a direct question.

'Go on . . .' said the other maid in a more whining tone. 'He was telling you what happened to that prying tidesman, wasn't he?'

'No, I durst not say. I promised Jem.'

'No one in the village has seen that Preventive for a sennight. They say Mr Thorne sent him back where he come from.'

'He was sent a sight further than that!' Nell gasped as the admission escaped her, then her voice dropped and was barely audible. 'And it were my brother that did it.'

'No! What he did do?'

'He rolled that man down Hangman's Hill, that's what he did. Jem and a couple o' the grooms saw him do it. He bound the poor man's hands and threw him down the steepest part of the hill – and he kicked him if he looked like coming to a stop. You know how steep that hill is – Jem reckons the poor devil were a mass o' broken bones by the time he reached the bottom. It were as much as he could do to wriggle like a worm. Then Ned dragged him all the way back up and rolled him down again.'

There was an awed silence in the room. I no longer noticed my cramped position or tried to think up excuses in case I was discovered. My head was too full of the red-headed man who'd saved me on the beach. Lieutenant Higgs – that was his name. I waited for Nell to say that he had survived the ordeal. But I could tell by the quality of her silence that he had not – and it made everything inside me cave in.

'Ned would've been in a fine fury,' Nell muttered at last. 'It were his job to guard that ladder, weren't it? An' somehow he got past him . . . so the poor devil had to pay for it.'

'Your Ned's not right,' the other maid whispered. 'Never has been. Do you remember when he fought those gypsies that camped here two years ago? There must've been half a dozen o' them set upon him, but he wouldn't give up fighting until they'd beaten him senseless.'

'I don't think he *can* stop. He may be my big brother, but I've always known better than to cross him – else I wouldn't be stood here now. He's like a fighting dog – he gets that same mad light in his eyes when his blood's up.' There were noises as if Nell had remembered she was supposed to be flicking her duster around the room and straightening the curtains. Before she went out of the room, I heard her whisper, 'An' what else does Mr Thorne use Ned for but a human mastiff?'

Her friend followed her, murmuring, 'You think it were Mr Thorne told him to do it then?'

'All I know is that tidesman were seen talking with Madam on the beach a week ago and one of the grooms heard the Master tell Mr Thorne it was beyond all bearing.'

The door closed upon the two of them and I stumbled blindly out of the closet. My head reeled and sickness churned inside me. Again and again I felt the strong freckled hand of Lieutenant

Higgs clasping my elbow, and I saw the concern in his face as he helped me to sit up. I might as well have murdered him myself.

I've no idea how I got back to my bedchamber – and I certainly didn't remember the ink. I lay down, feeling my bed dip and surge beneath me like a boat, while the flowers on the carpet swam like fishes. Not that I cared. My dizziness and sickness were nothing. All my feelings of guilt and remorse had multiplied so many times I couldn't think about anything else.

How could I live with this?

I couldn't. During the weeks that followed, I only existed. I dragged myself through each day like an undead thing. Taxidermy. My eyes became shadowed and sank into hollows. My skin faded to grey. My hands and feet swelled along with my belly, but my arms and legs were wasted. I was no longer recognizable as one of the fair-haired, pink petal-cheeked Marchant sisters. I had switched myself off inside, refusing to think or feel. My centre of gravity shifted and I lost my balance often – falling or fainting until my skin was mottled with bruises. My reflexes changed too. And sometimes I saw strange lights that weren't there. But it was easy to ignore them, for the world of Darkmere had become muffled and unreal.

There was no doctor in the village, so St Cloud engaged the services of an expensive accoucheur who lived at a town some ten or twelve miles distant. He arrived at Darkmere with his night-bag and his valet. He told me I was dizzy because I'd stopped eating. He scolded me for my lack of appetite as I watched him go swirling around the room. After that, he gave me laudanum drops and brandy to help me sleep. When I woke more listless and wretched than ever, he bled me and made me drink disgusting infusions of herb tea and other physics.

None of it made any difference. The Preventive's dead face continued to hang before me – too horrifying to let me eat or rest, and I heard the accoucheur tell St Cloud I might grow too weak to endure the birth safely.

'It's almost as if she does not *want* to have the baby,' he said, in a voice that frowned perplexedly.

I didn't! I didn't want it. I knew there would be something terribly wrong with it – and it would be my fault. Not because I'd fallen off a ladder, but because I simply didn't want it. Surely nothing so unwanted could possibly be born healthy. How could I *ever* want a child of St Cloud's, now I knew I'd never love or even respect him?

'It's a pity her condition does not permit a change of scene or some other distraction from her worries,' the doctor said. 'She's fretting away all her peace of mind over something or someone . . .'

'*No doubt you think me quite chicken-hearted,*' came the red-headed lieutenant's voice from the bottom of Hangman's Hill. '*But I truly cannot be found here.*'

'Could not Mrs St Cloud's mother be sent for to bear her company?' suggested the accoucheur. 'Or perhaps you would be able to spend more time with her yourself, sir?'

Sir would not.

Three days later, I raised myself to the window at the rattle of a carriage and – for a moment – believed that he had indeed fetched my mother. I saw St Cloud pull open the carriage door while a footman let down the steps, and they both stood waiting for the descent of an old maid in a concealing poke bonnet and dingy grey redingote.

She was familiar, but I couldn't place her until she looked up towards my window and I recognized the scars that ran through my sister's face like cracks in fine porcelain.

'*Anna!*' I exclaimed aloud.

I hadn't seen my sister for – what . . . ? More than six months, I supposed, and whenever I pictured her, I still saw her beauty unblemished. I remembered her perfect skin, wide blue eyes, and forehead as heartbreakingly beautiful as a child's. Now her damaged face shocked me all over again.

I forced the shock out of my face and lifted my hand in greeting. She didn't wave back and I realized she wasn't looking up at my window at all, but had caught sight of her own initial carved over the front door. Her expression didn't alter, so I couldn't guess at her emotions – on that face everything was a twisted sneer – but I felt as if a heavy stone had dropped into my stomach.

Minutes later, I heard her footsteps on the stairs, and then there she was, standing before me, untying her bonnet and tossing her coat on to the end of my bed.

'I hear you've been fancying yourself an invalid,' she said. 'Gracious, Ellie! You look quite dreadful!'

I wanted to say exactly the same thing. Anna's carriage dress was as ugly as the redingote and completely shapeless. Beneath her bonnet, there was no evidence of her glorious golden hair, for she wore it tucked into a linen cap. She looked ten or fifteen years older than I remembered her. She even walked with a limp as she went over to the window and threw it open.

'Faugh, it's like a sickroom in here! There, that's better, isn't it? I can't bear sickrooms; they remind me of . . .' She lapsed into silence.

'Are you better now, Anna?'

'Perhaps not as much as I'd like,' she said, recovering herself. 'But you're the patient this time, Ellie. And I must say that if having a baby were to make me look as ill as you do, then I'm glad I shall never have one myself.'

'But no one ever had so many suitors as you! Why, whatever became of Mr Milburn? Or – or – Captain Hartley?'

'This . . .' Anna gestured at her own face. '*This* is what became of them all.'

'But – but your figure must still be pleasing, and no one would guess it in that dress. You used to love pretty dresses. And why have you hidden your beautiful hair? You aren't nearly old enough for that cap.'

'Don't be a simpleton. I can't wear a pretty gown with a face like this.'

'But—' I stopped, bewildered.

'You don't understand, do you?' sighed Anna. 'No, I see that you don't. Nothing draws attention to my face more than a pretty dress or elaborately-dressed hair. It's the contrast, I suppose. I discovered it quickly enough when I began to go out again. Gentlemen would notice me from behind and seek an introduction . . . and then . . . well, I'll never forget the looks on their faces when I turned around. There was shock . . . dismay . . . even annoyance at having been taken in. No, Ellie, I don't dress to attract that sort of attention any more.'

'Oh, Anna . . .'

'Don't pity me.' She strode over to the bell and pulled it hard. 'I'll ring for the tea tray, shall I? And why on earth has no one come to take my things away yet? Are your servants always so slow?'

'Yes,' I admitted. 'Oh, Anna, I'm so glad you've come! I need your advice so badly.'

'What about? Is it your husband?'

'Yes . . . I . . . I . . .'

'What?'

'I hate him.'

'Oh no!' She made the oddest face, almost as if she were trying not to laugh at me. 'Is it really as bad as all that?'

'It's worse!' I lowered my voice and glanced over my shoulder – just as Lieutenant Higgs had done before he was caught – and I chose my words carefully. 'I'm afraid Mama was sadly mistaken in her estimation of his character.'

'As long as she wasn't mistaken in his finances, does it matter so much?'

'You don't mean that. You *can't*!'

'I do!' Flecks of spit flew from her slack-sided lips. 'I always meant it before and I mean it a hundred times more now! I'd accept any man who asked me, if you want the truth! But no one *will* ask me, so I must be a prop to Mama instead, and face her disappointment in me every single day.'

I looked down at my fingers, lacing them together nervously.

'I'm not making it easy for you to complain, am I?' Anna couldn't laugh any more because the corner of her mouth no longer lifted up. Instead, she had developed a kind of mirthless snort. 'Tell me what dark deeds and villainies you've caught him at.'

'I believe him to be involved with free-trading.'

Again came the bleak little snort. 'You're still reading those romances of yours then?'

'It's true! There was an officer, a Preventive—!'

I broke off as Nell burst into the room in answer to Anna's bell. She swung the door to with a crash, looked at me enquiringly and cast a quick glance at Anna. Then she looked back again with a gasp of horror.

I had known Nell's gasp was coming a second before it did. I suppose Anna knew it even before that. Because *this* – exactly *this* – was what had made my once-happy sister so hard and humourless. With real rage in my tone, I cried, 'Don't you dare stand there staring! Apologize at once.'

Nell blinked stupidly, then bobbed a curtsy. 'Sorry, my lady.'

'There's no need, Ellie,' Anna said lightly. 'I'm quite used to it now.' She moved closer to the astonished housemaid. 'Do you know, in one country house I stayed in, all the servants believed I was a witch? They thought that the devil had taken away my looks and given me the ability to curse people instead. Did you ever hear of such a thing?'

'Oh yes, miss . . . I mean . . . no, miss.' Nell backed away from Anna and her expressionless but somehow malevolent face.

'Well then, I shall rely upon you to quash any such fanciful rumours while I'm staying here.' Anna's voice held no trace of humour. 'We would like some tea, if you please. In fact, we would've liked it when I arrived ten minutes ago. Do you think you could bring it in less time that it took you to answer my bell – or would you prefer that we take it in the kitchen to save your legs?'

'No, miss – I-I'll bring it directly, of course, miss.'

Nell squirmed and stuttered and I watched the proceedings with my mouth open. What on earth had happened to Anna? The change in her was much more than skin-deep. Her famous *joie de vivre* was long gone now and she had become . . . almost *venomous*.

'Has my trunk been brought up and unpacked yet?' she asked.

Nell shook her head doubtfully and Anna turned to me, saying, 'I'd like the housekeeper to attend to my unpacking herself. I'm quite particular about my personal things and I've always found these country maids to be so clumsy and stupid.'

'Of course.' I felt slightly stupefied as I pictured the house-keeper's indignation. 'Perhaps you could tell Mrs Thorne, when you're fetching the tea, Nell.'

'And bring some bread and butter too,' said Anna. 'Are you hungry, Ellie?' Without waiting for an answer, she cast a disapproving eye over my slender arms and added, 'Yes, you're much too thin. We'll have a little cold meat and perhaps some fruit.'

Nell curtsied her way out of the room, looking every bit as stunned as I felt.

'That girl won't quash any rumours at all,' I murmured. 'She'll tell the entire household that you're a witch.'

'I know – it'll make for better service. Go on with what you were telling me about your husband.'

'Oh – yes! He writes letters to Papa demanding that the Preventives be stationed elsewhere, but I've seen their ships here. They look to be in pursuit of smaller, faster vessels that never stop for their signals. And though they look like fishing boats, they never seem to land any fish. I know some of the estate workers have been caught with smuggled goods, and they ought to be coming up before Papa quite regularly, but he and St Cloud always find a reason for their release before that happens. I even met an officer on the beach – and – and I'm afraid St Cloud had something *terrible* done to him . . .' My worries poured out in a rush and tears dropped on to my bedcover. It was the first time I'd been able to cry, although Anna didn't look much moved. 'And then there's St Cloud's treasure . . .You'll see for yourself the plate room downstairs; it's full of silver and valuables—'

'Everyone has family silver.'

'No, this room's like a pirate's cave. Besides the family silver, it holds gold plate, bronzes, goblets and ornaments studded with gemstones – oh, all sorts of things!'

'So . . . he has expensive tastes.' Anna wrinkled her scarred nose with scepticism. 'But it's not as if you've seen barrels of rum, rolls of silk or ropes of tobacco down there, is it?'

'No, there are bars at the windows and heavy doors, though. I believe those bars and bolts extend all the way down to the cellars.'

'Tell me about all the treasure again. Is there jewellery? Will you show me?'

I looked at Anna in surprise. Her voice was full of longing – I'd forgotten her love of *things*. My sister had the same expensive tastes as St Cloud. It wasn't her fault that she didn't understand, of course. She'd never heard that awful fear in Lieutenant Higgs's voice and she'd never cowered before Ned Scathlock.

'I'm sure St Cloud will show you if you ask him,' I muttered. 'Some of it, anyway.'

'Perhaps I will . . .' Folding her arms, Anna paced back to the window and gazed out at the sea. 'So you've decided he's using the cellars as a smugglers' store . . . No, I can't believe it – he's a *gentleman*!'

'Oh, you don't know St Cloud!' My voice rose in frustration. 'You wouldn't think me so silly if you knew him better. He refuses to follow other people's rules and he's capable of just about anything when the mood takes him.'

'You know, you're making him sound like a character from one of your romances.'

I gave a sigh that held many months' worth of regret. 'I don't read those any more.'

The tea tray was brought in then and I found I was hungry after all. I sat up and sipped my tea and ate a slice of bread and butter. I felt calmer and more hopeful. I wasn't alone any more – it was such a relief to have someone to confide in.

It wasn't to last, though. As we drank our tea, Anna told me all the news from home. Our neighbours, the Flinton-Fosters, were gone to Bath for the waters; a cousin had lost his seat as an MP to a popular radical campaigner; and the continuing rain had flooded much of the country around the village. The damp weather was being blamed for an outbreak of infectious illness among the villagers, although Anna theorized that they were probably expiring of disgust at how very muddy and odious the roads and lanes had become this winter. A young nephew of Mama's was believed to have lost a great deal of money through gambling – oh, and Nicholas Calvert had married abroad. A Frenchwoman no less, but quite respectable and an heiress into the bargain, so his father was perfectly satisfied with the match . . .

I let go of my cup and tea spilt all over my skirts. I could hear Anna exclaiming about it, but was unable to distinguish the individual words. Her voice seemed to be coming from terribly far away and the room wobbled like a heat haze. The dizziness had returned with a vengeance. And something was hurting.

Anna began to mop my wet skirt with her handkerchief, but I didn't care about the spilt tea. I could feel a stream of water coming from inside me and I started to scream.

Anna rang the bell without pause and servants came running. All was chaos and confusion and alarm. The accoucheur was summoned, the monthly nurse fetched from the village. St Cloud was informed. And – more than four months before I expected my confinement to begin – I started to have my baby.

Two days later he was born.

They were the worst two days of my life. The pain was prolonged and constant – I had no idea how to cope with it. It exhausted me, yet wouldn't allow me to rest. It coloured every minute and every hour. Day became night . . . became day . . . before fading to night again. The room was hot and stuffy. I groaned and wept and cried out until my throat was raw. My voice had begun to sound so strange as I pleaded for someone to help me. No one seemed to hear, though. I can remember their faces around me – they looked anxious or pitying or weary, or even ghoulishly curious.

CRASH!

My next memory was the sound of cannon fire. There were a couple of ancient cannon up on the castellated roof. St Cloud had bought them at an auction and vowed he'd fire them to announce the birth of his son. I'd assumed he was joking.

A moment later, lightning lit up the room and I realized I hadn't heard cannon fire at all. A storm had broken over the castle. I wished someone would open the window and let the rain in – I was so hot! As if I'd spoken aloud, someone began sponging my face with water and when I opened my eyes, I saw it was my sister. There was another sizzle of lightning and I noticed that the eyes of Mrs Thorne and the maids went straight to Anna. They looked fearful, and I remembered that a thunderstorm during childbirth was supposed to be a bad omen. *How funny*, I'd thought, through a haze of red-hot pain. *They really do believe Anna's a witch now.*

I couldn't bear it any more. I had to get away. I wanted to get out of this hot, hellish room more than anything. I would leave Darkmere. I would run away – go back home and find Nick perhaps. He would stop all this and make these people leave me alone. I managed to twist myself off the bed and on to my feet. But then I collapsed. Everyone exclaimed and scolded and lifted me back on to the rack that used to be my bed. And I remembered that Nick was married now . . .

Several times it was thought that I would die. Even the doctor thought so – I saw it in his face. After a while, I pleaded for it to happen. But fifty hours later, I lay in a sweat and blood-drenched daze and it was over.

I had a son.

He was frail of course, but perfect in every way that I could see. He looked like a child's doll. His eyes were shut tight. He had a scribble of dark hair and tiny fingers and toes. Perfect.

Perfect, except that he never woke up.

I knew, without being told, that he would never grow any bigger. Or take a breath. I'd never look into his eyes and see any recognition there – I'd never even know their colour. He'd never wiggle those fingers or make a sound. He'd never run around the rooms and passages of the castle.

He was never going to be St Cloud's heir.

Kate

It must've been obvious that something was going on between me and Jackson as soon as we re-joined the others at the castle. To be honest, I was pretty sure Lucie had figured it out before we'd even left.

We sat together with our arms or shoulders brushing. We held each other's eyes too long and we smiled all the time. It wasn't something we could help.

None of the boys seemed surprised. Jackson must've told them he liked me ages ago. It was Leo's reaction that I worried about, but he was friendlier towards us both than usual.

Too friendly, said a voice in my head.

By the following day, I was feeling unnerved. There was

something so *careful* about his smile – it never quite curled into a sneer. His eyes were guarded, but I caught a flash of resentment there every so often; and his giant knuckles would flex and twitch in a way that made me afraid of him. I could see how much he disliked me now, but I couldn't do anything about it.

'You're wrong,' Jackson assured me. 'Leo has never felt very deeply about anything or anyone. Not in all the time I've known him.'

But that was before he came here, I thought. *He cares about Darkmere. He cares what happens here.*

Darkmere affected Hat-man Dan and Lucie too – perhaps even more than the rest of us. Dan had lost all his coolness and languor. He spent hours pacing the clifftop and gazing out to sea. He haunted the pepperpot building too. We all knew who he was looking for . . . Sometimes, I think he saw her.

Lucie felt neglected and miserable. She was the kind of girl who was used to a great deal of attention, and she drooped like an unwatered houseplant when it was taken away. Her homesickness made her increasingly bad-tempered and we were all driven out of the castle by her tears and tantrums.

Jackson and I snuck off into the woods again. We discovered an abandoned quarry with steep stone sides covered in brambles and ivy with a perfect circle of sky overhead. We spread a beach towel in the centre and lay there together in a bowl of sunshine.

He was surprisingly easy to confide in. I talked about my

mum, feeling oddly detached now – as if she were someone I'd known a long time ago. I told him how hot and stuffy it would be in our basement flat in this weather and how she'd use the heat as an excuse to drink more. I found myself wondering whether she thought about me. Instead of feeling sorry for myself as I wondered this, I could only feel sorry for *her*. I suppose it was because I was happy now.

Jackson's home life didn't sound much better. While the rest of the gang all had that air of being loved, indulged and cared for, I could see – now I chose to look – he didn't have that any more than I did.

Eventually we talked ourselves to sleep – there in the old quarry. Above us, the sun burnt down hotter than ever. I hadn't taken much notice of the heatwave, simply because we were cut off from any exclamations about it. No weather reports or newspaper headlines. Not so much as a thermometer among us. But the boys wore only shorts and we had all begun to acquire glorious suntans. Apart from Beano, who freckled as if he'd been sprayed in short sharp bursts with a can of brown spray-paint.

It was hours later when I woke. My head *hurt*. I was bewildered by the pain of it; and when I tried to sit up, the ache in my shoulders made me yelp. Every tiny movement sent a fresh stab of pain through my forehead, which in turn made me lean over and retch – which, of course sent more pain through my head.

Jackson was burnt too, but his skin was naturally darker than mine. And since I had fallen asleep across his chest, I'd unwittingly shielded him from the worst of it. He picked me up and carried me back through the woods to my airbed in the Great Hall. There, beside my pillow – on a level with my flaming-red face – was my forgotten bottle of sun lotion. I looked at it and cried.

Jackson gave me a handful of Leo's codeines and sponged my back and forehead with cold water. He was quiet and gentle, but nothing he did made me feel much better. I whimpered and pressed my aching forehead into the pillow.

The next time I opened my eyes, I saw that Leo had come in and was watching Jackson look after me. His eyes had narrowed to slits under his great dark brows. That was when I realized for the first time just how *much* Jackson liked me. A chill slipped down my spine even though my skin was burning, and I buried my face back in the pillow.

It couldn't muffle the sound of Beano coming through the drawing room and emerging into the Great Hall, though. He was singing and hitting the wooden panelling with a stick of driftwood. He seemed to be existing in a state of perpetual drunkenness, trying to match Leo drink for drink all day long. As a result, he'd become louder, lewder and more aggressive than ever. But I noticed he now jumped and spun round at very small noises.

Lucie and Hat-man Dan came up from the beach shortly after. Bickering as usual. Their clamour hurt my head and the mingled smell of sweat, sun lotion and cigarette smoke that came off everyone made me feel sicker than ever. Right then, I hated them all.

'Looks like Kate needs some peace and quiet . . .'

It was Leo who'd spoken, and I twisted my head to stare at him in astonishment. He was pulling a crumpled flyer from the pocket of his shorts and smoothing it out. 'I took this off the wall of the pub when we were in town last.' He handed it to Beano. 'It says they have live music and dancing on Saturdays. Tonight! Who's up for a proper night out then?'

'There'll be women!' said Beano, capering about. 'I'm starting to get so desperate I'm not even going to look at their faces.'

Jackson rolled his eyes. 'You'd better hope one of them is following the same principle.'

'Dancing!' said Lucie, her eyes brightening. 'Dancing and drinking and dressing up.'

'Party time!' Hat-man Dan caught up her hand and twirled her under his arm. Lucie giggled and forgot to snap at him. Then her face fell and she looked across the room at me. 'You don't mind, do you, Kate?'

I shook my head. *Ouch.*

'She'll be fine,' said Jackson, smoothing a damp strand of hair behind my ear. 'I'm staying here with her.'

'What?' Leo looked him up and down. 'You're not serious . . . Are you?'

'Ward Sister Jackson!' shouted Beano, stumbling over his own bedding and falling in a heap.

Leo started to laugh. 'Do you want us to find you a little white nurse's hat, Ward Sister Jackson?'

Jackson's face closed up and he stared down at the water

bottle in his hands, rolling it between his palms. He didn't rise to Leo's mockery, but I couldn't help feeling like his jailer now.

I listened to everyone laughing and chatting and getting ready to go out. Lucie took for ever. After twenty minutes, she had spread the contents of her suitcase over most of the hall, but still hadn't settled on an outfit. 'Can I borrow your long green dress?' she asked me.

'I don't have anything green,' I muttered. 'And I don't really do *long*.'

'You know, the green swirly one – like a nightie sort of thing?' She rummaged through my crumpled assortment of clothing, frowning. 'I've seen you in it.'

I shook my head. 'Not me.'

She frowned disbelievingly and then turned back to her own clothes with a shrug. I turned away too, refusing to think about who or what she might've **seen**. Thinking made my head hurt.

After another ten minutes, I forced myself to sit up and sip from the bottle of water. The pain in my head had receded to a regular stabbing thump in the middle of my forehead, but there was still no way I would be able to go out drinking and dancing – I didn't even want to.

I wanted to confound Leo, though.

'I feel a bit better,' I said to Jackson. 'I think you should go to the pub.'

He didn't look at me. 'I'm not leaving you just because of Leo's bullshit.'

I knew he meant it, but it felt like a test. 'No.' I shook my

213

head, which still hurt a bit. 'I'm not going to spoil your evening out as well as my own.'

'Are you sure you won't be scared?'

'Don't be silly, Jackson,' I said. But his words gave me pause. *Would* I be scared?

He was watching me carefully. 'I don't know . . .'

'Look, it was my own stupid fault for falling asleep in the sun like that. I'm going to lie still and drink as much water as I can for the rest of the evening. So there's no point in you staying – you'd be bored to death, you know you would.' I found myself saying the words angrily – as if I resented him. But that was only because the words were so *hard* to say. I was in the miserable position of trying to persuade him to do what I didn't really want him to do.

'Maybe I'll go and have a drink or two, check out the band, then take a taxi back here before it gets too late. How about that?'

'Perfect.' I gave a sigh of relief. He'd be gone long enough for me to feel I'd done the right thing, but not too long.

After they left, I must've fallen into a doze, because when I opened my eyes again, the room was much cooler and almost dark. My headache had dwindled to a dull tingle flickering around the edges of my skull as if it were trying to find a way to get back in. I got up and stretched, monitoring my shoulders carefully. Ouch – still sore! I eased a clean T-shirt over my sunburn and then lit all the candles and a couple of camping lanterns. It was almost ten o'clock. I went and leant in the great arched doorway and looked over the dark hillside to the blue blur of the sea. It hushed and sighed at me in recognition.

After a while, I returned to my airbed and propped myself up on a generous heap of pillows. I reached for my bag of apples, and as I took one, I found my stolen auction catalogue. I'd been planning to read Lucie's abandoned *Grazia*, but my catalogue was more restful somehow and there was nobody here to call me a geek. So I allowed my gaze to drift up and down the numbered columns, picturing each empty great room filled with all the china, silver and furniture.

'South-west Bedroom & Dressing Room . . .' I read. *'Lot 992 Oak combination bed and hair mattress . . . 993, Sheraton inlaid toilet mirror . . . 994, Easy chair in pink silk brocade . . . 995, Antique copper warming pan . . . 996, Walnut and oak dower chest . . .'*

And so it went on, pages and pages of it. I'd always loved lists. Perhaps as a result of all the chaos and confusion of my home life, I loved the order, the method – the *neatness* of them. There was a rhythm there too. I heard it in my sleepy, slightly aching head with a beat similar to poetry.

'Library . . . Lot 272, Antique mahogany chair with cane seat . . . 273, Oak kneehole writing desk with nine drawers . . . 274, Boar's head and two antlers . . . 275, Sword stick and three other walking sticks . . . 276, Letter scales, one pair parcel scales and assorted weights . . .'

There was a sudden crunch of gravel from outside and I dropped the catalogue. Jackson was back! I turned a beaming smile upon the dark, open doorway, but after half a minute I could feel my smile faltering. No one had come in. What was he playing at? And why hadn't I heard his taxi?

How weird.

Frowning, I picked up a lantern and made my way to the front door. The moment I reached it, I hesitated. *'Are you sure you won't be scared?'* he'd asked me. And I'd scoffed at the idea. Maybe Jackson was playing with me – making me pay for my bravado.

Or – oh God! – could it be Leo, making me pay for Jackson?

I had a terrible suspicion that someone was lurking there – out of sight – waiting to pounce on me with a yell that would make me scream. I switched off my lantern and waited for a moment, listening as hard as I could. There was no sound closer than the whispering of the sea. Then, with one quick movement, I swung myself around the door frame and switched the lantern back on, whisking its beam up and down the driveway. It didn't catch anyone. The gravel shone whitely, and everything beyond the circle of light was darkness. At least there was no one there to see me making a fool of myself.

I leant back against the door frame and took a deep breath. I hadn't realized how hard my heart had been thumping. I set down the lantern and rubbed my sweating palms on the sides of my shorts, already beginning to be ashamed of myself.

That was when I heard the footsteps again. They were walking unhurriedly away from me around the side of the castle. I didn't stop to think, but I chased after the sound, limping and stumbling as the sharp stones dug into my bare feet.

'I know it's you!' I shouted, rounding the corner. 'This isn't funny! I'm going to lock the door – you'll have to stay out all night!'

There was no answer.

I wanted it to be Jackson so badly.

I swung the lantern as far along the side of the castle as its light would reach. I was standing beneath the mirror-windows of the strange tower room at the corner of the castle. To my right, the hillside fell away to the sea and impenetrable darkness.

There was a flicker of movement at the tower window. Was it a reflection of my lantern, or had I imagined it? Could someone be in there, watching me? My hand went to my mouth involuntarily and muffled a sob of fright. The castle was empty – I *knew* that – I'd been in there all evening . . .

Suddenly I wasn't sure whether I was safer inside or out. The darkness around me seemed full of moving shapes and shadows, so I scuttled back inside. My heart was beating hard again, but everything appeared the same as I had left it. The half-eaten apple and dog-eared auction catalogue lay on my airbed. The mound of pillows still bore the imprint of my head and shoulders. Everything was as it should be.

So . . . why couldn't I shake off the feeling that *something* had changed. I looked around more carefully, forcing my panic aside and focusing my eyes on each individual object. No, I couldn't identify the change. But the room *felt* different.

There was an alteration in the atmosphere – as if the air had been stirred. I could've sworn that someone had been in here; had passed through the room just a moment ago.

I turned back to the front door and closed it. The huge old key was still in the lock. That was Leo's way – he never locked anything. He kept the keys to the campervan either in the ignition or tucked into the sun visor. And whenever he dug in his pockets, a screwed-up twenty-pound note, a stray credit card or his phone was liable to slip out unnoticed. Material possessions came so easily to him, they meant very little.

I turned the key, but I didn't feel any safer. A hundred people could probably break in and creep around the castle and I wouldn't be any the wiser. *They could come up through the tunnels . . .*

As this comfortless thought occurred to me, I paced around the airbeds and mattresses, my arms folded tightly around my chest as if to contain the panic inside me. The pit of my stomach seemed to be actually *pulsing* with anxiety. Eventually I forced myself to sit down. There was nowhere to hide, no way to barricade myself in – so the lack of options was almost calming.

I leant back against my pillows and picked up the auction catalogue again. Maybe it would help to distract me.

'*Plate Room . . . Silver tablespoons, card cases, photo frames, epergne, porringer, sugar tongs . . .*'

Of course, the footsteps could have been made by a late-night hiker who'd strayed off the coastal path. Or – or the farmer who owned the farm on Hangman's Hill – perhaps *he*'d come to check up on us.

Scrunch . . . scrunch . . . scrunch . . .

Oh God! They were coming back again. My ears buzzed and my eyes focused upon the giant key in the front door until they watered. The handle creaked and turned. Rattled. And the great wooden door juddered as someone tried to come in.

I leapt to my feet and swayed. The insides of my legs had dissolved into liquid and hardly seemed capable of carrying me. Without taking my eyes off the front door, I stumbled across the hall and slipped through the dining-room doorway into the empty room beyond. There, I pressed myself against one of the long, arched windows that looked on to the drive-way, straining to see what was out there.

Scrunch . . . scrunch . . .

And that was when I saw my first ghost.

A tall figure came striding past my window and there was enough moonlight for me to make out not the fair-haired woman I was expecting to see – but the smuggler from the museum.

I felt as if I must be hallucinating. It was – quite literally – hard to believe my eyes. I didn't believe in ghosts – I really didn't. And yet one was walking right past me.

He had a blackened face, a filthy old smock and ancient boots – and he was holding that heavy wooden stave he used to club people to death. I remembered how funny I'd found him – I'd snorted with laughter. But I couldn't do it now. Somehow his ludicrous outfit made him all the more horrifying.

He looked so . . . *real*, and now I understood exactly why all those motorists from Hat-man Dan's story had thought the drowned woman was a real person and had reported her to the police. There was nothing unearthly about him. He stopped for a moment, and clutching his chest, began to cough. Even though the sound was muted by the glass and stone between us, it was a horrible, hollow, racking cough, and I recognized it at once – I'd heard it late at night and I'd heard it in the darkness of the underground tunnel. He'd been here with us all along then, lurking just out of sight.

Ned Scathlock. I remembered the name on the card. He was Ned Scathlock, who'd been hanged for murder. I clamped my hands firmly over my mouth in case any involuntary sound of terror should escape me.

He was here for me – I knew it. He would find a way inside the castle and then he would find me. I wondered about all the other missing people? Had their last moments been like this? The crunching footsteps followed by the appearance of this smuggler with his smudged and blackened face – and then . . . what?

What had he done to them?

I crept back into the Great Hall and hovered in the centre of the room, my gaze flicking to each of the darkly panelled interior doors in turn – then to the stairs, and then to the front door. Round and round endlessly. Where should I go? What should I do?

The room was completely silent. But instead of reassuring me that I was alone, the stillness convinced me that there was a creeping presence in the castle that had become intent upon sneaking up on me. It felt like a game of hide-and-seek. I don't think I was even listening for footsteps any more – I was listening for the sound of someone breathing as they stood quite still and watched me.

The room had grown colder and the air smelt of Leo's horrible lemony aftershave. I supposed he must've splashed some on before he went out . . . unless someone had been in here and knocked the bottle over. My eyes darted around again, but I couldn't see the source of the scent. Instead, I spotted Jackson's towelling robe, so I picked it up and wrapped it around me. It was warm and it smelt of him – which comforted me slightly.

There was a creak from somewhere above. It sounded as if someone was creeping along one of the upstairs passages and I froze, squinting up at the gallery. It was far too dark to see anything, of course. The upper storey of Darkmere were a nightmarish labyrinth of rooms and passages with rotten floorboards and crumbling, dangerous walls.

But down here, in the light and the open space of the Great Hall, there was nowhere to hide. I felt unbearably visible. Vulnerable. I longed to become part of the darkness like the watcher upstairs. Without thinking it through or giving myself permission, I went over to the mantelpiece and blew out the candles one by one. The room darkened and I threw one more glance up at the gallery. Had I heard a sound? A hiss, maybe? Or a whisper? I shook my head in denial, but when I reached out to switch off the lantern next to my airbed, I noticed that the coloured bands I wore on my wrists were shaking. Ugh! I was trembling all over.

Only one lantern remained alight now. I took it with me to the furthest corner of the hall, behind the oak screen and wedged myself into a crouching position. Then I switched out the light.

I disappeared.

Everything disappeared.

The noises seemed louder, though. I listened so hard that my ears developed a sort of tinnitus-drone and I was afraid that my own panic would cause me to miss something. But it didn't. A sudden whine, soft and familiar, came to my ears and made me catch my breath. It was the library door – it made that faint whining sound every time someone came through it.

I held my breath and bit down hard on the heel of my hand, trying to shrink even further against the wall. I made myself as small as I could – I even *thought* myself small. *Please . . . don't let him find me!*

Footsteps.

Quiet but close. Someone was in the room with me.

I could hear breathing too. There was a deep, lupine sniff as if someone was *tasting* the air in the hall. *Would he be able to smell me here?*

The steps came closer, soft and shuffling. They were accompanied by a gentle swishing sound like a cloak or a woman's long skirts. Inevitably, my eyes tried to adjust to the dark and I could discern movement as someone made their way around the hall. A figure – no more than that. But it was coming closer to me. It was standing on the other side of the carved screen, now peering through the tracery and looking at me as I crouched like a terrified child.

Oh God, I hated this. I hated it! I hated Jackson and Leo and all the others. Most of all I hated – hated – this fucking castle! Why had I come here? God – God – God! I'd give anything not to have come here – anything at all.

Then – miraculously – the dark shape was turning and walking back along the length of the hall. It hadn't seen me after all – and it was going away.

My head swam with relief – I honestly thought I might pass out.

The dreaded footsteps grew fainter and I followed the progress of the dark figure as it disappeared into the doorway of the drawing room. A second later I heard the breath of the heavy door opening, and then a rush of sweeping fabric passing through into the room beyond. I was alone again.

When I straightened up I didn't even have the strength to be ashamed of how weak and shaky I'd become. I took a deep, shuddering breath and tried to make my legs work. I couldn't stay here a moment longer. I tiptoed down the Great Hall, trying not to step on any of our possessions or make a sound.

At the exact moment I drew level with the drawing-room door, there was a thunderous smashing noise from the room beyond. A shattering-tinkling-crashing sound that exploded through the silence and darkness with a force that made me scream. I knew those rooms were empty, so I guessed it must be one of the windows that had been broken. It was horrifying.

I ran for the front door as the Great Hall rang with an aftermath of noise. I slammed into the solid, arched wood and my hands groped for the unwieldy old key sticking out of the lock. *I couldn't make it turn!* Another crash came from the room on my left and I cried out in terror. My fingers trembled and slipped and *fought* with the damn key.

Then the key gave way, the door swung open and I dived through it into the darkness beyond. I couldn't tell whether the ghost was coming after me or not – my only thought was to get away. I crossed the driveway at a run and then half-ran, half-slithered down the hillside. Too steep! I lost my footing before the bottom and all the breath was knocked out of me as I hit the ground. I didn't stop, though. I tumbled over and over, gasping great mouthfuls of salty air as I rolled towards the cliff top.

15

It was the hood of Jackson's robe catching on something that stopped me going right over the edge. There was a sickening moment of meeting nothing but air with my feet as I kicked and rolled and hauled myself back up to a halt on the rough grass that grew along the brink of cliff. After that, I was almost too afraid to move. I inched along the clifftop on my hands and knees, placing one hand in front of the other until I reached the pepperpot building. Then I crawled inside and wrapped Jackson's ratty old robe more tightly around me and – eventually – fell into a kind of trance, although I wouldn't have called it sleeping.

In the morning I was jerked up into a sitting position by the noise of an engine. For a second, I thought the walls of the Great Hall were closing in on me, before I realized I was in the tiny lookout building. I pushed my hair out of my face and rubbed my eyes. I felt stiff and battered, and my nerves were still jumping. I guessed the time was somewhere around eight o'clock in the morning and it was probably . . . Sunday. I was hopelessly tired and confused, and I hadn't even begun to think about what I was going to say to the others. Especially Jackson.

I picked my way along the shrubby clifftop and looked up at the golden walls of the castle in the morning sunshine. Darkmere didn't look in the least forbidding now and I knew, before I was even halfway up the hill, that I would never be able to make the others understand how frightened I'd been.

Above me, a taxi was turning and coming back along the drive. I watched it curling around the hillside until it had disappeared down the coast road. Then I sighed, half wishing I'd hailed it and let it take me away.

The front door of the castle was open, but there was no one else around. There was no sign of the campervan – and none of the usual ruckus made by the boys whenever they arrived anywhere. So who had the taxi driver brought to the castle?

Lucie. She was gathering up her belongings – make-up, magazines, clothes, towels, swimwear and shoes – and throwing them all into her duvet cover. Her hair was wilder than ever and there were deep rings around her eyes.

'Bloody *bloody* taxi driver!' she spat. 'Refused to drive me home, even when I told him my parents would pay him double whatever was on the meter. Said he has a regular fare on Sundays – some old granny he has to take to church or something. So I made him take me to the railway station, only to find there weren't any trains! I could barely scrape together enough money to get back *here*! I don't suppose you could lend me any money, could you?'

'What?' I shook my head – not in answer, but at the way girls like Lucie always assumed everyone else had plenty of money. 'Are you leaving?'

'*Yes!*' She pulled the plug out of her airbed and knelt on it to make it deflate. 'I've had enough and I'm leaving as soon as I can. God, I wish there was a mobile signal here. My mum would think of a way to get me back home. I can't stand having to rely on bloody Dan to drive me!'

'I think he's probably ready to go home too.'

'I don't give a shit what Dan wants.' She emphasized this point by stomping on her mattress. 'And he doesn't care about me any more either. He's turned into a total mentalist since he's been here.'

'I'm sure that's not true.'

'Where is he then?' She flung her arms wide to embrace the vast, empty room. 'And where's Jackson? Where are the rest of them?'

'But . . . but I was going to ask you that.'

'I'll tell you then. They're at the police station, that's where they bloody are.'

I sat down on the floor and held my poor, tired head in my hands.

After a moment, she took pity on me. 'They were all

arrested last night for being drunk and disorderly. Oh, don't look so surprised, Kate – they're always drunk and disorderly, aren't they? The only difference was that they all had to spend the night in the cells because of it.'

'Shouldn't we go and – I don't know – bail them out or something?'

'Ha! The longer they have to stay there, the happier I'll be.' Lucie laughed humourlessly and, plucking one of Hatman Dan's discarded socks out of her sunhat, she hurled it across the room. 'But if they need money, I'm sure Leo will have phoned *his daddy* by now.' She gathered all her things into a giant heap and began dragging them towards the door.

'Wait a minute!' I exclaimed. 'Hang on. What happened? And – and where did you sleep? Just tell me, Lucie!'

'OK – fine.' She folded her arms, her face truculent. 'We went to the pub, we managed to get served and we listened to the band. But it was all too tame for Leo, of course, and he started acting up. He criticized *everything*. He said the music was rubbish, the beer was bad and the locals were all inbred. He excelled himself actually. He wouldn't stop going on about how much better everything would be at Darkmere once he'd got it up and running. One of the regulars told Leo to shut up, so Beano threw his beer over him and we all got kicked out of the pub.'

'So why didn't you all come back here?'

'Because the local lad who'd got a faceful of Beano's beer had a gang of mates with him and they followed us all the way into the town centre.'

I groaned. 'Oh, no . . .'

'I was really scared – and Dan didn't look out for me at all! It was dark and I didn't know *where* we were or which way to go—'

'Sounds a lot like my night,' I said snappishly. 'Just tell me what happened.'

She curled her bottom lip. 'We ran as far as the town hall – you remember it's all covered in scaffolding?'

I nodded. There was a sinking feeling inside me as I guessed where her story went from here.

'They climbed it like a bunch of drunken monkeys and hurled abuse – and empty beer cans – on everyone underneath them. I stayed out of sight and waited for them to come down, but someone called the police before that happened.'

'How did the police make them come down?'

'I'm not sure you really want to hear this . . .' Lucie paused and gave a disdainful sniff, as if she were still holding Dan's dirty sock under her nose. 'Two policemen stood in front of the town hall and shouted up at them to come down. Which they didn't, of course. So the policemen folded their arms and waited . . .'

'*And?*' I prompted.

'And Leo felt the call of nature.'

I dropped my head into my hands for the second time.

'Yep,' she said. 'He pissed on a policeman.'

'Oh *God!*'

'Well, *you* may say that, but *he* found it hilarious.' She grimaced. 'Until a police van filled with every policeman in the entire town turned up. They were all dragged down and taken off to the police station. I found my way back to the camper-van and slept there overnight.' With that, she gathered up her duvet again and dragged it across the hall to the main door, where she piled it into a heap. 'As soon as those fucking asshats get back here, I'm going to make Dan take me home.'

'I'd like to go too,' I admitted. But I didn't want to leave without Jackson . . .

'You can! I'm going to insist that Dan drives me straight home – and there'll be plenty of room in the car for you. This place is creepy as hell. I'm pretty sure you've been seeing things . . . hearing noises . . . like I have. Like Dan has. There's something wrong here and it's making Leo into a monster. Do you want to come with us?'

Yes. Yes, I did. I wanted to leave Darkmere more than anything. But I couldn't say so. It would mean running out on Jackson. And I wasn't ready to give up on him yet. Lucie saw it in my face and her expression turned pitying. 'Jackson ditched you and came out with us the minute Leo asked him to, you know he did.'

'I told him to go into town. It wasn't Leo – it was me!'

'You mean, you did exactly what Leo wanted you to.'

Had I? I was too tired and confused to work it out. But I didn't want to fight with Lucie, so I gave her the most placatory answer I could come up with. 'Everyone deserves a second chance.'

'Pathetic,' she snapped, before flouncing off into the drawing room and banging the door shut behind her. I stood there for a minute, glaring at the door and feeling horribly afraid she was right.

It was a long, slow morning. I guessed Lucie had gone down to the beach, and I was too afraid to remain inside the castle on my own, so I locked myself in Jackson's car and dozed fitfully in the back seat. By lunchtime, I was going crazy with boredom. If only there were actual books in the library instead of all those empty shelves. Such high shelves too. How *had* people reached the books that were up there?

I climbed out of the duvet-nest I'd made inside the car and steeled myself to go into the castle and hunt for my phone – it was loaded with books, videos and podcasts and I missed it. The sun was high overhead now and the brightness outside made the Great Hall as dark as the underground tunnel when I put my head in at the doorway. Prickles of uneasiness ran up and down my spine, my breathing quickened and my heart thudded as I waited for my eyes to grow accustomed to the gloom. I stood there, looking at those swathes of dark wooden panelling and understanding hit me with a thump. I *did* know how those high library shelves had been reached!

Excitement overcame my fear and I went through the dining room and into the clock tower. Yes, I was right. Hidden among the panels, I could see those carved rosettes that worked as levers. And every time I pulled one, the panelling opened smoothly and another slim set of steps unfolded itself from inside the wall. It was ingenious.

The very last one I spied was set into the carved surround of the fireplace, and when I gave it a tug the wall above me moved. I let out a gasp and went skittering backwards. There was a nasty moment in which I thought of priest holes and hidden skeletons and torture chambers. Then I saw that the panelling over the fireplace had swung outwards like a door to reveal more shelves behind it – and they were still full of books!

In two excited bounds, I was up the nearest set of folding steps and leaning over the fireplace to take down volume after volume of the dusty, damp-spotted old books. Geek heaven!

For a while I forgot about Leo and Jackson and my longing to leave the castle. The books engrossed and soothed me more than anything else could have. I covered the mantel-piece with books too rotten to read, and every step of the ladder with only partly spoilt books. Then I sat cross-legged on the floor and examined a stack of the better volumes, one by one . . . *Newton's Sermons* from 1636 . . . the *English Baronetage* from 1741 . . . *Memoires de Casanova* from 1860 . . . and *Millais' British Deer and their Horns* from 1897 – this last making me smile: the St Clouds had been into antlers in a big way.

The books that I liked best were those which had been handwritten by the St Clouds themselves. I found household accounts, recipes, and records of how much game had been shot on the Darkmere estate. I even found a pencil drawing by someone called Mary St Cloud, sketched on the back of a recipe for *soupe à la reine*. It showed an old woman whose right eye was half-closed and whose right cheek was gathered and puckered by scars. On the left side, her face appeared to have sagged into a grotesque mass of folds and wrinkles. It was an image that gave me a feeling of pity and . . . indescribable sadness. The faded writing in the corner read '*Mother*'.

I was still staring at the image when Jackson and the others finally got back. I wasn't even thinking about them. I was lying on my front on the floor of the library, surrounded by stacks of disintegrating old books, while unfolded stepladders slanted in my direction from all around the hexagonal walls as if they had come down to see what I was reading.

Jackson put his head around the door and gaped at me.

'I found more stuff,' I said coolly.

None of the boys were as fascinated by my discovery as I'd hoped, but maybe that was because they were all hungover from the soles of their feet right up to the tops of their heads. Jackson and Beano were only interested in black coffee and ibuprofen. Hat-man Dan was still outside, throwing up in the driveway. And Leo, who had a stronger constitution than the rest, simply started drinking again.

I followed Jackson into the hall, steeling myself to tell him what had happened last night and to make him see that I couldn't stay here any longer. But Leo sat so close to us – his expression so damn *watchful* – that none of my words would come out.

Jackson told me that although Leo had been fined, the police had given the rest of them a caution and refused to let them go until they were sober enough to drive. He handed me my own mug of instant coffee and sank down heavily on to his airbed, grumbling under his breath about how Leo ought to get a proper coffee machine for the campervan.

'I'm just glad the van's back,' I said, sitting down beside him with both my hands wrapped around my coffee mug. 'I needed coffee too.'

His brow creased as if he was expecting recriminations. 'Everything just . . . got out of hand,' he said. 'I would've come back if I could. But the others were causing too much trouble for the police to let us go. I remember Beano throwing up in the police station. Then – I think – he slipped in his own vomit and fell over . . . only he accused one of the officers of shoving him and started shouting about police brutality.'

'And Leo?' I asked tonelessly.

Leo stopped pouring out his second Fernet and Coke and looked at me as if he was waiting for some sort of show to start.

'He was found in possession of cannabis and a phial of amyl nitrate,' said Jackson. 'Which is standard for Leo, but it meant he had to be searched pretty thoroughly. Do you know, I think Leo's accusations of sexual assault were even louder than Beano's protests about police brutality? God, what a nightmare!' He abandoned his coffee and – gingerly – moved himself back into a reclining position. 'One funny thing,' he added. 'That woman from the museum was there, at the police station. The one with the helmet hair. Do you remember her?'

234

'Oh no! She must've noticed how many papers and photos we stole.'

'Looks like it. I don't think she recognized me, though. She was in far too much of a state. She was making a fuss at the front desk as we were being signed out. I heard her claiming that several important historical artefacts were missing. *Artefacts* – Jesus! They were photocopies of old newspaper reports.' Suddenly Jackson sat up again and frowned at the floor around his airbed. 'Where's my robe . . . and my duvet?'

'Oh . . . they must be in the car. I-I was in there this morning.'

'But – did you—? I mean, what—?' He gave up and pressed the heels of his hands against his eye sockets. '*God!* I don't even know what question I'm trying to ask.'

'Look, I got scared . . .' I lowered my voice, even though I knew it would make Leo and Beano more inclined to listen. 'I thought I saw . . . well, *something* – and it scared me so much I ran out the door and almost went over the cliff in the darkness. I spent most of the night in the pepperpot building, and after that, your car seemed like the safest place to be. So don't you dare laugh at me! Not until *you*'ve spent the night in this fucking place on your own, OK?'

He didn't laugh at me.

'I don't think I can stay here any more,' I muttered, throwing a quick glance over at Leo and Beano to see if they were eavesdropping.

Beano was trying to light the wrong end of a cigarette, too befuddled to make any sense of our conversation, but Leo appeared to know exactly what I was talking about.

'Did the ghost walk last night, Kate?' he asked, his eyes alight with devilry. 'Did it put its horrible ghostly arms out – like this – and chase you down the driveway?' He lurched at me, sour alcohol on his breath and oozing from all his pores. 'Whoooo-*oooo*!' he growled. 'Whooooooo!'

I couldn't help it, I leapt away from him in revulsion, my skin *bristling* – as if it was covered with invisible hedgehog quills. I was unable to bear Leo's nearness.

Jackson stood up and pushed Leo away. 'Just ignore him,' he said irritably.

The front door opened then and Hat-man Dan stumbled through it. 'I can't find Lucie anywhere,' he moaned. 'Have any of you seen her?' With perfect comic timing, his gaze dropped to the great pile of Lucie's belongings at his feet and he gave a long, drawn-out groan of misery.

'I think she went down to the beach,' I said. 'And she wants to be taken home.'

Dan groaned again and staggered across the hall to the drawing-room door, one hand clapped over his mouth and the other pressed to his forehead. I thought he looked *really* ill – far more wretched than the others. Judging by their sniggers, they thought so too.

We all watched him disappear into the drawing room, and then – half a second later – we heard him exclaim, 'Whoa . . . why are all the mirrors in the tower broken?'

Leo jumped up with a howl of outrage and ran after him. Jackson turned to look at me without saying a word.

I held his eye. 'I didn't do it!'

'How did it happen then?' Jackson's light brown eyes were unfathomable. 'Was it an accident?'

'An accident?' Leo's voice wasn't loud, but it reached me from the doorway of the drawing room as he stepped back into the hall. 'Is that what it was, Kate? Did you *accidentally* trash my tower room because your boyfriend didn't come home? That's a pretty fucking spiteful accident!'

I drew in a deep, shaky breath and clutched at my temples. 'That's not how it happened.'

'You were the only one here,' said Leo.

I didn't care what Leo thought of me – I was *way* past that – but the confusion in Jackson's expression hurt like hell and I gritted my teeth in an effort not to cry.

'You smashed those windows and the mirrored panels which have been here – *unbroken* – for more than a century, because you were in a temper.' Leo advanced on me slowly. 'And now you're lying about it. Give it up, Kate – there's no way any of us are going to believe you. Even Jackson's not that stupid!'

'It wasn't me! It was . . .' What – a ghost? No, I couldn't say it. I wasn't sure I believed it myself any more. 'A maniac with a stick,' I said at last.

Leo was almost upon me now, and I began to edge away, my heart beating with a sort of hunted-animal panic. Then Jackson stood up between us.

'Back off, he said to Leo.

'Your girlfriend's a nut,' Leo said. 'You know that, don't you?'

They faced each other for a long moment of silence . . . until an increasingly loud series of bangs indicated that Lucie was on her way back up from the beach and was slamming every door she passed through as hard as she could. Leo shook his head and sighed. Jackson turned away.

Although Lucie was slamming the doors because she was furious, it became clear that she was also slamming them because the banging *really* hurt Hat-man Dan's head.

'Ow – ow – ow!' he said as he came in to the hall. Lucie followed him and slammed the drawing-room door almost off its hinges. 'Stop doing that!'

'I've had enough!' she yelled. 'I want to go home!'

'I know, but I'm not up to it, Luce – you can see I'm not. I'll drive you back first thing in the morning. I promise.'

Lucie stormed over to the main door and sat down on her heap of belongings, arms folded. '*You* brought me here and *you* can take me home. I want to go NOW!'

'Or what?' asked Leo, lighting a cigarette. As he inhaled, the end flared up and ignited a dangerous gleam in his eyes. 'You're not in much of a position to make demands as far as I can see.'

'Leave it, mate,' pleaded Dan. 'It's fine – it's under control.' His face was greenish and clammy-looking and he was absolutely shaking with hangover. He crawled over to his bed and flopped down. 'We'll go back tomorrow.'

The next couple of hours were strained. Lucie stayed right where she was, silent and unmoving, her face as hostile as if she were a prisoner of war. Leo smoked and scowled at her, while Jackson and Beano played cards. I flipped through my auction catalogue and fidgeted. Outside, the sky began to darken, and I glanced around at all the dark, shadowy door-ways and the high windows, knowing I couldn't be brave enough to sleep here again. I couldn't, I couldn't – I *couldn't*!

Suddenly Leo leapt to his feet and flung a Fernet-Branca bottle through one of the high windows over the front door, making us all jump.

'Fuck it!' he yelled. 'I'm going to start smashing windows and slamming doors too. It's got to be more fun than this fucking misery.'

'Come on,' said Beano. 'Everyone's tired and hungover, that's all.'

'Not Lucie or Kate,' he said, eyeing us both with frustration. 'You two have never liked it here, have you? You've been having a free holiday in a fucking castle and you're still not happy. Well, that's fine – that's totally fine! I'll drive you both back home first thing in the morning. But do you have to spoil our last night here?'

I looked at Lucie and she looked back at me. Then we both looked at the floor.

'I miss my mum,' she muttered. 'I can't help it – I want to go home.'

'First thing!' said Leo, prostrating himself theatrically before her. 'I promise! I'll write it in blood if you want me to. But will you please stop sulking and have a fucking drink?'

She gave a long sigh and then nodded her head at the

window he'd just made a hole through. 'I suppose a Fernet and Coke's out?'

Leo grinned and opened another bottle. After that, he got the fire going and Beano lit about a million candles. Someone else put Curtis Mayfield on at full volume and we began to feel better.

I could see now how amazing Darkmere would be as a party venue. When the walls were ablaze with heat and light, the dark panelling and the oak screen supporting the minstrels' gallery began to sweat and shine like melting chocolate.

Beano tried to dance with a beer can balanced on his head. Every few minutes, it fell off again as he kept hugging Leo and assuring him that he was the best friend he'd ever had – no one had ever understood him as well as Leo did. His earnestness made us all *howl* with laughter.

Over by the door, Hat-man Dan was sitting up and sipping some sort of tonic Leo had concocted for him. He was holding Lucie's hand and apologizing repeatedly for anything that came into his head.

'Should I be apologizing too?' said a voice in my ear.

I smiled and leant against Jackson's stubbled cheek.

'I *am* sorry,' he said. 'I'm sorry I wasn't here and I'm sorry you were scared.'

'I wish I knew how to convince you I had good reason to be scared.'

'Oh God, Kate, it's so *hard*, though! Can't you understand

how hard it is to hear about some maniac terrorizing you when I'd promised to be here? I really don't want to believe it!'

'Well, I need you to take my word for it, OK? I didn't smash those windows and I didn't lie about it – I wouldn't do that.' I gazed into his eyes, wondering if he still looked at me and saw only the short skirts, the bleached hair and the attitude. None of that was me – not really. I wasn't a troublemaker – I wasn't even very brave. 'Listen, I'm not as confident as . . . as I pretend to be.'

'Oh, I know that.' He sounded surprised. 'You're not at all how I expected. You're a total nerd in disguise. It's hilarious – the way you geek out over old books and photos. And the way you want to look at crumbling gateposts or spend an entire day at the museum.'

'And . . . um . . . that's OK?'

It was Jackson's turn to look away. 'Yeah . . .' He played with my fingers, lacing them through his own and tracing my palm with his thumb. 'Turns out, geeky is my type.'

We talked and talked. Slow and fast, deep and meaningful. Leo kept replacing our drinks faster than ever before. We sang and we danced – we couldn't stop moving. With hindsight, the fire and all the candles were a mistake. The Great Hall became unbearably hot. Beano opened a two-litre bottle of mineral water and began to pour it over his head, but Leo took it away from him and emptied it over the fire instead.

'To the beach!' he shouted. 'Time for skinny-dipping!'

'Naked swimming!' hollered Beano, heading into the

drawing room. 'Woo-hoo! Everyone to the beach!'

Once we were through the cellar door, I could no longer hear the thumping beat of the music. The coolness down here was blissful, but in my state of drunkenness, the darkness seemed . . . sort of . . . *darker*.

Hat-man Dan went by me and his camping lantern threw jerky arcs of light along the narrow walls. I saw faint golden tracers shoot after them as if to catch up. Everyone seemed to be talking at once, their voices bouncing off the walls and ceiling, overlapping each other and becoming a babble. My ears rang with it. I began to walk faster, feeling disorientated. We were almost at the beach when Leo stopped by the right-hand passage and held us up.

'I'm almost through that iron gate now,' he said. 'Come and see.'

So we all filed after him along the black and unfamiliar passage and watched as he directed the beam of his torch at the barred gate. He was right, he was almost through. The black and rusty iron bars glittered silver where he had sawn through them. He'd cut around two of the great hinges and there was only one left to go. This last was already torn-looking and jagged with teeth marks from the hacksaw blade.

'You've almost done it!' exclaimed Beano. 'Why did you stop?'

'Because my hand's fucked.' Leo shone the torch on to his huge right hand. His fingers were cut and scratched, his knuckles scabbed, and his palm was ridged with hard-looking blisters.

242

Beano kicked at the last hinge with his heel and the whole gate groaned. It didn't seem so impregnable any more. The last metal bar refused to give way, but several tiny chips fell from the rock of the wall in which it was sunk and I saw dust floating in the criss-crossing beams of torchlight.

I took a quick step backwards, but no one else did. They were fearless. All the boys hammered and kicked at the gate in a tangle of limbs and torch beams.

'Don't!' I shouted, hating the way they'd become a pack, one animal guided by a single brutish instinct. 'Please don't – it'll collapse on top of us!'

They didn't take any notice – they were too wired, too manic. They went on attacking the gate until its remaining hinge was wrenched out of the wall with a hideous grinding noise and the bars folded in on themselves.

There were whoops, yells and battle cries – then a great deal of coughing as we all breathed in the ancient rock dust. No one else seemed bothered about the possibility of a cave-in, and it seemed absurd for me to keep panicking about it on my own. So I followed them as they squeezed – one by one – past the battered gate.

The passage beyond sloped gently uphill. It was straight and wide but horribly airless. I wished it wasn't so dark. The odd lights and disjointed voices made it seem unreal, as if I were having a bad dream. At the end was a small bare cellar, more like a cave than a room. There were some ancient metal implements that looked a bit like pitchforks hanging on the wall, and a couple of broken barrels on the floor.

Nothing more.

'All that sawing!' moaned Leo, flashing his torch around everywhere. 'And there's nothing here! Un-fucking-believable!'

Beano sniggered and Leo hit him on the head with the torch.

'Hang on . . . I think there might be something . . .' Hat-man Dan was scuffing about on the floor with the toe of his sneaker. 'Here, under these bits of wood.'

Leo was at his side in an instant. I felt the rush of air as he passed me. All the torches were trained upon the uneven rock floor.

There was a trapdoor. It was made of rusty old iron with large studs around its edge, like the hatch on a submarine. There was an iron ring to pull it up, but it looked as though the trapdoor had sealed itself over the years. Its edges were corroded into the rock, held fast by a mixture of rust, metal oxides and sea salt. Leo heaved on the ring, then went staggering backwards as it came off in his hands.

'Ow – my fucking blisters!' he yelled.

'Let's leave it,' said Jackson. 'There's probably nothing down there anyway.'

That was when the trapdoor gave way and Hat-man Dan, who'd been standing on the edge, fell into the hole – just as if he'd been swallowed by a huge black mouth.

Although my thoughts *felt* fast and coherent, my brain had trouble processing what had just happened. Everyone yelled and swore and dropped their torches – and it was impossible to see much. I think Leo grabbed Hat-man Dan – but Jackson leapt for him too, and Hat-man Dan *s-c-r-e-a-m-e-d!*

There was a corresponding outbreak of choking and retching noises, because – *oh – oh – oh* – the smell! It was awful – *sickeningly* awful – and it filled that tiny airless room the moment the hatch gave way. I wasn't the only one who recoiled. The boys all pulled Hat-man Dan along with them as they fell back into the tunnel.

He was wet through. He had plunged down into seawater. And he hadn't been alone. We'd all seen it – in a single beam of torchlight. Something dark and rotten floating down there. Something dead.

16

Elinor

There was a ray of wintery sunlight coming through a chink in the curtains and it made me shift my head on the pillow. I lay for a moment between sleeping and waking, before putting back the covers and making a move to step out of bed. Then I remembered I wasn't allowed to do it.

'*She scarce leaves her room any more. I think she must be invalidish, don't you?*'

That's how Nell had described me months ago – just after I'd fallen off the ladder that led to the beach. And I'd hated her for it! Now, though, her words were an understatement. Only at night, when I was dreaming, could I still run and climb and dance. In the morning, I had to wait for Nell or Anna to come and open the curtains.

The accoucheur had advised a longer lying-in period than usual. He'd also warned St Cloud that I must never have any more children. So I was an invalid who had failed utterly at being a wife.

'You were too young,' said Anna, her cold fingers smoothing my forehead, then trailing down my cheek. Unthinkingly, she traced the pattern of her own scars across my unmarked face. 'That's what it was – you were too young for any of this. I remember you asked me to put off our London season for another year. I wish I'd listened.'

'Well, you listen now – and you make a wonderful nurse.'

She leant over me, prodding my pillows into shape and trying to raise me up a little. 'You've been looking much better these last two or three days, I think. Shall I bring you a book or some sewing perhaps?'

'Sewing? I hate sewing. My stitching is even worse than yours and you know it.'

'Never mind about that. You can sew something for the poor.'

'Trust me, no one in Merestone is that needy.'

'Very well, a book then.' She twitched my bedcovers into place with brisk, impatient movements. 'I want to make sure you're occupied. I've a great deal to do this morning. Mama and Papa will be arriving later today – did you remember?'

Of course . . . today was Christmas Day, and our parents were coming to stay at Darkmere until the New Year. Mama had wanted to come sooner when she'd heard how ill I was, but both Anna and St Cloud had written to dissuade her.

247

I couldn't be sorry for it. When I thought of Mama's reptilian look of disapproval – the way her eyelids snapped down like a candle snuffer, as she were trying to shut out a sight that disappointed her – I still cringed inwardly. This time, I knew I deserved that look.

But she couldn't be put off for ever.

So Anna wanted the castle made ready for visitors and she already knew better than to leave it to the housekeeper. 'Your husband may boast of his well-trained servants,' she complained. 'But I've found them to be lazy, surly and slovenly. Oh, they obey *him* all right – most of them seem to go in terror of him! But when you were really ill and I couldn't leave your side, I almost broke that bell pull ringing for hot water or clean linen that never came.'

'You must give orders on my behalf,' I said. 'I'm sure they'll take more notice of you than they ever did of me.'

'Well, I think so too. I mean to have the guest rooms made ready with lit fires, fresh water and properly aired sheets. I want holly boughs and trailing ivy brought in to decorate the hall. I'll need new tapers everywhere and the flambeaux burning outside. There should be a Yule log in the fireplace and hot punch waiting for everyone when they arrive.'

And so Anna went to war on the servants. I heard occasional snatches of her voice – soft and low but absolutely determined – as she moved about the castle, scolding the maids, chivvying the footman or giving orders. I admired her even more than when she'd been beautiful and had used her face to get what she wanted. My own spirit had been broken over the last few months and now I couldn't imagine myself standing up to any of these people – not any more.

Just before lunchtime, came the sounds of the inevitable clash between Anna and Mrs Thorne. First, I heard a howl of dismay that made me jump in my bed, followed by a loud childish sobbing. Nell Scathlock, I decided. Had she broken something? Or been caught slipping silverware into the pocket of her apron? Anything was possible when it came to Nell.

Sharp voices darted at each other over Nell's sobs and gasps. I heard Mrs Thorne, strident with indignation, and Anna, low and scathing. My heart sank as their exchange grew louder and clearer – they were coming along the passage to my bedchamber. I could hear their footsteps – the housekeeper marching angrily, while Anna's limp scuffed at the carpet.

'My sister is extremely fragile at the moment,' cried Anna. 'If you upset her in her present state of health, she may never recover – and I will hold you responsible.'

Mrs Thorne's answer to this was to tap upon my door and step into the room. 'I must tell you, ma'am,' she said in a burst, 'I am unused to having my own members of staff dismissed and turned out of their home by a – a—' She glanced at Anna in search of an epithet. 'A mere *visitor* to the house!'

'My sister speaks for me,' I said weakly.

'But she cannot speak for the master! And it was Mr St Cloud who agreed to Nell Scathlock's position here in the house. Nell is a faithful retainer who—'

Anna made a noise of disgust. 'She's a shiftless little slut.'

'Anna!' I exclaimed. 'What on earth has she done?'

Both women looked at each other grimly, and neither of them answered me.

'Nell may not be the ideal servant,' Mrs Thorne conceded at last. 'But the point is, ma'am, I cannot take it upon myself to make such changes to the household staff without ascertaining the master's feelings.'

'Very proper,' I said. 'But what has she done?'

Anna folded her arms. 'Take my word for it, Ellie, Nell Scathlock is not a proper person for you to have in the house. In fact, the entire Scathlock family has a most unchristian reputation, from all I hear.'

'But wouldn't it be more unchristian for us to turn Nell out of her home at Christmas?'

'No,' said Anna.

'Yes,' said Mrs Thorne, at the same moment. 'In her present situation, it would be considered unfeeling.'

'Her present situation is her own fault!' snapped Anna. 'And I don't see any reason for my sister to be troubled with it.'

But Mrs Thorne wanted me to know what was wrong with Nell – I could see it in the gleam of her eyes. There was a block of pressure building up behind my throat and nose. I swallowed hard, but it didn't help. My eyelids were prickling too.

'It's for the master to decide.' Mrs Thorne's eyes were still on my face, making me squirm. 'I believe he'd want to do what was right.'

'In an hour or two, my mother and father will be arriving with a party of guests,' said Anna. 'If any of them are waited upon by an unmarried girl whose gown no longer fastens around the

250

middle, my mother will succumb to instant hysterics. She will not be able to resist making the matter into a considerable scandal – trust me. So you'll either turn that chit from my sister's house, or I'll see that you're asked to leave along with her.'

Mrs Thorne drew in an audible breath like a hiss as she weighed Anna's words. It was plain she had no fear that St Cloud would ever dismiss her – she and her husband ran the estate for him – but neither would he appreciate the kind of domestic upheaval that Anna was threatening.

'Very well,' she said. 'Nell Scathlock isn't worth that kind of trouble. I'll tell her to pack up her belongings and clear out.'

But Anna's victory wasn't over Nell Scathlock. It was over the housekeeper herself, and both of them knew it.

'Right away then, if you would, Mrs Thorne,' said Anna, and her voice was smiling broadly even though her mouth could only leer. She moved away from the door to indicate that the other woman should pass through it.

The housekeeper left as abruptly as she'd entered. A moment later, I heard the wailing noises start up again and I guessed Mrs Thorne was taking her temper out on Nell.

'I don't believe the other servants will give me any trouble this Christmas,' murmured Anna. 'Not now I've got the upper hand of that old harridan.'

'She's . . . Nell's with child then?' I asked. My throat was too tight for me to breathe easily now. My eyes blurred and I told myself – sternly – that I had no right to mind about it. I hadn't wanted a child of my own, so why should it matter that mine had not survived?

'Anna, what do you suppose she meant about St Cloud doing the right thing?'

'I don't know.'

My sister's face was turned away from me, as she sorted through the little glass vials at my bedside. But she did know. I knew too.

It was the ultimate reproach.

I let her give me laudanum drops, knowing she wouldn't leave me if I refused. After she'd gone, I cried for the first time since they'd taken my son away. I had no right to cry – and I knew it – but at least no one could see me doing it.

I felt different now, that was the trouble. I was hollow with failure. I wrapped my arms around myself and wept – just as Nell was weeping somewhere outside my room. Where I'd grown accustomed to the butterfly-flutter of movement, there was a gaping nothingness. I'd assumed that if I never let myself acknowledge the stirring inside me, I could just go back to being the same person I was before the baby had ever existed. I *wanted* to go back. Instead, I felt as if a part of me were missing. I felt empty.

Before long, my tears were slowed by the laudanum and I drifted into sleep. By the time I woke up again, the light at the window had turned grey and my mother was there.

It was Christmas Day . . . still. I smiled groggily. Regular doses of laudanum – along with all the bleedings and purgings I'd had to undergo – had made my reactions slow and stupid. I was also far too thin and my entire body had long since been drained of all its colour. My mother looked appalled.

'Oh, Elinor!' she said, her face stiff with disappointment. 'What a wretched Christmas this will be for us all!'

She hadn't changed a bit.

'It needn't be, Mama. You brought people with you, didn't you? There must be quite a house party gathered downstairs.'

'But we wouldn't enjoy ourselves for a moment, knowing you to be up here alone at Christmas. You're the mistress of the house and you really ought to put in an appearance. I'll persuade St Cloud to bring you down after dinner, shall I? It wouldn't hurt you to spend an hour or two on a sofa before the fire.'

'Oh no, Mama! I couldn't!'

'Pray, think of your husband, Elinor – even if you won't consider the rest of us. Anna says the two of you seem quite *estranged*.'

I slid my hand over my eyes. 'He blames me . . .'

'Why should—? Well, no matter what you did, you're his wife and he'll forgive you in time. But some of the effort must come from you, my love. I'll ring for a maid to come and tidy your hair and find you a pretty dressing-gown to wear.'

Of course, she had her way and St Cloud came to my room after dinner. I was writing in my journal and I snapped it shut guiltily, tucking it inside my dressing-gown, out of sight. He stood inside the door, his arms folded and his huge shoulders resting against the frame. I couldn't read his expression, but he looked less daunting than usual.

'How are you feeling?' he asked. 'You look like a death's head on a pillow.'

'Thank you kindly. I'm feeling much better now.'

253

'Liar!' he grinned. 'Stop playing the martyr for one night. It's Christmas, you know.'

'Happy Christmas, St Cloud.'

He laughed. 'I won't be happy until it's over. Meanwhile, your entire family has taken over my house, so I don't see why you should escape.'

He approached the bed and put an arm around my shoulders, lifting me slightly. His hands were gentle, but I was all too aware of the strength that ran through him, and I held my breath as he touched me. St Cloud slid his other arm under my knees and picked me up without any effort at all. The effort was all mine – I bit down on my lower lip and forced myself to hold on to him, shivering as cold sweat trickled down my sides. There was a moment when he paused and looked at me and I had no idea whether he meant to hurt me or caress me. Either way, I was sure I would be sick.

But he'd noticed how hard I was biting my lip and he said, 'I don't think you're well enough to get up yet.'

'No, but my mother wishes me to be an asset to you.'

He snorted at that and bore me downstairs into the Great Hall. A crowd of people gazed up at me and I hid my face, wishing them – and my mother – a million miles away.

With my parents had come one of Mama's elderly cousins – the one who'd lost his seat as an MP – and his wife. There were also a couple of Papa's friends from the Board of Customs, who had come down from London with their wives, in order to shoot some deer on the estate.

With a sort of hen-house hustle and bustle, the women rose

from their places around the fire and began to arrange a mass of cushions against the arm of one of the long low sofas so that I could lie there in comfort. St Cloud lowered me down and I was immediately covered with shawls and offered cool drinks, hot drinks or various vinaigrettes.

To my dismay, I realized I was still clutching my journal under my dressing-gown. I shifted about as if I were trying to make myself more comfortable, and managed to jam it underneath the cushions.

'Are you close enough to the fire, my love?' asked Mama. 'The sea air is vicious at this time of year, and Darkmere's situation is so very exposed.'

'No, no, we're comfortable enough here at Darkmere,' put in my father. 'I must say I'm proud of you, Elinor. Everything is exactly as it should be. Comfort without extravagance, a good table and servants who are kept to their duties. Mr St Cloud must wonder how he ever got along without you.'

I didn't dare look at my husband's face. He was talking to one of the other men about guns, so I hoped he hadn't heard.

'It's Anna's doing,' I said.

'I'm sure your sister is glad to be of use to you now that you're a married lady,' said my mother. 'There's no more important role, for a woman.'

Oh, God. It really was going to be a long evening.

I had hoped to find a way to talk to my father about St Cloud's involvement with the free-traders, but now he was finally before me, I gave up the idea. Papa was older and greyer than I remembered, smaller somehow. His self-importance hung on him like a coat belonging to an altogether larger man, and as I watched him striving to engage St Cloud's interest with his every word – so eager to please and so afraid of giving offence – I suspected he and his friends from the Board of Customs already knew about the smuggling, but were too afraid to act. *Or too well paid perhaps.*

So I lay back against my bank of cushions and listened to the music and chatter. The Great Hall looked festive, bright and warm. The fire was blazing like a furnace and the wooden panelling glowed like bitter chocolate. Close by, a few of the men were playing cards and three of the couples trod a slow and stately measure up and down the hall.

Only Anna did not join in. Like me, she sat quite still and gazed into the flames. My mother had so enjoyed having two lovely daughters with limitless prospects before them. But now I felt the coldness of her lizard-eye upon us – her two damaged girls – and I understood why Anna had been so desperate to leave home and come here.

At midnight, there was a loud knock at the door, waking my father from his brandy-induced stupor and causing a flutter of exclamation among the ladies. The door was opened to reveal the vicar, leading an untidy procession of waifs who had walked up from the village in their ragged coats and scarves. The castle servants came in to hear them carolling, and Mr Thorne handed out coins and sugarplums. Then the musicians struck up an irresistible waltz and everyone swirled and spun beneath the glittering candles and swags of mistletoe.

Still Anna remained in her seat by the fire. She neither looked at the dancers nor appeared to be enjoying the music. Instead, she rested her forehead against her hand as if the noise gave her a headache. But I noticed her feet – half hidden by her skirts – tracing the unforgotten steps upon the polished boards before the fireplace, and my heart was squeezed with pity. I beckoned St Cloud and whispered a request that he or one of the other men, should dance with her.

He gave such a burst of laughter that everyone in the room looked round and several of them smiled at his amusement. 'Why, I'd liefer ask old Mrs Thorne to be my partner! She's by far the fairer of the two.'

'Hush, don't speak so!'

'Forgive me,' he said. 'Your request took me by surprise, that's all.' He turned to my sister. 'Miss Marchant, may I have the honour?'

'What do you mean?' asked Anna.

He bowed low and proffered a crooked arm. 'I mean, madam, that a sudden and uncontainable impulse to dance with you has overcome me.'

'No,' said Anna.

But he pulled her to her feet and led her out into the centre of the room. The other couples parted to make room for them and I saw that everyone else was equally amused by his choice of partner. I hadn't helped Anna at all.

St Cloud's eyes glinted with mockery – and far too much alcohol – as he drew Anna towards him, placed his hand at her waist and forced her to move with him. He was making her ridiculous. She was swept into the swirling romantic dance, with her hideous witch's face, her drab little gown like a governess's and her old maid's cap. It was a comical sight and people sniggered. Anna had never appeared so pitiable a creature. And this – *this* – was what she had tried to explain to me when she had first arrived here. *This* was the reason she had turned her back on society. *This* was why she no longer danced or wore beautiful gowns. So why on earth hadn't I listened to her?

Before the waltz was finished, Anna freed herself from St Cloud and ran from the room. I wanted to go after her, but when I tried to rise from the sofa, my legs felt boneless and my ears rang. I simply wasn't strong enough to do it. My mother scolded and all the other ladies fussed over me once again. Hating my own weakness, I fell back against the cushions and lay there watching distant shadows flicker across the ceiling.

When the party broke up, St Cloud returned me to my bedchamber. I wasn't in the mood to try to talk to him, and he put me to bed with all the impersonality of a postman delivering a parcel. Then he left the room. I wondered if he would walk all the way through the woods to the village smithy to find Nell Scathlock. I wondered if he loved her as he'd never loved me. Or if he'd acknowledge her baby.

I hoped so.

It would mean he was unlikely to come to my own room ever again. I shuddered at the thought – and not just because the doctor had told me I could die if I tried to have another baby, but because the memory of St Cloud touching me rose up inside me like bile.

I tossed and turned, but I couldn't sleep. I'd spent most of the day in a laudanum-induced doze and had taken no physical exercise for weeks. My conscience roiled uneasily at the thought of Nell Scathlock raising her child in the smithy, which was little more than a hovel. And with that murderous brother of hers too! My head throbbed. My legs twitched and cramped. My abdomen ached too – I found it hard to regard that part of my body as anything other than a coffin at the moment.

It was always in the early hours that my thoughts grew darker . . .

Usually I tried to distract myself by writing in my journal.

My journal!

I jackknifed into a sitting position. I'd left my journal downstairs under the sofa cushions. The Great Hall would be swept and tidied by one of the maids in a few hours' time. Those cushions would be moved and my private thoughts would be handed to . . . Mrs Thorne? Or St Cloud? Both of whom featured heavily in the journal. Oh no! My feet were on the floor before I was aware of it. But when I tried to stand, my legs gave way just as they had before.

I crouched on the floor and waited for the darkness to stop spinning around me. Perhaps it really *was* too soon for me to get up. Suddenly I was afraid. What if I was risking even more damage to my fragile body? What if it meant I'd never be well again – and would have to be carried around by St Cloud for ever?

But I needed that journal back. So I gritted my teeth and told myself my muscles felt weak because I hadn't used them in weeks. That was all. I staggered around the room, finding the tinderbox and relighting my candle, then resting again before wrapping myself in my shawl and setting forth into the passage.

My progress was slow and painful. The carpet felt strange against my bare feet – there was a numbness to my soles as if I were walking on a layer of fog. I hunched over and slid my hand along the wall for support. Puppet-strings of pain ran down my legs from the small of my back. By the time I reached the minstrels' gallery, there were beads of perspiration all over my forehead.

It was still warm and smoky downstairs. There was an orange glow from the Yule log in the grate and I could smell the ever-green scents of holly and mistletoe. Somehow I made it down into the hall, retrieved my journal from its hiding place and curled up on the sofa in relief.

I hadn't been there more than a few minutes when I heard a noise coming from somewhere in the direction of the drawing room. The door was ajar and I regarded it doubtfully. Perhaps one of the guests had left something behind . . .

I blew out my candle and waited for my eyes to adjust to the darkness before I crept into the drawing room. My guilty conscience told me it had to be Nell who was stealing through the darkness ahead of me. Nell had lost her home and would be feel-ing angry and vengeful. But what could she do? An awful picture of the castle in flames leapt into my imagination. But I didn't really believe it. No . . . Nell was capable of making mischief, but she wouldn't dare cross St Cloud to that extent.

Then came such a tremendous crash that I dropped my unlit candle in shock. I clutched at one of the armchairs and stood there in the darkness, my heart thumping and my ears straining. Nell must have reached the plate room. There was a tinkle of glass, a metallic clang, thuds and crashes, grunts of exertion that came close to being cries, and a kind of wild sobbing. Oh God! It sounded as if she was smashing everything in the room. I couldn't *not* look. All my own aches and pains were overborne by curiosity and I crept to the doorway of the plate room and peeped inside, my feet poised to dart away if Nell should see me. It was an astonishing sight. Everything was out of its usual place – smashed, broken, overturned. The room was flooded with bright winter moonlight coming through the barred windows in tiger-stripes. The mirrors and pictures and glass-fronted cabinets were smashed and the floor was coated with a sparkling powder of glass. Nell was already slipping and stumbling over some of the things she had smashed. She seemed to have taken leave of her senses. I watched her – a fevered black shadow – crazed and sobbing as she picked up vases, clocks, tankards – anything that came to hand – and flung each treasure against the wall.

I could understand how satisfying that might feel to an angry woman.

A sudden beam of light appeared in the doorway at the far end of the room and I drew back out of sight. It was St Cloud. His face was enigmatical as he raised his candle high and surveyed the damage to all his most treasured possessions.

I'd never seen him lose his temper, not in all the time I'd lived here, but I knew that men like Thorne and Ned Scathlock did whatever he told them to. They were not the kind of men who were easily mastered – and they didn't follow his orders simply because he held the purse strings. I knew that instinctively. They did what they were told because they respected – and feared – St Cloud.

Even as I turned to run, something held me and prevented me from disappearing into the darkness. It was . . . astonishment. Because I could see now – in the candlelight – that I hadn't been following Nell at all.

It was Anna. It was Anna who had just smashed the contents of the plate room. And it was Anna who was about to be murdered by St Cloud. Anna saw the murder in his eyes too. She collapsed into a crouching position, her hands over her head.

'It's no use,' she moaned. 'No use . . . I can't get away . . . I can't escape it.'

'Escape what?' asked St Cloud from the doorway.

'*My face . . . my face . . . my face . . .*'

'I see,' he said, lowering the candle and entering the room. I was unsurprised by his calmness. He had never stormed or shouted or acted hastily, so I'd known his anger would be a cold, controlled thing. It was all the more terrifying for that.

Anna was beyond all fear. 'It's always there,' she said, rocking backwards and forwards. 'Wherever I go. It's like some horrible, twisted hobgoblin leering at me from every mirror. It waits for me. It jumps out at me. And it still takes me by surprise even though I *know* my face looks like this now. Every time I see it I get another . . . jolt of horror. From windows and looking glasses and silver-plated dishes or spoons. It's everywhere, and I can't bear it! I want it gone! Beat me if you want to – kill me – I don't care any more. I just want it gone!'

There was a silence, broken only by St Cloud's footsteps as he crunched his way through the shards of glass and china and came to stand over his sister-in-law.

'I don't care what you do,' she repeated. 'I don't know what people live for when they aren't beautiful.'

'For me . . . it's the material things in life,' he answered, crouching beside her and picking up something from the wreckage. 'The things you just destroyed. You see this? It's a fragment from a valuable dish of the Yung Cheng dynasty. It was one of my favourites. Only you've just made it into a Yung Cheng jigsaw puzzle.'

'It's *things*!' Anna shrieked, scraping her face with her nails. 'Plates and vases and dishes – they're just *things*! They can all be replaced with new things or better things. But my face can't be replaced – it's ruined, and I can't go out and get a new one. My whole life is in pieces.'

'Much like my plate room.' St Cloud picked up an enormous shard of silver glass and held it to Anna's quivering throat. As if in sympathy, a sob of terror constricted my own throat. 'This must be from the overmantel mirror. I imagine you used to love mirrors, didn't you? They must have been a constant source of reassurance. And now they've all turned against you. Every one of them. You're like the wicked queen in "Snow White".'

Anna didn't move.

'Well?' he asked, caressing her skin with the jagged glass.

'Yes,' she said quietly. 'My reflection used to be beautiful. You wouldn't have spoken to me like this if I hadn't lost my looks. You would've married me. You would've given me anything I wanted. All this' – she swung her arm out across the room – 'you

263

would have laid it all at my feet if I'd asked you to.'

He dropped the glass then and took her face in both his enormous hands, studying her closely. One half of her face was puckered and crumpled with despair, but the other half stared straight back at him, impassive as a dead thing. It was an uncomfortable sight to witness, but St Cloud gazed at her as if intrigued.

'Perhaps I would . . .' he said, running his thumb down the long scar that sliced through her cheek. 'If I look hard enough, I can see how you might have been considered a beauty.'

Anna hit him.

Over in the doorway, I clapped both hands over my mouth in horror, but St Cloud only laughed and gave my sister a shake.

'Let me go!' she shouted, slapping every part of him she could reach. 'How dare you! Let me go!'

'I ought to give you the beating you deserve,' he said, shaking her again until she clutched at him giddily. 'I suppose this display of temper is because I made you dance with me this evening? Well, it wasn't my idea. It was your sister's.'

'She . . . *she* did that? After everything I said to her – after everything she took from me?'

'What did Elinor take?'

'She took the life I ought to have had.' Anna laughed bitterly and she gestured around the room once again. 'All this – the castle, you, everything. She stole my life.'

'Take it back then.' St Cloud slid one of his hands round to the back of her neck, working his fingers under her spinster's cap. The other he trailed down over the front of her high-necked unflattering bodice, cupping her breast and making her gasp.

'*I* always take whatever *I* want.'

Anna didn't fight him or protest; she appeared to be deliberating. St Cloud laughed and kissed her, and then he picked her up and carried her across the room to an elegant sofa that leant against the wall.

I watched them for a while with a kind of horrified fascination. And finally, I realized I no longer had to worry about him coming to my room at night. Nell had been replaced.

17

I dragged myself back upstairs to bed, but the pains in my legs were worse and my abdomen felt heavy as lead. The doctor had been quite right, of course – I'd got up too soon.

Weeks passed and different doctors were consulted. A misaligned pelvis, said one. Nerve damage, said another. Or perhaps compressed vertebrae. But they all agreed it was my own fault because I'd tried to climb down that stupid ladder. They told me that the shock of the fall had brought about an early and disastrous labour which had led to complications. And I said nothing of the shock that had *made* me fall.

I didn't know it then, but I was to spend the following year in bed.

It began, as these things always do, one day at a time. I came to know the exact number of flowers woven upon the carpet of my bedchamber. I knew each knothole in the panelling and the titles of all the romantic novels on the shelves, although it was many months since I'd read any of them. Jem — the kitchen boy — brought me books from the library instead: accounts of sea voyages or travels to foreign countries. I liked to read about places that were far away from Darkmere.

Jem could also be persuaded to carry my letters down to Mr Thorne's office, or bring me fruit from the hothouses or flowers from the gardens. Mrs Thorne disapproved at first, but Anna allowed him to wait on me, so he became a sort of unofficial pageboy. This meant that Anna herself no longer had to keep me company. Before long, I only saw her if someone carried me down to dinner in the evening, and then she never met my eye.

Mostly I was left alone, and over the months that followed I began to disappear. Hardly anyone noticed me or remembered I was there. I had no role at Darkmere any more. But neither had I anywhere else to go. In name, I was still St Cloud's wife, even if the initials inscribed upon the castle wall told the truth of the matter.

The castle was a place that lent itself to secrecy and silent observation, and little by little, I became as watchful as St Cloud. Sitting in the window seat of my bedchamber, I learnt about the weather, the tides and the seasons. I saw the servants go about their business and I listened to their chatter. At night, I heard the shriek of the owls in the wood and the muffled clop of horses on the driveway.

It was on one of these nights that I finally managed to stand again. The owls were screaming and the wind blew through the trees with a noise like the shuffle and whisper of a crowd. Next came a sound that I'd never yet accounted for – like the tramp of horses with cloth-covered hooves – and I shifted restlessly under my bedclothes. Then a clatter from right beneath my window! A clatter followed by a muffled oath and I jumped out of bed.

I was standing!

Only for a moment . . . before my legs folded and I landed with a bump on the carpet, but excitement and hope soared up into my chest and I felt sure I could do it again if I wanted to. At first, I was too frightened to try. What if I'd imagined it? Trembling all over, I tested my weakened muscles again and I found it was true – I was recovering! I wanted to tell someone – Anna perhaps. But she and everyone in the house had been asleep for hours. And then I thought of that someone who had dropped something under my window and cursed aloud . . .

I shuffled myself across the room to the window seat and peered out into the darkness. The driveway below was full of shadows. It took me a moment or two to understand what I was seeing, but then a bolt of terror shot through me so swiftly it took my breath away. The shadows were *men*.

In such numbers, they seemed like an invading army. It was too dark for me to see much, but my imagination supplied the missing details with pictures from history books and newspapers. Medieval castles under siege . . . the storming of the Bastille . . . the mobs of weavers and Luddites who'd burnt down mills and textile factories when I was only six years old. Now it was happening here.

The men's silence and their furtive movements made them

appear all the more menacing. They were robbers! We were being robbed. I had to rouse the house. Oh God – the plate room! I had to find a way to wake St Cloud . . .

There, my train of thought stopped dead. When I considered St Cloud and his reputation, I knew instinctively that no one would rob him.

I looked again more carefully.

It was Ned Scathlock's great size that made him distinguishable from the orderly mass of men with their dark clothing and blackened faces. He also had a recognizable swagger and he carried his hateful wooden stave against his shoulder. I shivered at the sight of it, knowing that he would have no compunction or restraint if there should chance to be dragoons in the woods.

Here at last was the proof that Lieutenant Higgs had wanted: this was a smugglers' run. And the goods were coming through the house.

I leant closer to the window, bending my knees. The muscles in my legs were feeble, but they still worked. I had to start using them again if I ever wanted to get away from Darkmere. The carpet prickled the soles of my feet distractingly. The harder I looked, the more I saw. There were quick glimmers of light thrown by the shaded lanterns carried by some of the men. The lights illuminated wooden clubs hefted over burly shoulders and occasionally the glints of pistols or knives worn in the men's belts. Almost every man from the village must have been down there, including some of our own servants. And if St Cloud sanctioned the trade, what other choice did they have?

I could discern the authoritative figure of Mr Thorne –

pointing and gesturing, directing the train of horses and wagons supposedly used to transport stone from the quarries on the estate. The men marched silently along the driveway and into the trees. The heavily laden horses went with them and I wondered how far they meant to travel. Would they make for some lonely farmhouse miles inland? Or would they walk all night, making for the nearest town?

The idea of informing against them was in my head before I'd watched the last of them disappear, but I was as dependent upon St Cloud as everyone else. I would have to wait and I would have to watch. I was already invisible – especially to my husband. He'd never notice if I was able to walk again.

Night after night, I slipped out of bed and paced about my room, stretching my aching spine and switching my weight from one leg to the other, learning to balance again. Rebuilding my wasted muscles. I wouldn't be able to escape the castle until I was strong enough to walk and run and ride again. St Cloud had men in the woods, lookouts on the cliffs and a spyglass trained upon the beach. Who knew how far I'd have to go before I found someone who would help me stand against him?

Meanwhile, I recorded the smuggling in my journal. I began to recognize when the wind and the tide were right to land a cargo. I knew that the next moonless night afterwards might mean a run. And when the 'owls' began to shriek more than usual, I went to the window and wrote down everything I saw.

But who could I hand the book to? My father was the only person I could think of. As a magistrate, he'd be unable to ignore written proof of another man's wrongdoing. It had been almost a year since I'd seen him and I'd done my best to forget the way he'd fawned upon St Cloud last Christmas. This time when he visited, I would talk to him – *seriously* – and explain how unhappy I was at Darkmere. Surely my mother and father could be persuaded to take me home with them.

Christmas Day emerged through a sheet of water. I peered out of my bedroom window and saw that rain was hitting the driveway so hard it was bouncing back up again waist high. It drummed on the window panes, pattered noisily on the leaves of the trees and bushes, and hurtled down the hillside in a tiny millstream.

When the carriage emerged from the woods, I marvelled at how wet everything was! The coats of the horses streamed, water poured from the roof of the coach and the brim of the driver's hat – and the windows were all steamed up behind the streaks of rain. There were outriders too – their faces sunk into their collars – and a covered wagon which sagged miserably under the downpour.

The butler and footmen were outside with umbrellas before the forlorn little cavalcade had come to a halt. Grooms raced to lead the horses round to the stables and dislodge the luggage. I sat down quickly on the window seat as I heard the knock of the footman who'd been sent to carry me downstairs, so that I could greet the guests.

We met with all the bustle of arrival. Greetings were exchanged and orders shouted to servants. Rushes of cold air came from the front door, wet boots stamped across the flagstones and streaming coats were carried away. There were several visitors I didn't recognize. A tall man standing in the shadow of the carved oak screen caused my heart to give a tremendous thump of shock, although I couldn't have told why. My father was already chatting to St Cloud and helping himself to a glass of hot wine. Anna was directing Mrs Thorne to go and make Mama a restorative of her own particular recipe.

The hall could hardly have been warmer or more welcoming, but none of the credit belonged to me, of course. Mrs Thorne and the other servants now went in as much fear of Anna as they did of St Cloud. Fires and candles were lit before they were requested, bells were answered promptly and any desire for food or drink was anticipated in advance. Still Anna grew more exacting every day. I believe her only real pleasure lay in finding fault with her inferiors. Mama herself was close by the fire, a crease of displeasure running between her eyebrows as she divested herself of all her shawls and heaped them into a maid's arms.

The footman settled me on the sofa and helped to tuck a shawl of my own around me. Mama came and kissed my cheek.

'Elinor, my love, there you are! Such dreadful weather! And oh, *what* a journey – I've never been so knocked about! It was abominably damp and draughty in that coach. I can feel twinges of rheumatism in every inch of me. Thank heavens you have a good fire.'

'It's good of you to come, Mama.'

'If I didn't make the effort to come all this way, I can't help but wonder what sort of a Christmas you'd have here. There are never more than the three of you at Darkmere, and yet Christmas is a time to be surrounded by – well, not only family, but friends and neighbours too. You must excuse my speaking so plainly, my love, but it's up to you – even with your . . . limitations – to assemble such a party. However much St Cloud may enjoy the company of others, a man rarely exerts himself to send out the necessary invitations.'

'Mama?' I was regarding her with suspicion now. 'Who else have you brought?'

'Oh, we've brought the Flinton-Fosters with us again, as you see – and Cousin Charles and dear Augusta. And you remember Sir Hector, of course? A most charming neighbour – he sent me a little note asking if he might bring his son who's at home. Now, my dear, I could scarcely refuse him. And poor Nicholas really had nowhere else to go this year. I was sure you wouldn't mind since the two of you used to be such friends.'

Nicholas?

My eyes had been alighting upon each of the new arrivals in turn, but here they stopped and I turned my head to look at the tall dark man standing in the shadow of the screen. *Nick?* Could it be? My heart gave that strange thump of recognition again. It had been almost two years since I'd seen him and he looked so different now.

'Hello, Ellie,' he said, and his voice brought a rush of tears into my eyes because I knew it so well. It really was him.

There was a severity to his face that had prevented me from knowing him at once. His expression was guarded and there were new lines around his eyes and mouth. Those sleepy eyes I loved so much now looked terribly weary. His face was wet with rain; and drops of water separated his eyelashes like starfish. I longed to hug him, to say something, but my throat had tightened and I couldn't say a word. *Nick . . . ?* I said with my eyes. *Nick . . . ?*

Aware of my distress, he came to me, crouched down and took my hand, brushing it with his lips. 'Was I wrong to come?'

'Wrong? Oh no, Nick! I'm glad – so *very* glad to see you.'

'I couldn't stay away any longer.' His face tightened and all the new lines grew a little more pronounced. 'We were always the best of friends, Ellie, and I need a friend right now.'

'I heard you'd married . . . ?'

'Yes. I was married and widowed. The . . . the baby died with her.'

'Oh, *Nick*!' My eyes held his with a sudden fierceness. 'If friendship can be of any comfort at all, then you have mine. Always.'

He squeezed my hand and the guarded look dropped from his face for a moment. His eyes were as wet as my own and he looked quite tortured. 'But what happened to you, Ellie? You look . . . so . . . so—'

I gave a gurgle of laughter. 'I look much better than I did this time last year, I assure you.'

It was true. At least I was dressed and sitting up now.

'My wife's rather pale because she doesn't go outside any more,' said St Cloud, approaching to be formally introduced. He shook Nick's hand, showing no sign that he remembered him from their last meeting. 'Elinor is no longer able to stand or walk unaided.'

'Well, we've brought the remedy for that!' exclaimed my mother. 'Where's Elinor's Christmas present? My dear, the luckiest thing! The poor Flinton-Fosters lost the dowager this year

274

and they've given us her Bath chair. Tell those men to go and fetch it out of the wagon!'

I clapped my hands to my mouth as the footmen returned with an enormous, dripping wet bath chair. It had a folding hood, an upholstered seat, huge back wheels and an air of dignified hauteur reminiscent of its late owner. It was the most *absurd* gift for an eighteen-year-old girl!

I think this was the first time I'd ever laughed at Darkmere. 'Oh, I must try it right away!'

St Cloud took a step forward, but I'd instinctively stretched out my arms to Nick. Because no matter how tall and strong my husband was, Nick was the only person in the room who existed for me now that he was here.

It no longer mattered that my sister wanted me confined to my bedchamber until I disappeared from her life altogether. Nick was here now and he'd *always* wish to see me. And I wouldn't have to talk to my father about St Cloud's smuggling exploits, because Nick was here and he could advise me. Nick would make everything all right again.

Grinning widely, he lifted me into the Bath chair and pushed me around the Great Hall while I attempted to steer with the long handle. It was like sitting inside a giant high-heeled shoe and the thought made me laugh again.

'Let me show you the house,' I called over my shoulder. 'Push me through that door – there! That's the dining room.'

The butler held the door open and Nick whizzed me around the long, polished table as I clung to my new chair delightedly. One of the small, spindle-legged dining chairs caught on my back wheel and was dragged along with us. I laughed harder than ever. I hoped it was broken!

'To the library!' I cried, pointing at the next door. There were steps to the library and Nick had to tilt the bath chair, allowing me to smile up at him. 'How good it is to see you again,' I said. 'You're the best Christmas present they could've brought me.'

'I'm flattered – since they also brought you this admirable chair.' He parked it before the fire and wandered around the room, inspecting the spines of the books.

'Do you remember,' I asked him, 'how I ruined the rug in the library of the rectory?'

'You smashed a bottle of my father's favourite Chambertin all over the floor.' He grinned. 'The whole room smelt like a tavern for months! It never quite recovered its atmosphere of sobriety. I wonder what the new rector makes of it.'

'New rector? Nick, you don't mean . . .'

He nodded, his face creasing into lines of sadness again. 'My father was in poorer health than he ever allowed me to know. When I returned to England, my father was taken from me before I'd been home a month. The new incumbent was ready to move into the rectory, so Sir Hector invited me to stay with him, since his son is an old school friend. I'd lost everything and I didn't have anywhere else to go.'

My heart was wrung. 'Does it bother you to think of a stranger there – in your home?'

'No, it didn't feel like home once my father was gone. I couldn't wait to get out, to tell the truth. Do you know, whenever I tried to conjure up a vision of home, I always thought of you?'

'Oh!' I leant out of the chair towards him and took his hand, bringing his palm up against my cheek. 'That's how I always think of you too.'

'Don't, Ellie.' There was a bleakness in his voice that I hadn't heard before. 'Your home is a magnificent castle.'

'This? This has never been my home. It belongs to St Cloud and it's run by my sister.'

Nick stared at me, clearly taken aback by my candour. He shook his head wordlessly.

'I'm sorry, Nick.' I smiled up at him. 'I never learnt to guard my tongue with you, did I? And I'm supposed to be showing you the library.' I pointed at the panelling below the bookshelves. 'Go and twist that wooden rosette in the panelling – yes, just there – then stand back.'

As he did so, there was the click and scroop of a set of polished wooden steps unfolding itself from between the bookshelves.

Nick laughed. 'Upon my word, that's a neat little trick!'

'Wait, there's more!' I stretched out my arm and twisted the device that opened the panelling above the fireplace.

'More books,' Nick exclaimed. 'Hidden ones.'

'Well, you can never have too many books.' I took down a couple of volumes and ran my hands over the leather bindings, breathing in their scent. 'I think the smell of books and spilt wine will always remind me of your father. Shall I ring for a bottle of burgundy and pour it into the carpet in his memory?'

He shook his head, laughing harder than ever. 'What on earth does your husband do when you say things as nonsensical as that?'

'I could never talk to St Cloud the way I can talk to you.' I shoved the books back into place. 'In fact, I seldom talk to St Cloud at all.'

'All this time I've been steeling myself to see you happily married and to pretend I can bear it. But somehow this feels worse.' He moved behind the Bath chair so I couldn't see his face. 'I'm sorry, Ellie – I wish you really *were* happy with your husband. That would be easier than seeing you so sad.'

'I'm not sad,' I said, feeling the tears start to my eyes. 'Not now you're here.'

'Then it *was* wrong of me to come.'

'Mama would never have brought you here if there was anything improper about it. I never dared hope she'd forgive you for the scene you made at her party that time.'

'She's forgiven me everything since I inherited my wife's fortune. I can now afford to cause as many unpleasant scenes as I choose. She brought me here on this visit because she wanted me – and my fortune – for your sister. And I allowed her to think it might happen because I wanted to see *you*.'

I gave a sudden snort of laughter and clapped a hand to my face to smother it. 'Anna? I didn't realize. Oh, dear God, how ironic! And I suppose she wanted you to see what a splendid match she'd made for me into the bargain. What a detestable old horror she is.'

'Yes, we'll aim to run her over with the Bath chair. Where do you want to go next?'

'Back through the hall, I suppose. There's a plate room full of treasure I can show you, and a sort of spying room in one of the towers. St Cloud has rigged up this ingenious sequence of mirrors which show him every angle of the cliffs and the beach.'

'A spying room? Why would he want a spying room?'

'Any number of reasons. He can watch for his latest shipment of untaxed brandy . . . he can keep an eye out for the Customs men . . . he can even watch the maids bathing if he wants to. That's the kind of man he is, Nick.'

'I can't tell if you're in earnest or not.'

'I mean it! I don't care about the smuggling so much, but the violence that goes hand in hand with it is intolerable. I have to do something about it.'

'But your parents? Your sister?'

'My father's as afraid of St Cloud as everyone else. As for Anna . . .' I dropped my voice to the barest whisper. 'She wears gowns of French silk. She smells of expensive French scent and there are diamonds in her ears and around her neck – that's how Anna feels about it.'

'I see.'

'Oh, Nick! What am I going to do?'

'We'll think of something. Why don't you show me the tower room to start with?'

We took the doorway far too fast. Nick had forgotten the steps that went back down into the dining room and the front wheel dropped down so suddenly that I flew out of the Bath chair like a bird. My mood was already on the edge of hysteria and it was too much for me. Too ridiculous and too undignified. I lay there shaking with laughter, tears pouring down my face.

Nick gave an inarticulate cry and fell to his knees beside me on

279

the carpet. 'Are you hurt? Oh God, you must be terribly hurt! Tell me where you're hurt, my love.'

'Here!' I clutched at my side. 'Oh, I'm getting a stitch!'

'A-a stitch? But your injuries? You must be hurt!'

I reached for him and put my head in his lap, still laughing and sobbing and wiping my wet cheeks. 'I haven't laughed in such a long time – and now I can't stop! This is how it used to be, though, isn't it? When we were together, we never stopped making each other laugh. I'd forgotten. Being married to St Cloud has left me so battered and bruised it hurts my sides to laugh now.'

Nick cradled my head and it felt exactly as I'd said: like coming home.

'So you're truly not hurt?'

'Of course not! This carpet's perfectly soft.'

I felt him exhale with relief and it almost started my tears again. I wanted to sit there on the floor hugging him for ever, but he was also the one person I could never lie to. So I placed my hands upon his shoulders and pushed myself up on to my feet.

He gasped and reached out to support me, but I didn't even sway.

'You see? I've been recovering steadily for the last few months. But no one ever asked me if I was getting any better, so I never told anyone. I know you're thinking I'm insane, but this kind of subterfuge is all I have left now. It's my only advantage – and perhaps the only way I'll ever be able to escape from here.'

Nick looked shocked. I searched his face for additional signs of disapproval, but didn't find any. His eyes were all confusion and concern. 'I-I'm glad you're better.'

'Thank you,' I said. 'For reserving judgement, at least. I think you'll understand when you know my husband a little better.'

He helped me back into my dowager's chair – not a moment too soon, for the butler came in to lay the table for dinner just then, and Nick and I resumed our tour of the house. Later, at dinner, I was trapped between my father and the boorish Sir Hector, while Nick was placed at the far end of the table in between Anna and Aunt Augusta. But my gaze went to him often.

Every glance at him recalled a time when I was younger and the future had been something to look forward to. When he raised his wine glass very slightly in my direction, I remembered again the time I'd spilt wine all over the rectory rug and Nick had taken both the blame and the punishment in my place.

When I watched him bite into a peach, I remembered the summer's day he'd thrust his battledore racquet into a hedge, disturbing a wasps' nest and we'd both run screaming in terror into one of the hothouses. I chuckled at the memory and Sir Hector stared at me from under his bushy eyebrows.

And when he wasn't doing anything in particular – just meeting my eye and smiling at me as if I were the only person in the room – I remembered how he'd asked me to be his wife on that windy day in the park. And I wished I'd said yes. *Oh God, how I wished it!*

I was in love with him. I knew it without question. Not because of any 'falling' sensation or butterflies in my stomach or romantic music playing in my head. None of the things I'd read about in the novels I'd long since abandoned – just the engulfing *whoosh* of realization that I had always loved him. Always. There was no 'falling' because I was already there.

It was a happier Christmas than I'd ever thought to spend at Darkmere. Although I tried not to show it, I could feel the happiness *radiating* from me. I woke in the morning eager to be with Nick again, and when I went to bed at night I was already looking forward to seeing him the following morning. Nick's hard, bleak look began to fade and I became more animated every day.

St Cloud noticed.

Even when I saw his gaze fixed upon me with barely concealed anger, I couldn't stay away from Nick. Oh, the blessed relief of being myself again – the way I used to be! We spent entire days sitting before the fire and talking. Sometimes we played cards or looked through my favourite travel books in the library and planned tours of Europe or sea voyages to the Far East. Whenever it wasn't too cold or too wet, he tucked me into the Bath chair and we explored the woods, the village and all the surrounding countryside.

We were watched, though. There were keepers in the woods who materialized from the behind the trees when we strayed too far – and they sidled ever closer to us until we gave up and turned back. In the village, it was the same. Local labourers, quarrymen and estate workers all appeared on street corners, talking in low voices and eyeing us as we passed. It was clear there was no easy way out of Darkmere.

'By sea then,' said Nick, on the last evening of the Christmas visit. 'I'll have to leave here with your parents, but I'll hire a fishing boat at the nearest town and I'll sail straight back for you. There's only one landing place, of course. Do you think you'll be able to meet me on the beach?'

I shivered at the thought of those dark tunnels and the passages through the cellars but St Cloud had ordered one of his men to smash every rung of the ladder off the cliff face months ago and there was no other way. So I nodded. Somehow I'd make it down to the beach.

'How long will you be gone?' I asked. 'And how will I know when to meet you there?'

'I'll come back as soon as I can, you have my word. It shouldn't take more than a day or two to hire a boat, and a chaise to continue our journey. But I've no idea how to let you know when to meet me. Is there no one at Darkmere you can trust to carry a message?'

'Jem,' I said. 'He's the kitchen boy and a particular friend. You must take him with you. No one'll notice if he hides in the wagon – no one ever takes much notice of Jem.'

'That's settled then.' He sighed 'Although the thought of riding away without you is tearing me into pieces – I wish there were another way.'

'I'm afraid St Cloud will come after us,' I said. 'Not because he wants *me*, but because he needs my father. As long as he has the magistrate's daughters, he has the magistrate too. So he'll react as if you've stolen one of his possessions and come after us. I know him.'

'He won't find us. We'll travel. Go abroad somewhere.'

'We'd be outcasts,' I said, gazing at the frosty hillside, my hands knotting themselves inside my old shawl to keep out the cold. 'No one will speak to us – or even acknowledge us.'

'I don't care what anyone else thinks.' Nick was standing very straight beside my wheeled chair. A lock of hair blew across his forehead and made him frown, furrowing his brow. He looked older – capable and determined – and the temptation for me to fling myself into his arms was almost overwhelming.

But someone was bound to be watching.

Mr Thorne. Or perhaps Ned Scathlock in his pepperpot look-out building. Or even St Cloud himself in his little tower room. Someone was *always* watching.

'I don't mind for myself,' I said in a low voice. 'But I can't help regretting everything you'll have to give up. Respectability . . . position . . . family . . . everything. I can't even give you any children.'

'I told you, I never imagined any of that in my future. I only ever wanted to be with you.' He crouched beside me and wiped away my tears with his fingers. 'I was married before, remember? I was married to a sweet, young girl who did everything to please me. She suffered so dreadfully to bear me a son. She suffered and died trying to please a man who didn't really love her. Because I still loved you, Ellie. My wife didn't deserve that. She ought to have married a man who could love her properly. Each of us belongs with the person we love.'

I began to sob in earnest. The tears rose up hot beneath my lids and I felt them cool in the freezing air as they spilt down over my cheeks. Nick swore furiously. 'I'm going to take you back in now,' he said. 'I can hear the dressing bell and you must be cold, and – *damn it* – I can't stand seeing you so upset and not be able to comfort you properly.' He strode back to the house so fast the wheels of the Bath chair fought with the gravel and I bounced up and down on the seat. 'I swear I've kissed you a thousand times since I've been here,' he muttered, 'and not one of those kisses has existed outside my own imagination!'

He hadn't loved her, I told myself over and over. *He'd loved me, always.* I hadn't known it would matter so much, but it did. It felt as if the whole world had shifted.

18

Kate

We ran.

We ran without pause, like a herd of startled animals, all the way back up to the castle. I barely looked to see where I was going and my torch dangled in my hand, making useless patterns on the floor. At one point, I turned a corner too sharply and caught my hip bone on the rocky wall, but I didn't even slow down.

Music – loud and fast – was still pounding away in the Great Hall. The mood was completely different now, though. No one felt like dancing or laughing or even listening to it, but it didn't occur to any of us to turn it off. We paced around the room or stood and stared at each other in horror.

I couldn't get that terrible smell out of my nose. I walked up and down, shaking my head, sniffing and snorting as I went, but it seemed lodged in my nostrils.

'What *was* that?' I asked of no one in particular. 'What *was* that? What *was* that?'

Hat-man Dan had torn off his wet jeans and T-shirt and rubbed at himself with a towel. He kept on rubbing and scrubbing long after he was dry. He was muttering to himself and grinding his teeth. He looked half crazy with panic.

'It was her,' he was saying. 'It was that blonde girl . . . with the green dress. This is why she haunts the castle – it's because she's still down there.'

I shuddered at the thought. Then I found I couldn't stop shuddering and I folded my arms tightly around myself. Jackson turned the music off and we all jumped and looked round at him. The silence stung my ears.

'Are you sure it was . . . human?' he asked.

'I saw her,' repeated Hat-man Dan. 'She was floating in that black hole in the floor . . . I was in there with her – I touched her. Her eyes were open and her hair looked just like that yellowish seaweed. Only . . . the water had made her body . . . all swollen and bloated.'

'You can't have seen that,' said Jackson. 'You imagined it because you were panicking.'

'She must have been down there all along . . . she must've been down there while we slept and ate and made stupid jokes . . . all that time, she was down there floating in the dark . . . underneath us.'

'No!' said Lucie, marching over to Hat-man Dan and

slapping his bare chest. 'No – no – no!'

'There aren't any ghosts!' said Leo impatiently. His face was white in the brightness of the hall, and his eyes glittered with a sort of perverse fascination. 'I'll prove it – I'll wait for the stink to clear and then I'll go back and see what's really down there.'

'Oh God, no!' said Beano. 'Oh God, oh God – you can't!'

'I'm not asking you to come.' Leo squinted as if he was looking down into that black hole again. 'But I need to get a better look. What about you, Jackson? Are you coming?'

Jackson grimaced, but nodded staunchly. Beano wavered, his face working, and then he followed them out of the room.

After a moment, I realized that Hat-man Dan was crying. Lucie had turned her back on him, so I went over and touched his arm.

He looked at me blankly. Then he took my hand and placed it against his chest. 'Can you feel that?'

I nodded. Beneath my fingers, his heart was beating so fast it felt like a vibration inside his chest.

'Do you think there's something wrong with me? Do you think it could be a heart attack?'

'No, I think it's probably a panic attack.'

'Oh, Jesus! This is the worst holiday ever.'

'We're going home soon. Try to breathe more slowly. You've just got to stay calm and ride it out. You'll soon be back to normal.'

He pulled off his hat and used it to wipe his streaming eyes. 'Oh, Kate, there is no normal here . . .'

I sat down beside him and hung my arm loosely around his shoulders. It felt awkward and I wished I was better at comforting people. Because I really *did* understand how he was feeling – all the shock and the fear.

'I know,' I said quietly. 'You're not the only one seeing things. I wasn't alone here last night, I know it.'

My confession didn't seem to help. Hat-man Dan buried his face in his arms, his shoulders convulsing under my useless arm.

'It's OK,' I persisted. 'I was petrified too. If the others had seen the ghost, they'd all be freaking out as much as you are.'

'You didn't see what you thought!' He shrugged my arm off his shoulders and looked at me for a long anguished moment before tugging a carrier bag out from under his pillows and handing it to me. Inside there was a bundle of crumpled clothing and some . . . *hair?*

'It's the museum smuggler's costume,' he said, still sniffing wetly. 'You sent Leo some photos from the museum, remember? He dared me to break into the museum and steal one of the costumes while the others were in the pub, so I was never arrested along with the rest of them. I told Lucie I'd hitched a lift back to the castle and fallen asleep . . . but I was meant to frighten you first.'

'*It was you!*' My mouth opened in slow motion, but I didn't think to draw in a breath until my head started to spin. 'There wasn't a ghost at all . . . it was *you!*'

'Leo said that if I gave you a scare, you and Lucie would start to appreciate us boys a bit more. I was drunk enough to find the whole plan hilarious. That was the trouble – I'd had far too much to drink and I couldn't find you anywhere. I didn't think you'd even seen me. I'm sorry, Kate.'

Sorry? No, it wasn't enough. I'd been trying to comfort him! I sprang away from him, glaring and breathing hard. Then I slapped him across the face.

'*You bastard!*'

'Ow! Jesus! I told you – it wasn't my idea.'

Leo . . . of course.

'It was you who came in here and crept around until I was so frightened I could hardly breathe!' I said out loud. 'And you who smashed those windows in the tower room! Well, you can bloody well make sure Leo knows it was you – because he nearly had a fight with Jackson over it earlier on.'

Wincing, Dan shook his head. 'I didn't smash anything. I couldn't even get in here – you locked the door, you know you did. I walked around the castle two or three times and found that every other door and window was locked too. Eventually, I sat down in a corner of the kitchen courtyard and passed out. That's where I was when I woke up this morning. I was still wearing that stupid costume and I was almost too ill to move. God, I'm never drinking again, I swear. I've done too much drinking and smoking this whole holiday. Too much everything. That's Leo's problem as well – always too much of everything.'

Lucie was watching us avidly from across the room. 'What's he done now?' she called to me.

'More than he's owning up to,' I shouted back.

290

'Then you should keep on hitting him,' she suggested disloyally. 'Until he says something one of us can actually believe.'

Hat-man Dan started to protest, but I stalked off to another corner without listening. We sat in silence, glaring in different directions, until the others came back upstairs. None of them noticed the resentment swirling around the atmosphere – perhaps because the air down in the cellars was so poisonous.

'A dead seal,' said Jackson, throwing himself on to his airbed. 'Must've got stuck down there ages ago.'

'The water is jammed with carcasses,' added Leo, who had followed Jackson into the hall. He held one of the strange long-handled forks that had hung on the wall of the cave-like room. With his muscular build, wet clothes and hair tangled into dreadlocks, he looked like Aquaman or someone who'd emerged from the deep. 'Seals or dolphins mostly, I think. There must be some kind of littoral cave inside the cliffs that filled up with water and trapped them there. Maybe I'll get hold of some diving equipment and explore.'

'God,' moaned Beano. 'That'll be like swimming around in the waste bucket of a really gruesome fishmonger's shop.'

Leo prodded him with the long fork, but Beano lay face down on his bed and didn't respond. It was late – almost midnight. Everyone was tired and slightly sickened by the smell coming from the cellars. No one wanted to party any more.

Leo didn't give up, though. He attempted to cheer every-one up the only way he knew how – with more alcohol. He produced a bottle of absinthe and made bright green cocktails. They tasted extremely strong and inspired us to play a version of the Rizla game in which we each had to represent a famous absinthe drinker, such as Ernest Hemingway or Vincent van Gogh. The game ended in dispute when Leo insisted that Frank Sinatra had been an absinthe drinker and Hat-man Dan said that was bollocks.

One by one, the boys began to crash out. Jackson fell asleep beside me with a smouldering joint in one hand and a cigarette paper stuck to his forehead with *Toulouse-Lautrec* written on it.

'Night-night, Toulouse,' I whispered, stubbing out the joint for him.

The night hours ticked by slowly – like a clock that was coming unwound. I hadn't slept for a long time but I couldn't relax here any more. My eyes ached with tiredness and still the minutes continued to tick by.

Tick . . . tick . . . tick . . .

When the ticking became too irksome for me to ignore, I went to the door and looked out. The hot weather had finally broken. Not with thunder and dramatics, but with the slow, rhythmic ticking of raindrops. There was a soft pad of footsteps and Lucie came to stand beside me.

'I wish we could go home,' she said.

'We will in the morning.' I nodded at the blackness and rain. 'Summer's finally over.'

'I hate waiting.' She wrapped her arms around herself with

a grimace. 'What the hell are we going to do with ourselves until morning?'

I tried to think of some way for us to pass the time together and absolutely *nothing* came to me. Then I realized it didn't matter. I didn't have to be like her, or any of the other Denborough Park girls – not any more. Jackson had made me feel OK about who I really was. So I smiled and said, 'I'm going to go and look at the books in the library.'

Lucie pouted, but followed me when I picked up a camping lantern and made my way across the hall. I didn't mind – I preferred not to be alone in any part of Darkmere now. Leo, who was still awake and tinkering with his makeshift bar, called us both over to try some new alcoholic creations he'd made.

'One of my specialities,' he said, smiling at me from behind a glimmering multitude of glass bottles. 'It'll give you sweet dreams.'

Which was enough to convince me he'd spiked it with something hallucinogenic and I had to force my hand out to take it from him. I don't think he noticed my reluctance, though. Leo, who had always been so adept at reading people or persuading then to do whatever he wanted, appeared wholly unaware of my mistrust. Perhaps he was tiring at long last . . . I gave him one more backwards glance and saw that his smile had widened into something utterly sinister.

In the library, books were still piled in dusty great heaps on the floorboards and the mantelpiece. They made the room smell like a second-hand bookshop – all damp-spotted paper and musty leather bindings.

'Pooh,' said Lucie, wrinkling her nose. 'Mouldy old books.'

'Don't complain,' I said. 'It's better than the smell coming from whatever's in the cellar.'

We both shuddered.

Lucie went over to the panelling above the fireplace and played with the rosette mechanism. 'It reminds me of my great-grandma's house,' she murmured. 'All this dark wood, dust and damp plaster – it smells of . . . of *oldness*.'

'It doesn't remind me of anything,' I said, after a moment's reflection. Everything in the flat I shared with my mum was made of plastic. 'I'm just happiest in libraries, that's all.'

I looked through the books on the floor, while Lucie examined those on the mantelpiece, talking all the while and sipping her drink. Every time I tried to lose myself in the words, Lucie would jerk me back again with some complaint about Hat-man Dan or an observation about how her next holiday would be somewhere less remote than Darkmere. Siberia possibly . . . or Greenland. She flitted from one volume to another without reading any of them, and she spilt some of her drink over a whole heap I hadn't looked at yet. At last, she unearthed a small notebook with a marbled cover which seemed to hold her interest, but she began to have trouble turning the pages. There was a tissuey ripping sound and a muffled snort of impatience.

'What are you drinking?' I asked sharply.

'Oh God, is this yours?' She peered into her glass and

giggled. 'I'm sorry – I thought it was mine. I've left mine up there on the mantelpiece, look.'

'I wouldn't drink that if I were you,' I said. 'It's one of Leo's specialities and you know they're not to be trusted.'

'Oh, I might as well finish it now.' Lucie smiled radiantly, and there were more tearing sounds as she struggled with the delicate pages of her book. 'It seems to be taking the edge off my nerves. Do you know, I reckon Leo's got the right idea – we came here to have fun. So we shouldn't fall out with each other. Not when we're all such good friends. I think we'll always be friends after this holiday, don't you?'

'Um . . . I didn't think you liked Leo all that much . . . ?'

'Well, he's more of a man than bloody-big-stupid-hat Dan!' She giggled naughtily. 'Did you see the way Dan was crying earlier on? It was *embarrassing* and I'm not at all sure I want to keep on going out with him.'

'Dan cares about you a whole lot more than Leo does.'

'I don't know . . .' Lucie drained the rest of her glass, then cocked her head on one side, considering. 'I think Dan cares more about *her* than he does about me. But there's nothing I can do about it. I can't compete with some imaginary dead girl. It's . . . it's just sick!'

'Are you feeling OK, Lucie?'

'I am, I *really* am.' She pushed her hair back from her face with both hands and held it there. 'Can you see my forehead? Dan says it's the same shape as Josephine Baker's forehead. He's never said that about *her* forehead, has he?'

'I think you need to start drinking lots of water now, Lucie.'

'But my forehead—?'

'Yes, Hat-man Dan's right. It's lovely.'

Lucie clawed at the pages of her book like a kitten playing with string. 'I can't read this any more,' she said, hiccoughing with laughter. 'The writing's too faded and all the words are swimming about.'

'What's so funny?' Leo put his head in at the door.

'Oh, *you!*' she said, giggling and swatting at him with the book in her hand. 'Kate doesn't trust you, Leo. I do, though.'

'Yeah, I can see that.' His eyes twinkled as they went from me to Lucie's empty glass to Lucie herself, swinging the little notebook wildly and not even coming close to hitting him with it. 'I'm glad somebody trusts me.' Leo's feet were bare and dirty, and his T-shirt showed a gaping hole under the arm. He sat down very close to Lucie and took the book away from her.

'I think you're mister – mister—'

'Misunderstood?'

'*Yes!*' Lucie beamed at his wondrous telepathy and pushed her hair back. 'Do *you* like my forehead, Leo?'

'I dream about it,' he said solemnly, making her laugh. He slid one of his huge palms around the back of her neck and pulled her face towards him, planting a kiss on her forehead. She looked quite tiny in his hands. I caught myself staring.

'And you don't think I've been giving Dan too much of a hard time?' she asked him. 'Because you look like you do sometimes.'

'Maybe I'm jealous.'

She giggled and played with the raggedy hole in his T-shirt. His arm was around her now. I was tired and confused and a couple of steps behind, but I was beginning to grasp what was going on.

'Maybe we should all go and ask Hat-man Dan about it,' I suggested.

'Dan's asleep,' said Leo, then he turned his head and spoke into Lucie's ear. 'He probably thinks you're asleep too.'

'I don't feel like sleeping,' said Lucie, tugging at Leo's hair. 'I feel like having fun. We *came* here to have fun, didn't we?'

'How about a swim then?'

'I'm too drunk – I'll drown.'

'We'll go and make sandcastles then.'

They were touching each other all over now. Leo didn't look remotely turned on though; he just looked amused. His eyes were crinkled with silent laughter as he started to French kiss her shoulder. Ugh – I remembered exactly how *wet* that felt, but Lucie just shook with helpless laughter. I had no idea what I ought to do.

'Stop it,' I said. 'You need to stop it. You're not being fair to Hat-man, you know you're not.'

'No one's forcing you to watch, Kate,' murmured Leo. And then he tossed me the little book Lucie had found. 'Here, we'll leave you to your reading.'

He scooped Lucie up easily and set off out of the room. He didn't even sway. He must have had more drugs and alcohol in his system than the rest of us put together, but he remained outwardly unaffected.

How much would it take? I wondered. How much would it take to weaken him? I pictured some sort of elephant tranquillizer gun, as I followed the two of them through the Great Hall, where everyone else lay sleeping. Leo and Lucie giggled and shushed each other with suppressed hilarity, before disappearing through the door on the other side of the room that led to the tunnel.

So what should I do? I couldn't go down to the cellars after them – *God*, I could still smell the dead things from here! All I could do was wait. I told myself they would probably go down to the beach, run around shrieking and splashing each other for a while, then come back and pass out. No one but me would ever know and no harm would've been done.

I decided to go up to the minstrels' gallery, where I'd be able to see them come back but my light wouldn't wake the other boys. I carried the lantern, the book and my pillow up the stairs and settled down to wait.

I turned the little book over in my hands and riffled through the pages. They were closely covered with small, old-fashioned handwriting, but I was too tired and too twitchy to read any of it. It looked like a diary. And then a name leapt out at me and gave me a start – *Elinor*. I was holding Elinor St Cloud's diary. It had been written almost two hundred years ago by a girl who had walked through the same rooms and passages that I was living in right now. She had recognized the soft whine of the library door and the scrunch of gravel that meant footsteps upon the driveway. She had known the secrets of the panelling and the tunnels deep beneath the castle. She had even cursed the castle – and maybe haunted it still.

Before I could read a word, I heard a soft scuffle from somewhere below me, in the darkness of the hall. Beano had woken up and was crawling over to Jackson's sleeping form. I peered through the banisters, watching as Beano shook Jackson awake and whispered something. He gestured to my empty bed and then to Leo's. He whispered again – more emphatic this time – then he sat back on his haunches, waiting for Jackson's reaction. But Jackson just looked across, then turned over to go back to sleep.

He didn't care.

Upstairs, I sat looking down at him, and my stomach felt like a deep, hollow well. I closed Elinor's book and squeezed it hard enough to make my knuckles crack. My interest in the long-dead past was gone just like that. Because Jackson thought I was with Leo and he didn't care.

Then I saw his tousled head silhouetted – even darker than the darkness – as he sat up, and I had to stifle a sob of relief. Part of me wanted to run downstairs to him, but I sat still, holding my thankfulness tight inside me, until I'd at least seen him get out of bed.

He stood up slowly and ran his hands into his hair, looking around the room with an expression that I recognized as a frown, even though I couldn't see it. Then he disappeared into the dining room – he'd gone to see if I was still reading in the library.

Moments later he was back, his bearing more alert and

upright. Beano gave a mischievous little chuckle and followed Jackson through the opposite door into the drawing room. I was smiling even as I scampered downstairs after them, enjoying myself now. I could hear them stepping over the shards of glass in the tower room with the window that spied on the beach and I gave them time to climb the steps and stare out into the darkness. They must've been able to see something – or someone – out there because I heard Jackson swear.

'Looking for me?' I asked, peering around the door with my lantern held high.

Jackson turned and I could see the relief that I'd been feeling mirrored in his face. It was one of those moments that made all the heartache and uncertainty worthwhile. Then he elbowed Beano right off the top of the steps and watched him crash to the floor with satisfaction.

'Arsehole,' he said.

'But . . . but . . . *then who* . . . ?' Beano was comically confused. He looked from me to Jackson and back again. I wouldn't have been surprised if he'd scratched his head.

The only thing that prevented it from being funny was Hat-man Dan looming behind me in the doorway. He was bug-eyed with sleepiness, his hatless hair ludicrously on end.

'What's going on?' he asked. 'And where's Lucie?'

Although none of us spoke, I suppose our faces must have answered his question. He went up the steps in silent disbelief, pushed Jackson aside and gazed into the remaining pieces of the right-hand mirror for a very long time. And that whole time none of us said a word.

'Leo doesn't even like her,' he said dully. 'He's a bastard really.'

'I don't think he wanted the girls to come here with us in the first place,' said Beano. 'They're always trouble. But you two wouldn't listen.'

'I hate him,' said Dan. 'He always has to prove he's better than me – he thinks it's *funny*! I really fucking hate him right now!'

I felt desperately sorry for him. What Leo had done was inexcusable and I should've knocked him on the head with one of those heavy old books – or . . . or . . . thrown cold water over them both.

Why hadn't I?

Hat-man Dan returned to the main hall and switched on a couple of camping lanterns. Then, slowly and methodically, he began to pack all his belongings into his rucksacks and holdalls before piling them next to Lucie's things by the door. It took him a while. He moved with precision, like a robot programmed to pack things.

I peered along the dark, empty passages that led towards the kitchens, wondering when Leo and Lucie would come back. Even this far from the tunnel there was a strange citrus scent mixing with the stench of decay. I could taste it, sharp as lemon peel on my tongue. I still didn't know what it was, but I no longer thought it was Leo's cologne or the perfumed candles down in the tunnel. With the scent came a draught, as if someone had walked right by me. It was so close I almost screamed.

Ugh – this place!

I bolted back through the doorway into the Great Hall, my heart hammering crazily. None of the boys looked at me or said anything. No one but me seemed to have noticed the sharp new scent or the coldness in the air. I stood there trembling, watching Dan wring out a pair of damp shorts and stuff them into his rucksack. The atmosphere had been painfully awkward a moment ago, but now . . .

Now it was filled with despair.

The lemon smell swirled around us, bitter and deadly as poison. And I knew – with absolute certainty – that something really bad was going to happen.

19

Deep in the early hours, Leo and Lucie returned. Hat-man Dan had finished his packing and was leaning against the wall, chain-smoking, when we heard their footsteps. Their clothes and hair were wet through and they were plastered in sand. Leo had his arm around Lucie's shoulders and she was still giggling intermittently.

Hat-man Dan dropped his half-smoked cigarette and straightened up as they came into the hall. Leo took in his expression, the rest of us looking on, the silence and tension in the great room and the piles of packed bags by the door. And he smirked.

That's when Hat-man Dan turned away. He looked so thin and gangly next to Leo that I couldn't really blame him for backing down. But I was wrong. He only retreated as far as the fireplace, where he picked up a glass bottle and smashed it against the dirty marble of the mantelpiece. Then – with that purposeful robot-expression – he went for Leo.

There was an explosion of red where Leo's features had been, screams and shouts, gasps of disbelief: I stared and felt myself swaying with horror.

Turns out, faces bleed a lot.

The blood was horrible. It was dark and viscous, yet somehow it ran *everywhere* – Leo's chest was streaming within seconds. Jackson pulled his T-shirt over his head and handed it to Leo who buried his face in it. The damp white cotton turned a sort of raw sienna colour that reminded me of uncooked meat. That was when my knees gave out and I slid down the wall.

Hat-man Dan turned and walked away, pulling Lucie with him. As she went, she continued to scream – shrill, hysterical screams that filled the Great Hall and echoed around the beams in the ceiling. I heard him put her into his car and then he came back for all their belongings. Five minutes later came the sound of the Beetle being driven away.

'Fuck 'em,' said Leo in a muffled and bloody voice. 'I hope they fucking crash.'

'You're going to need stitches,' said Jackson. 'I'll drive you over to the hospital.'

'I'm not going.'

'You have to.' Jackson sounded weary. 'I'll go and get the first-aid kit out of the camper first.'

Leo lifted his face out of the bloodied T-shirt to watch him go and I stared at his injuries. To my relief, the glass had missed his eyes. I hadn't eaten or slept for . . . well, I wasn't sure how long . . . but I couldn't have faced a punctured eyeball at this point. It was his nose – large, arrogant and aquiline – that had borne the worst of it. The jagged gashes over his nose were still oozing.

'Mate,' whispered Beano. 'Your nose looks like it's going to come apart.'

'The holiday's over.' Leo turned on him, eyes yellow and glittering. 'So why don't the rest of you fuck off as well?'

'*Me?*'

'Of course, *you*. Since when have *you* been my best fucking friend?'

'But, mate . . . *mate* . . .' Beano hid his bewilderment badly, his face twitching as if Leo had slapped him. He half rose and looked at the open door, plainly wondering whether to leave or not. Then he turned his back on Leo and jammed his hands down into his back pockets, whistling tunelessly through his teeth.

Jackson came striding back through the door with the first-aid kit in his hand. He sat down next to Leo and unzipped it, inspecting the contents by the light of a camping lantern. 'Right . . . I've got plasters . . . surgical tape . . . antiseptic wipes – which are, um, three years out of date.' He tossed that packet over his shoulder. 'A roll of bandages and a dressing pad. So . . . I'll put the pad over your nose and try to stick it down with everything else . . . what do you think?'

'I think my face is fucked. Just leave it, Jackson.'

'Sounds like he's in shock,' said Beano, still facing the other way.

'Why are you still here?' asked Leo nastily.

'Come on,' said Jackson. 'You didn't give Dan much choice.'

'Yeah?' Leo glared at him. 'What if it had been Kate? Would *you* have glassed me?'

'No.' Jackson fiddled with the reel of surgical tape and I bit my lip. Not that I wanted him to cut anyone's face open on my account, but Leo had a way of making me feel bad about the *stupidest* things. Leo began to laugh, an ugly humourless laugh, as Jackson added quite coolly, 'I would've punched you, though.'

'I'd have made you regret it pretty quickly.'

'Not if you were standing on the edge of the cliff.'

'Yeah? Is that how you've been imagining it?' Leo was bloody-nose to nose with Jackson and I could barely breathe. 'It must be haunting you – all the near misses I've had since we've been here, and I'm still alive. Still the king of this castle.'

'OK, so the party's over,' said Beano, swinging round again. 'Fine, we get it. Just let Jackson tape your nose and we'll all go back home together.'

'This is my castle. I'm staying here.'

'I swear to *God*!' Jackson flung the first-aid kit across the room. Then he clapped his hands to his forehead, pushing his head right back on to his shoulders so that he was gazing up at the black ceiling of the cavernous great room. 'I swear we will leave you here on your own. Like this – all cut up and bleeding.'

'I'll stay,' said Beano. 'I don't want to leave you, Leo. We might even have a laugh.'

'What sort of a laugh?' demanded Leo. 'More wrestling and play-fighting, you mean? The sort of laugh where you keep on touching me all the fucking time – is that what you mean?'

There was a silence, although I think Jackson may have sighed very faintly.

'Very funny,' said Beano.

'I'm not gay,' said Leo, his face red and glistening in the light of the camping lanterns. 'So you're going to have to stop pestering me.'

'*I'm* not gay' said Beano, his voice rising higher and higher – panic coming up to the boil. 'I'm *not*! Is that what you're going to tell everyone? You are, aren't you? When we get home, you're going to tell everyone that I'm gay? I'm not – I'm *not* gay!'

'We won't tell anyone,' said Jackson.

'No, no, that makes it sound—' Beano gave a yowl of frustration. 'There's nothing – *nothing* – not to tell!' He began to charge about the hall in the darkness, gathering clothes and belongings into his arms.

'Why would we tell anyone?' asked Leo. 'It's obvious enough for everyone to see it for themselves.'

'*It fucking isn't!*'

Leo lit a cigarette. His fingers were bloody and shaking, but his voice remained steady. 'Yeah, well, it will be when you find a boy who returns your love, won't it?'

'I hate you!' Beano was crying audibly as he went out. 'I really fucking hate you, Leo!'

I listened in bewilderment. I couldn't understand why Beano wasn't laughing at Leo's teasing the way he usually did, then wondered if he hadn't always overplayed the blokeyness a bit.

'*Is* he gay?' I whispered to Jackson.

'I don't know – he hasn't admitted it to himself if he is . . .' He paused, watching the front door swing shut. 'Do you think I should go after him? It's a long walk back in the dark.'

'You should at least go and tell him he still has a Rizla paper with *Oscar Wilde* on it stuck to his head,' I said helpfully.

'He doesn't have any intention of walking into town,' said Leo.

'Oh God!' I started up. 'You think he's going to throw himself over the cliff?'

'Nope.' Leo flicked cigarette ash in a deliberate arc across the room. 'I saw him pick up Jackson's car keys on his way out.'

'Fuck!' shouted Jackson, sprinting for the door.

But we all heard the Polo's engine firing up before he got outside. There was a scrunch of gravel, a painful grinding of gears and the engine stormed away down the hillside.

Jackson kicked the door shut again and slumped against it. 'Fuck,' he repeated quietly.

'And then there were three . . .' said Leo.

'No,' said Jackson. 'Then there were *none*, because we're leaving. I've had enough of this shit.' He started throwing clothes and shoes and random possessions into his sleeping bag. 'Come on, Kate. We'll shove as much of this stuff into the camper as we can, then we'll drive Leo into town to get his nose stitched or glued or whatever they want to do with it. Then we can go home.'

'OK,' I said.

'I'm not going home,' said Leo. 'I'm going for a swim.'

'What?' yelled Jackson. '*What*? Are you insane? You can't get salt water in those cuts! And it's dark, it's raining. It's—'

'It's typical,' I murmured under my breath.

Leo heard me and shook his head, spattering drops of blood. 'What would *you* know about *me*?' he snarled. 'This would've been the best holiday ever, if Jackson hadn't persuaded me to bring you along.'

'Shut up!' said Jackson.

I tried to stare Leo down, but I couldn't help remembering how much trouble I'd caused. I'd refused to travel here in Jackson's car, I'd rejected Leo, and I'd drawn everyone's attention to Lucie and Dan having sex on the beach. Maybe I *had* ruined everything.

'You have a massive fucking chip on your shoulder, don't you?' Leo padded closer and even his breath smelt of blood. 'Because we have more money than you do. You tried to humiliate all of us.'

'I mean it!' Jackson yanked on Leo's elbow. 'Enough!'

'It still bothers me, you know?' said Leo, ignoring him. 'The way you switched from me to Jackson. How calculated it was. It still bothers me.'

Jackson put himself in between us. 'Just go and get in the fucking van, Leo!'

Leo turned away. He slung a towel around his neck and headed for the front door. 'That's not the way you really want it. Because if anything happens to me you'll get your hands on my castle and Kate's gamble will have paid off, won't it?'

I slumped back against the wall as if I had been physically battered by his rage. 'Gamble?' I echoed, looking at Jackson blankly.

In place of an answer, Jackson gave me one of his shrugs and leant against the wall beside me. We listened to Leo's footsteps going across the gravel driveway until there was only the sound of the wind and rain in the chimney.

'He's not even making sense any more,' I added. 'How the hell would *you* ever get your hands on this place?'

'He's my cousin,' muttered Jackson.

'*What?*'

'He's my cousin.' Jackson spoke in the same dull tone I used whenever I mentioned my mother. 'Not on the crazy-St-Clouds-of-Darkmere side, but on his father's side. That's how I got the bursary for Denborough. His father was too ashamed to let his nephew go to a state school, so he didn't give me any choice.'

'I can't believe . . . I mean, why would you not tell me this?'

'Because it isn't something I boast about, all right?' He stood up again and kicked a couple of empty bottles into the fireplace so hard that they smashed into a cloud of raindrop-sized fragments. 'But it isn't a secret. Everyone else knows – and Leo certainly seems to think I've told you about it.'

'You're . . . you're the next heir?'

'I'm not like Leo.'

But I shrank from him even as he said it. The shock was chilling and I started to shake. I couldn't be sure who *anyone* was any more.

'OK – whatever,' snapped Jackson. 'I'm going to have to go after him and make sure he actually does get in the campervan and come home with us. He's still my cousin – whether I own up to it or not.'

He left the castle and I exhaled slowly, rubbing the goose-flesh on my arms and waiting for my heartbeat to slow down. After a moment or two, I scooped up the rest of our belongings and went outside to wait in the campervan. There was no sign of Jackson or Leo, so I climbed into the back seat, put the light on and left the door open.

I wanted to go home.

Where were they?

Where had Leo gone? Into the woods? Down the hill? And why hadn't Jackson persuaded him to come back yet? I was so wrapped in weariness, the panic was slow to reach me, but when it finally broke through, it hit me hard.

I ought to have gone after him. No matter who he was related to, he was still Jackson. And if he really was Leo's cousin, he was as much in line for the curse as for the castle.

I jumped out of the campervan and stood in the drive. Although the dawn hadn't broken, the sea and the woods and the birds seemed unnaturally quiet and it frightened me.

'*Jackson?*' I shouted.

I was answered by a rumble of thunder, then silence.

I had sensed that something bad was going to happen – and I'd assumed it had happened when Dan glassed Leo's face. But what if that *wasn't* what I'd sensed? What if there was even worse to come?

'*Jackson!*' I shouted again, beginning to run down the steep hillside. '*Jackson? Where are you?*'

Nothing.

He was nowhere in sight and I couldn't shake the feeling that Leo had won after all. It was a fear that rode me all the way to the edge of the cliff, where I stood and listened to the sea. The in-out swoosh of the waves was no longer soothing to me; it held a hungry, sucking undertone that heightened my feeling of dread.

'*Jackson!*' I screamed, attempting to throw my voice far out across the water.

It seemed for a moment as if I caught a cry in reply, but it was drowned by the waves and the heavy, rain-soaked wind that whistled around the rocks. The only thing I knew for sure was that Leo had announced his intention of swimming, but had not gone through the drawing room and the cellars and the tunnel to the beach. He had gone out through the *front door* and there was only one way down to the water from that direction.

I ran all the way to the lookout point, pushing through brambles and nettles, slipping and sliding on the damp grass and gasping for breath.

I could hear his voice in my head: '*I'll do it before we leave.*

I'll get totally wasted and do it on the last day.'

And that's where I saw them.

Jackson and Leo were standing on the roof of the pepper-pot, apparently still arguing. The long-established ground upon which their friendship was built had been shifting and a row was inevitable. But not up there . . .

'Come down,' I shouted, as I ran towards them. 'It's dangerous! Come down!'

And that's the moment I've replayed in my head a thousand times since it happened. I've imagined countless other ways I could have approached the two of them.

Would it have changed anything?

Who knows? And I can't undo what I did.

I came charging along the cliff in a panic and shouted at them to come down.

Leo couldn't stand being told what to do.

I saw it in his reaction the moment my words reached him. He leapt to the edge of the roof, and turned his head to look down into the churning water. Jackson put a restraining hand on his arm.

'Don't!' I shouted, and Leo gave me one final look of loathing before he turned and jumped.

Jackson tried to stop him, but Leo was bigger and stronger, and they both went over the edge together.

20

Elinor

The long dining table had been laid for three.

St Cloud sat at its head and Anna had taken the place at his right hand. She was wearing one of the expensive silk evening gowns that had been made for me during my confinement. There were diamonds at her throat and she smelt of the expensive new scent that St Cloud had bought for her. *Verveine.* Whenever I breathed it in, I felt my mouth go dry and my skin go clammy.

My place was set further down, almost hidden from view by two branches of candles and an enormous silver epergne loaded with fruit and flowers from one of the hothouses. We had just begun the soup course when a strapping middle-aged woman in a begrimed cap and apron, yanked open the dining room door and marched in.

'Where's Jem?' she shouted. 'Where is he? What've you done to my boy?'

'And I thought this was to be our first quiet evening at home,' murmured St Cloud, his soup spoon paused at his lower lip. 'Thorne! Remove this creature from my dining room.'

The steward and his wife were upon the woman in an instant, seizing her arms as they delivered a string of apologies and explanations to St Cloud. Two footmen and one of the maids grabbed at her shoulders, her skirts and her waist, as they wrestled her through the doorway. Mrs Barrow fought as if she was trying to get to St Cloud through a gale. Her hair worked loose from her cap and tears slanted from her eyes. She looked and sounded utterly demented.

'*I won't! I won't! What about my Jem? I know this is your doing!*'

One of the footmen forced his arm around her throat and her words took on a strangled quality. The others began to drag the woman backwards.

'Wait!' I cried. I'd started from my chair the moment she'd burst in, but everyone had been staring at Jem's mother and had failed to notice me behind the epergne. Now I forced myself back down into my seat before they saw me and realized I was able to stand unaided. 'What about Jem? What's happened?'

'Which one's Jem?' asked Anna, looking at St Cloud.

'I suspect Elinor is referring to the boy who cleans the boots. In which case, this conversation would be better held with the housekeeper than with me.'

315

'I beg you, my lady,' choked Mrs Barrow, trying to hold my eye. 'Mrs Thorne won't tell me what's happened to him. He's missing and I don't know what to do. He's all I've got.'

'Oh no!' I was gripped by guilt and foreboding. What had I done?

Anna spoke to Mr Thorne. 'See that some kind of search is made, would you?'

St Cloud began to look impatient. 'That kitchen boy was an idle, gossiping simpleton who probably tripped and fell down the well.'

A horrified gasp broke from me. 'What do you mean *was*? Surely he's not—?'

Mrs Barrow began to howl as if she were in terrible pain. Even after they'd hauled her out of the room, I could hear it.

'What happened?' I hissed. 'You know, don't you?'

'Why don't you tell me what you suspect, Elinor?' St Cloud set down his spoon and met my eye. 'This is your fault, after all.'

'Well, if I've done wrong, why must Jem suffer? He's just a child, St Cloud – a little boy!'

'Shouldn't you have considered that when you decided to make use of him?'

'Oh God, what did you do to him?'

'You know I won't tolerate disobedient servants and yet you encouraged – *deliberately encouraged* – that boy to defy me.'

'Then punish *me*, for God's sake! Punish *me*!'

'I am,' he said, and resumed sipping his soup.

My breath was coming in short, sharp pants. I glared at him helplessly and everything inside me churned with fear and hatred.

316

I wanted to attack him – claw at his face, beat his chest, bite him even. I *longed* to hurt him physically!

'You're not going to tell me what's happened to him, are you?' I said. 'You're torturing me – and Jem's mother – just by staying silent. If you've harmed that little boy you're a monster and a-a murderer! Do you know, I couldn't bear the thought of giving birth to a child of yours – because I was afraid he might be like you?'

'Be careful, Elinor.' St Cloud's face barely moved – if anything it was more expressionless than before – but somehow it conveyed a sense of increasing danger.

Anna sat up straighter, her hands folded under her chin, her *soup à la reine* cooling in its plate. 'But perhaps the baby wouldn't have resembled St Cloud at all,' she said slowly, tasting each word. 'After all, you were going to marry Nicholas before you met St Cloud.'

I looked at her without understanding. She was sitting beneath a heavy chandelier of lighted candles and she'd left her head bare for once. She was not beautiful – she could never be that again – but she was arresting nonetheless. The light turned her blonde curls into a dazzling silken halo and her ruined eyes flashed with pleasure at my confusion.

'Nicholas Calvert proposed to you a couple of months before you married St Cloud, didn't he?' she continued. 'Why *was* he sent away in such disgrace? Mama never did tell me all the details.'

I felt my face burn as understanding and revulsion rushed over me. I looked at St Cloud to see that he was not remotely surprised

317

by Anna's insinuations.

'And your child was born *far* too early,' he remarked, holding my gaze. 'As you said, he was much better dead.'

'How . . . how dare you! Oh, how *dare* you! You know quite well there was never anyone before you!' I couldn't come any closer to reminding him how much he'd hurt me that first time. The memory still twisted in my stomach like a jagged thing.

Anna gave half a yawn. 'Some women can be so clever about these matters.'

It was too much. I lunged at the huge epergne, tipping it over and sending the fruit, flowers and water all over my sister and her plate of soup.

'Only women like you!' I shouted. 'Women who scheme and lie and betray other people! I've heard you creeping into his room, night after night – and I've noticed the way you've had to let out all your gowns to hide your waistline because of it. That's why you've started to leave off your old maid's caps, isn't it? They're hardly suitable for a woman in your condition! Are you hoping for my wedding ring as well? Is that what this is about? Have you been dripping this poison into his ear in the hope he'll have me shut away somewhere – or worse?'

'That's enough.' St Cloud stood up and came around the table, seizing my arm. 'Since Calvert's visit, you've behaved in a far more indiscreet manner than your sister. It seems that I married the wrong woman after all.'

I struggled, but was unable to break his grip on my arm. 'Just as I married the wrong man! Curse you, St Cloud – and any son of yours who inherits this hateful place!'

My cries made no more impression on him than my attempts to free myself. He strode out of the dining room and I was dragged along the floor at his side. Instinct would have forced me on to my feet if he'd given me any opportunity, but he believed my legs were useless and so hauled me along as if they were. I could've been a sack of firewood or feed for the horses.

He strode across the hall and into the drawing room, where the butler was laying out cards, straightening newspapers and maga-zines, making the room ready for us to use after dinner. He pretended not to see as St Cloud dragged me almost over his shoes and I felt the indignity burn across my face. We went on through the music room and the plate room without stopping, then past the estate manager's office. My arm was aching under St Cloud's fingers and my protests began to take on a pleading and fearful note as he strode on past the housekeeper's room and through the kitchens. There, more servants who had long been trained to avert their gazes, concentrated on their domestic tasks with far more than their usual intensity, only to peer after us when it was safe to do so. It was nightmarish.

When St Cloud unlocked the door to the cellars and dragged me down into the darkness, I knew a sick feeling of absolute terror. 'Stop, I beg of you, I'm sorry for what I said! Oh, for God's sake – stop!'

There was a silence as he picked up a lamp that was hanging on the wall and lit it. I massaged my arm and looked back towards the brightness of the kitchens, wondering whether to scream for help or try to claw my way back up the steps.

'No,' he said, inclining his head in the direction of the

underground passage. 'We're going that way.'

'To . . . to the beach?'

'No. You wanted to know where Jem was, so I mean to show you.'

St Cloud threw me over his shoulder and carried me past store rooms and smaller tunnels, and the air grew ever more fetid. Wild fears seized me and I thought perhaps he meant to keep me down here as a punishment. Could poor Jem be trapped down here somewhere too? Was he locked in one of the tiny cell-like rooms, a prisoner in the darkness? A frightened sob burst from my lips as I wondered if I would ever see daylight again.

'Stop making that devilish noise.' St Cloud's voice was low but quite implacable. 'I will not tolerate a wife who disobeys me, and the same goes for my servants and tenants. I'm going to show you what happens to those who attempt it.' We reached a fork and he turned to the right, unlocking a barred iron gate set deep into the stone walls and dragging me through. My skirts were torn and dirty, and one of my slippers was gone. St Cloud was perfectly at home down here, I could tell. Like some predatory animal in its lair, he was at ease in the close, dark secrecy of these tunnels under the earth.

The end of the passage had been hollowed out to form a small round room containing tools, winching equipment and fishing nets. St Cloud hung up his lantern and I flung myself against the rough stone wall furthest away from him. I was shaking and sweating all over. The room felt slimy and what little air there was smelt foul.

'Ned Scathlock's been itching to get his hands on that kitchen boy of yours for a long time,' said St Cloud. 'He rather enjoyed himself this afternoon . . . and the boy confessed to all sorts of things.'

'Oh no – *no!*'

'He said you sent your friend Calvert a letter. But you'd been talking to Calvert all week, so what else could you possibly have to tell him? Do you know, I began to be afraid that letter held some sort of written records . . . or is my imagination running away with me?'

'No, I sent Nick pages from my journal.' I pushed myself up on my arms and made my voice sound brave. If St Cloud was handing me a weapon, I was determined to try and use it against him. 'I've been writing down the times and dates of every run of smuggled goods I witnessed from this house. Along with the names of everyone I recognized. So if anything happens to me – if I don't come back up from these cellars for instance – Nick will send copies of those pages to every lawmaker in the country.'

His eyes glinted in the blackness and the line of his mouth was ugly. 'Yes . . I was afraid it was something like that.'

I didn't notice the hatch in the centre of the floor until St Cloud levered it open and the stench of salt and decay immediately worsened. I clapped my hands over my mouth and nose.

'We're right over the sea,' said St Cloud, watching my face to see if I understood him.

I shook my head helplessly, neither attempting to make sense of his words nor taking my eyes off him.

'Look,' he pointed down at the square hole in the floor, 'you can see the water beneath us.'

I glanced down at the blackness that gleamed in the lamplight. 'How . . . how can that be?'

'The cliff is hollow and it's full of seawater. You can smell it, can't you? There's a littoral cave right underneath us and the entrance is below the sea level, so hardly anyone knows it's there. I discovered it. It's like a vast black lake under the ground.'

'Dark . . . *mere*?'

'That's right.' He laughed and it was a horrible echoing sound in the eerie little cell. 'But it's more than just a secret lake, you know. It's the landing point for goods for which I've no intention of paying any duty.'

'*Smuggled* goods, you mean?'

'Yes, that *is* what I mean.' He was amused by the accusatory note in my voice. 'You've seen the ships hovering off the shore, haven't you? They hover there for hours while the crews of the Revenue cutters wait for the cargoes to be unloaded or run ashore. That's when the tidesmen like to step in. But I prefer not to give them that chance.'

I could hear the fervent rattle of the obsessive in his description. He talked as if smuggling were a hobby rather than a criminal offence for which the sentence was a long spell in gaol and a reputation irredeemably ruined.

'The sea itself is the perfect hiding place,' St Cloud explained. 'The seamen wrap the kegs or ropes of tobacco in oilskins and weight them to float just below the surface before tossing them over the side of the ship. At first, I had a man swim out to steer them inland, but I soon discovered that anything tossed overboard in just the right spot – when the tide is on its way in, mind you – will generally be washed right into the cave mouth by the curious little undertow around the cliffs. And no one any the wiser.'

'I believe you're mad. It would all be smashed to pieces!'

'No, the current holds the barrels deep underwater and the walls of the cave are thick with seaweed. I think you'd be surprised how few cargoes I've lost that way. Of course, I've made a few improvements of my own. I've used ropes and fishing nets to line the rocky walls where the cargoes might get damaged in rough weather. I made this hatch and the shaft below by boring through the rock – right down into the cave, so we can hook up the barrels from here without ever setting foot upon the beach. And, perhaps best of all, I've designed a sort of underwater gate to the mouth of the cave.'

'W-why would you need a gate?' I asked, my voice trembling. Was he going to drown me in the awful black lake inside the cliff?

'To prevent anything from being sucked back out, of course. The gate swings inwards under almost no pressure at all, but the hinges only move one way. It works like the opening of a lobster pot – that's where I got the idea. The gate is made from an iron mesh, shaped to fit the mouth of the cave. A raft of barrels will be carried through it easily, but there's nowhere else for them to go until we're ready to winch them up here.'

He leant back against the wall with the air of a performer waiting for applause. His frilled white evening shirt, high collars and pristine white cravat gleamed in the darkness, making his face seem more shadowy than ever. No words of praise occurred to me. All I could do was cringe against the wall, wondering if I was about to die.

'Nothing can get back out through that gate,' he reiterated slowly. 'A school of dolphins got trapped down there once and they battered themselves against the gate for hours, but it didn't give an inch. We had to fish each of them out this way, one by one.'

'St Cloud, don't tell me any more.'

'When one of the sailors was tempted to keep a little of the tobacco back for himself, the master of the ship had him tied to the barrels and thrown overboard with them. Of course he ended up down there too, and once again the gate held fast. I daresay he's down there still.'

My lips were dry and my tongue stuck to the roof of my mouth. Every word I uttered was a struggle. 'Why are you telling me all this?'

'You asked me, remember? You demanded to know what had happened to the kitchen boy.' He stepped forward and leant right over the black hole in the floor, peering into its depths. 'Do you want me to poke around with one of these hooked creepers and see if I can find him in there?'

'Oh no – not Jem! Oh, I can't bear it!'

'There's one particular spot up on the cliff – where I built my lookout shelter in fact – that drops straight down into the treacherous little current that swirls into the lake. That's where Ned Scathlock threw the Preventive you got so friendly with last year. It's where he disposes of anyone else who angers him or attempts to interfere with my trade.'

I covered my face with my arms and wept unrestrainedly. St

Cloud came close enough to speak right into my ear. 'And it's the fate that awaits your friend Calvert when he gets here.'

'No!' I wailed. '*No!*'

'He cuckolded me in my own house and he's planning to have me arrested for smuggling! What else do you expect me to do?'

I screamed as he seized me and made as if to throw me down through the hole in the floor. My toes grew wet at the touch of the cold stinking seawater beneath me and I was so afraid I could barely breathe.

'The boy had a note for you – from Calvert,' he said, shaking me so that every other weightless second I expected to be swallowed by the icy black water. 'It says he's coming here tomorrow morning and you're to meet him on the beach – *my* beach – at sunrise.'

Then he tossed me on to the hard rock floor beside the hatch. 'Only you won't be on the beach to greet him, I'm afraid. I'm going to be making up the welcoming committee with Ned Scathlock. You'll stay here until I have those smuggling records safe – I can use your life to bargain with. The next time you're with your beloved Calvert again, you'll both be in the lake. Goodnight, Elinor.'

As he finished speaking, he closed the metal hatch in the floor with an echoing clang, turned on his heel and strode away from me along the passage, taking the lantern with him.

It was a long time before I was able to pick myself up off the floor. At first, I could only lie there weeping, shocked and afraid. But I needed to get to Nick. The thought of him tugged at me.

Even if I couldn't save Jem, I could still protect Nick. So I stood up in the darkness and staggered back along the tunnel. I stumbled and reached out to run my hands along the rough walls as I went. I could neither see nor hear properly. My senses were numbed by a sort of debilitating disbelief.

It was night – the easiest time for me to make my way through the cellars and the kitchens unseen. I would leave the castle and creep through the woods. I would hide in ditches on my hands and knees if I had to. I no longer cared how cold or dark or terrifying the journey would be. I needed to get to Nick, and if I just kept walking I would have time to reach him. Somehow I'd find the nearest town. I would ask at every inn – wake everyone – until I'd found Nick. I would do whatever it took to stop him from coming here!

Only . . . St Cloud had locked the gate.

Of course he had.

I gave a moan of agony. I was trapped in this underground dungeon. I shook the gate and kicked it and hurled myself against it. But the gate shrugged me off with what sounded like a burst of metallic grating laughter.

I couldn't stop Nick from coming. He would be butchered on the beach – along with the fisherman hired to help him. They'd disappear. And the boat would probably be sunk or hacked into pieces of driftwood. I pictured Nick's face at the moment he would set foot upon the beach and realize I'd let him down. I was sure he wouldn't try to run. I knew the set of his shoulders and could imagine the way he would clench his fists as he tried to fight St Cloud. Then I remembered Ned Scathlock's giant cudgel and shuddered with horror.

For the first time, I wished to God that Nick's wife hadn't died. He would've loved her more than he loved me in the end. It wasn't in Nick's nature to short-change anyone. He ought to be living contentedly in a manor house in France, bringing up sleepy-eyed children and growing old surrounded by his family. That was the life he deserved – *not this*!

I wrapped my arms around my head, but the thoughts and images continued to find a way in. I wondered if I'd hear the noises – shouts or screams – from the beach when it happened. Would I know when Nick was killed? Would I feel anything? Unawareness seemed impossible when I loved him so much.

Hours passed but I barely noticed. The intensity of my pain dislocated me from the reality of time and place. I grew accustomed to the hard, wet floor and the stench of decay. I was so exhausted I even slept for a few hours, curled at the foot of the barred gate.

I was woken by the vibration of St Cloud's footsteps and the sound of the key in the lock.

'Not much longer for you to wait now, Elinor,' he said, swinging the lantern over my crumpled figure. 'No time to try and crawl away. Ha, we'll be back soon with Calvert.'

I knew then the sun was coming up. I struggled to raise myself off the ground. My limbs were knotted and cold, and the sudden light from the lantern had dazzled me. When I rubbed my eyes, dozens of ghost lanterns scrolled across the darkness. I was hopelessly disorientated, but I could tell that St Cloud wasn't alone.

The mutter of men's voices and the tramp of their boots

reached me from the end of the passage. I went scrambling after them. My stiffness made me too slow to see much more than their retreating shadows. But I knew one of the men was Scathlock, for his hulking shape was bent double under the low ceiling and I could hear the drag of his wooden stave along the floor. The others must have been a couple of the rougher-looking keepers and our burliest footman.

I didn't follow them to the beach.

Of course, if St Cloud had been aware I was able to follow them anywhere, he might not have unlocked the gate. I suppose he'd merely been ensuring that all the evidence of whatever was about to happen would be disposed of quickly and cleanly. He was chillingly practical that way.

So I groped my way back through the cellars and up into the kitchens. To my relief, the door wasn't locked and I waited behind it until the maids were out of the room, and then I escaped through the little kitchen courtyard. I clung to every wall. I tried to melt into every shadow and I crawled through the kitchen garden like a mouse. By the time I'd reached the hillside, my other slipper was missing and my stockings torn to shreds. Every inch of my body was protesting, but I gritted my teeth and hurried on. The sky was lightening with every second.

Nick must be on his way now.

Although the castle grounds were deserted, I knew I might be seen from the windows at any moment, so I gave up on stealth and attempted to run. I fell – twice . . . no, three times – on my way to the pepperpot. My legs were bruised and one of my elbows was bleeding freely. My eyes were watering, I couldn't tell whether the salt wind was stinging them or I was crying.

Inside the tiny lookout, I leant out of the window opening, trying to catch my breath and frantically scanning the sea. There was a sail in the distance and the sight of it broke me completely.

'*Oh no!*' I turned my face into the wall so that I wouldn't see it come any closer. '*Oh no – no – no – no!*'

If only I hadn't involved Jem. If I only I were creeping through the cellars while the rest of the castle slept. If only I'd woken in my own bed and packed a few belongings in a bag – toothbrush, journal, my favourite old shawl – and slipped down to the beach to meet Nick as we planned.

If only. If only. If only.

I looked again, and already the sail had become a fishing boat and it was heading towards the Darkmere beach as surely as if it were a toy boat pulled by a string. Nick was coming for me just as he'd said he would. I turned my back upon the sight and left the little room. Outside, the wind seized my hair and made my eyes stream again.

I found the roughly built wall easy to climb, even though my hands and knees were shaking. I stood up straight on the roof and took the few remaining steps to the edge. When I looked down, the sea was so far down I wobbled and almost fell.

I'd run all the way out here to look and see if he was coming. But there was one more thing I could do. I loved him so much I didn't really have a choice.

I wouldn't let him down again.

I unfastened what remained of my dress and stripped it away. The cold wind bit into my bare arms, but I knew the water would be far colder and I didn't want my skirts to drag me down. I wondered *how* cold the water would be. Bitter. Wintry. Cold enough to knock all the breath out of me. I looked down at the churning grey waves. Would the temperature paralyse me before I could reach the boat? Would I die before I could even start to swim?

I didn't want to do this – I really didn't.

Oh God, now I really was crying.

I was *so* afraid.

I didn't want to die. But what if the alternative was to watch Nick die? I looked at the fishing boat, all by itself on the infinite sea. It was closer now than ever. I could make out a couple of tiny figures on board. And one of them was him.

I glanced behind me. The beach looked empty and innocent. But dark shapes lurked in the blackness of the cave's mouth. Waiting . . . waiting. Soon they would see the boat.

One more step. I couldn't feel my toes at all.

Smuggled cargoes and lifeless bodies couldn't swim against the deadly undertow, but with the tide on the turn, surely *I* could. And I would – I'd make it to Nick's boat before it came too near the beach.

But I'd have to do it now.

Oh God . . . I couldn't . . . I couldn't . . . I couldn't . . .

I wasn't even a very good swimmer.

Panic engulfed me and swept all my resolve away. It was blind and illogical but it was too strong for me. I took a step away from the edge and I knew I was about to fail.

Then I heard a cry from the clifftop. I saw a fluttering green dress and golden hair. It was my sister. She must have been wondering how on earth I'd got all the way out here by myself. Perhaps she thought St Cloud had brought me here – his way of getting rid of me.

'*You can have him now,*' I told her silently. '*He was always your husband really.*'

She raised her arm and shouted again. I could see she meant to stop me, but instead she had distracted me from the terrible panic. There was no time left now – there was only Nick.

And I wouldn't let him down again.

I jumped.

Kate

It was my fault!

My mouth opened in a shuddering gasp of horror. *It was my fault – again!*

Somehow I ran to the edge of the cliff. The sea churned and raged and hurled itself upon the rocks. I could see someone in the water – someone tiny and helpless.

'*Jackson!*' I yelled, and for a hideous second I felt the urge to dive headlong into the water. But I fought it, turning on the spot and pelting back towards the castle. All the way back, I could see that tiny, drowning figure in the water. *This is how it happened before*, I thought, remembering the story in the newspaper about the two boys who'd tried to climb down the cliffs. One had fallen and grabbed the other – his cousin. *One of them had died on the rocks and the other had never been found.*

It was uphill going back. By the time I'd regained the castle, my chest was heaving. There was broken glass all over the floor, and bare-toed footprints in trails of blood. I grabbed a lantern from out of the mess and ran through all those rooms I knew so well . . . the drawing room . . . music room . . . plate room . . . the estate office and into the kitchens. Then down into the cellars, where the air still smelt so dreadfully of dead things and the floor was slippery with seawater and gore.

Jackson! Jackson! Jackson! He was the one thought in my head. I'd never been more focused in my life. As I ran, he was drowning. *If only I could run faster!*

I burst out of the tunnel on to the beach and bent double, drawing great jagged breaths into my aching lungs. My chest hurt badly and it took valuable seconds before I was able to straighten up and scan the expanse of sea before me. Still gasping and holding my ribs, I hurried over the sand and waded into the water. It was the first time I'd gone into the sea without squealing or making a sound – my jaw was clenched too hard.

I looked this way and that. I could see black shadows being dragged and rolled by every wave – and each shadow took on the shape of a drowning man. There were hundreds of them and I felt dizzy as I tried to focus on each one. *There! No – over there! Or, wait – was that a body further out?*

Then I saw it. A dark thing way out on the water. I couldn't define the shape of whatever I'd seen. Could it have been a head and shoulder? An arm or a leg? Or simply a piece of driftwood? It had been a glimpse so fleeting that it caused me to doubt myself almost immediately. But I kept on striding towards it.

When the waves were up to my chest and threatening to tip me over, I dived forwards and began to swim, half blinded by the dark salty water. This was different to the times we'd come down to the beach for moonlit swimming parties. This was lonely and scary. I had to fight my way through the sea, and the whole world tilted with the waves until even the sky seemed liquid.

I could feel the current sucking at my legs, turning me this way and that. I had to force myself to swim closer to the cliffs, where the undertow pulled even harder. Eventually it dragged me so far down my knees were grazed by rocks hidden under the surface.

What was I doing out here?

I wasn't even a very good swimmer.

I was too afraid to kick much so close to the rocks. I splashed with my arms and tried not to swallow the seawater as I went down further. There was a ball of pressure building inside my chest. I wasn't sure whether it was a need for air or just pure panic. Suddenly the current relaxed its grip and I came up for air. The body in the water was almost on top of me. All I had to do was make one final, exhausted leap and hold on to it.

It felt like Jackson.

Sobbing with relief, I put my arms around him and floated,

trying to get my bearings before I went under again. But the whole world had become cold, murky water and Jackson's weight was dragging me down.

My arms were numb and my chest hurt with a sharp, jabbing pain – as if something inside my lungs was fighting to get out. My ears hurt too – the feeling of *pressure* was unbearable. Every instinct of self-preservation I possessed was screaming at me to let Jackson go.

I gritted my teeth and held on tight.

I'd heard that drowning was painless – like falling asleep. Somehow the thought terrified me and I fought harder than ever. *No, no, no – kick, kick, kick.*

The water threw us up to the surface unexpectedly and I gasped too fast to take in as much air as my body needed. I think someone shouted. Lightning flashed across my vision and I shook my head to clear it. Then I caught sight of Leo. He was still in the water too, and even closer to the cliffs than we were.

'Help!' I tried to shout. 'Help us!'

He *must*'ve been able to see that Jackson needed help – and yet he didn't come. He shouted again, but I couldn't hear his words.

Why wasn't he helping? *Why?*

He was a stronger swimmer than any of us.

God, I hated him then. He was prepared to watch us drown. Why? Because we'd argued? Because of his face? Because of his ruined holiday?

I wouldn't forgive him. Not ever!

I think the fury helped me. Holding on to Jackson, I pumped my legs without pause until I was steering a course back towards the shore. At last – at long last – more benevolent waves found us – lifted and carried us and spat us on to the beach.

Was he breathing? I was gasping so hard I couldn't tell. I tried everything I could think of to bring him round. I pounded his chest, shouted at him and slapped his face. I remembered how he had revived Leo by tipping water over him, but Jackson was already soaking wet. I gripped his shoulders and shook him, but I knew that the sea had already shaken him around much harder. Nothing worked. I was failing him.

'Oh, please, Jackson . . . please!' My voice came out ragged with hysteria. 'I don't know what to do! You have to help me – please wake up!'

But Jackson wouldn't wake up and, as the waves lapped at his lifeless body, I realized I'd have to do *something*. I wanted to run for help, but I couldn't bear to leave him on his own. Not here. I'd never leave anyone alone at Darkmere.

I buried my hands under his armpits, repositioned my legs wider apart – knees bent – at each side of his shoulders, braced every muscle and heaved.

He was so heavy!

The expression 'dead weight' came into my head uninvited. I gave one horrified shudder, then clamped my lips together and breathed in through my nose. I was *not* going to let him die. It hurt me too much to even think about it.

That was the reason I hadn't been able to let go of him in the sea. The reason I couldn't leave him here on the beach. I'd fallen in love with him.

So I dragged him, my arms tight around his chest, water trickling from his mouth. I lifted and tugged – I staggered backwards and collapsed – then I lifted and tugged some more. I pulled him into the tunnel and along the passage, sliding on my bottom and pushing at the rocky floor with the rubber soles of my Cons. Stop . . . start . . . Stop . . . start . . . Still going backwards and weeping now from the pain in my back.

I made it all the way to the stone steps. Then I hooked my hands under his shoulders and heaved. I felt his body lift and begin to move upwards for just a fraction of a second before my wrists gave out. It was a horrible feeling and I was swamped with utter despair. I was never going to get him out of here. I couldn't save him.

I'd always hated this tunnel, and right now it felt more hostile than ever. Someone really had cursed this place – I could feel it.

As the thought came into my head, one of those sinister, icy draughts rushed over me, freezing the sweat on my arms and legs and raising goosebumps all over my skin. It wasn't a real wind or any kind of sea breeze, I knew that at once. It was something that smelt sharp and citrus and colder than the sea itself. Something long dead.

We were no longer alone down here in the tunnel. Whatever it was circled us and sighed, slicing through my hold on

Jackson's body like the blade of a guillotine.

I tried to lift him again and now his body was colder in my arms than before. Colder and lighter, as *someone else* lifted and carried him up each rough stone step with me and into the kitchens.

I lay with him on the floor. There were deep hollows beneath Jackson's cheekbones, his hair was caked with wet sand, and his skin was as bloodless as a death mask. But around us skirts were swirling, enveloping us in the lemon scent.

'Elinor?' I whispered, beyond any feelings of foolishness now, beyond anything. 'Help me . . . please help me . . . don't let him die.'

Shadows thickened and twisted themselves into a shape bending over Jackson's body. Head bowed. A haze of green silk.

'Elinor?' I said again.

She lifted her head and just for a moment I saw not the pretty, teenaged Elinor of my imagination, but the scarred, old woman from the drawing in the library.

'No – leave him alone!' I shouted.

But already she was nothing more than shadow and my words fell upon an empty room. Had I imagined her? That dead, nerveless face, puckered with scars?

'Who *are* you?' I could hear the tremble in my voice. 'Don't hurt him. Just please, don't hurt him . . .'

That was when the atmosphere changed. It filled with an emotion that wasn't mine but I felt it so strongly it swept away my fear and made me groan. It was remorse.

Remorse that went far beyond guilt or sadness or regret. It was pure torment. Whoever she was, she was sorry. So sorry that even now, all these years later, she was desperately trying to make things right.

The shadows snaked around me again. Was that a gleam of pale hair? Was she there, kneeling by Jackson in the darkness and cradling his injured head? I cried out inarticulately.

His eyes opened.

There was an explosion of shock – and hope – inside my chest. I went hot and cold and shivery all at the same time.

He was staring right at me.

'Please, please, please!' I whispered, holding him closer. 'Oh, please be all right – please!'

In answer, his chest heaved and his face scrunched up. He tipped on to his side, coughing and retching painfully, until the woman's outline faded and we lay alone on the cold stone flags of the kitchen floor.

From the distant driveway came the sound of an engine.

It was a police car. Away from Darkmere, Hat-man Dan must've felt bad about what he'd done to Leo's face and contacted the police. Or maybe he'd simply wanted to deny Leo the satisfaction of reporting him.

The policemen radioed for an ambulance for Jackson then went through the tunnels to the beach to help Leo. In a surprisingly short time, the driveway filled up with coastguard trucks, ambulances and police vehicles. Men in uniforms or disposable overalls surged like an army through the filthy old rooms, and I could hear the buzz of a helicopter overhead.

I wondered if Leo could hear it, wherever he was. It was the sort of attention he'd find gratifying. I thought he'd probably already gone to ground somewhere – the woods perhaps – like a wounded animal. The last twelve hours seemed to have completely unhinged him and I couldn't help hoping the police would find him before his path crossed my own again.

I was more worried about Jackson. He seemed shaken and disorientated. Paramedics had treated his head wound in one of the ambulances, while I was interviewed by the police. After that, they told me he had to give his own account of our holiday. So there was nothing for me to do but wait.

My whole body ached for the numbness of sleep, but I was too overwrought to close my eyes. Sitting outside on the grassy slope, I leafed through Elinor's journal and after a minute or two, my mind made an escape into Elinor's life, as if it had borne enough of the present. I read about her arranged marriage, her arrival at Darkmere and her growing suspicions about her husband. Had she managed to escape? I wondered, running my fingertips over the ragged edges where pages had been torn from the book.

I wanted to believe so.

But I don't think her sister ever knew if she had. The woman with the scarred face from the drawing in the library. *Anna . . . Mother*. She'd had St Cloud's children, continued the line, but she hadn't been able to forgive herself for the part she'd played in Elinor's apparent suicide. Anna had become a victim of her own bitterness.

A breeze rippled the pages and attempted to play with my hair, but my hair was too salty and tangled to move. I looked around, half expecting to see a hazy figure in green drifting down the hillside. Instead Jackson emerged from the archway.

'How's your head?' I asked him.

'Bit sore.' His voice was hoarse from the sea and he touched the dressing on the side of his head with careful fingers. 'I wanted to go back down to the beach, but they wouldn't let me.'

He went into the camper and made us both coffee. It tasted awful because there wasn't much coffee left, but it gave Jackson something to do. He paced around the hillside, holding his mug, while I continued to sift through the journal.

Around lunchtime, a middle-aged policewoman came out to talk to us.

'The divers found a cave under the castle,' she began.

My heart began to thump.

'It's a death-trap, and there seem to be bones down there . . . But they've recovered a body . . .'

I couldn't look at Jackson, couldn't move at all.

'I'm sorry – we believe it's Leo Erskine.'

I shocked myself by bursting into tears.

Leo was not immortal after all.

Jackson walked away from us, his face turned to the sea. I wasn't sure what I could say to him. He was probably the only person whose approval Leo cared about. They had been friends as well as cousins.

'We've already been in touch with Leo's father,' the police-woman went on after a minute. She'd unclipped a notebook from her belt and was reading from it. 'We've spoken to your friends . . . Daniel Delaney and Lucie Adu, and they've been telling us about the last few days. It seems as if you've been having a fairly eventful holiday down here. We also talked to Benjamin Nolan, the boy who was involved in a car crash on the motorway in the early hours.'

'I don't know who that is,' I managed.

She frowned at her notes. 'It says "Beano" in brackets.'

'Oh . . .' *B-No* – he'd given himself a street-tag. I wanted to laugh, but my mouth couldn't go through with it and I ended up crying again. Leo had rejected him so viciously. 'Is he OK?'

'He was lucky. The car he was travelling in is a write-off.'

'But that's . . .' I was going to say that it was Jackson's car, but then I saw Jackson's face as he turned back and my words dried up.

'I should've stopped him.' Jackson sat back down beside me and put his head in his hands. 'I shouldn't have let him take my car keys. I should've stopped Leo from jumping too. I was right there with him – next to him – touching him!'

'Why did he jump?' asked the policewoman. 'Was it some sort of game or a dare? I suppose you'd call it *tombstoning*?'

The term sounded awkward on her lips. She resented having to use it. I could hear her disapproval of teenagers and their stupid, dangerous hobbies in every syllable.

'That's not how it happened!' I said. 'I shouted at him to

come down – that's why he jumped. He always did the opposite of what anyone told him to do.'

'I threatened him,' put in Jackson. 'I told him I'd wait until he was standing right on the edge of the cliff and then I'd hit him. He must've thought I meant it – that's why he wouldn't let me help him. He must've died thinking it was what I wanted.'

The policewoman flipped through her little book again. 'Your friends have each claimed it was their fault as well. Perhaps you should try not to be too hard on yourselves . . .'

But I knew. Leo had said he would jump off that lookout point and so that's what he had done. Leo was just being Leo.

'I have to ask you to come and identify the body,' she said. She looked genuinely sorry about it. 'And afterwards, you should go home. I'll contact your parents and arrange for someone to drive you.'

She even gave us the numbers of counsellors we could talk to. Considering the amount of trouble we'd caused since we'd been at Darkmere, she was very kind to us.

At last she went back inside. Jackson and I got up, but we didn't follow her right away. My cheeks were wet and Jackson's jaw was rigid. We stood there on the hillside and gazed at the castle.

It looked just as it had the first time I'd seen it. Beautiful – with long arched windows and creamy-coloured towers and turrets emerging from ancient swags of ivy. It was magnificent and unchanging. Impervious.

'It's yours now,' I said to Jackson.

'Yes . . .' he said. 'And I know exactly what I'm going to do with it.'

'What?'

He stared up at his inheritance and frowned. I'd never seen him look like Leo before, but the resemblance was startling as he gazed at Darkmere.

'I'm going to burn it. I'm going to come back here after everyone's gone, pour petrol into every single room and burn this fucking place to the ground.'

I couldn't tell whether he meant it or not.

Overhead, the sky was white and flat as paper. A gull wheeled and screamed, and the air smelt rotten. But I imagined the castle burning and turning the whole sky orange. That rotten stink would be inhaled into an endless cloud of smoke and ashes. It would be the biggest bonfire this place had ever known, and I said the only thing I knew for certain:

'Leo would've loved that.'

ACKNOWLEDGEMENTS

Huge thanks to Barry Cunningham for all your enthusiasm and hard work. Thanks to Rachel Hickman for endless advice and support. Thanks to Helen Crawford-White for such a beautiful cover. And thanks to Kes Lupo, Jazz Bartlett, Sue Cook, Laura Myers and Laura Smythe for making the whole process so much fun.

Thank you to Rachel Leyshon for working as hard on this book as I did. I couldn't be more grateful for your kindness, patience, humour and brilliance. You deserve more *thank yous* than I can fit on the page.

Thank you to Rowan Lawton for reading the manuscript and helping me to shape it into a story rather than a gigantic tangle of words. Rowan and Liane Louise Smith at FurnissLawton have given me editorial advice, a publishing contract and a brand new job description. Thank you both so much.

Special thanks too – to my writing friends Hayley Hoskins, Amanda Reynolds and Kate Riordan for being excellent company and providing constant help and encouragement. Thank you to the inspirational Judith Green for telling me I didn't need anyone's permission to become a writer (which I took as permission to become a writer). Thank you to my first readers Charlie Chitty, Ali Corder, Loraine Evans, Sally Glover, John Matheson and Sam Redfern – all of whom gave me the confidence to show it to someone else.

The #UKYA community is jam-packed with awesome authors, reviewers and bloggers – far too many to list, but I want to mention the coolest YA author around, C. J. Skuse, who read the book early on and said nice things. Similarly Keris Stainton for her boundless generosity to new authors everywhere. I fell completely in love with the unstoppable force that is Michelle Toy – thank you so, so much, Chelley – also Jim Dean, who makes the internet all kinds of fun. Thanks as well to the lovely Suzanne Furness for encouraging me from the beginning.

Thank you to my parents and in-laws, extended family and friends. And thank you most of all to my husband and two sons, who make me proud every single day. I heart you.